The
KEY
to the
ISLAND
HOUSE

BOOKS BY AMANDA LEES

WW2 RESISTANCE SERIES

The Silence Before Dawn

Paris at First Light

The Midwife's Child

The Paris Spy's Girl

STANDALONE NOVELS

If I Can Save One Child

AMANDA LEES

The KEY to the ISLAND HOUSE

Bookouture

Published by Bookouture in 2025

An imprint of Storyfire Ltd.
Carmelite House
50 Victoria Embankment
London EC4Y 0DZ

www.bookouture.com

The authorised representative in the EEA is Hachette Ireland
8 Castlecourt Centre
Dublin 15 D15 XTP3
Ireland
(email: info@hbgi.ie)

ISBN: 978-1-83618-940-4
eBook ISBN: 978-1-83618-939-8

For D.
I am so proud of you.

PROLOGUE

THREE YEARS BEFORE, ENGLAND

NADIA

She sat staring through the window at the fountain, watching the water cascade as the music washed over her, taking her back there, to where it all began. Where it ended too. Cairo. Or more specifically, the island in the middle of the Nile. Gezira, Zamalek – call it what you will. The oasis where she had found and lost so much, including Eden, the villa that had stolen her heart.

Eden was still there, decaying by the day, but she could never go back. There were too many ghosts wandering its corridors, getting up to high jinks in the garden where an identical fountain played, or dancing in the ballroom just as she and Tom had once danced to this very music, the chandeliers showering them in a thousand stars of light. She smiled, swaying her shoulders in time to the beat, whirling in his arms once more, head and heart spinning too.

'Nadia?' He was standing in the doorway clutching his briefcase, a look of concern on his face. 'Are you alright?'

She sat up straight in her armchair, the memories retreating into the recesses of her mind. 'Yes, yes of course. Come in, Ben. How are you?'

So like his great-grandfather, Freddie. Kind, dependable but with that added spark. She'd known she could trust him even before she instructed him. Old ties never die, and he was one of them, in the same way Sophie was. That the two of them would be tied together was only fitting. It brought things full circle. Almost.

'I'm fine, thank you. I rang the bell several times, but you didn't answer. I hope you don't mind me just walking in like this.'

She glanced at the briefcase as he placed it on the table. 'Good heavens, no. I asked you to come. I'm afraid I didn't hear the bell. This was one of Tom's favourite records, you see. Mine too. Would you like some tea?'

He smiled gently as he took the seat opposite her and poured from the pot she had ready. 'Glenn Miller, if I'm not mistaken?'

'You're absolutely correct. But I didn't ask you here to talk about music. It's time, you know, to set a few things straight.'

He pulled his pen from his pocket, attentive now. 'I see.'

'First, though, I want to give you this.' She opened her hand to reveal the ring nestled in it. A most unusual gold ring set with an indigo gemstone on which a goddess and a feather were engraved. 'It's for Sophie,' she went on. 'I know you've talked of getting engaged, and I wanted her to have this as her engagement ring, if she'd like to have it. I quite understand if you'd rather not. It is somewhat unusual, after all.'

'No, no. I mean, yes, I'm sure Sophie would love it. She loves anything from you, and this is truly special.' He took it from her, holding it up to the light. 'Is it Egyptian?'

'Phoenician originally. It's very old.'

'So I see. Thank you, Nadia. We'll treasure it.'

She looked at him, this young man who had won Sophie's

heart, as handsome in his way as Tom had been, with that same sense of honour. A man of his word. Not like the other one who had come to see her pretending he was there on behalf of some charity. He'd even had the cheek to park himself in her chair. She'd sent him packing, of course – but not before he'd clocked the photograph on the mantlepiece. She'd realised then she had to act fast; to summon Ben before it was too late.

She picked up the large manila envelope on the coffee table and handed it to Ben. 'In here you will find a letter and a photograph. You are to give the letter to Sophie on your wedding day. It's my final gift to you both.' She held up a hand as he opened his mouth to protest. 'I want you to send the photograph to the address on the other envelope. And please don't trouble her by telling her about our conversation today. You know how she worries.'

Ben gave her a reluctant nod. 'May I?'

She nodded, watching as he extracted the items, looking first at the sealed envelope with Sophie's name written on it and then at the photograph of a young man laughing into the lens, his fair hair tousled by a sea breeze, the sun highlighting his cheekbones and strong, straight nose, his gaze fixed on the person behind the camera. Ben glanced at the mantlepiece. 'Isn't this the photo of Tom you normally have up there?'

'Yes. I took it by the Red Sea. We sneaked away, you see, for a day at a beach. Such fun. I think it's my favourite picture of him. In fact, the only one I have of him, although what's perhaps more important is what's written on the back of it.'

Ben turned it over, studying the numbers written there. 'What is this? Code?'

'They're coordinates – or at least half a set. You'll find the rest at the address on the other envelope. I've left more instructions for you there, along with some clues. I know you and Sophie love to read, so I'd start in the library, if I were you.'

He stared at the address on the other envelope. '"Villa

Eden". Isn't that where you used to live in Cairo? The place you told me about?'

'It is indeed.' She faded for a moment, lost momentarily in the past or perhaps the music again, before she snapped back to the present, leaning forward with more urgency. 'I want you to take the letter now and the other envelope. The photograph I will keep with me until the end. I need to have him with me when I go. I hope you understand.'

'I understand what you're saying, but I don't think you're going anywhere soon, Nadia. Look at you. You do more than most twenty-year-olds I know.'

She chuckled. 'That's a lie and you know it. Yes, I've done a lot in my life, but it's important to know when to stop. Now, listen to me. When I do stop, I want you to post the photograph. Will you promise to do that?'

'Of course I will.'

'Good.'

He held it out to her. 'Here, why don't you put it back in its frame for now?'

She took it from him, trying to hide the tremor that came and went these days, placing it carefully on the arm of her chair. Not carefully enough. To her dismay, it teetered and then slid down between the cushions. Her precious photograph. She reached down, her fingers scrabbling for it, closing around it, her fingertips brushing something else, something small and hard. She knew at once what it was. So her instincts had been right. The same instincts that had saved her time and again out in the field. No need to alarm Ben. She palmed the device and dropped it into her tea, stirring it to cover the faint *chink* as it hit the bottom.

She took a sip. 'That's all settled then.'

Ben tucked his pen back in his pocket. 'Don't worry about a thing. I'll take care of it, Nadia.'

She sat back, closing her eyes for a moment. A sigh escaped her lips, a siren call to the spirits.

He frowned. 'Are you sure you're alright?'

Her eyes flew open, shining now with unshed tears. 'Absolutely sure. Better than I've been for ages, in fact.'

Better now she knew she would see him soon. See them all, just as she had out there, through the window, flitting across the lawn, their laughter audible beneath the tinkling of the water, forever young. Forever free. As she soon would be. Home to her Eden.

To Tom.

1

PRESENT DAY, CAIRO, EGYPT

SOPHIE

Two enormous bronze lions gazed at me, guarding the bridge that spanned the Nile, stretching into the gathering dusk. A sea of people swept towards me on the footpath while car horns honked and blared. It must have been so different in Nadia's day. Back then, this place was an oasis. The island at the beating heart of Cairo where our new life was supposed to begin. Ahead of me, I could see couples wrapped in one another's arms, gazing out over the river, alight now with a fireball of orange. They were cocooned by their love as I would have been, should have been.

If only.

I stopped, gripping the rail, a wave of nausea rushing through me. The river flowed below, a carpet of gold, sailing boats weaving and darting across it like moths. Overhead, a bird soared, flying straight into the sun as it slipped down the sky. A night heron maybe. Or a cormorant. Ben would have known. I always teased him about being a bird nerd. Teased him about many things. God, how I wished he was here with me. Or even just alive somewhere.

Was this how Nadia had felt too?

She'd loved Tom until her dying day. I could tell by the way she spoke of him, with deep longing and yet such affection. Almost as if he were still alive. She, of all people, would have understood. How I ached for them both, Ben and Nadia. The two people who had meant the most in the world to me were gone. Now all I had was their legacy – or rather, Nadia's legacy. I still found it hard to comprehend that she'd left it to me. Her villa. The place she'd been happiest. Where she and Tom had met and where they'd fallen in love. The place where he died. And where, somehow, Nadia had carried on even after the war, although those years were shrouded in secrecy. All she would say was that she felt Tom was there, still. Until the day she could bear it no more.

At least she'd had those final moments with Tom. I didn't even get to say goodbye to Ben. All I had was his last, urgent text. The one that still didn't make sense: 'Go to Cairo.'

We were going there anyway, on our honeymoon.

Moments after he sent that message, he was dead.

I felt the air stir as someone leaned on the bridge beside me. Turned my head. There was no one there.

'I got here,' I whispered. Alone, but I'd done it.

Now, perhaps, I would find out why.

The ball of fire slipped below the horizon, the shadows it left behind reaching out to me, melding with the darkness in my heart. Beside me, I felt nothing but an emptiness I knew only too well. The aching void that claimed me in the small hours when I turned to reach for him, only to remember and turn away again, my arms empty. Ben was dead. It was time to go.

I had to cross Opera Square to get to the hotel, running the gauntlet of the men muttering and smacking their lips as I passed. I pulled my scarf tighter around my shoulders. They would never have behaved like this if I'd had Ben with me. Then again, if I'd had Ben with me, we'd have been heading to the opera, hand in hand, laughing and talking. Instead, I was heading back to the hotel to dine alone.

I lifted my chin, daring them to accost me, holding my head proud, my heart thudding so hard I thought it might burst. Just a few more steps. I could see the hotel entrance now. All I had to do was get across the road. Lights on red. Perfect timing.

I stepped out and someone grabbed my arm. I tried to wrench it away, spinning on my heel to scream at him, my other arm clamped tight over my bag.

He hauled me back on the pavement. 'You could have been killed.'

I looked where he was pointing, at the cars racing down the road towards us, speeding through the junction where I'd been about to step out, motorbikes weaving in and out of them, horns blaring.

'But the lights were on red.'

He released my arm. 'That doesn't mean a thing here. Let me walk you across.'

He sounded American. In fact, under his tan he looked American – taller and broader than most of the locals, his hair light brown rather than black, green eyes looking at me with concern. 'I'm fine, thank you.'

'You're obviously not.'

I'm not sure what it was that undid me, maybe the note in his voice. Perhaps just hearing someone speak English or the fact he reminded me of Ben. Not so much in his looks, but there was something about him, the sense that I could trust him. It was one of the things I had loved most about Ben – his integrity along with his kindness. This man evidently possessed both too.

I could feel my eyes welling and dipped my head. Too late. He glanced at me then took my arm more gently this time, waiting for a break in the traffic before guiding me across and all the way to the hotel steps, where the doorman stood sentry.

'Please take care of madame,' he said, slipping a crumpled note into his hand.

The doorman sprang to attention. 'Yes, of course, sir.'

I turned to thank him, but he was already halfway down the steps. I called out after him. 'I'm sorry. I didn't even catch your name.'

He smiled and gave me a half-salute. 'It's Josh. Have a good evening.'

Then he was gone, swallowed up by the lights and the crowds moving in a torrent as unstoppable as the river Nile that flowed through this insane city. I gazed after him for a moment, feeling lonelier than ever. For a few seconds there, I'd felt safe. But safety was a mirage as much as any of those in the desert. And yet there was something about Josh that felt all too real.

2

The streets around the hotel were filled with modern shops and high-rises. I peered helplessly at the map on my phone. The villa must be around here somewhere, if it still existed – although, looking at the tower blocks that surrounded me, it had probably been razed to the ground many years before.

I walked as fast as I could in the morning cool, shoulders back and eyes fixed straight ahead, although daylight seemed to mute the stares. Even so, as soon as I could, I darted down a quiet side street that led away from the main boulevard, striding in the general direction of the opera house, trying to pretend I wasn't hopelessly lost. I pulled out my phone again and stared at the blue dot on the map. If anything, I was heading away from the street where I thought the villa was located, which now appeared to be miles away. Admitting defeat, I trudged back to the hotel.

'Excuse me?'

The concierge was young, but he radiated an air of efficiency. 'How can I help you, madame?'

I held out my phone. 'I'm trying to find this street. There's a villa there called Eden that my great-aunt used to own. Her name was Nadia. She lived there during the war and for a while afterwards. To be honest, I'm not even sure if it's still there.'

He studied my phone for a moment. 'Nadia, you say? Could you wait here please, madame? I have someone who might be able to help.'

I watched him cross the vast lobby, through the well-heeled tourists gathered in clusters working out their itinerary for the day or waiting to be scooped up by a guide. Nadia had paid for the hotel in advance, insisting it was her treat, or I would never have stayed here. It was too luxurious. Too Nadia. At least we had turned down her suggestion of the honeymoon suite. There was that.

'Here, madame.' The concierge was back with what looked to be one of the doormen, although he appeared too old to carry anything more than a handbag.

He bowed when he saw me. 'It is an honour, madame.'

I smiled, unsure what to say next.

'This is my grandfather, madame,' said the concierge. 'All my family have worked at this hotel for generations, although in the old days it didn't look like this.'

'I see.'

'My grandfather remembers that villa. In fact, I think he remembers your great-aunt too.' He turned to his grandfather, speaking now in Arabic.

The old man nodded, his face crinkling into a toothless grin.

'You knew Nadia?'

The grin faded slightly, replaced with a look of sorrow. There were tears shimmering in his eyes. Tears that matched my own. Instinctively, I took a step forward, holding out my hand to him. He clasped it between his, gazing at me as if I had emerged from a dream, murmuring something in Arabic.

'He knew her for many years, from when he started working here as a young boy of fourteen. He says you look like her,' explained the concierge.

The old man nodded. 'Yes, yes.'

'Many people say that. To be honest, she was more like a grandmother to me. She brought me up after my parents died. Here, I have a picture of her.'

I scrolled through my phone, holding up that last picture of her, the one I loved. The old man stared at it.

'But you probably remember her like this.'

This was a photo of a much younger Nadia, taken in England in the 1950s, after she returned from Egypt. I had the original at home, but I kept a copy on my phone too, a reminder of why I was here.

His face lit up as he looked from this photo to me.

'Nadia,' he enunciated before turning to his grandson once more, gesturing as he spoke.

'He says she was so beautiful, as you are beautiful. But you have the same sorrow in your eyes.'

'Tell him that's because we both lost the men we loved.'

The old man digested this for a moment, then stepped forward and placed his palm on my cheek, his eyes infinite pools of sorrow, his touch filled with love. There was something else too. A hint of a question. Maybe an answer as well. He turned and said something to the concierge, who scribbled on a piece of paper and handed it to me.

'My grandfather says that you are to go to this café on the corner of these two streets. It has no name, but you will recognise it because it's in the traditional style. Not some modern coffee shop. It's near to the villa, and you should find a man there who can help you, an Englishman called Mr David. He's there every day at around this time. In fact, his assistant came here to speak to my grandfather only yesterday, so I'm sure he's here, in Cairo.'

I looked from him to the piece of paper. 'Thank you. How does he know this man can help me?'

Another rapid-fire question. This time, the old man's eyes welled up once more.

'Apparently, Nadia told him to tell you that. They corresponded from time to time, you see, but then the letters from Nadia stopped coming. Now he knows why.'

I stared at them both, feeling another touch now, the sense of Nadia's hand reaching out to me from beyond the grave, showing me the way even now. A hand whose touch conveyed great love. And a warning.

3

The taxi driver dropped me outside the Bulgarian embassy in the north-west of the island, just as the concierge had instructed him. I'd memorised the route from there, watching his finger trace it on the paper map he'd given me. A right at the corner after the embassy, then a left and another left. It looked so easy when he showed me, but, of course, I was soon as lost as before.

All the streets around here looked the same, the villas that lined them older, with glorious gardens that stretched to the road. Most of them were ochre, their walls reflecting the desert that surrounded the city, while others were pale monuments to a colonial era that was long gone. Date palms rose behind wrought-iron gates, soaring above the acacias and sycamores that shaded the street. It was calmer here than at the other end of the island, although I still walked as fast as I could, my eyes scanning this street and the next and the next, searching for the café where some mysterious man would help me find Eden, the villa Nadia had once called home. The villa that was now mine.

Around another corner. Wait. Hadn't I been here before? I recognised the house on the corner and the van parked in the road. I'd been walking in circles. Frustration rose, thick in my throat. No point in screaming. It was now mid-morning and the temperature was rising.

I glanced across the street and there it was, a traditional café on the opposite side of the boulevard, wooden chairs set by tables under an awning that offered shade. This had to be the place the old man meant.

I scanned the tables, all of them occupied by men whiling away the morning over tiny cups of tea or coffee, some engaged in a game of backgammon, others setting the world to rights. I made my way over to the vacant table in the corner.

'You need a hat.'

I had barely sat down and ordered a coffee when the elderly man at the next table put down his newspaper and squinted at me from under his own straw fedora, his voice curiously old-fashioned, as if he were a BBC announcer from a bygone age. He was the only European in the place. It had to be him. I threw him a tentative smile. 'Are you Mr David by any chance?'

'My name is David, yes. And you are?'

'I'm Sophie. The concierge at my hotel told me I would find you here. I think you knew my great-aunt Nadia.'

That was all the invitation he needed. He moved his chair so that it was closer to my table than his. I caught the waft of whisky fumes on his breath. 'You don't mean Nadia Pulaska?'

'I do.'

He was dressed in rumpled white linen, a shock of hair that was equally white standing up from what had once been a noble brow. His eyes were pouched, his nose bulbous and riddled with broken veins that spread out across his cheeks, the sure sign of a drinker. His gaze, however, was sharp, taking me in just as I was studying him. 'You have a look of her. How is Nadia?'

'I'm afraid she's dead. She died two years ago.' With Ben and me at her bedside, holding her hands. I was glad we were both with her at the end. At least she hung on that long. It was thanks to her that we'd met, after all.

I sometimes wondered what my life would have been like had she not chosen Ben to represent her. He'd done a good job getting her compensation. Of course he had. That was Ben all over. He particularly loved those cases, representing people whose property had been taken during the war, helping them get it back or at least get what they deserved. In a way, he felt as if he was carrying on what his great-grandfather Freddie had started back then, working alongside Nadia, fighting for justice. He'd handled Nadia's will too, although I didn't know that until the day it was read and I learned I was the sole beneficiary. Another mystery.

Nadia had other relatives who were still alive, a brother among them. I suppose she may have looked on me as the daughter she never had, but it was still a shock to discover that I was the owner of a villa in Cairo, as well as the proud possessor of a lifetime's worth of books and bric-a-brac. The rest I gave to her remaining family, including her compensation. It was only right, after all. They had lost their home and lands in Poland too. The villa, though, was another matter, and Ben was oddly insistent I not only take on its ownership but that we visit it for our honeymoon. The honeymoon we never took.

The man was dabbing at his eyes with his napkin. 'Nadia is dead. Dear, dear. I suppose she must have been very old. We're all old now. At any rate, if you want to see the villa, it's just over there, down that street.'

I looked across the road – he was pointing at a side street I hadn't yet ventured down.

Eden.

At last.

4

I must have looked bewildered because he repeated his instructions, making them even clearer. 'Go down that street and then take the first right off it. A left after that and then another left.'

I was on my feet almost before he'd finished speaking. 'Thank you so much. I'm sorry – I didn't introduce myself properly. I'm Sophie...'

I stumbled, my lips unable to form my surname. It should have been Sophie Gibson by now. After much banter, I'd agreed to take Ben's name.

'You don't like my name?' he'd teased.

'I love your name. I just think it's an archaic practice, taking your husband's surname. They don't do it in other countries. I'm not your personal possession, you know.'

He'd started to kiss the back of my neck, sending sparks of desire shooting through me all the way to the pit of my stomach. 'How about this? Is this an archaic practice?'

'Stop it.'

'You really want me to?'

'Oh God, no.'

David rose from his seat too, jerking me back to the present. 'It's lovely to meet you, Sophie. You really do remind me of Nadia. In fact, I'm working on a book about her right now. Well, not just her – it's mostly about my family history, some of which involves the villa.'

I gaped at my new friend for a second, torn between finding the villa and finding out more. Right now, though, I just wanted to get there, to Eden.

'I wonder... perhaps we could have another drink. Here, let me give you my number. I'm here for a while yet.' I began scrabbling in my bag for a pen and a scrap of paper. He pulled a hip flask from his pocket and added a healthy dash of its contents to his coffee with a trembling hand. 'No need, my dear. You can find me here every day at this time. Isn't that right, Hassan?'

He looked up at the proprietor, who placed my change on the table. 'Yes, indeed, Mr Molyneux.'

I left the change where it was. 'In that case, I'll go and find the villa and then I'll be back. I'd love to talk to you some more about Nadia, if that's alright.'

He slurped his coffee, his eyes fading out of focus once more. I had a feeling he was seeing not me but Nadia. 'Yes, yes. Off you go.'

Dismissed, I scurried across the street, dodging the taxi hurtling towards me and the scooter coming down the wrong side of the road, taking a right where he had indicated and then the first left followed by another left. It took me to a dead end. I retraced my steps, thinking that perhaps I had got it wrong. But there was no other left off the original street, just another avenue of villas, some modern and some restored. I returned to the dead end, a high wall surrounding what looked to be a larger villa than most, finally spotting the narrow alley beyond a rusted gate to my left that stood open, an errant vine winding through its curlicues, obscuring the entrance.

I hesitated, looking over my shoulder. There was no one

around and no other form of left turning. This must be what he'd meant. Then again, the stench of whisky on his breath had been overwhelming. This might not be the place at all.

I peered down the alleyway, which was almost blocked in places by the shrubs and branches that overhung it from the garden behind the wall, silently cursing David, wondering if I should risk it or not. Sod it. I'd come this far. The worst that could happen was someone shouting at me for trespassing.

I shoved at the gate, but it didn't budge, so I squeezed my way through the gap, ducking low where the branches made the pathway impassable until, finally, I emerged in another street. Straight across from me stood another villa, its garden so overgrown that I couldn't make out the sign on its gate until I parted the leaves that covered it.

'Eden,' it read in hand-painted letters, the colour faded to such an extent that it was the only word I could make out.

'My God,' I whispered, gazing up at the gaping windows. Their shutters hung uselessly, the glass smashed in some of them, while others were intact. The front door was a washed-out, peeling green, the steps leading up to it treacherous and crumbling in places. I tugged at the rusted old chain around the entrance gate. It snapped within seconds. The gate itself gave easily, swinging open with a sigh as if it had been waiting a long time for me to arrive.

I picked my way up the path and then the steps, holding my breath as I turned the knob on the front door. Locked. Of course it was. This place might have lain abandoned for years but it wasn't about to give up its secrets so easily. No doubt Nadia's property manager here could supply me with a key, but I had yet to track him down.

I stumbled back down the steps, trying to remember all the stories Nadia had told me about this place, the tales of hard partying in between their missions.

'Oh, darling,' she'd say, 'we had such fun. We even had a

ballroom, and we invited absolutely everybody over. The king came a couple of times to our parties, although he preferred to be out in the garden having a smoke, you know.'

I could only imagine.

As I stood on the path facing the front door, the garden extended around the back of the house to my right, a tangle of weeds, trees and overgrown shrubs that must have been glorious at one time. Another path was scarcely visible through the scrub, leading to what looked like a derelict courtyard, its mosaic tiles as faded and worn as the rest.

I worked my way along it, holding aside branches and keeping an eye out for any snakes who might have decided to take up residence, stepping onto what was once a lawn but was now a carpet of weeds. A set of French doors opened onto it from the house, although these, too, were barred and bolted from the inside. Further round, however, another door was hanging off its hinges. I jerked it open and stepped into what appeared to be the kitchen. Dishes and tagines were still arrayed on open shelves. A cupboard door stood open, displaying the rusting tins inside. I reached out to touch one, imagining Nadia here, laughing as she always did, whipping up some inedible meal or, more likely, a cocktail.

'They're medicinal, darling,' she would say. 'A cocktail makes everything better.'

I wasn't so sure about that. After Ben died, I tried to drown my sorrows. It didn't work. I could still smell him in every room, on all his clothes that I couldn't bear to give away. I saw him out of the corner of my eye, a flash of movement that, when I turned, was nothing more than wishful thinking. Above all, I heard him in every note of the songs he played, over and over, on the piano he bought me as an engagement present, promising to give me lessons. The piano I'd always wanted. The one that meant nothing now he was gone.

I could hear him playing now, his fingers dancing over the

keys. No, that wasn't him. Of course it wasn't. But there was someone playing a waltz, and it sounded as if it was coming from inside the villa. I ran my hand through my hair, feeling the sweat on my forehead, droplets of it clinging to my skin. Just my imagination. The heat. My memories. No, it wasn't. I could definitely hear music. The three-four timing was insistent, compelling, demanding that I dance.

My feet were moving to it as I followed the sound out of the kitchen and through what appeared to be a salon, its couches and chairs covered in dust sheets, looking for all the world like crouching ghosts. I carried on, pushing through another set of double doors, stepping into a ray of sunlight that sliced through two vast chandeliers above, sending sparkles like diamonds glittering across the ceiling. This must be the ballroom Nadia had loved so much. The place where she had danced with her Tom.

A parquet floor stretched before me, dust motes rising from it, gyrating like sprites in time to the music I could hear in my head. At the far end of the room stood a grand piano, its lid down. Between me and it, flashes of colour that took form as they swirled, heads thrown back, laughing, their voices mingling now with the music, the sunlight ever brighter, filling my vision now, my head whirling too. Dancing towards me, a figure I would recognise anywhere, holding out his arms.

'Ben, what are you doing here?' I whispered.

He looked different, somehow, his dinner jacket cut in a way that reminded me of old black-and-white movies, a moustache adorning his upper lip, his hair combed back in a style I'd never seen him wear. Ben's hair flopped over his forehead, or at least one stubborn cowlick did.

I reached up to touch it, longing to tug out that lock of hair, to see my Ben again. As I did so, a shadow passed over the sunbeam, erasing it, plunging everything into darkness. White noise filled my head like static. Beneath it, whispers, distant voices calling out to me, murmuring like sirens, singing of gold and of treachery. Of passion and curses. Of undying love. And murder most cold.

'Ben!'

I called out his name as the floor rushed up to meet me, my outstretched arms breaking my fall before the world faded to black.

5

16 SEPTEMBER 1942, CAIRO, EGYPT

NADIA

The truck roared off, leaving me at the gate with my suitcase and the girls on their leashes. I pushed it open and walked up the path past the rose bushes that lined it, breathing in their scent along with that of the eucalyptus trees that dotted the lawn. There were more roses scrambling over the wall that surrounded the villa, twining through the hibiscus in bloom. A faint breeze tickled the bamboo rushes, their gentle swishing an accompaniment to the sound of trickling water from the inevitable fountain. I inhaled it with all my senses. After the cacophony of central Cairo, this place was an oasis of peace.

As I put my foot on the first of the steps that stretched up to the house, the front door was flung open and a fair-haired young man bounded down, an Alsatian puppy at his heels. He might have stepped straight off the playing fields of Eton or Harrow, although there was a battle-hardened look in his eyes that belied his years.

'Tom Molyneux,' he drawled, picking up my suitcase. 'You

must be Nadia. Welcome to Eden.' He glanced at the girls. 'What the devil do we have here?'

'These are my pet mongooses. Their names are Kochanie and Malenka. Kochanie means "honey" in Polish, and Malenka "little one".'

The puppy was staring at the two of them, rigid with fear. He ventured a sniff but backed off, whimpering, when Malenka bared her teeth. 'It's alright, Pixie,' Tom soothed, adding, 'I hope they don't take after you.'

'Fortunately, I have a much friendlier disposition.'

Especially when faced with someone like Tom. Jacqui might have warned me he was this attractive when she extended his invitation to lodge at the villa, although, to be fair, she was kept so busy between entertaining at the embassy, running the Red Cross and tending to Sir Miles that I sometimes wondered how she did it all. Somehow she managed everything with her customary warmth and style, insisting I must take up this invitation.

'Gezira is much quieter and safer than downtown Cairo, darling. You'll be able to get more rest there, and I understand there are two other women who are also moving in.'

Now that I was here, I could see what she meant. Although looking at Tom, I wasn't so sure about the rest part. I followed him up the steps and into the villa, where a manservant in full regalia hovered.

'This is Miss Nadia, Abbas,' said Tom, handing him my suitcase. 'She's in the Cleopatra room.'

'Very good, sir. Please come with me, Miss Nadia.'

'Abbas is our butler. He takes excellent care of us,' added Tom. 'You'll meet the others later. Drinks at six o'clock sharp in the garden room followed by dinner at eight.'

I glanced at my suitcase. It contained a swimsuit, an evening gown and my uniform. 'I assume you dress for dinner?'

'Naturally.'

'I'll see you at six then.'

He gave me a brief smile. 'Very good.'

I decided then and there that I'd give Tom Molyneux a run for his money. By my reckoning, he was a few years younger than me. He might have a veneer of sophistication, but I suspected that hid a certain vulnerability, especially around women. The sensitive mouth was a clue. The softness in his gaze another. Then there was the disturbing realisation I was thinking about him even while I was dressing for dinner. I pulled out my notebook and scrawled a new entry. It consisted of two words: Tom Molyneux?

6

He was standing at the bottom of the stairs, head bent over a book, as I descended in my one evening gown.

'Are you waiting for me?'

He looked up, snapping the book shut as his mouth fell open, a schoolboy blush burnishing his cheeks. Admittedly, my gown was low-cut but not so low as to be indecent. That décolletage had served its purpose several times, loosening tongues. It looked as if it was doing the opposite on Tom Molyneux.

'I, uh, no. I was just in the library,' he stuttered.

'There's a library here too? You'll have to show me.'

He smiled, equilibrium returning, and tucked the book under his arm. 'I'd love to, but first let me introduce you to everyone. The garden room is this way.'

I could already hear the chatter from it along with the sound of a gramophone playing Glenn Miller. As we entered, I also caught the earthy, sweet whiff of cigars, along with a hint of cologne. Or perhaps that was Tom, standing beside me. He cleared his throat. 'Gentlemen, this is Countess Nadia Pulaska of the Polish Red Cross. She will be joining us for the duration. What can I get you to drink?'

'That martini you're drinking looks perfect.' I glanced at the others ranged around the room, all of them male, Pixie the puppy asleep beneath a couch. 'How do you do?'

A darker, more scholarly-looking version of Tom pulled the pipe from his mouth and held out his hand. 'Freddie Gibson. Delighted to make your acquaintance. This reprobate here is Nico Casanoff.'

'Casanoff?'

The swarthy man who had been hovering by the French windows bent low over my hand. As his lips brushed it, his cologne filled my nostrils. I recognised the heady perfume over-laid with musk. It spelled danger. And mischief.

'Enchanted,' he murmured, his eyes raking my face. There was a gleam in them that I also recognised.

I smiled. 'Likewise.'

Tom handed me my drink, but my lips had barely touched it when the double doors to the garden room were flung open and a man dressed in an American uniform strode in.

His gaze fell on me. 'I guess you're the new arrival.'

Out the corner of my eye, I saw Kochanie come scampering in after him. Damn. She must have broken out of my room.

'Hello, I'm Nadia.'

I got the impression he'd inspected me and found me wanting in thirty seconds flat. 'Jim Taylor. Good to meet you.' All at once, Kochanie launched herself at him, jabbering with rage. 'What the hell...?'

I grabbed her, pulling her off him. 'It's alright. This is Kochanie, my pet mongoose. She gets very jealous.'

From behind us, a burst of laughter and then an exquisite creature floated in, her black hair curling around a face that reminded me of Ava Gardner, although this woman was even more exotic, her emerald eyes framed with dark lashes in striking contrast to her olive-toned skin.

'Charmed another girl, have you, darling?' She smiled

mischievously as she took in the scene. 'He's absolutely irre-sistible, you know,' she added, dropping me a wink.

Ignoring the undercurrent to her tone, I scooped up Kochanie and took her back to my room, which looked as if it had been burgled, the sheets ripped from the bed and one curtain hanging drunkenly from its railing, dipping lower and lower as Malenka swung from it.

'You're both very naughty,' I admonished. Tomorrow, I would find better quarters for them. Right now, I needed to get back downstairs and unravel the web of intrigue I could already feel tightening. The enigmatic Casanoff was definitely not who he said he was. But then, so many of us operated under code names. As for the handsome American and his companion – the electricity between them positively crackled with promise, although of what I couldn't yet tell.

Her gaze fell on me the moment I re-entered the room.

She advanced, a slender hand outstretched, the diamonds in her bracelet catching the light as she reached for mine. 'I don't believe we've been properly introduced. I'm Colette. You must be Nadia. Tom said you'd agreed to move in.'

Her touch was cool, her perfume heady. 'I am and I have. Do you live here too?'

'Oh good heavens no, darling. I have my own apartment in Garden City. Tell me, what is it you do? Tom said you were living all alone in some ghastly hotel.'

'I work for the Polish Red Cross here in Cairo. And you're right. The hotel was rather ghastly. It was Jacqui – Lady Lampson – who suggested I move in here. The British ambas-sador's wife. We work together sometimes.'

'Really?' She extracted a small, silver cigarette case from her purse and flicked it open, offering me one. I glanced at the insignia on it as she snapped it shut again, a gold spearhead set in a black oval. I'd seen it somewhere before. 'Do you have a light?'

'Allow me.'

Nico appeared as if from nowhere brandishing a lighter. Colette smiled her thanks. While she applied the tip of her cigarette to his flame, I studied her more closely. That symbol. I remembered now where I'd seen it. It was the insignia of the Office of Strategic Services, our American cousins in spycraft.

'Another drink?'

I looked up to see the American, Jim. At least, that was what he said he was called. He had those fine, even teeth all Americans seemed to have. They were bared now in a smile.

'That would be lovely.'

'Why don't you come with me? Tell me exactly how you like it?'

Colette was laughing at something Nico was saying, although he kept his voice too low for me to hear.

Jim brandished the gin bottle from the drinks trolley. 'She's quite something, isn't she?'

Caught out, I smiled boldly into his eyes. 'Indeed she is.'

'I trained her, you know.'

'I'm sorry?'

'Let's not play games, Countess. You spotted her cigarette case. I saw you. Which means you know she's working for us.'

Still, I prevaricated, unsure where this was heading. 'Us?'

He snorted. 'OSS.'

'You work for them?'

'I don't just work for them; I train them. Colette was one of my best students, if not *the* best, although I have a feeling you'd be pretty good too.'

I heard a by now familiar drawl in my ear, one that sent an unexpected thrill through me. 'Too late, old boy. Nadia already works for us.'

7

PRESENT DAY, CAIRO, EGYPT

SOPHIE

Someone was calling my name from far away, over and over. I was floating underwater, the weight of it muffling their voice, its constant swooshing filling my ears.

'Sophie!'

I sighed. It was much easier just to float here.

They called it again, louder: 'Sophie. Wake up. Come on, Sophie. That's it.'

I forced my eyes open and shut them almost immediately. The lights were still whirling on the ceiling. Or maybe that was my head.

With a groan, I pushed myself up on my elbow. 'What happened?'

'You fainted. Don't try to stand up. Here, sip this.'

He was handing me a bottle of water. I took a gulp and choked on it, spluttering most of it out again. 'S-Sorry,' I stuttered.

There was something familiar about him. His voice. That

accent. What the hell happened? I put my hand to my forehead, feeling the bump on it where it hurt.

He slid his arm around me. 'Here, lean on me. Let's get you up.'

That was when it hit me. 'It's you.'

He was depositing me gently in a chair, clouds of dust rising from it all around me. 'We really must stop meeting like this,' he quipped.

I swiped the specks from my eyes, gazing out over the dance floor with smeared vision. I thought for an instant I could see him again. *Them* again. Then I blinked and they disappeared once more, swirling back into my memories, or perhaps another time, one I had stumbled into. Hot tears welled, spilling as I stared and stared, willing him to come back. 'They've gone,' I whispered. 'He's gone. No, Ben. Come back.'

There was a cough from behind us and then another voice, one I also recognised. 'Josh, dear boy, do you think we should take her to the hospital? She might have concussion.'

I shook my head. 'No, no. I'm alright.'

Nothing now save an empty room stretching before me, the piano at the far end lifeless, music no longer playing in my head. Instead, there was the endless silence that had filled it since they'd taken me into a side room at the hospital and told me that Ben was gone. 'Pronounced dead on arrival,' was how they'd put it. I'd shaken my head then too. They were wrong. Ben couldn't die. Not my Ben. It wasn't until they'd let me see him and I'd stroked his lifeless cheek that I'd known. Ben was never coming back.

Except he had, right here in this dusty ballroom. Or maybe just in my mind and heart.

I could sense the two men hovering, wondering what to do with me. I smiled my thanks to the younger one – Josh if I remembered right. Then at the older man. Our conversation in the café felt like a lifetime ago.

'I found it,' I said. 'Nadia's villa.'

'Yes, you did,' he murmured. 'I suspect you stirred up a few ghosts too.'

I stared at him and then beyond him, desperately hoping to see them again, to see Ben, knowing that the old man was right. They were nothing more than mirages in my mind, phantom glimpses of what might have been, ghosts of love lost conjured by the longing in my own heart.

8

'Shall we go out the front door?'

The room swirled again as I stood.

'Here.' Josh was holding out his arm. 'Lean on me.'

'No, really, I'm OK. It was just a blood rush. I think the front door is locked – at least it was when I tried it.'

Sure enough, it was both locked and bolted. Whoever left here last had gone out through the back.

Josh tried the handle again just to make sure and then spotted something on the ancient doormat. He bent to pick it up. 'A letter. Addressed to a Sophie Barclay.'

'That's me.'

I stared at the envelope in his hand, mired with dust and grime. I'd know that handwriting anywhere, the way Nadia formed the letter 'S' in sinuous curves, as bold as she was.

'Looks like this letter has been here a while.' Josh was gazing at me, questions written in his eyes. I averted mine, reaching out for the letter, hating myself as it shook like a leaf in my grasp.

'Two years,' I mumbled, gazing at the postmark, seeing the date and feeling the shock of it sear my bones. 'Two years almost to the day. He must have posted this the day he died.'

I could see him now, announcing he had to carry out an errand as he tucked an envelope into his pocket. An envelope which looked very much like this one. Nadia's last wish. The one he insisted he couldn't tell me about before he walked along the lane to the nearest postbox, leaving me furious and bewildered. It was one of my biggest regrets – that my last words to him were in anger. They found him in the ditch just along from the postbox, left for dead.

'Who did?' Josh's voice was gentle, concerned.

'Ben.'

'Ben? Who's Ben? You were talking about him as you came round.'

I barely heard him, my heart was pounding so hard. Whatever was in this envelope might hold a clue. It was one of the last things he'd ever done, posting it. It had to have been important. And why was it addressed to me here? Was it some kind of a surprise for our honeymoon? The villa had been a big part of that, after all. Discovering Nadia's gift to me. To us. So many questions. The answers could be inside the envelope. Still, I couldn't bear to open it. If he hadn't gone to post the damn thing, he might still be alive today. My Ben. My life.

'I think perhaps we should take Sophie back to the apartment,' said David. 'She looks as if she's had quite a shock.'

'Apartment? What apartment?'

'The one where my wife and I lived until she passed on. Now it's just me. And Josh for the moment. He's helping me write that book I told you about, you see, the one all about my family history here in Cairo and after that. Don't worry, my dear. You'll be perfectly safe with us. Nadia came to visit us there several times when she was still here. It's not far.'

'A book? You're a writer?'

Josh inclined his head. 'That's how we first bumped into one another. I was at your hotel to meet a contact.'

I met David's quizzical look. 'Josh rescued me from being run over.'

David snorted. 'Sounds like something he would do.'

I gazed at them both, my instincts telling me I could trust them. David had known Nadia. They were friends. That was enough of a recommendation for me. Besides, if I was with them, I didn't have to open the envelope. Not yet. The genie could stay in its bottle for a while longer. Or rather, the djinn. That was what they called them here, the spirits that could be good or evil, created from smokeless fire, or so the legend went. Whatever was in the envelope could be one or the other too. I'd find out soon enough. I tucked the envelope in my bag, my fingers fumbling with the clasp, my whole hand shaking with the effort.

'You're right,' I murmured. 'I'm not feeling too good. Let's get out of here.'

The apartment was on the second floor of what had once been a colonial mansion. The fan that rotated in the ceiling created a welcome breeze. After a few minutes in the blissful cool, I was feeling more in control.

'Are you sure you wouldn't like to lie down?'

I was propped against silk cushions, my feet on a footstool in front of the wicker peacock chair in which I sat, a tall glass of iced water on the inlaid table beside me. In the chair opposite me, David was rifling through a cigar box of old photographs while Josh leaned against the windowsill, a look of concern on his face.

I smiled. 'No, really, I feel so much better now.'

'David has boxes full of these old photographs,' said Josh. 'Don't you?'

'They were given to me for safekeeping,' muttered David.

'By whom?'

David's face clouded. 'By my father.'

'Was he friends with Nadia too?'

'In a way.'

Those three words hung in the air, resonating through the room. David sighed, a heartfelt quiver that shuddered through him as he dropped his head, evidently overcome. Josh stepped forward and took the box from his hands. 'What David means is that his father was Tom's brother.'

Tom. The love of Nadia's life. The man she never got over. She would talk about him sometimes, her eyes misting, generally after a third glass of wine. She had certainly never found anyone to replace him. Instead, she poured all her love into me.

David raised his head, speaking with some effort. 'My father was Tom's younger brother. After Tom died, quite a long time after, my grandfather was sent these boxes full of his papers and photos.'

I frowned. 'I don't understand. Who sent them to him?'

'The British embassy.'

'Why on earth did they have them?'

'The SOE office here in Cairo passed them on to the embassy after the service was wound up,' said David. 'Apparently, they then sat gathering dust for years until someone thought to contact my grandfather.'

'Why him? Why not Nadia?'

'As you probably know, Tom and Nadia were never married. In fact, Tom was still legally married to someone else when he died. My grandfather was the next of kin.'

'Wait a minute.' Another memory tickling at my brain, bursting through in a rush of revelation. 'I remember Nadia telling me now. Wasn't it your father who stole Tom's wife from him? His own brother? Didn't they have a child together?'

David's face clouded. 'Unfortunately, yes. That child was me.'

The man in the photograph bore a passing resemblance to Tom too, but his chin was weaker, his gaze turned inward rather than towards the woman who stood beside him cradling her baby. Their baby.

'This is me,' said David. 'Eight months after I was born. They had moved by then to their own place away from the family estate. My grandparents eventually came round, long after they were finally able to marry, but my father felt guilty until the end of his days.'

He didn't look guilty. In fact, he looked rather pleased with himself, while the woman in the photograph, David's mother, appeared somewhat dazed. I could understand how she might have been lonely while Tom was away at war, and they had married very young. Too young. Even so, to steal your own brother's wife was a betrayal too far. Whatever the pair of them had done, their child, David, was the innocent victim of their selfishness. And it was selfish beyond belief.

I could never, *would never*, have betrayed Ben in that way. We'd talked of having children, of course, whispering in the dark of how they would look and what we would name them. I wanted a boy and a girl. He didn't care.

'As long as they're healthy and look like you,' he would say as I admired his fine profile, longing for the children who would resemble us both in perfect fusion. The children who would never be.

I turned my attention back to David. 'Did you have brothers and sisters?'

'One of each. They're a few years younger than me. My parents waited until they were married before they had more. You know, you really do look extraordinarily like Nadia when she was young. Let me see if I have a photograph of her in here.'

He rummaged in his cigar box again, sifting through the piles of photographs in there. 'Here we go,' he cried, passing me one. 'This was taken at a party at the villa.'

I turned the photograph over. 'Eden, 17 September 1942,' was scrawled on the reverse in copperplate, the ink faded to sepia. The photograph, too, was faded, one corner creased and another spotted with age, but the image was clear enough. A group of people standing under a tree in the garden, drinks in their hands, their faces bleached by the flash. I could make out Nadia standing next to a tall man who looked to be Egyptian, a sash bisecting the long coat he wore over a white shirt in place of a dinner jacket. On his head, a fez. Adorning his chest, a medal. Across his face, an expression of pure delight as he smiled down at Nadia.

'That's the king,' said David, leaning forward to jab at the photograph. 'Farouk. Nadia knew him quite well. I believe he liked her very much.'

Nadia was laughing up at him, caught, it appeared, mid-conversation. Whoever had taken this photograph had done so unawares.

'And that's Tom.'

I stared at his handsome, smiling face, his eyes only for Nadia. 'I've never seen a photograph of them together before.'

'I believe this is the only one.'

So much still to understand, but I was fighting the waves of exhaustion washing over me. It had been quite a day. Too much of a day, and I still had the envelope to open. I could feel the privacy of my hotel room calling to me. 'I think I've taken up enough of your time. I'd better be getting back to the hotel.'

Josh stepped forward. 'Let me take you.'

I hesitated. There was something in his eyes that told me to agree. An invitation perhaps. Or a dare. 'There's really no need.'

'I insist. You were unconscious for quite a while. It would be negligent of me to let you go alone.'

David was gathering up his photographs, his fingers lingering over one or two as he stacked them back in their box. In his eyes, regret tinged with a great sadness. The sadness, maybe, that had driven him to drink. In the face of it, the last vestiges of my anger disappeared. All I could see was a frail old man who was haunted by the past. 'Then I accept. Thank you for showing me your photos, David. It means a lot to see Nadia so young and happy.'

He looked up at me with eyes clouded by time. 'She was very happy there, you know. So happy and so alive. We all loved Nadia. I know Tom did, very much.'

'I'll go back and secure that door for you,' said Josh. 'The rest of the place too. The least we can do is make sure the villa is safe.'

It was all I could manage to whisper, 'Thank you.'

So many questions, but they were for later, if ever. Right now, I needed to be alone, to think, to try to unravel what I had seen in that ballroom. I let Josh lead me out and into the street, where he hailed a taxi.

It was only when we were safely inside the cab that he turned to me and said, 'It was the gold, you know, that killed

Tom. If they hadn't gone after it, they would probably have had years together, him and Nadia.'

I stared at him. 'The gold?'

'She never told you about it?'

I shook my head. 'She told me many things but also kept quiet about a lot, mostly things she couldn't bear to talk about. Tell me what happened.'

He studied my face for a second as if he was trying to work something out. 'All in good time.'

'Oh come on! You have to tell me now.'

He stared straight ahead of him, through the taxi windscreen, although his focus was somewhere else. 'I don't believe in this kind of stuff, but I'll tell you one thing. That gold was definitely cursed.'

10

17 SEPTEMBER 1942, CAIRO, EGYPT

NADIA

The champagne bottles lay discarded on the floor, glasses scattered across every surface. Dinner was a distant memory, although I seemed to recall much laughter over the endless parade of glorious dishes served up by Abbas. I gazed out into the garden through the French windows, seeing nothing but silhouettes and shadows. Colette was stretched out on the couch, Jim's head in her lap. I could hear the pitter-patter of the puppy's paws as it followed Tom across the room. He pressed a tumbler into my hand. I took a sniff, inhaling the wood, vanilla and caramel notes that signalled a fine cognac. 'Nightcap for you.'

'It's almost dawn.'

It was true. The silhouettes of the trees outside were now tinged with the rosy glow of the approaching day. As if on cue, a lark started to sing.

'"It was the lark, the herald of the morn / No nightingale," ' I murmured.

Tom picked up where I left off. "'Look, love, what envious streaks / Do lace the severing clouds in yonder east.'"

I smiled. 'You know your Shakespeare.'

'I was reading English at Magdalen before all this started up. *Romeo and Juliet* is one of my favourite plays. We have a fine copy of *The Complete Works* in the library here. Let me show you.'

The puppy trotted after us as I followed Tom back to the main entrance hall and through a door that led off it at the spot where I'd seen him standing, his head bowed over a book, the evening before. The door opened onto a room so golden I thought at first the lights must have been left on. Leather-bound books lined the shelves that covered each wall, their spines lettered in gold. The air was filled with the smell of them along with that musky scent of pages long loved. On the desk beneath the window sat a reading lamp, also gold, while the armchairs that occupied the corners had plump cushions decorated with golden thread. I gasped aloud, my eyes drinking it all in. 'What a lovely room.'

'Isn't it? This villa belongs to a family of academics, although they are in Paris now, unfortunately for them. I try to take great care of their books.'

I inhaled their scent once more. It took me back to another library, the one we'd had at home in Poland. 'My husband also loved Shakespeare,' I said. 'We used to read his sonnets to one another.'

'Your husband?'

'He was killed in 1939. Shot by the Nazis.'

'I'm so sorry.'

I gave him a bleak little smile. 'Thank you.'

What else was there to say?

Andrzej's fate was sealed before the Germans even entered Poland bearing a list of nobles, politicians, actors, scholars, doctors, priests and intelligentsia, among others, all of whom were to be summarily executed. Andrzej's name was on that list, along with mine as his wife and those of my entire family and his. Fortunately for us, we fled our country estate before the Nazis got to it, driving south to Romania and on across the Balkans until, finally, we ended up in Mandatory Palestine, from where I travelled to Cairo while the others set sail for London and safety. By then, I knew Andrzej was dead.

Dead too was our only child, my little boy Alexander. Barely ten months old, he did not survive the journey. In the space of a few short months, the Nazis had taken everything from me. It was why I did what I did, the memories fuelling the fire that never died within me, although sometimes the flames threatened to consume me whole. I'd thought of them when I pulled that trigger in Paris. Andrzej and Alexander. My family. My everything.

I heard Tom, beside me, clear his throat. 'Are you alright? You've gone awfully pale.'

'Yes, yes of course. It's just... please show me some of these books.'

Sensing I needed the distraction, he reached up and pulled a red volume from the shelf. '*The Complete Works of Shakespeare*. Here we go: "Night's candles are burnt out, and jocund day / Stands tiptoe on the misty mountain tops. / I must be gone and live, or stay and die."'

The moment Juliet realised that Romeo must leave after their night of lovemaking. And he read it so well, his voice mellifluous, gliding over the words as if they were his own thoughts. Perhaps they were. We all lived on a knife edge, never knowing what the next day could bring. Or if there was even to be a next day. It was why so many fell in love fast. Or at least in lust. Might as well seize the moment while you had it in your grasp. Or before it was snatched from you by a Nazi firing squad.

I smiled. 'Act Three, Scene Five. You really do know your

Shakespeare, although I'd have thought you were more a *Julius Caesar* man.'

'Why? Because I put you in the Cleopatra room?'

There was devilment in his eyes now. A challenge. Perhaps I'd underestimated him. 'Well, now, that would only be a reason if you intended to visit my chamber. Which, of course, you won't be doing.'

He laughed – a deep belly laugh that brought a smile to my face. 'I was warned about you. It appears it was all true.'

'By whom?'

'The king.'

I raised an eyebrow. 'What would he know?'

'You can ask him yourself at the party tonight.'

The sky was lightening now to a pearl grey. Soon, the sun's rays would filter through. Another dawn in Cairo, the city I'd refused to leave despite the German armies on its doorstep before we routed them. Not for the first time, I wondered if that had been a mistake. Maybe Romeo was right. 'What party?'

'The one we're throwing to welcome you to Eden.'

'Are you serious? I have to go to work today. There are still hundreds of evacuees arriving.'

'So? The party's not until the evening. You can have a little snooze before then. Besides, the party is work too, of a kind. Speaking of which, we'd better go and wake the others. There's a lot to do before tonight.'

A lurch of disappointment deep in my gut. I was enjoying this time alone with him, here in this golden library, the zig and zag of wordplay between us. I liked that he loved words too. In fact, there was a lot to like about Tom, including his perfect manners as he stood aside with a gallant little flourish to allow me through the door first.

I glanced around the garden room as we entered, at Jim and Colette now curled up together, asleep, at Freddie bleary-eyed but still blustering from his armchair, bending the ear of Nico, who nodded sagely through the smoke rings he was blowing. This villa, this island set in the middle of the Nile – they were worlds apart from the reality out there. Every single day, more of the wounded arrived from the desert. Not all the wounds were physical. Some had quite literally lost their minds along with everything else they had. I had no idea how I'd held on to my own sanity, but as I looked around at this place, these people, I had a sense I was coming home.

11

Later that day, I cornered Tom in the study, where he was just replacing the telephone receiver. I glanced at it then at him. He looked back at me, guileless. I was dying to ask him who he'd called, but discretion won out. Besides, I had another bone to pick with him. 'Why did you tell that American I work for you?'

He smiled at me lazily. 'Because you do.'

'No I bloody don't. I work for the Polish Red Cross and Agency Africa. That's it.'

He walked round from behind his desk and took my arm, leading me over to the window. 'Look out there. You see that?'

I stared out at the dazzling orb of the sun, hotter even than the warmth from his flesh upon mine, half-blinded by the sight. 'What?'

'Exactly. No planes in the skies over Cairo. No German tanks rolling through the streets, and if we want it to stay that way, it's all hands on deck, darling. Including yours. We've agreed to work together – SOE, OSS. Your lot. It's the only way to win.'

I stretched out my fingers almost as a distraction, gazing at my nails, cut sensibly short. They were workmanlike hands. Peasant hands, I'd always thought.

Tom closed his hand around mine, enveloping it. 'So will you do it? Work with me?'

His tone was softer now, and there was a pleading note in his voice. That heat was building, his hand all-encompassing. And yet, I preferred to work alone. I always had, even in Paris. Especially in Paris. He was right though. All the espionage agencies had agreed to work as one, even mine. 'I suppose so.'

He squeezed my hand. 'Splendid. I knew you'd say yes.'

I extracted it from his grasp. 'Did you now?'

There it was again, that endearing flash of a boy barely out of short trousers. A sophisticated boy, but a boy nonetheless. 'I didn't mean... I just thought you'd want to do the right thing.'

'Ah, but is this the right thing?'

'You know it is.'

He was standing awfully close for a boy. Perhaps I should revise that assessment again. I could feel his breath on my cheek as he leaned towards me, my eyes half-closing, expectant, my mouth opening up to him, the temperature now at boiling point.

'Sir.'

My eyes flew open again. I could have ground my teeth in frustration.

Tom bit back a sigh. 'What is it, Abbas?'

'Sir, there is someone here to see you.'

'Who?'

'Captain Peter Noel, sir.'

A pause. An eloquent, sideways glance from Tom.

'Show him in.'

I'd seen Peter Noel before at parties and the Turf Club. He had the brilliantined hair and supercilious air of a British officer, although the set of his mouth under his moustache spoke of more depth to his character. There was no trace of anything other than urgency as he strode into the room, cap in hand, stopping short when he saw me.

'It's alright, Peter – she's one of us,' said Tom. 'Do take a seat.'

'Thank you, but I can't stay long. I came to warn you that we have picked up a source who is supplying the Germans with highly accurate intelligence from right here in Cairo.' He glanced at me. 'Obviously, that information does not go beyond these four walls.'

'Indeed. Do we have any idea who it might be?'

'Not yet, although whoever it is knows you are hosting a party here tonight. That was included in a message Bletchley decoded, along with a reference to His Majesty King Farouk.'

'The king is expected to attend. What exactly was this reference?'

'Only that he has been invited.'

I looked at Tom. His face mirrored what I was thinking. 'Do you think the Germans are planning to assassinate the king?'

'I wouldn't put it that bluntly. They're certainly watching his movements, but it doesn't serve them to kill the king. He has little interest in political or military affairs, as you know, but his parliament is pro-German, if anything.'

'So what are they up to then?'

Noel's moustache twitched. 'For now, we have no idea. We may well find out more at this party of yours. I take it you'll have briefed Miss...'

I smiled sweetly at him. 'It's Countess. Countess Nadia Pulaska.'

'Countess. Yes, of course. We met at the Turf Club I believe. You were with Lady Lampson.'

'I was. We work together with the Red Cross.'

'But now you are here?'

He raised an eyebrow at Tom, who gave him a level look. 'I

took this place in preference to Hangover Hall and invited a few chums to share. Nadia agreed to move in along with the other chaps.'

Noel's moustache really was most expressive. Right now, it was practically standing on end. 'But there are other ladies here too?'

'Yes, yes of course,' I stuttered. 'I have a chaperone. Madame Khalifa. She is unfortunately indisposed at present.'

'I see.' Clearly, he didn't. 'Well, I'd better be getting along. Keep your eyes and ears open at this party of yours. I shall expect a full report.'

With a brisk nod to me, he marched from the room. I barely managed to hold back until I heard Abbas close the front door. 'Who on earth does he think he is?'

'The second in command of A Force, that's who. They're a military deception unit tasked with feeding the Germans false information and bloody good at what they do. They've managed to camouflage hundreds of tanks in the north and create fake ones in the south along with a fake pipeline which has the Germans thinking our attack will come from the south rather than the north and not for a few weeks. Little do they know we're about to mount a massive counter-attack. It's another reason for the party tonight. To send our boys off in style.'

I bit back a retort. 'Yes, I know all about A Force, but why him and not someone from SOE HQ?'

'Because, as you may also know, our operation here is a shambles. I wouldn't trust half of them to sabotage a donkey cart. I prefer to work with Peter and his boss, Dudley, as well as Jim, on occasion. We're all on the same side, after all, especially now.'

He'd acted so nonchalant as he'd replaced that telephone receiver. Too nonchalant. 'Are we?'

His eyes narrowed. 'What do you mean?'

'You heard what Noel said. Someone is sending intelligence to the Germans. That someone could be anyone. It could be one of us. It could be me. Or you.'

You could have cut the silence with a knife.

'Well then,' he said at length. 'We'd better find our rat, hadn't we?'

12

As I locked the door to my room, I could hear the party in full swing.

'This time, stay there,' I muttered. God only knew what Kochanie and Malenka would get up to while I was gone.

Music was drifting up from the garden room overlaid by laughter. Abbas was waiting at the bottom of the stairs to greet guests as they entered with a tray of champagne glasses while his young nephew stood sentry at the door.

'Thank you, Abbas.' I scooped a glass from the silver tray and scanned the crowd loitering in the entrance hall. I recognised a couple of British officers, along with a small group from the Swedish legation, a scruffy war correspondent with a delectable young woman on his arm and a gaggle of the kind of party-goers who graced, or rather disgraced, every event in Cairo if they could gain entrance.

I locked on to a pair of emerald eyes watching me, catlike, from an alcove and squeezed through the throng, giving the war correspondent a sharp dig with my elbow when his hand brushed my hip. 'Hello. Are you having fun?'

Colette brushed my cheek with hers. 'I am, yes.'

I could see her discreetly scoping the hallway and the room that led off it over my shoulder, selecting her marks.

'Has the king arrived yet?'

'He's in the garden. He brought a crate of champagne with him and the usual hangers-on.'

I smiled. I was beginning to like Colette more and more. 'Shall we go and join him?'

'You go. I need to work the crowd. I'll catch up with you later.'

With that, she melted away into it, leaving me to descend the stone steps that led from the French doors to the garden, where people strutted like peacocks across the lawn, a dazzling array of Cairo's finest reprobates mingling with uniformed officers from across the globe, spotlit by the lanterns that hung from branches and the flaming torches dotted around, adding to the bacchanalian atmosphere. If the Underworld had risen from the depths, it might well have looked like this. Alluring on the surface but oh so dangerous underneath, each sideways glance a warning and every smile a potential trap.

I could make out King Farouk standing under a jacaranda tree, his handsome figure towering above the group that surrounded him, laughing dutifully at his every remark. The soft purple boughs that dipped behind him were suitably regal, the scattered blossom on which he stood a worthy carpet for a king. Even so, there was something about Farouk that always made me think of him as a lost child despite his height and stature. He must have been about the same age as Tom and yet he appeared far younger at times, at others wily beyond his years.

'Your Majesty.'

His face lit up when he saw me. That was the other thing about Farouk. He could be immensely charming. 'Countess. How very good to see you. But what are you doing here?'

I smiled. 'I live here now, Your Majesty.'

I felt rather than saw Tom appear at my side. 'The party is to welcome Nadia to our humble abode, Your Majesty.'

The king flung an arm wide. 'I would hardly call this humble.'

'In comparison to your palaces, Your Majesty, it most certainly is.'

Farouk inclined his head graciously. 'Have you met these two gentlemen? They were just telling me about their exploits in the desert. They are explorers, you see.'

Farouk's English was perfect, a product of his time spent in Surrey attending the Royal Military Academy, when he felt like it.

Tom stiffened a fraction, not so that anyone else would notice, his gaze sharpening as he surveyed the two. 'I see.'

The older of the two, a blonde, bearded man in his mid-thirties, took a step forward. 'Erik Carlsson,' he said, shaking Tom's hand. 'This is my colleague, Dr Ghaffar.'

The saturnine Dr Ghaffar threw me an inscrutable look. Although he went by a local name, he did not appear to be entirely Egyptian or even North African.

'It's a pleasure to meet you,' I murmured, then turned back to Carlsson.

'Are you Danish?' I asked.

'Swedish.'

'What luck. There's a party from your embassy here.'

His smile tightened at the corners. 'I know. We've already said hello.'

A flash, momentarily blinding me. The official photographer, making his rounds. 'Say cheese,' quipped Farouk, and I couldn't help but laugh. For a king, he could be such a big kid at times.

I noticed the two so-called explorers slinking away out of shot and dug my elbow into Tom, who looped his arm through mine. 'On that note, we'd better go and greet some more guests, Your Majesty.'

Farouk was already regaling his audience once more as we backed away and wandered across the lawn, Tom steering me towards the fountain courtyard where he stopped to apparently admire the play of the water against the light. I stared at it too, well aware that his eyes were on me.

'Care to dance?' he murmured, taking my silence as assent, along with my hand, as he led me back into the house and through the throng into the ballroom where couples were dipping and swaying around the dance floor, gay smiles on their faces in defiance of what was to come.

We slipped in among them, feet moving to the beat as the music sped up, exhilarated now, jitterbugging with the best of them, slowing and swirling into a rumba, then a foxtrot and finally a waltz, each time Tom's embrace claiming me more and more, our bodies finding each other's rhythm, dancing as one.

The music ended as the band took a brief break, but he held on to my hand. 'Can I get you a drink?'

'Champagne please.'

Still we stood, staring at one another, as people pushed past us, heading for the bar. You could feel the determination in the room to party until we dropped, to live this night as none of us had ever lived, with no regrets, no doubts. We all knew what was to come. Tonight, though, was for us. All of us. For Tom and for me.

I gazed at him, seeing him perhaps for the first time, really seeing him, the sweetness behind that veneer of confidence, the invitation in his eyes, written across his lips. It took but a moment to lean up just a little and brush his lips with mine, to feel his intake of breath and then the warmth of his mouth claiming me. I opened my eyes for a second, dizzy with the delight of it, dazzled by the lights from the chandeliers, which couldn't match the light in his eyes. He was looking at me too, from under his lashes, and what I saw there made me stifle a gasp.

I knew that look. I'd seen it before what felt like a lifetime ago. I never thought I would see it again. And yet here I was with Tom looking at me as if he really saw me too, his gaze naked, unafraid. Full of something I hardly dared name.

Even as the thought flitted into my mind, I felt the beat of other wings, the brush of a claw against my cheek, a talon hooking into me. I took a step back, but there was no escaping its shadow or its cries, calling out to me across the centuries, flying on the wings of pain, warning me this love was cursed.

13

PRESENT DAY, CAIRO, EGYPT

I gaped at Josh. 'Cursed? What are you talking about? What is this gold anyway? And how come you know so much about it?'

'I've discovered all kinds of things researching David's book, including a great deal about the gold. Turns out it was pivotal to events.'

'Is Nadia in this book? And Tom?'

'Of course. They're a huge part of it. Not just because of what happened between the brothers but what happened to Tom and Nadia. And the gold.'

'I see.'

Even I could hear the frustration in my voice.

Josh held up his hands. 'Look, I'm not holding out on you. It's just that I'm still very much at the research stage, but I promise I'll show it to you when I've written it. It probably won't even get published, to be honest, but it's important to David. I hope you're not upset. I know how much you cared about Nadia, and I assure you, I will honour her memory.'

Nadia and Tom's story preserved. A legacy for all of us. 'I'm not upset. It sounds like a wonderful project. I'd like to be part of it, if I may.'

He smiled, looking relieved. 'I'd love you to be, especially as you were so close to Nadia. I'm surprised she never told you about the gold.'

I looked at him more sharply. 'I'm not. She never talked about the war or her time here. She was of that generation.'

He looked back at me. 'Right.'

'You don't believe me?'

'I'm sorry. I didn't mean to seem sceptical, and you're absolutely right. Those folk were trained not to talk. It was a matter of life and death to them. It's just... I was trained not to believe people.'

'How come?'

He looked away then, out the cab window, staring at the endless stream of traffic. 'I'll tell you sometime. Looks like we're stuck in this. Why don't we get out and walk? Maybe grab some dinner?'

I glanced at my watch. Gone seven. It had been hours since I'd last eaten. My stomach rumbled as if reading my thoughts. 'Sure.'

Josh glanced around. 'I know where we are – there's a great place right on the river. Want to try it?'

My stomach rumbled again, so loud that I was glad of the honking from hundreds of cars along with the music that blared from most. 'Lead on.'

As it turned out, the restaurant was actually floating on the river. 'A boat,' I exclaimed.

'You like it?'

I could see the lights on the opposite bank starting to twinkle as the maître d' led us to a table overlooking the water. 'I love it.'

The place was swanky but also upbeat and fun, the crowd young and the music pumping. Not at all what I had expected of Josh. Actually, I wasn't sure what I expected of him. He was a conundrum, by turns displaying a delightfully old-fashioned gallantry, while at others blurting out things that suggested he'd had a whole other life. As soon as we had our first drinks in front of us, I tackled him on that. 'How many books have you written?'

He looked at me over his menu. 'This is my first.'

'Oh. Right. So why did David ask you to write this one?'

He laughed. 'You think I'm too much of an amateur?'

'No, not at all. I just wondered how he found you. Did he advertise for someone?'

The waiter appeared to take our orders, and I hastily chose the first thing on the menu, my attention focused on Josh. He looked as if he was wrestling with something. A secret probably. Ben had always worn the same look when he was embroiled in a particularly juicy case and could only share snippets with me. Maddening and yet intriguing at the same time.

'We have a... mutual connection,' Josh finally mumbled.

Curiouser and curiouser. 'Who?'

He sighed. 'My grandma, as it happens.'

'Your grandmother? Are they friends?'

'In a way. Actually, Nadia and her mother were friends. My great-grandmother, Colette. My grandma told me how, when she was a little girl, she nearly died because of the gold, but Nadia saved her.'

I stared at him. 'Wait... you're saying you have a connection to Nadia as well? To me, in a way?'

His smile lit up his face, already illuminated by the glow from a thousand lights and the last, golden moments of the setting sun. He looked straight into my eyes and raised his glass. 'I certainly hope so,' he murmured.

14

The sun had long set by the time the waiter appeared again with the dessert menus, the stars now studding the sky, tiny diamond chips above the neon city lights reflected in the river flowing before us. 'Just a coffee for me,' I said.

'It doesn't keep you awake?'

I threw back the dregs of my wine. 'I hardly sleep anyway. I haven't since Ben died.'

A moment as Josh took this in, his eyes alight with compassion. 'You were saying his name as you came round back in the villa. I'm guessing he was important to you.'

I looked down, partly to hide the tears pricking dangerously, threatening to spill. 'He still is. Very much.'

Josh's hand touched mine, the lightest brush of his fingers that was so much more. 'Is that why you wear this?'

I glanced at my engagement ring, then at him. 'Actually, I'd stopped wearing it before I came here, but I felt it was only right to put it back on. This was meant to be our honeymoon, you see. Here, in Cairo. Two years ago. The hotel and airline let me change the dates. To be honest, it's also come in handy warding off the local men.'

'It's an unusual ring.'

I held out my hand. 'It was Nadia's. She gave it to Ben to give to me. I believe it's very old and possibly even from here. Knowing Nadia, she'd been saving it all that time.'

The ring was fashioned from one piece of solid gold inset with an indigo gemstone. A goddess was engraved into the gemstone, along with a feather. It was unusual and quite lovely. Very Nadia.

'It looks Egyptian,' said Josh, examining it more closely. 'Or possibly Phoenician. I believe that's the goddess Maat, the goddess of all life and truth.'

His words echoed Nadia's the day she told me about the ring, having engulfed us both in her embraces. 'It suits you. I knew it would. That's the goddess Maat, darling. She'll look after you both.'

If only she had.

'Well, she's doing a good job keeping the local Romeos at bay.'

A brief smile. 'They can be very persistent. Your honeymoon?'

'Yes. We chose Cairo because Nadia had left me the villa and, well, Ben insisted. He was adamant. You see, his great-grandfather lived there too, with Nadia and the rest of them. We had to come here and get to know the real story behind it. The same as you're doing, in a way.'

'Really? Was that how you two met? Through your family connections?'

'It was through Nadia. She was his client. She hired him to help her lay claim to the property the Nazis stole from her family during the Second World War. She did it because she knew he was Freddie's great-grandson, but she liked him the moment she met him and insisted he come round for dinner. I suspect she planned it all from the start. Nadia was a great planner.'

A smile now tugged at the corners of his eyes. 'So I'm beginning to learn. Was it love at first sight?'

I laughed. 'Not at all. I thought he was a pompous lawyer type. It was only later on I came to realise he was shy beneath it all. Shy and incredibly caring.'

'You loved him very much?'

'I did.'

'So... how did he die?'

His words were so soft they were almost carried away by the background music. 'A hit-and-run, three weeks before our wedding. A terrible accident and the driver probably panicked. At least, that's what the police said.'

'But you don't think so?'

I shook my head, vehement now. 'No way. There is no way Ben would just step out in the road and not see a car coming. It was a quiet country lane and he was a very careful person. Besides, according to the police he was running away from the direction the car came when he was hit.'

At least Josh wasn't giving me that look, the one people usually gave me. The one the police had given me. 'You think it was deliberate?'

I looked him right in the eye. 'I do.'

'But who would want to kill him and why?'

I stared down at my coffee, watching the dark liquid swirl, almost black. As black as the water below us now. 'Good question.'

15

The music was cranking up inside the boat, the beat harder and more insistent. 'This is on me,' said Josh, ignoring my protests. 'Come on – I'll walk you back.'

The night was young, the evening air balmy, the city streets around us alive. It felt good to stroll them with someone else rather than on my own, head down, trying to look as if I knew where I was going. 'You know the place well,' I said. 'How long have you been here?'

'A few months, although I've visited Cairo before.'

'On holiday?'

'For work.'

There was something about the way he said it that told me not to push for more. We paused in front of a bar. 'Fancy a nightcap?'

I smiled at him. 'Why not? Although I think the bar at my hotel looks nicer.'

The moment I said it, I realised how it sounded. Josh, though, seemed to take it at face value. 'Your hotel it is. We're only about ten minutes away in any case.'

The mile or so we'd walked had passed in a flash. Josh was

an easy companion. More than that, he made me feel safe. This island was a whole different place with his friendly presence beside me. Perhaps the goddess was looking over me after all. It had certainly been a day of happy accidents. Not so happy was the sense of that envelope sitting heavy in my bag, still unopened. I set it beside me as we settled in the hotel bar, taking up a couple of comfortable chairs. I'd look at it later, in the privacy of my room. Another drink or two could only help. Give me some Dutch courage.

The goddess must have had other ideas, or perhaps it was just Josh. He looked at me across the table. 'Aren't you going to open your letter?'

I felt myself colouring up. 'Oh, that. I'd forgotten all about it.'

'Yeah. Right.'

'OK, maybe I hadn't. I just don't feel up to opening it right now.'

'Want me to do it for you?'

The air left me in a rush, my shoulders sagging. 'Would you?'

'Of course.'

I don't know why I found it so hard to even hold that envelope, but the moment I pulled it from my bag and handed it to Josh, a great sense of relief washed over me. Maybe it was because I knew whatever was inside would change everything. Or possibly because I already had the sense I was on a road that led somewhere dark and forbidden. Josh had been my guiding light tonight. He had shoulders broad enough to take this too.

'It's a photograph,' he said as he extracted it from the envelope, holding it by the edges. 'There's something written on the back.'

As he turned it over to show me, I knew. This was it. There was no going back.

16

17 NOVEMBER 1942, CAIRO, EGYPT

NADIA

I was getting used to the rhythm of this place, to the frenetic partying that punctuated the long days at my official job, dealing with the welfare of the wounded brought back from the front, and the even longer nights disseminating the intelligence, keeping tight-lipped about our deception operations while murmuring the right things so the Axis spies in the restaurants and nightclubs we frequented kept believing the lies we spread to confuse the enemy.

Now, at last, it was all over. At least here in Egypt. Monty's Eighth Army had done it. Rommel's troops were retreating into Tunisia, while more of our troops had landed in Morocco and Algeria, attacking the enemy on two fronts. We had the victory we so badly needed. Churchill's words, crackling over the radio, still rang in my ears:

'This is not the end. It is not even the beginning of the end. But it is perhaps the end of the beginning.'

Perhaps. For the wounded who came streaming back from the front, it would never end. For those who now lay forever under the red Egyptian earth, there would be no more beginnings. For us, our work continued. We might have routed Rommel in the desert, but the enemy was still out there, still fighting, as the war raged on and within. I was acutely aware that we still hadn't winkled out our rat.

All of which meant it was more important than ever to keep our eyes and ears to the ground, to sniff out the slightest hint of enemy plans that could scupper our own ops while remaining alert to enemies closer to home. It was demanding work, and as we gathered around the breakfast table, I could sense the weariness under the adrenaline that drove us on. We were living on fumes, pushing ourselves beyond limits even while we partied on.

Half of us hadn't even made it to bed after the soiree at the Gezira club last night. I had never felt so alive and yet so exhausted at the same time, and a big part of that was down to Tom. As each day passed, I could sense the pull between us grow more demanding. As much as I tried to deny it to myself, I was falling for him, and I knew he felt the same. I could see it in his eyes, sense it in the way he sought me out, his presence electrifying the air as it was now.

'When do the first guests arrive tonight?' I asked, reaching for the coffee pot.

Tom handed it to me, our fingers grazing. 'The invitation said from seven onwards. We're expecting quite a crowd.'

Everyone wanted to celebrate, even the walking wounded. We'd waited so long for this victory, but I still felt a twinge of anticipation. Silly of me. It was only a party, after all. And yet, the thought of it sent my nerves jangling. Maybe another cup of coffee wasn't such a good idea.

I felt rather than saw Abbas enter the room. I was beginning to get used to his presence – or rather omnipresence. He was everywhere and nowhere, our silent guardian, immaculately attired in his uniform in spite of the hour. For once, he seemed ruffled. 'Sir.'

'What is it, Abbas?'

'Sir, I am sorry to disturb you, but this arrived for you.'

Tom took the message Abbas held out on his silver tray, his forehead creasing as he read it. 'Shit. Forty German aircraft have landed in Tunis. They're expecting more. Bastards beat us to it.'

Jim stared at him, his eyes red from lack of sleep. 'Crap. Who sent the message?'

'Your office. You're to report there immediately.'

Colette's face had turned ashen. 'I must leave too. My family is there.'

I looked at her, aghast. 'Your family are in Tunis?'

'There and in Djerba. It's an island south of Tunis. I have to find out what's happened to them. If they are alright.'

She wasn't looking at me now but at Jim.

'There's no way in hell you're going to Tunis or any other part of Tunisia,' he said. 'Not now. If those Nazi bastards get hold of you, they'll shoot you on the spot.'

She stared back at him mutely, exuding defiance, although wisely she said nothing more.

I looked round the room, taking in everyone's expressions – or rather lack of them. 'Do you think we should cancel the party?'

'Don't be silly,' said Tom. 'And let the Germans know we're bothered? We've invited all their favourite spies. Isn't that right, Nico?'

Nico smirked. 'Every single last one of them.'

'In that case,' I said, 'this is going to be fun.'

The room was filling fast and yet it felt emptier with so many missing faces, some still out there, in the desert camps, or back here in hospital, others never to return. I plastered a smile on my face and greeted each and every one as I wove through them, searching for those I knew and, more importantly, those I didn't. The Swedes were here again. The war correspondent too with a different girl on his arm. On the surface, we were celebrating, and yet the gaiety felt forced, a palpable sadness permeating it. We had won and yet we had lost so many. It was a thought written on almost every face.

I wandered out into the garden, the music following me, and caught sight of Tom pretending to pause for a cigarette while his eyes scanned the crowd. The king was out here too, in his favourite spot under the jacaranda tree, holding court. I counted his bodyguards. All present and correct. My eyes swept across the royal party and landed on Tom's, locking on. He jerked his head, indicating I should follow before disappearing back into the garden room where couples were ensconced on the couches and in the armchairs. A pair from the Swedish delegation were deep in conversation. In one corner, a man was kissing someone I knew to be someone else's wife. Nothing out of the ordinary, and yet any one of them could be an enemy agent.

Tom smiled at me. 'Care for a cigarette?'

As I leaned in for him to light it, I could feel eyes upon me.

'Fellow to your right,' muttered Tom.

I slid my gaze sideways, blowing out smoke so that it masked me. There was a man standing on his own, half-hidden by the palm in an enormous ceramic pot that graced that corner of the room. A man I recognised with a jolt. I had to rip my eyes away before he sensed I was watching him. What the hell was he doing here? More importantly, how the hell was he alive?

I moved closer to Tom so that he masked me, taking a second look to be sure. It was him alright. Ice-blue eyes, so pale they were almost white, set in a thin, vulpine face, his mouth a cruel twist under a nose that had been broken more than once.

'You know that man?' muttered Tom in my ear as he placed a hand on my back and steered me out into the garden once more, out of his sight. 'Who is he?'

'His name is Felix Vulke of the SS.'

'How do you know this?'

'Trust me, I know. What I don't understand is how he's still alive. I thought I'd killed him in Paris over a year ago.'

The world seemed to kaleidoscope. Nothing was making any sense. I could hear music drifting from the house. The sounds of laughter and chatter. And something else. Something I couldn't quite identify at first. Then I realised what it was. The sound of someone choking and gasping, struggling to stay alive. Then a single, swiftly muffled cry.

18

We found her lying by the perimeter wall. The sound of us crashing through the shrubs to get to her must have scared off her attacker because there was no one to be seen. I crouched and placed my fingers gently on her pulse, watching her chest rise and fall.

'Thank God. She's alive. Colette, can you hear me?'

A low moan escaped her lips. I could see the marks on her neck, livid, where he'd tried to strangle her.

'Who did this to you?' I muttered, though I could make an educated guess.

'We need to secure the house and grounds,' said Tom. 'Although they might already have got away.'

She was moving now, her head twisting from side to side. 'Hush,' I murmured. 'It's alright, Colette. Lie still.'

Her eyelids trembled.

I looked up at Tom. 'Go. I'll stay with her. You need to alert the king's bodyguards.'

'I don't want to leave you on your own with an assailant on the loose.'

'I'll be fine.' I reached under my skirt and pulled my gun from its holster. 'See?'

Tom stared at it then at me. 'Right you are.'

He was off and running back towards the king and his bodyguards, the music and the party chatter covering the sound of him crashing through the trees and shrubs, just as it had the sounds of Colette struggling. If I hadn't somehow heard her gasping at that precise moment, God only knew what might have happened. But then, I was attuned to that sound. I'd heard it all too often in the hospitals and out in the field.

'Nadia.' Colette's eyes were open. She appeared dazed as she tried to sit up. I put my arm around her shoulders, helping her while I kept the gun trained on the bushes in front of us. 'What happened?'

She coughed, her hands flying to her throat.

'Someone attacked you. They tried to strangle you. Did you see him? Did you recognise him?'

She shook her head. 'He grabbed me from behind and dragged me into these bushes. He had his hand clamped over my mouth so I couldn't scream.'

She was rubbing her throat as she spoke, twisting her neck from side to side, looking agitated.

I tried to reassure her. 'Tom's making sure the place is locked down, although he might already have got away.' Colette looked at me then scrambled to her feet, swaying slightly as she stood. I grabbed her by the elbow. 'Steady now.'

'What about the king?'

'Tom's warning the bodyguards. They'll get him somewhere safe. We have to be discreet. This place is crawling with spies, and the last thing we want is anyone panicking.'

'That's good, although I don't think the king is the target.'

'You don't? Why?'

She stalled, her eyes darting from side to side. Shock probably. 'I-I remember he said something before I passed out, the man who attacked me. He spoke in French: '*Souviens-toi de Paris.*'

Remember Paris.

She was looking at me now, her eyes calmer. 'What do you think he meant?'

A warning bell in my head, that niggle that had been there since this morning now gnawing at me. Remember Paris? How could I ever forget Paris? Now it had come back to haunt me.

'I have no idea.'

19

Tom locked the door behind him. Outside it, the party was staggering to a close, the last revellers dotted in heaps around the lawns and in armchairs, too drunk to dance or too tired to even try. The king was safely on his way back to the palace, protesting loudly at missing the rest of the party. His bodyguards were having none of it, fearing his advisors far more than the young monarch. The rest of the throng scarcely noticed, drunk on champagne and life. Here, in the study, the atmosphere was far more charged.

Tom motioned to a chair. 'Sit.'

I stayed standing, trying to work out what was behind this sudden change. The gentle, charming Tom I'd come to know was gone. In his place was this man, staring me down with basalt eyes.

'I said sit.'

I glared at him. 'How dare you? You don't get to order me around.'

'I do when I suspect you of being a foreign agent.'

I laughed, incredulous. 'You think I'm a spy?'

'I know you're a damn spy. The question is for whom.'

'You said it yourself. I work for you.'

'We both know you don't. At least not yet.'

He pulled the chair closer to me. I took a step back. 'I have a gun.'

'I know that too, but you're not going to use it.'

God but he was sure of himself. 'How do you know?'

'What would be the point? If you wanted to shoot me, you'd have done it by now. You obviously wanted to get close to me, or rather us, by moving in here. Killing your source wouldn't be a wise move.'

He was right. And so very wrong. With a sigh, I sank into the chair. 'Does that make you happier?'

'Not much. It's time you started talking. How is it you know this Vulke? And what was that cock and bull story about shooting him in Paris? From what I can see, he shows up here in Cairo and almost immediately another agent is attacked. How do I know it wasn't you who told him about this party? It seems to be one big coincidence.'

I gaped at him. 'You seriously think I somehow contrived to get Felix Vulke into this party and then attack Colette? For what reason?'

'You tell me.'

I stifled a sigh. 'Felix Vulke was my target in Paris. I was there on an assignment, tasked with assassinating him. He's one of Hitler's favourite assassins after all, so it only seemed fair to send me after him.'

'What are you saying? That you're Churchill's favourite assassin?'

'I'm certainly one of the first people they ask when it comes to assignments like that. Or I was, until General Sikorski asked me to come here and work with Agency Africa, using the Red Cross as a cover. My father taught me how to shoot when I was a girl, back home in Poland. I'm a crack shot. I have a perfect success rate. At least, I thought I did. It seems I was wrong in Vulke's case.'

He was chewing on his lower lip now, taking in every word I was saying. I felt as if I was on trial, stating my case for the prosecution. It wasn't a pleasant feeling.

'How do I know you're telling the truth?' he demanded.

'You don't. You have to trust me. You can radio London of course, or Lisbon, but your communications are already compromised, so if you do that, you'll compromise me too.'

He was weighing it up, deciding on the lesser of two evils. Let me live and prove myself, or shoot me now and possibly make a serious mistake. We both knew that there was no room for error. An enemy agent had to be eliminated as soon as possible. We might have won at El Alamein, but the war in North Africa was far from over, especially now that Rommel had taken Tunis. The Desert Fox was a wily opponent, more than capable of planting a spy like me. Somewhere in our system there was an intelligence leak that had to be swiftly plugged or the results would be catastrophic. If Tom let me walk out the door, I might disappear into the labyrinthine streets of Cairo. Except that someone like me couldn't just disappear.

'Think about it,' I said. 'Shoot me and you'll be answerable to Sir Miles and Lady Lampson, along with the king. Do you really think the Nazis would plant someone like me here?'

I saw it then, the ruthless streak that set Tom apart. It hardened his eyes for a moment and then evaporated as if it had never existed. 'No,' he murmured. 'I don't. It's just... there's been a lot going on tonight. That incident with Colette threw me. And with that Vulke turning up... I don't know what I thought. That maybe you knew one another and had planned the whole thing. I'm sorry, Nadia.'

I stood. 'Don't be. I do know Vulke, in a way. As much as you can any target. But that's as far as it goes. You did the right thing. It's exactly what I would have done if the situation was reversed.'

'Marched me in here and threatened to shoot me?'

I matched his rueful smile. 'If that was necessary, yes. What I don't understand is how Vulke is still alive. I got a clean shot to his heart. I saw him hit the ground.'

I could still see him now, one leg twitching as he lay, his arms flung wide, blood seeping from his chest, already pooling around him as I walked away. Felix Vulke, the golden boy of the SS, and I had killed him. Except I hadn't. And now he was back, very much alive. Which meant I would have to kill him all over again.

20

We were all gathered in the study now, still in our party clothes, a large pot of coffee to hand. Through the window behind Tom, I could see a couple of bodies prostrate on the lawn, passed out from too much drink. Beside me, Colette sipped at her coffee as she studied the map of Tunisia in front of us. Freddie appeared rumpled, Nico immaculate. All of us hung on every word Tom was saying.

'As we know, the Operation Torch landings last week were intended to secure the Vichy territories in Morocco, Algeria and Tunisia. We had anticipated the Axis forces would try to take Tunis after those landings, but unfortunately for us, they moved faster than we expected. We lost the race for Tunis, and now we face losing control of the Mediterranean and possibly the entire war unless we can stall them on land and at sea. For that, we need first-rate intelligence along with as much sabotage as we can muster. And that, ladies and gentlemen, is where we come in.'

Colette took a slug of her coffee. I had to hand it to her – she was a tough cookie. 'What do we have so far?'

Tom looked at me. 'Nadia, perhaps you can tell everyone what you told me?'

I glanced around the small group. 'I recognised someone at the party, a man by the name of Felix Vulke, although he goes by several others. He worked for Reinhard Heydrich of the SS and is Hitler's favourite assassin. He's a very dangerous individual, as you can imagine. I believe it was Vulke who attacked Colette tonight. I thought I'd killed him in Paris, but apparently not.'

Freddie raised an eyebrow. 'You thought you'd killed him?'

'Yes. I shot him from the Pont des Arts. He was on the path beside the river, on his way to meet a contact who was about to give him the location of one of our safehouses. I took him out before he could rendezvous with that contact. At least, I thought I had, until Vulke turned up here tonight, very much alive.'

Nico flicked his ash into the copper salver filled with sand that was studded with a hundred butts from the night before. 'Are you sure it was him?'

'Absolutely sure. It's just Vulke's style to turn up like that, bold as brass. The question is, what does he want? He never does anything without a good reason, and to come here like that, it must have been a compelling one.'

'Do you think he was here to track you down?' asked Tom.

'Unlikely. My cover at the Red Cross is watertight. I'm almost certain Vulke has no idea it was me who shot him. How could he unless someone betrayed me? Though there is always that possibility.'

Colette took a drag of her cigarette. 'Almost certain is not one hundred per cent certain, darling. Especially when you consider what happened to me and what he said. "Remember Paris."'

She put her hand to her throat. The marks on her neck were turning a nasty shade of purple. Vulke's claw marks.

'There are far too many unanswered questions,' said Tom. 'Which takes me back to my first point. We need better intelligence. And we're going to get it.'

We all looked up as Abbas burst into the room, breathless. 'Sir.'

Tom rose from his seat. 'What is it, Abbas?'

'Sir, I apologise, but you must come at once.' He glanced from me to Colette, evidently uncomfortable. 'There is a man on the lawn, sir. I'm sorry to have to say this, sir, but he is dead.'

21

He was lying on his side in a semi-foetal position. From a distance, he looked just like the others I'd seen sleeping it off on the grass, but as we drew closer, I could make out the dark stain soaked into the ground around his head and his throat, which had been neatly cut.

'Have you touched him, Abbas?' asked Tom as he kneeled to examine the man.

'No, sir.'

'That's good.'

'Shall I call the police, sir?'

'No. Not yet. I think perhaps we need to call his embassy first. If I'm not mistaken, this is one of the Swedish crowd.'

I tore my eyes away from his throat to his face; I recognised him as one of the group who'd clustered in the entrance hall. His eyes were open, staring up at a sky he would never see again.

Tom leaned forward and gently closed them. 'Does this look like Vulke's work?'

I grimaced. 'I'm afraid it does. Neat, efficient, silent. Those are his hallmarks.'

'But why kill someone from the Swedish legation?' mused Colette. 'They're protecting German interests here, aren't they?'

'He might have gone further than that,' said Tom. 'It could be he was working for the Germans and Vulke was sent to silence him. One of the German spies we caught a few months back had a high-ranking Swedish diplomat among his contacts. Vulke might very well be carrying out a clean-up operation.'

'You think someone was about to blab?' asked Nico.

I caught the barely perceptible shake of Tom's head. For whatever reason, he wanted me to keep schtum about our earlier discussion.

'Vulke is methodical,' I said. 'In my experience, he thinks well ahead. If he had the slightest suspicion there was any danger of someone talking, anyone at all, he would eliminate them without a second thought. And he'd do it in such a way that it sent a message, as it did here.'

My eyes slid back to Tom's and held them for the briefest moment before I looked away again. Let him think what he liked. There was a leak somewhere. It was also my experience that it was usually somewhere, or someone, close. Which meant I might as well deliver a warning. If there was a traitor among us, they'd do one of two things: ignore it – or act on it. Time would tell which.

22

PRESENT DAY, CAIRO, EGYPT

SOPHIE

I woke the next morning with the sense that I was not alone. Sure enough, as I prised open my eyes, I saw it on the next pillow. The photograph, the one that used to sit on Nadia's mantlepiece. The one she'd held to her heart as she'd died. I'd recognised it the moment Josh pulled it from the envelope. Tom's face smiling up at me, handsome and eternally young.

A sudden rush of grief swept over and through me. Ben was forever young too. He would remain so, in my memories. And yet I wanted him to be so much more than that – a spectre who would fade as the years went by, my imagination filling in the gaps, the might-have-beens, the if-onlys. I picked up the picture and studied it, gazing into those eyes that laughed back at me across the years, full of merriment and something else.

'You really loved her, didn't you?' I whispered. 'Well, she loved you too. So much.'

A tear plopped onto the photograph before I could stop it. I swiped it away. No damage done. The writing on the back was similarly well preserved. Not surprising when it had sat in its silver photo frame all those years. Someone must have removed it from that frame after she died and sent it here. Not someone. Ben. But why on earth he had done that was a mystery to me. And posted it the day he died. It was almost certainly his final act, although the question remained. Why?

It was a question that rattled my brain as I took a shower and dressed for the day ahead. I remembered wondering where it had gone, but that thought had been swept away in the tsunami of Ben's death, so soon after Nadia's.

Focus, Sophie. Deal with the day ahead.

The yellow dress. No, maybe the blue. What did it matter? I was only meeting Josh at the villa to take a good look around it and see what else we could find that might provide a few answers. There had to be a reason Ben had sent the photograph there. He was not a man who left anything to chance. He could have sent it to our home in England or anywhere else, but he chose the villa. Then there was his text message. The last one he ever sent me. 'Go to Cairo.' Did he know, even then, that he'd never make it to our honeymoon? That I'd end up here alone?

According to the police, Ben had been running when he was knocked down. Running from what? The car about to mow him down? They dismissed it as him hurrying back to me, but that wasn't like the calm, confident Ben I knew. Something or someone had spooked him right before that car hit him. I couldn't bear to think of him afraid. No. Ben was fearless. The only thing he ever worried about was me.

It was what had kept me going, the thought that I had to be as brave as he was. Ben wouldn't have crumbled in the face of anything. Except, perhaps, my death. Well, I was the one who had to live now, for both of us. As well as for Nadia. She was no sentimentalist. She'd left me the villa for a reason beyond the fact she'd once loved the place and loved the man she'd met there. I knew that in my bones. Coupled with Ben's insistence I come here, it added up to one thing: there was something I had to find at the villa beyond this photograph. Something veiled in the secrets of the past that still resonated to this day. A veil Josh and I would, with any luck, begin to lift today.

He was waiting for me on the steps of the villa, brandishing a set of keys. 'For the lady of the house,' he said. 'I've put locks on all the doors for you and changed the one on the front door. We have no idea who else might have had keys, so it should be more secure.'

I smiled at him. 'Thank you. How much do I owe you?'

He waved a dismissive hand. 'Don't be silly. All part of the service. Shall we?'

I took the keys from him and unlocked the front door. It slid silently open, smooth as you like. He must have oiled it too.

Inside, the hallway offered a number of other doors I hadn't yet opened. I chose the one at the bottom of the stairs at random, its handle turning with reluctance, as if it wanted to hold on to whatever lay behind the door.

When it finally gave, I gasped. The room before me was a temple to books, the dust that covered them unable to hide the gleam of the spines and the glint of the gold thread embroidered through the cushions adorning the easy chairs. This side of the house faced south, the sunlight pouring through the window, burnishing everything. Whoever had designed it had cleverly arranged the shelves so that they stayed out of reach of those gilded fingers, preserving the leather and cloth covers so that they were scarcely faded.

I pulled one from a shelf at random, a fine copy of Perrault's fairy tales. The dust flew off it as I opened it, the motes forming letters and words in the air, or so it seemed as the sunlight caught them. The text was in French but I easily recognised the titles. '*Sleeping Beauty... Cinderella... Little Red Riding Hood*,' I read out in delight, the illustrations as evocative as those stories I remembered from my own childhood.

Josh smiled. 'Let me guess... you were a bookworm as a kid?'

'Absolutely. I always had my nose in a book, and my parents read to me too. After they... were gone, Nadia did as well. I can imagine her in here, reading for hours.'

I glanced around the room, aware that my voice had faltered as it always did when I spoke of my parents. All these years later and it was still raw. But then, as I'd learned with Ben, grief never really goes away. It merely softens with time, now and then sharpening at a word or a song or even the briefest, most inconsequential reminder of that person who once walked so tall in your life and who had now shrunk to nothing more than a memory. A glimpse of what once was.

For a moment, I could have sworn I saw Nadia, in that armchair by the window, curled up with a book. If I half-closed my eyes, I could imagine my mother too. Perhaps even my father. He was the hardest to conjure up, possibly because of the bond we had shared. My parents always called me their little miracle. They'd waited years to have me, and then, just when they thought it was too late, I arrived. Maybe it was because I was their only child, but my father doted on me, in his own quiet way. My mother too, of course, but I knew he worshipped the ground I walked upon.

'Your parents passed away?'

Josh's voice broke the spell.

I turned back to him. 'They were killed in a sailing accident when I was ten. They got caught up in a squall and the boat went down, taking both of them with it. I was staying with Nadia while they were away. I will never forget her telling me.'

'That's awful. I am so sorry.'

He was staring at me, stricken. I shrugged in that way I always did to try to make other people feel better about my tragic backstory. Truth was, I got tired of it myself sometimes. Always living in the knowledge that I was still here while the people I loved the most were all dead. 'The inquest said it was human error, but my dad was a brilliant sailor. He would never have gone out if he thought the weather would turn like that, and my mum would never have gone with him. Just one of those things, I guess. A freak accident.'

It felt obscene, almost, to utter those words in this golden room. This sanctuary. I'd felt it the moment I walked through the door. I was sure Nadia must have felt the same.

'They happen,' said Josh. 'I've lost people that way. People I thought were indestructible. One moment they were there, the next gone. It hits you so hard, and it's even harder to understand. Life is cruel like that. It flips on a dime. I don't think you ever really get over the shock, but you learn to accept the consequences, however painful they are.'

'Was this family?'

'Friends. Colleagues. I used to work in the field. Some people might call it the front line. It's a dangerous place to be.'

His gaze was shuttered now, guarding him from the pain of the past. I brushed his arm with my fingertips. 'I'm sorry.'

I didn't know what else to say.

'Don't be. I was privileged to know those people. Privileged to work with them. It was my greatest honour to serve my country that way. To try and keep it and the rest of the world safe.'

'I often think that's how Nadia felt when she was here during the war. Tom too. Both of them working undercover, risking their lives every day for a greater cause. It's incredibly brave what they did. What you did.'

His eyes held mine. 'Not as brave as you, Sophie. You've lost everyone you love and yet you're still here, still standing. That takes courage. And heart.'

Something had shifted between us in that sharing of pain. I felt exposed, raw and yet relieved at the same time. I could see the same vulnerability in the way he was looking at me, his tenderness reawakening my deepest instincts underpinned with a truth that pierced my heart.

I glanced away again to break the spell, my eyes raking the shelves and falling on *The Complete Works of Shakespeare*. I pulled that, too, from its shelf, and it fell open at *Romeo and Juliet*, Act Three, Scene Five. 'I bet he read this to her,' I murmured.

'Who?'

'Tom. I bet he read this to Nadia. Look, you can see how the page is worn and creased. She always said *Romeo and Juliet* was his favourite play. He was an English scholar at Oxford, you see, before he went off to war. She told me how he read so beautifully it made her want to cry. Nothing ever made Nadia cry, so that's saying quite a lot.'

Josh took the book from me, his eyes scanning the lines. All at once, he started to read, the words rolling off his tongue as if he had just thought of them. '"Look, love, what envious streaks / Do lace the severing clouds in yonder east. / Night's candles are burnt out, and jocund day / Stands tiptoe on the misty mountain tops. / I must be gone and live, or stay and die."'

His voice fell away, leaving that last line hanging between us, the truth in it raw. I looked at him, really looked at him for maybe the first time, sensing the pain behind his eyes, the tumult beneath that steady exterior.

'That was beautiful,' I murmured.

'You're beautiful.'

Two words that changed everything. Two words that resonated through me, sending an answering cry from my heart. And still we stood, a few feet apart, the invisible magnet that I could no longer deny pulling us together, tighter and tighter, until our souls touched.

23

I had to look away. It was too much. I stared at those damn shelves again, blind to the books on them, pretending I hadn't heard what he said. That way, the world remained unchanged, even though it was, forever. Words can do that. Change everything. They always had for me at any rate, wrapping me in a cocoon into which I could escape after my parents died, one which Nadia reinforced with her love of them and of me.

She would read to me all the time when I was younger and then recommend books as I grew older. 'You must read this,' she would say, pressing Simone de Beauvoir or Tolstoy into my hands. It was thanks to her that I'd wept over *Anna Karenina* and marvelled at the worlds Shelley, Orwell, du Maurier and Dickens had opened up. I spied one of them now on a shelf, retrieving it with a cry of recognition. '*Rebecca*. My favourite book ever. Nadia lent me her copy. It looked exactly like this one.'

Josh glanced over. 'Du Maurier. One of my favourites too. *Rebecca*'s a masterpiece, but I also love *Jamaica Inn* and *My Cousin Rachel*.'

'So you're a reader as well as a writer.'

He arched an eyebrow. 'Is that so surprising?'

'Not at all. I should have guessed.'

Nadia had a special fondness for Shakespeare of course, largely because of Tom, but we read everything and anything. As I examined the shelves properly, I could see more and more of those books here now, in this magical library, some of them in English. Another caught my eye, and I eased it out from where it sat nestled between several more children's books beside Perrault.

'*The Secret Garden*. I love this one too.' I flicked through the pages, all too aware of Josh's eyes on me. Safer to look at the book than at him.

He moved to my side, reaching into the shelves. 'What's this?'

I glanced at the book he was holding, one that looked different from the rest. It had a home-made cover that someone had carefully wrapped around what appeared to be a journal, the image on it depicting two children, a little boy and a little girl, playing in the sand. I recognised the style of it at once. Nadia had sketched like this, doodling away on scraps of paper almost without thinking. And every single one of her doodles had included a small boy or girl exactly like these.

'May I see?'

I took the book from him with trembling hands, the image a gut punch to my memories, ripping Nadia from that ephemeral place she now occupied and right here, into this room. I could feel her, smell her, that scent of roses and jasmine that accompanied her wherever she went. She always said it was to remind her of here, this villa, with its garden full of roses and jasmine. Now that I was here, I could smell it too, pervading the place, seeping in through the windows and soaking itself into every corner of the house.

Or maybe that was Nadia, her spirit still wandering the rooms, ever restless, searching for her Tom, finding him in the ballroom where I had seen them dancing together, reunited at last.

I flipped over a page and read the inscription: 'For Gaby and Alexander.'

That was it. Nothing more.

'That's funny,' I muttered.

'What is?'

'My grandmother was called Gabriella – Gaby for short – although she died long before I was born. I know Nadia had a little boy called Alexander, but he died while he was still a baby. They buried him in Palestine by the sea. Maybe this is her imagining him playing on the beach there with a friend.'

I stared at the cover again. There was something about the nose and chin, the shape of this little boy's face. The girl's too.

'She looks a bit like you,' said Josh.

'You think?'

Now he mentioned it, I could see the resemblance. My mum always used to sigh and say I was unlucky to have inherited the family nose. Actually, I liked it, along with the tiny indent in my chin. They were the marks that branded me as my mother's daughter. As family. The same marks I could see clearly in the picture now I looked.

'I wonder...' I murmured, half to myself, flicking through more pages while Josh waited patiently. 'It's a collection of children's stories. See here, this one's about Gaby and Alexander finding treasure in the garden. I love the illustrations. They are so Nadia.'

'Those are beautiful,' Josh breathed over my shoulder.

I gazed at them some more, a thought surfacing. 'Josh, the research David asked you to do for the book is on his family, right?'

'It is. Mostly on Tom and his story here.'

'And Tom was his uncle?'

'Correct.'

'The thing is, Nadia and Tom never married. They weren't together long enough, and besides, he was still married to the wife who ran off with David's father.'

'Yes, although after Tom died, they did get married.'

'Convenient.'

He looked at me. 'I know.'

'Nadia told Mohammed to send me to David when I got here. That means she must have trusted him beyond just helping me find Villa Eden. After all, she could have simply left me a map. I think she wanted us to meet for a different reason, something to do with Tom possibly. It feels to me as if she's still trying to tell me something from beyond the grave, but what?'

'You think Nadia orchestrated all of this? That it's not just about you inheriting this place?'

'I do. I think there's far more to it. That there are secrets here she couldn't reveal to me when she was alive for whatever reason. Questions I never knew to ask. And I believe the answers are somewhere in the family history you're investigating. Will you help me find them?'

He placed his hand on mine, on top of the book I was still holding. 'Of course I will.'

24

19 NOVEMBER 1942, CAIRO, EGYPT

NADIA

The man holding court at the Long Bar in Shepheard's would have passed unnoticed in any crowd. He was not particularly tall and of average appearance. The perfect person for his job, in fact, because Dudley Clarke was a master of deception.

I tilted my cheek to receive his kisses. 'Dear girl. What brings you here? No, don't tell me. Let me guess. A martini. No olive but a twist of lemon. Am I correct?'

'You are.'

He slapped his thigh and guffawed. 'Never fails. Good to see you, Tom. I had no idea you two knew one another.'

His eyes were shrewd above his paunchy cheeks, taking in everything around him as he kept up his jovial stream of chatter. Behind him, Joe, the legendary barman, nodded a greeting while staff dressed in white robes and red tarbooshes bustled backward and forward under his watchful eye, serving the cocktails he mixed with consummate expertise. To one side of us, an officer was slumped forward from his bar stool, staring into the depths of his drink as if it somehow contained the answer to goodness knows what. Another man sat at the table nearest the bar, fingers tapping in impatience, occasionally glancing at his watch. All at once, he sat straighter, plastering on a smile as a woman swept up to the table swathed in a fur coat against the evening chill, waiting until her chair was pulled out for her before she dropped her fur onto it in one sinuous move.

Then there was Tom and me. God only knew what to think about us. About Dudley too, for that matter. I certainly didn't. You could meet a hundred people and they would all know a different Dudley Clarke. This one was his most frequent incarnation – benign barfly.

'Tell me, to what do I owe the pleasure?' he asked, his attention finally focusing on us now that the masquerade of chatter had served its purpose, gesturing to us to accompany him as we followed the waiter, who had magically appeared to lead us to a table discreetly set in an alcove graced on either side by potted palms. The location was perfect, affording an uninterrupted view of the room while effectively curtaining us from prying eyes and ears. Dudley's usual table. Like everything he did, it was planned down to the last detail.

My martini slid past my teeth, its sourness bringing everything into sharp focus as it collided with my taste buds. 'Vulke is here. In Cairo.'

Dudley barely blinked, but I could almost hear his brain whirring. 'Felix Vulke?'

'He's alive. I saw him for myself. At a party two nights ago. Our party, as a matter of fact.'

'Nadia is, as you know, now lodging with us at Eden, sir,' interjected Tom. 'The excuse for the party was to celebrate El Alamein, although it was, of course, the usual affair.'

Dudley nodded absently, his gaze fixed somewhere else, somewhere far from here. 'Naturally.'

I sat back as he pulled a cutter from his pocket, slicing the end of the cigar the waiter had brought before applying a silver lighter to the end of it until it glowed, a thin spiral of smoke obscuring Dudley's eyes for a second. When the smoke cleared, they were fixed on me, intent. 'Does he know?'

I let out the breath I'd been holding. 'I don't think so. Maybe. There was something he said when he attacked another agent at the party. To be honest, I'm not sure, which is why I wanted to talk to you.'

I could feel Tom beside me, burning with questions, but they would have to wait. Besides, Dudley would deflect them as he always did, with a joke and a smile, although right now there was no trace of mirth on his face, which was uncharacteristically sombre.

He sucked on his cigar once more. It had always been one of his most useful props. I'd seen Dudley deploy it in Lisbon, where he posed as a flamboyant journalist, and in his supposed role here as head of the escape and evasion network MI9, although it was as a master of deception that I knew him best. Dudley was a magician, the man who conjured up fake information and non-existent battalions to deceive the enemy. Not even Dudley, though, could bring a man back from the dead. Which was why we were here now. Something had gone badly wrong.

'I saw him hit the ground in Paris, Dudley. He was dead. I would swear it.'

Dudley tapped the end of his cigar on the cut-crystal ashtray that adorned our table. 'You saw what he wanted you to see. It's easily done, Nadia. A steel breastplate. A vial of fake blood. What that indicates to me is that he knew you were coming and wanted to get you off his back. Don't blame yourself. Felix Vulke is a spy like no other. He's also a brutal killer. If he's popped up here in Cairo, then it will be on direct orders from Berlin. The question is why and whether he already knew you were here. Or at least the person who tried to kill him is here. We don't know if he knows it's actually you.'

'Whether he does or not, he's going to try to find out and then kill me.'

'Of course he is, but we won't let that happen.'

'Too bloody right we won't,' muttered Tom. 'We'll kill the bastard first.'

I threw back my drink. 'You bet we will.'

25

Dudley's office was not, as you might have expected, at HQ, where he reported to the commander-in-chief, but further along the street opposite, below a brothel, a situation he found highly amusing. Since the authorities had closed down the brothels in the Berka – or Wagh El Birket as the red-light district was more formally known – after two Australian soldiers were killed there, prostitutes had become a little more discreet, plying their trade from anonymous office buildings such as this one. Even so, I strutted through the door as if I was a lady of the night turning up for work, only throwing aside my headscarf when I was safely inside the cluttered room that was the headquarters for Dudley's A Force.

Tom's task was somewhat easier. All he had to do was stroll in acting as a punter, closing the street door to make sure no one saw him dart along the corridor that led to the A Force entrance rather than carrying on up the stairs. In some ways, it was easier to be a man in this war. In others, much harder. The Germans and their allies maintained an air of macho superiority that could not countenance a woman being anything other than a Madonna or one of the whores upstairs.

That suited me just fine. Let them think we were fit for nothing except domesticity or another kind of drudgery. And drudgery it was, judging by the constant stream of men who mounted those stairs to be serviced by girls who were often co-opted into what was virtually slavery, seeing to the needs of men who were so brutalised or broken by what they had experienced on the battlefield that they were scarcely human anymore.

Sometimes, I knew, all they wanted to do was talk. I heard it so often from the men I'd tended while working with the Red Cross. War, above all, is lonely. You might be serving alongside men you consider brothers in arms, but when it comes down to it, it's every man for himself. And every woman. We were here too, doing our bit in so many ways. I included those young women upstairs in that. After all, my job wasn't so different from theirs in that I had to read people and act the appropriate role, sometimes purely to stay alive. Only there was no role I could play that would save me from Felix Vulke. I hated to think what it would be like to have to service him.

'You alright, old girl?'

I could feel Dudley's gaze, taking in every thought that crossed my face. 'Yes, yes of course.'

'Cup of tea?'

I glanced around, looking for a chair on which I could sit, lifting a pile of files off the nearest one and depositing them with the rest on Dudley's desk. There were files everywhere, teetering on the tops of cabinets and tables or fanned out on the floor, under the cage which housed a particularly belligerent parrot Dudley had rescued from a departing Admiral of the Fleet and which could swear fluently in half a dozen languages.

Tom perched on the edge of the desk as Dudley filled an ancient kettle, for once in silence. I shifted in my seat. Silence wasn't good as far as Dudley was concerned. It meant things were far more serious than we thought.

Sure enough, he handed me a chipped cup, the tea already slopped into the saucer, and took up his position on the other side of his desk. His setting might have appeared chaotic, but I knew it was all part of the act. Dudley had a mind that filed everything into neat compartments, sifting and sorting so he knew exactly where to find the facts.

He reached for one now, pulling it off its mental shelf with precision. 'From our intercepts, we understand that Vulke is in Cairo on his way to Tunis to join Colonel Walther Rauff.'

'Head of the SS there?'

'Correct. Rauff was supposed to be in charge of Einsatzkommando Egypt, but the Nazis dropped that idea after El Alamein. We know he reports directly to Rommel but apart from that appears to have a remarkably free hand in Tunisia. We can only imagine how he will utilise a killer like Vulke.'

Einsatzkommando. A killing squad, with Jews, the disabled and anyone else the Nazis considered undesirable as its targets.

'Wasn't Rauff one of Reinhard Heydrich's closest aides?' I asked.

Dudley pulled a real file from the pile on his desk. 'Also correct. Take a look at this.'

Tom pulled his chair alongside as I flipped it open. I stared at the image of Rauff, his prominent nose and flat, hard eyes at odds with his flaccid jawline. More memories stirring, this time of intelligence smuggled directly out of Poland. 'I remember him now. Rauff is the one responsible for the gas vans. He helped design them.'

Tom glanced at me. 'Gas vans?'

'Mobile killing chambers. The Nazis used them in Poland to kill patients at psychiatric and other hospitals as well as children and women they classed as prostitutes. The people are forced inside and the vans are sealed. They then pump in carbon monoxide using the exhaust pipes. There is no escape. They do all of this while driving them to a burial site.'

'How very efficient.' Dudley's tone was as cold as dry ice.

I snapped the file shut, blocking out Rauff's hateful face. 'Indeed.'

'I'd like you to eliminate Rauff before he gets a chance to really crack down in Tunisia. We know what he's capable of, and we also know that killing him will be a much-needed morale boost for our troops and everyone back home. The tide is turning in this war but not fast enough. All I'm waiting for is word from London and then we can make a plan.'

I lifted my eyes from the file. 'It will be a pleasure.'

26

The terrace of the Gezira Club was as busy as ever and yet it was far more serene than Shepheard's, the tables set wide enough apart so that I felt as if I could breathe out here. Overhead, the lights strung between the acacias were just beginning to twinkle as day turned to dusk. They could not dispel the deep sadness that had overwhelmed me since leaving Dudley's office.

'Shall we eat here?'

Tom's tone was matter-of-fact, although I could detect the concern in his eyes.

'Yes, why not?'

Two cocktails down and still I saw their faces. Andrzej and Alexander. In my imagination, they were intertwined. First one, then the other. Somehow I never saw them together, but then, we'd had so little time as a family. By the time Alexander succumbed to his fever, Andrzej was already dead. At least he had been spared that, knowing his son did not survive his flight from the evil bastards who took his own life. It was a cruel twist of fate but better than the way Andrzej had suffered.

I had no doubt Andrzej had died with dignity. He was an

officer after all, as well as a true gentleman. As Tom was now, avoiding the subject in that oh so British way of his.

I picked up my glass, finishing the dregs of my Suffering Bastard, savouring the lime juice that cut through the bourbon and the warming effect of the ginger beer. Not as good as the one made by Joe at Shepheard's, but then he'd invented it as a hangover cure for the troops. Now it was more the fuel on which many of them fought. Too bad it couldn't cure a broken heart.

'They brought a list to Poland, you know. The Nazis. My husband's name was on it, as well as mine. They wanted to eliminate everything that was good or noble in our country. Anyone that would stand up to them. That was Andrzej. He hated those murdering scum.'

Tom reached for my hand across the table, not quite touching it. 'That was also you, Nadia. It *is* you. And you're alive, which means you can fight on for him. For all of us.'

'For my son,' I whispered.

He looked at me, stricken. 'You had a child?'

'A little boy. Alexander. He caught a fever and died on our way to Palestine. After we buried him there, I came to Cairo. The rest of my family and his are now in London, but I couldn't go while a single Nazi still lived and breathed. I swore then I would do everything I could to stop them. I have stuck to my word.'

His fingers were still inches from mine. 'You have in spades, my darling. Dudley told me a little of what you've achieved.'

I met his gaze. 'Did he now?'

I felt the air around us still, as if someone standing right behind me had taken a deep breath, inhaling it all. It seemed so real that I glanced round, half-expecting to see someone at my shoulder, but there was no one there. No one visible at any rate. Maybe I had been in Egypt too long, but it seemed to me this was a city of ghosts, the past haunting the present, casting an inexorable shadow, the weight of history all around us as we battled to sustain the present, to keep it safe for future generations, just as Andrzej had done. It was him I felt standing there now, quietly watching. I could almost see him, that half-smile of his, the approval in his eyes.

'If anything happens to me,' he'd said, 'I want you to find someone.' He'd lain a finger on my lips as I'd protested that could never, would never happen. In the same way I was pressing my own finger to my lips now, blowing a kiss to the spectre of happiness I could sense fading from me. He was gone. I dropped my hand to the table, alone again. No, not alone. Tom's fingers finally touched mine, intertwining, holding on. I leaped back as if I'd received an electric shock.

He said nothing, merely addressed himself to the menu, allowing me a moment to gather myself. When our food arrived, he kept up the sort of light chatter at which Dudley was so accomplished. I had to hand it to him. There was a sensitivity to Tom that belied his years.

When we had both finished eating, he offered me a cigarette.

'There's something I feel I must tell you,' he murmured as he lit mine and then his.

I felt it then, that plummeting in my stomach that warned me what I was about to hear would change everything. 'Go on.'

'I'm married too. Unlike in your case, my wife – if you can call her that – is still very much alive.'

I gaped at him. 'You're... married?'

'Yes. Is it so surprising?'

'No. Not at all. It's just...'

He threw me a rueful smile. 'We met when we were children and married still far too young.'

'Do you have any children of your own?'

'My wife and me? No. Although I believe she is expecting a child with my brother.'

I exploded in a fit of coughing, only able to speak once it had subsided. 'Your wife is having a baby by your brother?'

As he dropped his head, the light from the candles on the table made his eyes glisten. No, not the light. Those were real tears he was holding back. I reached out and took his hand once more, this time for comfort. 'I'm so sorry.'

'Don't be sorry. I'm not. They're made for one another. As it appears you were for your husband.'

'Andrzej and I, we were children too when we met. And yes, I loved him, very much. I believe that love never dies, but it loses that intensity, you know? It becomes something you hold dear just as you held dear that person, but life must go on. And I intend to live as well as I can to ensure others do too.'

He raised our entangled hands, dropping a kiss onto mine. 'What about love? Is that part of living?'

I gazed at him, spellbound, hearing the whispers all around me – Andrzej's voice urging me to find someone, the heart-shattering cry of my child. I could see in Tom's eyes all the pain I had endured too. Was enduring. Could two damaged souls really help mend one another?

'Perhaps.'

27

PRESENT DAY, CAIRO, EGYPT

SOPHIE

Josh sat back in his rattan chair. 'Tell me about Ben.'

I blinked, taken aback. 'What do you want to know?'

The lights were starting to come on, their orbs on top of wrought-iron stands glowing in the twilight. Out here, on the terrace, the air was cooling, although it was still warm enough to sit without a coat or jacket. I was wearing the same dress I'd had on back at the villa. It was Josh's idea to come here for dinner, and I'd worried it wouldn't be smart enough for such a fancy-sounding place. As it turned out, the Gezira Club was far less stuffy than I had imagined – or perhaps that was Josh's presence. Everyone here appeared to know him, even the frosty female at the reception desk. But then Josh had an effortless charm to match his good looks.

'Forgive me,' said Josh. 'That was a little blunt. I feel like he was such an important part of your life. Is such an important part. I just wanted to hear more about him.'

'What is there to say? He was Ben. Good, kind, handsome. The man who was meant to be my husband. He didn't deserve to die, and I didn't deserve to lose him, but it is what it is. As Nadia would say, all you can do is keep going. Keep living. Even though at first I wanted to die too.'

He took my hand, the warmth flooding from him into me. 'I'm sure you did, but instead you're here. You should be proud of yourself. I know Nadia would be.'

'You met her?'

'No, but I feel like I did after listening to David and now you. My grandma met her when she was a little girl.'

'I remember you saying your great-grandmother knew Nadia. That Nadia saved your grandma's life. So your grandma was here, in Cairo?'

'I believe they visited with Nadia in England. Grandma went there with her dad, although she doesn't talk much about it. Family trait. We also have our secrets.'

His eyes were clouded now, grey with remembrance. I wondered what had happened to cast this shade over him. Life no doubt. Except it was more than that. There was a real ache in his eyes, in his voice. It seeped from him.

'Another drink, sir, madame?'

Our waiter gave us a little bow as he cleared our glasses. He reminded me of the concierge's grandfather. Another old retainer who had no doubt seen and heard many things in his service. Not for the first time, I wished I could have seen Cairo through Nadia's eyes, in its heyday. 'What do you recommend?'

There was a glint in Josh's eye now as he turned to the waiter. 'How about a Suffering Bastard?'

The waiter chuckled. 'Very good, sir. For the lady too?'

'Of course. She needs to try one at least once. I believe it was one of Nadia's favourite cocktails,' he added, turning to me.

I caught a hint of recognition in the waiter's expression before he dropped his professional mask over it, discreet to the last. 'Two Suffering Bastards. Right away, sir.'

As soon as he was out of earshot, I rounded on Josh. 'What on earth is a Suffering Bastard?'

'It was a cocktail invented during the war by Joe Scamolini, the barman at Shepheard's Hotel. Joe was a chemist who became a mixologist, one of the best in the world. The Suffering Bastard was his masterpiece, invented as a hangover cure for the troops, although it quickly became the most popular cocktail in Cairo.'

'How do you know all this stuff?'

'Book research.'

'Ah, yes. Your book. Am I going to be in it too?'

'I should think so. The story is still unfolding.'

His eyes held mine just a fraction too long. I looked away first, almost relieved to see the waiter arrive with our cocktails. There was an intensity to Josh tonight that I didn't quite understand. It was unsettling.

'Two Suffering Bastards.'

The waiter hesitated a moment before placing our drinks in front of us. I didn't blame him. The air was crackling in the way it does before a storm, heavy with what was to come.

I took a sip. 'So what's in this famous drink?'

'Bourbon, gin, lime juice, angostura bitters and ginger beer. I make a mean one myself, as it happens.'

I looked at him, all trace of suffering dissipating in his grin. It lit up his face, stripping years from it. I could imagine him as a little boy, playing on a beach just like the one on Nadia's book cover. The book I had tucked in my bag. 'You should do that more often.'

'What?'

'Smile.'

He cocked an eyebrow. 'I will if you will.'

I held my hand out for him to shake. 'It's a deal.'

He took it and dropped a kiss on the inside of my wrist. 'Sealed.'

28

The slapping and clapping of a nightjar filled the air, followed by a soft *coowhit* as it settled on a branch, calling out to its compatriots, who called in return. It reminded me of those lines from *Romeo and Juliet* as each tried to convince the other it was the nightingale or the lark that sang, one prolonging their night of love while the other heralded the dawn when they must part. Was Josh trying to convince himself of something too?

I stared at him, his face half-hidden in the dark, his eyes unreadable. All I could see in them was the candlelight reflected from the table, the dancing flame obscuring his thoughts. He was still holding back in spite of the kiss that had left its imprint on my wrist.

'Tell me about it, about whatever it is you're not telling me.'

A sigh. 'I can't. You already know too much.'

Something was off here. I could feel it. Never mind what he'd just said, it was obvious he was struggling against a far greater weight. That of secrets. 'You can't or you won't?'

He looked at me then. 'I can't. It was my job, you see. My great-grandad's job too, as it happens. I'm sorry. I'm not trying to be difficult. It's just...'

'You can't. I get it. There were times Ben couldn't tell me about his work. OK, so let's talk about what you do now. Why did you decide to become a writer?'

'Oh, that's simple. As you know, I love reading. Always have. And I'm forever trying to work out what makes people tick. Hangover from the old job. So it seemed like the ideal thing to do when David suggested it.'

'Are you enjoying it?'

He leaned forward then, into the light, flashing that captivating smile. 'Absolutely. I've met you through it, for one thing.'

I laughed. 'I guess, in a roundabout way, you have.'

'And there's still so much to discover.'

'About me or about the whole story?'

'Both.'

A heartbeat. Then another. A bottomless gulf yawning before me. I could fall into it. That would be so easy and, on the other hand, so impossible. After Ben, I resigned myself to never falling in love again, and yet here I was, on the edge. There was something in the way he uttered that word that broke through my last reserves. I could feel the ice that had encased my heart for so long start to splinter. 'There's not much to learn about me. What you see is what you get.'

'I see someone whose whole world was shattered but who's still holding on, doing her best to live for the people she's lost and to do the right thing.'

'It's what Ben always did,' I whispered. 'The right thing.'

'You think that's what got him killed?'

My shoulders sagged. 'I don't know. Maybe. It was just so odd, a hit-and-run on a straight country road. Whoever it was must have seen him in the road, running, but they still hit him and then just drove off, leaving him lying there. Dead.' I heard myself stutter, stumbling over that awful word. 'That alone makes me think it was no accident, no matter what the police say. I know they think I've lost my mind with grief. That it's all

in my head. But it doesn't add up, does it? He told me he had to
do something for Nadia right before he left her house. He must
have gone straight to the postbox to send the photo here, and
then he sent me a text insisting I come to Cairo moments before
he was hit. It's all very weird.'

'It does seem strange, but accidents do happen and people
do panic.'

The familiar sting of disappointment. He didn't believe me
either. Maybe they were all right. Maybe I really had lost it.

'OK, but how do you explain the photograph? Something so
important he felt he had to post it even then, when he was
clearly frantic. Why else send me that text? That wasn't like
Ben at all. I think he knew something was about to happen to
him and he only had enough time to send that. He might even
have heard the car coming and realised it wasn't going to stop,
which is when he started to run. But why knock him down?
None of it makes sense.'

My voice cracked. Shit. Any moment now I'd be sobbing. I
gulped, trying in vain to swallow it all back.

Josh picked up his folded napkin and handed it to me.
'Here.'

I covered my eyes with it, wiping away the tears and trying
to compose myself. 'I'm sorry.'

'Don't be. You lost someone you loved very much. I can see
that. It's brutal.'

I blew my nose on the napkin. 'It sounds to me as if you
know what that feels like.'

He sat back, gazing up now at the stars that studded the sky,
diamonds that glittered, so alive, although they might already be
dead. Just like Ben. And, perhaps, someone who had meant a
lot to Josh.

'It's not the same as for you. She didn't die. She just left me.
For someone else. My best friend, as it happens. At least he was.
Turns out they started seeing each other while I was away,

working. They have a kid now and they're married. Very happily, so I hear. It's one of the reasons I can empathise with Tom so much.'

It was there in his voice now, the ache I'd seen in his eyes. He was trying to make light of it, but there was no disguising a pain like that.

'That's worse, in a way. At least I have closure.'

'It doesn't sound as if you do. Have you got that photograph with you by any chance? The one Ben sent?'

He obviously didn't want to talk about it. Fair enough.

I pulled the envelope from my bag. 'It's here.'

He studied it while I studied him surreptitiously. He and Tom were not so very different. I could understand why he empathised with him. Both had lost their women to another man, in Tom's case while he was away fighting a war. As for Josh, from the little he'd said, I got the impression whatever he'd done as his previous job was for the greater good too, even if he'd hated it. Well, more fool those women. From what I knew of Tom, he'd been a thoroughly decent man. As was Josh. There was none of that pretence or game playing. He was who he was – a gentleman, just like Tom. Someone worth holding on to.

'There has to be more to it,' he murmured. 'A photograph of Tom, who once lived at the villa. Random numbers written on the back of it. And Ben sends it to the villa on Nadia's instructions shortly before he's killed in a hit-and-run that you don't believe was random. From what you've said, you don't think any of this is random. We're missing something. Maybe we need to go back and look at the villa more carefully. Find whatever it is, if it's there.'

The nightjar called again; its eerie churring rattled my brain along with my thoughts. So many thoughts.

'You're right,' I said. 'We got distracted by the library. We need to take a proper look at the whole place. But what's the point? Everyone thinks I'm crazy.'

'I don't think you're crazy.'

The *coowhit* pierced the air, a plaintive cry that shot through my heart like an arrow. 'Really?'

He leaned forward across the table, his face no longer hollows and plains but filled now with light and something else. Tenderness. Compassion. 'Really. If there's one thing I've learned, it's that things are never as they seem. Not when people want you to look the other way. And it sounds to me as if someone set it up so that everyone is looking the other way but you.'

I bit my lip. 'You really believe me?'

'I not only believe you – I want to help you.'

'But how?'

I could see him wrestling with his thoughts and then he took a deep breath. 'That job I used to do? Let's just say it was for the United States government.'

I stared at him. 'You were secret service?'

'Just like my great-grandpa. The one who was out here, working with OSS. The Office of Strategic Services. Have you heard of them? They later became the CIA.'

'Now you mention it, it rings a bell. Nadia said something about OSS once or twice, although only in passing. She said very little about the war, but then she was of that generation.'

Josh nodded. 'Just like my great-grandpa. Most of them took their secrets to the grave. And that's where we're going to start tomorrow. At Tom's grave. I haven't been there yet, although I know where it is. I doubt there's anything to discover, but you never know. And it feels right we pay our respects before we start digging into the past, don't you agree?'

I smiled at him. Decent, just as I thought. 'I do.'

'What is that quote – to know your future you must know your past? My grandma loves that one. But then, she has quite a past. Apparently, she was drowning when Nadia saved her in Tunisia. Dived into the water and pulled her out.'

'That sounds like Nadia. What were they doing in Tunisia?'

'It was some kind of top-secret operation, but that's all I know. Like I said, my grandma is one of those old-school types. She says very little, even though it was her mom who was the spy and not her.'

'Her mother was a spy too?'

'That's how she and Nadia became friends. Her mother, Colette, was killed sadly. On the mission in Tunisia. How or why I have no idea. She's buried there with her people. One day I'd like to visit her grave too.'

I smiled. 'I'm sure you will.'

'Maybe you could come with me?'

'Maybe I could.'

Inside me, a tiny flame began to grow, brighter and brighter, sending its warmth and light through me. The flame I'd thought had been extinguished. The one called hope.

29

28 NOVEMBER 1942, CAIRO, EGYPT

NADIA

Colette's eyes blazed, the lashes that ringed them jet black against her skin, from which all the blood appeared to have drained. 'I will not stay here while my family are in danger. I am going to Tunis, I tell you. Tonight.'

Jim slapped his hand down on the table in frustration. 'No you are not. It's too dangerous right now. I'm not going to let one of my best agents walk into a deathtrap.'

I could sense it again, that tension between them, an elastic band of emotion pulled so tight it was about to snap. She was rooted to the spot, a gazelle frozen in flight, her limbs trembling with emotion as she faced him down. There was obviously so much more between them than just a professional relationship, although quite what it was I couldn't yet tell. Something told me it was far more complicated than it appeared. But then isn't everything?

'Sit down,' he said softly.

She shook her head, defiant.

'I said sit down,' he snarled, hands on hips.

And still she stood, glaring at him, unyielding.

The rest of us were rooted to the spot, watching in morbid fascination from our positions around the room where only a few moments before we had been discussing tactics. This was no game. It was full-out war.

'Sir.'

Tom kept his eyes fixed on the scene playing out in front of him. 'What is it, Abbas?'

'Sir, Lieutenant Colonel Clarke is here to see you.'

'Show him in.'

The moment Dudley walked through the door, I felt the hostility in the room subside. He swept in with his customary bonhomie, full of smiles and good grace, although his gaze took in everything as he dropped kisses first on Colette's cheeks and then on mine. 'You're all here. How marvellous. Saves me having to repeat myself.'

Nico uncoiled himself from the couch on which he had been sprawling. 'You have news?'

'Indeed I do. Tell me, what does a chap have to do to get a drink around here?'

Tom held up his hand. 'Don't worry, Abbas. I'll get it. What do you fancy, sir?'

Dudley waved an expansive arm around the room. 'I hope you'll be joining me. We have something to celebrate.'

'We do?' I was all ears. It was about time we had some good news with Vulke on the prowl and the intel from Tunisia growing gloomier by the day.

'Felix Vulke has left Cairo and is on his way to Tunis.'

Colette whirled on him. 'You call that good news?'

'Come, come, darling. At least it means he isn't here, trying to pick you all off one by one.'

'No,' she spat. 'He's there instead, picking off my people.'

I clenched my fists, fighting back the fury. 'It also means we've lost our chance to eliminate him.'

Dudley cocked an eyebrow. 'And I thought you were resourceful. There is more than one way to skin a cat, as they say.'

Resentment rose like bile in my throat, burning the back of it. My fists coiled tighter, fingernails digging into my flesh. 'So what do you suggest?'

'Oh, it's quite simple, darling. You're going in after him.'

30

I pressed my fingers to my forehead, feeling the pulse beating there. Thud, thud, thud. Matching the tattoo of my heart. All around me, raised voices, shouting, talking all at once. In here, inside my skull, an eerie silence broken only by that pulse. Thud, thud. One, two. One, two. *Slow down, my love.* That's what Andrzej would have said. He'd been saying it since we were ten years old and running wild through the forest, trying to creep up on the deer and the boar that inhabited it. I was trying, God help me.

'Will you all just be quiet?' I cried. 'I can't hear myself think.'

Startled faces turning to me, none more so than Dudley's.

I took a breath. 'That's better. Now, can we please speak one at a time. Dudley, what exactly do you mean by "you're going in after him"?'

'Precisely what I said, although I admit I omitted the details, and that's because we don't yet have a plan. That's what I want you all to come up with. A plan. We have the go-ahead from London. You are to get into Tunisia and eliminate Walther Rauff.'

'Wait a moment,' I said. 'Rauff? I thought we were going after Vulke.'

Dudley kept his expression carefully blank. 'Your official orders are to eliminate Colonel Walther Rauff, the head of the SS in Tunisia. Should anyone else get caught in the crossfire, so to speak, that would be unfortunate, but such is war.'

'Let me get this straight,' cut in Jim. 'You want my agents to go after a German colonel behind enemy lines?'

Dudley rubbed at his ear. I noticed a faint smear of what appeared to be dirt in front of it. Curious. Dudley was usually so pristine. 'That's about the size of it, old chap,' he said.

Jim's eyes glittered from under his brows, his mouth drawn into an unyielding line. 'Over my dead body.'

That smear wasn't dirt. It was make-up. I would swear to it. I'd heard the rumours about Dudley, of course, but had yet to see any evidence of his preference for dressing up as a woman. Until now. Come to think of it, his lips looked unnaturally pink, as if he'd recently had to rub lipstick from them. It seemed he'd rushed over here in something of a hurry.

'Why has London suddenly decided we're to go in now?' I asked.

'Not just that, who the hell issued the order in the first place?' snarled Jim. 'I thought this was a joint mission. Now it seems you Brits want to run the show.'

Dudley bared his teeth in a smile, revealing a smear of pink on one incisor. Careless of him. 'Not at all,' he murmured. 'But as you ask, the order was issued from the highest level. On both sides of the Atlantic.'

Jim lowered his head, a bull about to charge. 'Are you telling me that President Roosevelt sanctioned this along with Churchill?'

'Something like that,' said Dudley.

Jim snorted. 'I call bullshit.'

'You can call it what you like. The fact remains that in this theatre of war, we have agreed to work together and that includes on our intelligence ops. If you want to call the White House then please go right ahead, but I suggest that, in the meantime, we all get on with planning this mission.'

I caught a note then in his voice, one he had been carefully disguising until now. One that sent a ripple of fear through me. 'What's so urgent about this, Dudley?'

The mask dropped. His eyes were sombre, his tone hushed. 'Rauff has already started to herd people into his infernal camps. Worse than that, a dozen or so of his gas vans arrived in Tunis yesterday. I have no doubt that Vulke has gone to assist him in a mass extermination campaign which will start any moment now.'

Colette's hand flew to her mouth. My heart twisted as I saw the panic in her eyes.

'The vans are Rauff's invention,' added Dudley. 'His hatred of Jews and other people he despises is well known. Rommel, on the other hand, loathes Rauff's beliefs and the consequences of them. If we can eliminate Rauff, there's a very good chance we will save many lives.'

Lives like my Andrzej's. My baby Alexander. I looked round the room. 'Then what are we waiting for? Let's get planning.'

Colette looked from Jim to me, then moved to my side and slipped her arm through mine. She was so close I could have sworn I heard her heart beating too, her chest rising and falling too fast as she breathed. 'Let's do it,' she said. 'Let's take that bastard down.'

As I smiled at her, I saw her lips form a couple more words that hung in the air between us. Words that would return to haunt me. 'Thank you,' she mouthed.

31

The bathroom was filled with steam, the tiles slick with it. Perched on the edge of the bath, Colette and I listened while Tom drew out a rough map on the mirror, his finger cutting through the misted-up surface. I couldn't help but notice his T-shirt clinging to his torso, outlining every muscle, his bare skin gleaming with sweat. Jim leaned against the shower head while the others crouched on the floor, Nico picking his teeth in apparent boredom.

'Brandon Mission is situated here, on the outskirts of Algiers. We can liaise with them to pinpoint the best route into Tunisia based on the latest intelligence. They get that from Agency Africa, the Franco-Polish intelligence operation that's based in Algiers too.'

'They're the best in North Africa,' I said. 'I should know. I've worked for them. And they know how these bastards operate. Both Rauff and Vulke worked for Reinhard Heydrich, carrying out the exterminations in Poland. Over one hundred thousand people were murdered on his orders, including my husband. If anyone can give us insights into how best to take them out, it's Agency Africa.'

I could hear the slow drip-drip of water from the bath tap into the pool of silence that spread from my words. Colette placed her hand on mine, a gentle touch that signalled solidarity.

Tom cleared his throat. 'Maybe Nadia should contact Agency Africa directly. Get the intelligence first-hand.'

'Absolutely not,' snapped Jim. 'Our orders are to work with Brandon directly, and that's what we do. Those are our own people. We know we can trust them.'

I glared at him. 'Are you suggesting we can't trust Agency Africa?'

'Not at all. I'm just saying this is a clandestine mission and we need to keep it that way. The fewer in on it, the better.'

I took his point. We still had no idea who was passing on intelligence to the enemy, which was one reason for this meeting, here in the bathroom of all places, away from prying eyes or ears. I would trust Abbas with my life, but you never knew who else might be listening among the parade of people who passed through this place day and night. Still, I bristled.

'Major Słowikowski, who runs Agency Africa, is a fine officer. We used the information his organisation gathered to plan the Operation Torch landings. If it's good enough for Eisenhower, I suspect his intelligence will be more than adequate for us.'

Jim stiffened. 'Of course. I meant no disrespect. But we want to keep this tight. Which is why I'm confining the task force for this mission to the people in this room.'

'Hold on now,' protested Tom. 'This is a joint op, remember?'

'Oh for God's sake,' I cried. 'Can we just stop the chest beating? You're absolutely right. It's a joint op. So let's work together and not waste time proving who's top dog.'

Colette clapped her hands. 'Bravo! Well said.'

They both had the grace to look shamefaced. 'Agreed,' said Tom. 'Shall I continue?'

He didn't wait for Jim's nod, and I suppressed an inward sigh. This was going to be an interesting mission, if it ever got off the ground.

'Nadia has already mentioned Heydrich who, as you know, was assassinated by Czech agents trained by SOE back in June. The plan in his case was to ambush his car using snipers. Although it didn't quite go according to plan, that is how we're going to carry out this assassination as well.'

'Are you nuts?' said Jim. 'For one thing, that op was a serious screw-up, and for another, it resulted in those two agents shooting themselves and the executions of hundreds of people.'

'Including eighty-one children in Rauff's gas vans. Yes, I know,' said Tom. 'But we're not going to screw up. We're following the basic MO, but we're going to do it better, starting with the agents we embed weeks before we even attempt this to gather information on Rauff's daily routine so we can ambush him at the right time and place. Colette and Nadia, that will be you two.'

'No way. Absolutely not. I forbid it.'

Jim was in Tom's face now, fists clenched.

Colette rose to her feet. 'It's alright, Jim. Tom's right. I should go undercover. I'm Tunisian, after all. I know the country and the people. It will be easy for me to pass unnoticed. I can help Nadia blend in too. We women find it far easier.'

Jim turned and looked straight at her, his hands no longer clenched into fists but upturned, almost pleading. 'What about Céline?' he murmured. 'What if you lead them to her?'

I saw his words hit home. Colette blinked, a single tear spilling from one eye. 'That's low, Jim. Very low.'

The atmosphere was so charged I could feel the hairs on the back of my neck rising in spite of the damp. 'Who is Céline?' I whispered, already half-knowing the answer.

'My baby daughter,' she answered. 'My life.'

32

Out in the garden, the air was dry in contrast to the steamed-up bathroom, redolent with the smells and sounds of the night. A waft of jasmine as we strolled past the fountain; beyond that, the perfume of the roses, still abundant even at this time of year.

Colette stopped to stroke one, her fingers drifting over its velvet petals. 'I almost called her Rose,' she murmured. 'But when she was born, she seemed more like a Céline. It means "heavenly", and she is, she really is. Such a good baby. My parents adore her.'

The longing in her voice tugged at my heart. I knew what it felt like to ache to hold your child in your arms again, to smother their vanilla-scented skin with kisses and to feel their tiny fingers curl around your own. The difference was that Colette could still do that. Her baby might be hundreds of miles away, but at least she was alive. Alexander was rotting alone in a grave in Palestine, his tiny body covered in dirt. I would never know his warm weight in my arms again.

'What happened to your husband?'

It came out rougher than I intended, my voice rasping as I struggled to suppress my own grief.

She snapped the head off the rose and buried her nose in it. 'He was killed, just as your husband was. You see, we have that in common too. Our particular reasons for hating those bastards.'

The moonlight was bathing her in its silver glow just as it had that other night, the night of the party. Only then, she had been lying crumpled on the ground, thanks to Vulke. 'Remember Paris.' All at once, I felt a surge of blind fury such as I'd never felt before, not even when I heard Andrzej had been murdered or when, just a few weeks later, I had to close his son's eyes knowing that he would never grow to see his father or his homeland again.

'We do, and that's why we have to make this happen. I understand if you feel it's too much of a risk, given your daughter is right there, but I will go in alone if necessary. I'm sure I could pass as you. After all, Vulke seems to have mistaken you for me or at least thought you were the person who shot him in Paris.'

She laughed. 'I'm sure you couldn't pass as me or as a local without me. The fact my daughter is there gives me all the more reason to go in. To make sure those monsters can't destroy other families. Are you with me?'

I took the rose she was offering me. 'All the way.'

Behind us, the fountain flowed, its water an eternal symbol of Paradise. I so wanted to think that Andrzej was there now, holding Alexander, but I'd seen too much suffering to believe in anything other than the here and now. At least in this life, I could make a difference. The next would just have to take care of itself.

Colette smiled as if reading my thoughts. 'The sound of life,' she murmured. 'Do you believe in it? The afterlife?'

'No. I watched my baby die and there was nothing. No light, no angels, just a little boy who was no longer there. I've watched men die too, in the field hospitals. They're no more than boys, many of them. Someone else's son. I've held their hands. Tried to comfort them. Most of them cry out for their mothers. And when they're gone, they're gone. Forever. The only thing I believe in now is vengeance. I will not stop until I get it. I know I should be fighting for peace, but the truth is that I have no peace. All I know now is pain and loss. Yes, we cover it up with drinking and partying, but the truth is, that's how we all feel. Isn't it?'

Her hand was cool on my arm, the lightest of touches, like a night moth. 'Yes.'

As if to emphasise my words, I could hear the sound of bottles and glasses clinking in the garden room. The men were celebrating, as was their way. Better, I suppose, to celebrate what lay ahead than to mourn what lay behind us. All the grief in the world wouldn't bring them back, any of them. We had to look ahead. Keep living, come what may.

I heard someone calling to us from the open French doors and looked up to see Tom standing there, silhouetted in the moonlight. We gazed at one another through the darkness, two night creatures finding one another. I felt our eyes meet. Not just our eyes. Something more.

He said nothing, just raised his hand.

'I'm coming,' I said.

33

PRESENT DAY, CAIRO, EGYPT

SOPHIE

Josh handed me a glass of tea. 'Take me through it from the beginning.'

Somewhere in the apartment, David was sleeping, but out here, on the balcony, I had never felt more awake, every nerve and synapse firing as I remembered. 'The police came to the house at around five o'clock. Ben should have been back long before then. The postbox was only down the lane, maybe ten minutes' walk at most. I thought maybe he'd decided to carry on walking and get some fresh air. I knew before they even told me that Ben was dead.'

Josh nodded, his eyes never leaving my face. 'Go on.'

'They wouldn't let me see him at first. I think it was because of his injuries, but when I finally did get to see him, he looked as if he was asleep. A couple of bruises to his face but that was all I could see. What I didn't know then were his brain injuries. The doctor told me he would have died instantly, and I'd like to believe that. I held his hand for a moment, but it didn't feel like him. It was cold. Lifeless. And Ben was so full of life.'

'The life you'd planned to spend together.'

I swallowed hard. 'Yes.'

'And you think the last thing he did, or one of the last things, was send the photograph here?'

'Like I said, it's postmarked the day he died. He sent me the text at 3.32 p.m. He was found in the road at just after four. By then, he was already dead.'

'No witnesses?'

'None. There was an elderly man who saw a car speeding away from the scene of the crash, although all he could say was that it was black and some kind of hatchback, and that the driver was wearing a red baseball cap. He wasn't even sure about the time. The other was a woman who was walking her dog along the road and found him. She was the one who called the ambulance and stayed with him until it came. It was too late, but I will always be grateful to her, to think that he wasn't all alone.'

I choked back a sob. Yes, the doctors told me he'd died instantly, but I was never sure if that was just to make me feel better. After all, how did they really know? It gave me some small comfort that she was there, even if Ben was already dead. They say the spirit lingers, and I believe that. I see and hear him all the time, out the corner of my eye, at the edge of my vision. It was another reason I wanted to come here, away from all that, from the home that no longer felt like one but more like a living tomb. A big part of me died along with Ben.

Josh rubbed his chin, his eyes lowered. When he looked up at me again, it was with a new focus. 'So we have a photograph of Tom with some numbers on the back of it. A photograph Nadia gave to Ben. Had you ever seen it before?'

'Yes. Nadia used to have it displayed on her mantlepiece, in a silver frame. She insisted on having it with her when she died. She said she wanted Tom close to her.'

'Did she say anything else about it?'

I heard it then, the tiny but insistent sound of a bell ringing in my memory. 'As a matter of fact, she did, long before she died. She told me it had been one of the happiest days of her life, a golden day, and to keep the photo safe and to treasure it after she was no longer around. I thought at the time it was a little odd, but then we're talking about Nadia. She was a free spirit. An eccentric, you know.'

He smiled. 'So I've heard, but I don't think she said that because she was being eccentric. I think Nadia was trying to give you a clue.'

34

'A clue to what?'

'A clue to this gold I keep talking about. I know it has something to do with my family and I think it has to yours too, or at least to Nadia. I'll explain, but first I want you to take a look at this.'

He opened David's cigar box and drew out another photograph. Like the others, it was black and white, the man in it smiling uncertainly, as if he'd been caught unawares.

'This is Nico Casanoff,' said Josh. 'Although that's not his real name. It was invented by his British handlers. He also went by several other names although everyone at the villa knew him as Casanoff.'

'What was his real name?'

'Ivan Bosko. He was Serbian. A lawyer as well as a spy. He was also a double agent, working for the Abwehr as well as for us, although he remained loyal to the Allies.'

I looked closer at him, trying to discern any duplicity in his open gaze. To be honest, I couldn't see anything other than an ordinary man. 'He looks so normal.'

'That's what made him such a good agent, although he was

anything but normal. From the reports I've read, he was flamboyant. An adventurer. The life and soul of any party and a real hit with the ladies.'

I glanced at Josh. 'Which is presumably why they called him Casanoff.'

'Yep. Typical British humour, especially in those days.'

I handed him back the photograph. 'What exactly has Casanoff got to do with anything? Apart from being a double agent?'

'Casanoff was there when Tom was shot. He'd gone with them to recover the gold. There's a chance he might have had something to do with it.'

My mind was already tilting on its axis. 'All I heard was that Tom was shot during a mission. Nothing more. Nadia could never bear to speak about it, even all those years later.'

Josh refilled my tea glass. 'It's quite a story. They call it Rommel's gold, but it's really Rauff's. He stole it from the people of Djerba, demanding it in exchange for letting them live. Over fifty-eight million dollars' worth in today's money. Among it there was a very special jewellery collection which a family on the island had kept safe for centuries, passing it down the generations. My family, or at least my grandmother's. That collection was thought to be Dido's gold, dating from Carthaginian times.'

I sipped at my tea, the mint clearing my head while the sugar in it gave me a much-needed boost of energy. It was past midnight. We'd been talking for hours, although that was no hardship. I was enjoying Josh's company even though these revelations were coming thick and fast. 'I thought Dido was a myth.'

'She's a mythical figure, yes, but there's sufficient evidence that she not only existed but so did her gold. Have you heard of the Douïmès medallion?'

I shook my head.

'It's a small gold pendant that was found in the Douïmès cemetery in Carthage in what is now modern-day Tunisia. It was inscribed with a six-line epigraph that mentions Pygmalion and is dated 814 BCE. That ties in with the dates of Dido's story, although the original story doesn't mention Aeneas. It says that she killed herself rather than marry a neighbouring king.'

Dido and Aeneas. The legend of a powerful queen who killed herself over the man who abandoned her. Somehow I'd never bought that part of the story, although I'd listened to 'Dido's Lament' over and over after Ben died, the agony in it chiming with my own unbearable loss. I felt abandoned too, although I knew it wasn't through choice. We had so much to live for together, Ben and me. So many plans. The children we would have. The places we would go. All of it obliterated in one senseless act. Or was it?

'I get that this gold had something to do with Tom's death, but are you trying to tell me it also had something to do with Ben's?'

Josh handed me a piece of paper, a printout of a rough map with what appeared to be coordinates written on it. 'Maybe.'

'What's this?'

'Those are the coordinates which were found scrawled on the back of a photograph of an SS officer retrieved from Dachau. They are supposedly the coordinates of where the gold was dropped overboard. Divers have tried to find the gold using those coordinates and come up with nothing. I think there might be a second set.'

'I'm confused. What are you saying?'

'That there is another set of coordinates, possibly the real ones, written on the back of another photograph. Nadia's photograph of Tom. Although those don't appear to be a complete set but rather half.'

'The photograph that was sent here?'

'Exactly.'
'And you think that's the reason Ben died?'
'I do.'

35

21 DECEMBER 1942, CAIRO, EGYPT

NADIA

Three weeks since we had made our plans in that steamed-up bathroom and still we were waiting for the go-ahead. An interminable wait, especially for Colette. I watched her cheeks become thinner by the day as she paced, desperate to be there, to help her family, knowing that timing was everything and we couldn't blow it. Not now.

I was watching her through the window, tracing and retracing her footsteps across the lawn, her fingers twisting as she walked, head bowed when I felt rather than saw Tom come up behind me. Like an animal sensing danger, I knew it was him, the hairs on the back of my neck standing up, electrified, while I fought to keep my breath steady. Stupid. So stupid. But he had that effect on me. 'I hate to see her like this,' I said.

'Then don't. There's nothing you can do until we get our orders. Nothing she can do either. Why not come away with me for the day? I have an idea.'

I swivelled, my eyes glancing off his. *For God's sake, Nadia, look at him.* But I couldn't. 'Oh?'

'How about we head off to the beach? Forget about all of this?'

'The beach? Are you mad?'

His grin illuminated his face. Everything, in fact. Including my heart. 'Not at all. I know an excellent beach a couple of hours' drive from Cairo. We could get Abbas to make us a picnic. Oh, please say you'll come.'

I thought I was immune to his boyish charm. Apparently not. 'Very well.'

To be honest, the thought of a day at the beach was tempting. I was suffocating here, watching and waiting. Dudley wanted me to lie low until we departed for Algiers, so even my work with the Red Cross was curtailed. The idea of the sun and the sand, even on these cooler winter days, instantly lifted my spirits. And then there was Tom, his eyes widening as he took in my acceptance. 'You will? That's wonderful. I'll go and tell Abbas. Just one thing – let's keep it between ourselves, eh? I need to get away from all of this for a while, if you know what I mean.'

I grinned back at him then, a partner in crime. 'I know exactly what you mean. I'll go and get my things.'

Forty minutes later, we were sneaking out the side door to the street where the car was parked, my swimsuit stuffed into a bag along with a towel. Abbas had not only provided a splendid picnic, but he also promised to look after both Pixie and the girls, who were now happily ensconced in the summer house, tearing that to bits rather than my room. Now and then, Abbas would look at me forlornly as I handed him yet another item to mend, although he knew how much I loved the pair of them. Still, it would take a largish bribe to ensure he cared for them while we were gone.

I left all of that behind as we sped through the streets of Cairo, heading out of the city and towards the coast. In all my time here, I'd only gone the other way, into the desert. I realised with a jolt that the last time I'd seen the sea had been in Palestine when we buried my baby within sight of the blue waters of the Mediterranean. Perhaps paddling in other waters would help me feel close to him once more. Some days I could barely remember what it had felt like to hold him, but the one thing I had never forgotten was how to love him. That I would do until the end of my days.

'We're here.'

I turned my head from the window where I'd been gazing out, mile upon mile of rock-strewn desert rushing by along with my thoughts. There, ahead of us, was a glimpse of dazzling turquoise waters. 'The sea,' I breathed.

'It certainly is.'

The road swept round to our left, following the curve of the bay, until it finally ran out before a promontory where we parked. As I emerged from the car, I could see the distant bulk of a warship patrolling the Gulf of Suez. Not too far from here, the canal over which we still held control. This was the Red Sea, clear as glass, its pink coral beds visible as I ran down to the shoreline, whooping in delight.

'What's the water like?' Tom called out as he deposited our picnic basket on the sand and started to lay out a rug.

I pulled off one shoe and dipped in an experimental toe. 'It's lovely.'

After pulling off the other, along with my now soggy stockings, I wandered back up the beach to him, luxuriating in the scrunch of the soft, white sand between my toes and the sea breeze stirring my hair, whipping it around my face as I threw myself down beside him.

He handed me a steaming glass. 'There you go. Hot toddy to warm you up after our swim.'

'But we haven't been swimming.'

'Not yet we haven't. Consider that insulation.'

I knocked it back, relishing the liquid fire of the whisky

igniting my throat, seeping all the way to my fingertips as I fumbled for my swimming costume while Tom stripped down to his trunks, gallantly turning his back as I got changed.

'Ready,' I called out, jumping to my feet.

He turned, did a double take and then, sweetly, that same blush I'd seen when we'd first met crept once more across his face. 'Come on – I'll race you.'

He sprinted off.

'Cheat!' I yelled after him, laughing as we both ran towards the turquoise expanse in front of us, my legs working hard to keep up with him, both of us whooping like children as we plunged in, splashing at one another. Tom struck out first, heading for darker patches of coral offshore, and I followed, my arms slicing through the water, matching him stroke for stroke.

He stopped, treading water and pointing below the surface. 'Look down there.'

I dived, my eyes open, taking in the colours of the coral and the fish darting between the fronds that waved from it like hands beckoning to me. Electric blues and yellow, reds and deep greens.

Lungs bursting, I broke the surface once more. 'It's so beautiful.'

Tom held out his arm, steadying me. 'My God but you are beautiful.'

Our limbs were entwining now, two sea creatures becoming one. He was so close that the slightest movement of the tide would bring our lips together. I stared at his mouth, that soft, wide, kissable mouth, and dived back below the water.

36

The sea was swirling all around me, tiny fish circling, darting this way and that, my mind whirling with it. Then another, larger shape. Tom, swimming down towards the coral, those long, athletic limbs scarcely moving, the sunlight filtering through the crystal-clear water, rippling across his back. God, how I wanted to touch that back, to run my hands over it. *No. Don't go there, Nadia. That way madness lies.* And I had known enough madness for a lifetime. It never seemed to end.

I kicked upwards, emerging into the sunlight, so I could catch my breath, my heart pounding. All I could see was Andrzej's face. That look he would give me. Somewhere beneath the thudding of my heart, I could hear his voice, commanding me to be happy, to find someone to love me if anything ever happened to him.

Something, or rather someone, grabbed at my ankle, and I shrieked, the spell broken.

Tom popped up beside me, laughing. 'Gotcha.'

'You bastard.' Out the corner of my eye, I caught a movement, mock indignation forgotten. 'Over there! Look.'

Perhaps fifty feet from us, a dolphin leaped from the water, poised for half a second in effortless flight, soaring free, followed by another and another. A school of dolphins dancing for us across the bay, or so it felt. We gazed at them, transfixed, until their sleek forms disappeared beyond the horizon.

'Race you back,' I called, striking out for shore and beating him by an arm's length.

'Now who's the cheat?' he grumbled as we threw ourselves once more onto the sand, the towels Abbas had packed for us a welcome shield against the breeze.

'Sore loser. Is there any more of that toddy?'

He unscrewed the flask and poured me a generous measure.

'Trying to get me drunk?'

'If that's what it takes.'

We were both teasing, and then, all of a sudden, we weren't. I could feel the undercurrent, stronger than any riptide, pulling me into dangerous waters. They always say you should never try to swim against a riptide, and yet I did.

'Did you love your wife?' I blurted. The moment I said it, I could have slapped myself.

He sat up straight, looking now not at me but out to sea. 'I did, as it happens, A great deal.' His jaw was working, a muscle going in his cheek. When he looked at me once more, I could see the wound I'd reopened.

'I'm sorry,' I whispered. 'That was unforgiveable of me.'

'Not at all. I loved her, and then I didn't. It happens.'

'Yes, I suppose it does.'

'But not to you. You loved your Andrzej until the day he died.'

I swallowed. 'Yes, I did.'

'Then you are fortunate.'

The break in his voice nearly broke me. I reached out to touch his cheek, right where that muscle had been pulsing. 'I am, in many ways. Fortunate to have found him. Fortunate to have met you.'

He sat so still I thought for a moment he'd ceased to breathe. 'Do you really mean that?'

'Of course I do, but...'

'But what?'

'It's complicated. We live together. Work together now. We have a mission to complete. I'm not even sure we should be here now, doing this.'

'Doing what?'

'You know...'

'No, I don't.' His hands were cupping my face now, drawing it towards his, his mouth murmuring against mine. 'Do you mean this?'

'Oh God, yes, yes I do.'

'And this?'

His hands roamed ever lower, caressing my sides, my stomach, tracing every line and curve, insistent, demanding. I arched into him, into the hollows and planes of his body, his warm, damp limbs tangling with mine, his tongue hot in my mouth, seeking me out. I moaned as his fingers traced my nipples under my swimsuit, feeling them harden at his touch. I was sinking now under the white-hot waves of desire, wanting this, wanting him so badly, knowing that we were making a terrible mistake.

'I can't do this,' I muttered, pushing him away from me. 'I'm not ready. I'm so sorry.'

He rolled onto his side, still cradling me in his arms. 'Don't be sorry. I'll wait. For as long as you need.'

I think it was at that moment I fell in love with him totally and completely. A love that scared me as much as it cried out to me with a call that had to be answered. But not now. Not yet.

37

We got back that evening, sun-kissed after our day at the beach. Kissed in other ways too. I ran a hand through my tousled, salt-splattered hair as we wandered back up the steps, languorous in the way that only the sea and lovemaking can instil. Not that we had done anything more than kiss, although that felt dangerous enough. We had stopped at the edge of the precipice. One I was still staring over. And yet, if anyone looked too closely, the burnish on my cheeks would be a dead giveaway, a glow I could detect on Tom's face too. We exchanged a smile of complicity as we stood before the door, which unexpectedly swung open to reveal a flustered Abbas.

'Sir, madame. You are to leave at once.'

I dumped my bag on the hall floor. 'Leave for where?'

'They said to tell you the Mena training camp. Everybody is waiting for you there.'

I glanced at Tom and raised an eyebrow. 'We'd better do as he says.'

'Yes, indeed. Abbas, could you take care of our things please?'

'Of course, sir. Would you like me to pack your bags too? I have done so for the others.'

This was getting serious. Our mission was underway. 'Yes please, Abbas,' I said. 'It shouldn't take you too long.'

I glanced down at the shorts and shirt I had changed back into after our swim. Along with my desert boots, they would do. I'd acquired nothing since my arrival at the villa apart from that lurking sense that I was falling into a chasm from which I would never be able to clamber out. An abyss that was far deeper than the mere prospect of a love affair.

As we turned and headed back to the car, bags in hand, that inexplicable feeling of dread dogged my footsteps.

'You're very quiet,' said Tom as he navigated the back-streets, doubling back a couple of times to make sure we weren't being followed. Vulke might have departed for Tunis, but who knew what he'd left in his wake? Aside from him and his under-lings, there were all the other eyes on us, including those of the traitor who was still somewhere in our midst. Our mission might already be compromised. We could all be walking into a trap. And yet we had to go on. There really was no other option.

I could see the suburbs giving way to desert as we headed in the opposite direction to the one we'd taken earlier, inland towards the great pyramids of Giza, where the military camps, including the British Political Warfare Executive, nestled at the foot of the Sphinx, who now guarded them with a wall of sand-bags built between her paws to protect her from enemy bombardment in return. We passed a sign in multiple languages pointing us towards the camp along the Mena road, dust kicking up in clouds as we drove, although it couldn't obscure the magnificence of those vast tombs rising from the desert.

Tall palm trees delineated the camp, shading us as the guard on the gate took his time inspecting our papers.

'Captain Thomas Molyneux?'

'That's right.'

'And who is this?'

I gave him my frostiest glare, the one that generally worked on men like him. 'Countess Nadia Pulaska of the Polish Red Cross.'

He stared back at me, unimpressed. 'The Red Cross you say?'

Tom sighed. 'Oh come on, man. We're late for a meeting. The countess is here on official business and that's all you need to know.'

A belligerent gleam appeared in the guard's eyes. 'One moment, sir.'

We watched him return to his guard hut and pick up the phone. Five minutes later, he was back, just as belligerent. 'You can go through.'

I took my papers back from him with the most charming smile I could muster. 'Thank you.'

We roared up to the main tent, Tom's face like thunder. 'For God's sake, what did he think you were? Some kind of foreign spy?'

'Well, I am if you think about it, although some of these men still don't believe a woman can actually fight a war. I'd say he was more concerned you were bringing in your fancy woman.'

'My what?'

'You know.'

He cut the car engine. 'I'm not sure I do. Perhaps you'd care to show me?'

I would. I very much would. And yet I couldn't. 'We have a meeting, remember?'

'Ah, yes. Blasted war. I almost forgot about it.'

Still we sat there, the heat in the car building even as the air outside cooled.

At that moment, the unmistakable figure of Dudley swathed in what appeared to be native dress emerged from the tent, a vast canvas structure that was more akin to a sizeable building. 'There you are at last. Come on in. We've been waiting for you. It's game on.'

I opened the car door. Saved by the war.

38

Resplendent in his kaftan and keffiyeh, Dudley appeared as laconic as ever, although I detected an underlying edge. More than once, I'd seen someone mistake his studied nonchalance for lack of care. They never repeated their error.

'I'm sorry, Dudley,' I said. 'We only got back to the villa an hour ago.'

He grunted and beckoned us to follow him through to an inner tent where the others were sitting in front of a large map of North Africa. Jim was standing before it, wielding a pointer, tracing the route he was describing. He glanced at us as we took our seats behind Colette while Dudley joined him up front. 'Good of you to join us.'

Colette whispered, 'Hello.'

Apart from that, all eyes were on Jim.

'You will be dropped here, at this airstrip. It's around forty kilometres from Algiers. You will be met and transported to Brandon Mission, our joint OSS and SOE station conducting operations into Tunisia. From there you will be taken along the coast to Cap Serrat by submarine to our post there. No. 1 Special Forces will get you into Tunis. There will be no contact with other SOE or OSS agents on the ground. This is a deep cover operation.'

Nico raised his hand. 'What about backup?'

Dudley folded his arms. 'I think I can answer that. There is no backup. This mission is completely deniable. You are effectively an assassination squad, which means it lives or dies with you, as does the Geneva Convention.'

'So what is our plan?' asked Tom.

'Your target, as you know, is Colonel Walther Rauff. What you may not know is that Rauff was the commander of the SS extermination unit set up after Tobruk to follow Rommel's Afrika Korps. His mission was to carry out "executive measures on the civilian population", which essentially means mass murder. Fortunately, our victory at El Alamein put a stop to that mission, but it also precipitated Rommel's retreat to Tunisia where Rauff is in command, leading an SD Einsatzgruppe – or extermination unit.'

'Sounds like a lovely chap,' muttered Freddie.

Dudley pinned a photograph to the map in front of us. 'Quite. This is Rauff. Not exactly a handsome devil, as you can see. Killing Rauff will deprive Rommel of the man in charge of the SS in Tunisia at a crucial turning point in this war. Perhaps more importantly, it will also have the same propaganda effect as the assassination of Reinhard Heydrich, spreading fear among the Hun as they realise they're not invincible.'

I gazed at the photograph, recognising the small, hard eyes peering from an otherwise expressionless mask. 'But hopefully not the same reprisals.'

Dudley nodded at me. 'Indeed, which is why we have devised this plan to ensure that no locals can possibly be blamed for it.'

'Fritz will do that anyway,' muttered Tom.

'Probably, but we intend to make it look as if his own men

attacked him, ambushing his car before getting away and disappearing into the desert.'

'That's what they did to Heydrich,' I said. 'It didn't end well. Won't the Germans be watching out for another ambush like that one?'

Dudley smirked. 'The Germans think in a very linear way. They won't imagine we'll carry out another attack like that. We've learned from the Heydrich case, so we've refined our plan to cover all eventualities, which is why, from first light tomorrow, you'll all be in refresher training, including close combat.'

A collective groan rumbled across the room.

'I'm not exactly built for close combat,' quipped Nico. 'I mean, look at me.'

I glanced at his linen shorts and shirt, immaculate in spite of the desert heat and dust.

'You speak fluent German, so you will be the designated driver during this mission,' said Jim. 'Your chief role is to get you all through roadblocks and the like. It's essential you know what to do if anything goes wrong. As for the rest of you, you'll be given your roles in due course. For now, I want you to rest up in preparation for the morning. Any questions?'

This was my last chance to raise the spectre of Vulke even though I knew they weren't going to like it. I couldn't let it rest, though. I had to finish what I'd started in Paris. I took a deep breath and raised my hand. 'What about Vulke?'

'What about him?'

'Surely we should take him out too?'

'As I said, your target is Rauff.'

'But—'

'No buts. Any more questions? No? OK then. We'll see you in the morning, 6 a.m. sharp.'

I stayed seated while the others rose, looking down at my hands, remembering. I'd had my chance in Paris and I'd missed.

I wasn't going to lose another one. Forget what Jim said. I was going to hunt down Vulke and finish him off. It was the only way I could make sure he, along with Rauff, couldn't hurt anyone else the way they'd hurt me. The way they intended to hurt and destroy so many in Tunisia now. That was their mistake. They hadn't destroyed me, despite taking everything I loved. I was still here to save others from suffering, and that was exactly what I was going to do. Whatever it took and no matter how high the price I had to pay.

39

'Come on, darling – cheer up. Things aren't that bad.'

I looked up to see Colette hovering, waiting for me. Behind her, Dudley, who moved to block our path as I rose from my seat.

'A word, ladies, please. In private.'

I glanced around. Jim was still there too, beside his map, but other than that, everyone else had left. 'There's only us here.'

He smiled. 'You know what they say, my dear. Walls have ears. Especially canvas ones.'

I got his drift, falling in beside him as he strolled from the tent and out into the fetid air, Colette on the other side of me. He wandered over to a cluster of palms fifty yards or so beyond the tents, under which someone had lashed together a few old oil cans covered with rush matting to serve as a bench. Dudley sank onto it with a sigh, patting it to indicate we should join him. 'All very cloak and dagger I know, but the problem is we still have not caught our rat.'

'You think it could be someone here?'

Dudley tapped his nose in that theatrical way of his. 'Anything is possible, although I don't, as it happens. I imagine our rat is scuttling around one of the embassies, safely hidden.'

'Probably,' murmured Colette.

A thought occurred to me. 'Do you think the villa is bugged?'

'We sweep it regularly, and so far it's clean. But we're not here to talk about rats. Unless we count Rauff.'

I sniffed. 'He's a particularly vile specimen.'

'Agreed, although even someone like Rauff has his weakness.'

'And you know what that is?'

Dudley smiled as if he was pulling a rabbit from a hat. 'Indeed I do. You two.'

I glanced at Colette. 'Us?'

'Well, not specifically you two but women. Rauff was discharged from the German Navy thanks to, shall we say, an entanglement. It seems the Germans frown on adultery where their officers are concerned.'

'I see. You're saying he's susceptible to women? Or was it just this one woman?'

Dudley chuckled. 'From what we know, he always has at least one or two on the go. Randier than any pharaoh.'

Looking out from under our palm tree, I had a view of the Great Pyramid of Cheops rising above the tents and huts that formed Mena Camp. It was, in fact, a tent city divided into smaller camps for the various battalions that were based here. Shouts rang out across sandy parade grounds, along with the occasional burst of machine-gun fire. A drill no doubt. At least, I hoped so. Keeping the men sharp until they were deployed somewhere across the Western Desert or further afield, much as we were about to be put through our paces.

The tang of smoke filled my nostrils as Colette lit up a cigarette. At least it would help keep the infernal flies at bay. 'So you want us to act as some kind of honey trap?'

Dudley shook his head. 'Rauff is too wily to fall for that one. I understand he has a couple of local women to keep him occupied at the moment. I want you to make friends with them, find out what he does and where he goes when he's not running his killing squad.'

I took the cigarette Colette was offering me and lit up too. 'How do you propose we do that?'

'His Majesty the Bey has graciously agreed to house you both at the palace where you will be safe. He's no fan of the Germans, as you can imagine. Your cover story is that you, Colette, are employed as a tutor to Muhammad VII's grandchildren, while you, my dear, are there on behalf of the Red Cross. As part of your duties ensuring food supplies to prisoners, you need to liaise with the owner of an oat merchant in Tunis, supplying a company in Algiers.' Dudley chuckled at my obvious bewilderment. 'The company is an oatmeal manufacturer run by a certain Rygor Słowikowski.'

'Rygor? Of Agency Africa?'

'The same. Rygor now works with us. He operates the oatmeal business as his cover, along with a few other businesses, including a pig farm near Casablanca. Canny bugger has managed to turn a nice profit out of all of them. His Tunis outpost was compromised last February. It has taken all this time to establish this oat merchant as the new Tunis outpost, only for the blasted Boche to invade.'

Dudley flicked at the flies clustering around his eyes with the edge of his scarf, to no effect. 'These women I want you to befriend are both wives of Vichy officials, one of whom is a businessman who frequently deals with Rauff. A Monsieur Rivaud.'

I was beginning to get the picture. 'So Monsieur Rivaud services the Germans while his wife services Rauff?'

'Indeed. He's a shrewd operator. There's a lot of profit in supplying Berlin. The other is a Monsieur Darlan, a civil servant for the Vichy government. The two couples frequently attend palace functions, where you will both also be present and where you can engage them. They're bored colonial wives. It shouldn't be too hard to get them gossiping, find out about Rauff's daily routine, that kind of thing.'

'That's all very well,' said Colette, 'but I can tell you now it will never work. They might be bored colonial wives, but those women are the worst snobs of all. They'll never consort with a hired tutor, even one employed by the palace, and would probably draw the line at the Red Cross too. At best, they'll gossip about us rather than to us.'

'Not if they believe you have the ear of the king. The Bey has already secretly declared his loyalty to Roosevelt while trying to send the French resident-general packing. He's also protective of the Jewish population, especially professionals and businessmen. Tunisia is technically neutral, or it was until the Germans occupied it. If there's one thing a Frenchwoman like these two can do, it's sniff out which way the wind is blowing.'

He had a point.

'I suppose taking the local German commander as a lover would, in that case, be a smart move. Even smarter to make friends in high places who can perhaps pass on information that they could then feed to that lover as pillow talk.'

Dudley beamed. 'Exactly.'

'How do we two know each other? What's the story for that?'

'Stick to the truth. You know each other from Cairo, where Colette already has a cover story as a tutor and you are widely known to work for the Red Cross.'

It sounded plausible enough.

'So let me get this straight,' said Colette. 'We will be making friends with these women while gathering information from them about Rauff and his daily routine?'

'Information we will then use to carry out his assassination?' I added.

Dudley's smile was almost beatific. 'Yes.'

40

My legs felt like jelly as I rolled over and over in the sand, my head spinning in the midday heat, and still the instructor kept shouting. 'This isn't a bloody party. It's a bloody war. Kill or be killed.'

A refresher course, Dudley called it. There was nothing refreshing about it. As for Christmas, forget it. The only thing we would be celebrating was the start of our mission.

Three days until we got on that plane heading for Algeria and I had my doubts. Our weakest link by far was Nico, who kept complaining about the heat, the flies, anything but his own poor performance. We needed him along though. He was the only one of us who spoke convincingly fluent German, which meant he was vital to the entire plan.

At last the instructor blew his whistle, and we staggered off to wash our hands before mustering in the mess tent.

'Stop right there, darling,' hissed Colette as I bent over the basin. I felt her pluck something from my hair. 'Scorpion.' She crushed it under her boot before pulling her lipstick from her pocket. 'Here you go. Might brighten up your lovely smile.'

I peered into the tin square that served as a mirror and burst out laughing at my sand-streaked face. 'I'm not sure anything's going to help.'

'Oh I don't know, darling. From what I've seen, you don't need much help on that score. All you have to do is look at that handsome young man and you start glowing.'

I stared harder into the mirror. 'I don't know what you mean.'

Colette snorted. 'Yes you do. As for the way he looks at you...'

I tugged a few hairs into place in a futile effort to smarten up. 'What utter rubbish. We work together – that's all.'

I strode ahead of her into the mess tent and ducked under the mosquito net, fuming. What an idiot I was. So unprofessional. If Colette had noticed, then who else might have?

Belatedly, I realised absolutely everyone had as they silently shuffled up so I could sit next to Tom. I caught Colette's wink as she sat opposite us and hastily started tucking into my rations. Bully stew. Again. Cooked to a pulp with potato, onions and adorned with the usual flies for an exotic touch of extra protein.

I ate steadily, doing my best to ignore Tom's thigh inches from mine, his flesh under his khakis. The same warm skin that had wrapped around mine as we lay entangled on that beach, exploring one another. I could feel my skin tingling in response to his proximity, along with a deep ache in my belly. I wanted him so much, and yet I didn't. This was all wrong. We were setting off on a highly critical mission, one that could turn this war around. Agents were discouraged from entering into relationships for their own safety and that of their comrades in arms. And yet we did, thrown together in extreme danger, our senses heightened along with the knowledge that it could all end tomorrow – *we* could end tomorrow – so why not live for today?

There were so many reasons why not.

An agent caught up with another was bound to be

distracted. The very ties that bound two people together could turn out to be a noose. If the enemy got hold of both and detected they were a couple, they would use that knowledge relentlessly to gain information. I knew of agents tortured in front of their lovers to make them talk or even shot on the spot to break them. Then there were the others to think about, those who fought alongside you and who would inevitably be compromised by a love affair in their midst. In a firefight, who would you protect first? The person by your side who was simply another agent or the one with whom you shared your bed? And of course, always there was Andrzej, my lost love. I wasn't sure I would survive another loss like that.

All of this ran through my mind, and yet... and yet, I yearned to touch him. To reach across those few inches that separated us and stroke his thigh until I felt him respond. To feel his mouth, hot, upon mine. To move into his embrace so that we fitted into one another like two pieces of a jigsaw, skin on skin, breath mingling, coming in pants and gasps. It was no good. I had to get out of here. Get away from him. I slammed my spoon down into my bowl and fought my way out from under the mosquito net, muttering something about not feeling too good.

Tom found me outside, on the same bench where we'd sat with Dudley, and handed me a cup of water. 'Here. This might help.'

I squinted at it. Anything but look at him. 'Is that from your rations?'

'Never you mind. Just drink it. Water is life. At least it is out here.'

Water, flowing from fountains in the gardens here to represent Paradise. And life. Although this godforsaken place was no paradise. We were rationed to four and a half litres a day, including washing water. The cup was full to the brim, which meant he was making quite a sacrifice. 'I can't. It's your water. You need it.'

'Not half as much as I need you.'

I blinked up at him, half-blinded by the sun, unsure if I'd heard right. 'What did you say?'

He sank onto the bench beside me. 'You heard. Now drink up.'

Truth be told, I was starting to feel a pounding at my temples and a band tightening around my scalp. It was so damn hot. We'd hardly slept, or at least I hadn't. Tom was right. I was dehydrated from what had been a tough morning. I took a gulp and then another, feeling the water wash away the sand and the flies, although it couldn't quite assuage the longing.

'I want you,' he murmured, a mirror for my thoughts. 'All the time.'

I choked, spluttering out some precious drops.

He laughed and patted me on the back. 'I'm sorry it's such a horrible idea.'

'Not at all. Quite the reverse.'

Dear Lord, the sun must have melted my brain because all of a sudden, I was stumbling over my words, reaching for them.

'You mean that?'

'Yes, I do.'

'Meet me after lights out. Here. I'll be waiting for you.'

From the main tent, a whistle summoned us back to class. From deep in my gut, a warning bell rang. But when had I ever listened to that?

'I'll be here,' I murmured.

41

If I'd thought the morning was hard, the afternoon's training proved even tougher. Escape and evasion across scorching sand with nowhere to hide, nowhere to run, weighed down by a gun and a backpack with Jim as our instructor. 'You'll thank me for it,' he called out as we staggered through the motions, 'when Jerry's coming after you.'

'Gratitude will be the last thing on my mind,' I hissed.

Colette sniggered. 'Because obviously they're not going to spot a woman out in the desert carrying all this stuff.'

Jim's eyes pinned her down. 'What was that?'

'Nothing.'

'Nothing, sir.'

She stood, ramrod straight. 'Nothing, sir.'

His eyes raked her before he turned away. She carried on staring straight ahead, the perfect operative.

What the hell was it between those two? It wasn't even a flirtation. More of a tension that hummed between them like an overtightened wire. We all cracked jokes now and again, even in the worst of it. Especially in the worst of it. Humour was what got us through many times, and yet he pulled her up on everything.

I was still trying to figure it out as I splashed water frugally over myself later, the hard little bar of soap we'd been given scarcely lathering at all, dirt apparently ingrained into my face. A final slick of our one, shared lipstick and it would have to do. I changed into the clean fatigues we'd been given, emerging from the wash area into the tent I shared with Colette. She was sprawled on her cot with her nose in a book, the lamp casting eerie shadows up the canvas walls. 'What's that you're reading?'

'*L'Etranger* by Albert Camus. You look nice. Going somewhere?'

I smoothed my hair, suddenly self-conscious, pulling on my jacket to ward off the evening chill. 'I thought I'd go out for a stroll.'

Her lip curled in mischief. 'A stroll?'

'Yes. Just around the camp. It's been so hot today. I need some fresh air.'

'If that's all you need.'

She was on to me and we both knew it. 'I have no idea what you mean.'

'I think you do. Don't worry, I'll cover for you if necessary.'

Colette's grin said it all. I slipped out of the tent and padded past the others, heading for the bench. He was there already, watching me as I approached, as still as the Sphinx a few hundred yards away. I could feel the intensity of his gaze, the question in his eyes as he stood up and took my hand. We walked in silence until we were beyond the next encampment of tents and almost at the foot of the great pyramid soaring above us, thrusting into the starlit sky.

There were so many stars. More, I think, than I had ever seen. I'd spent nights in the desert before, marvelling at the carpet of stars above, but none as breathtaking as this. Tom was leading the way now, carrying on around the base of the pyramid, out towards the open desert. A cluster of shapes loomed to our right, growling in that low, guttural way only a camel can, their humped silhouettes huddled around a fire as they hunkered down for the night, some lying, others standing to protect the herd.

We wandered on under our carpet of stars, the pyramid now behind us as we surmounted a hillock and then half-skidded, laughing, into the natural hollow that lay below it, scattered with rocks.

'Sit here,' said Tom, indicating the largest rock. I sank onto it as he crouched and applied his lighter to a pile of what looked like twigs. As I watched the flames take hold, I could see it was a fire he'd already laid, set neatly in a circle of stones. He reached behind the rock and pulled out a bottle and two glasses along with a blanket, which he laid at our feet.

'What on earth?'

He popped the cork, then filled a glass and handed it to me. 'Champagne for the lady. I'm sorry it's not quite as chilled as you might like.'

I stared at him, at the firelight dancing in his eyes, dusting his cheekbones with its lustre. 'How did you manage all this?'

'A good agent never tells. You should know that. Although it helps to have friends in useful places.'

He raised a glass in the direction of a building the other side of the pyramid, its tall palms stark shapes against the lights shining in its windows. 'The Mena House Hotel. It was once a royal hunting lodge. Right now, it's being used as a hospital. I happen to have a chum working there.'

'Of course you do.'

He dropped a kiss on my lips, still wet with champagne. I could taste it on his too as he murmured, 'One day I'll take you there.'

'Oh, you will, will you?'

My laughter bubbled up, as fizzy as the stuff in the glass he took off me and carefully placed on the next rock, along with his, before taking me in his arms. 'Yes, I will. We'll go there for our honeymoon.'

My breath caught in my throat. Instead of answering, I leaned in, kissing him deeper and harder until he moaned with impatience. 'My God, woman, what are you trying to do to me?'

To be honest, I wasn't sure. All I knew was that I couldn't bear the flutter of hope he'd conjured with his words, a butterfly as doomed as any of that species. It was a beautiful thought that would die as quickly too. I trailed a finger down his face, touching first his temple, marvelling at the sweep of his lashes before moving it, featherlight, along the edge of those sharp cheekbones and down to the corner of his mouth, tracing the edges of it and then pushing between his lips. His teeth bit down gently as he drew me into his warm, wet mouth.

He sucked hungrily on my finger for a few seconds, reaching for me, his hands caressing my breasts, working under my jacket, my shirt and then my underwear, pulling me onto his lap, where I could feel him, hard against me. I twisted so I was straddling him, cupping his face between my hands as I kissed him deeper and deeper, our tongues intertwining, setting off a trail of fire that ran all the way to my loins. He stood, my legs still wrapped around him, then sank onto the sand beside the fire, laying me down gently as he reached behind the rock once more and produced another blanket.

'You really do come prepared, don't you?' I murmured.

He undid my belt and eased off my trousers. 'I try.'

He did more than try. As our bodies melded together, it felt so right, so natural, that all other thoughts were driven from my mind. Thoughts of Andrzej. Of Alexander. Of Tom's wife who had left him. All the memories and complications were swept away in those perfect hours beneath the stars in the shadow of the Great Pyramid. As I cried aloud in ecstasy, I could have sworn I heard a nightjar echoing me from the desert, its eerie cry shivering through me even as my shudders died away and I lay, spent, in Tom's arms, tasting the salt from my tears, alive again at last.

42

PRESENT DAY, CAIRO, EGYPT

SOPHIE

The graves stretched into the distance, rows and rows of them, as regular as the ranks of soldiers, sailors and airmen they commemorated, although I noticed the names of women too, nurses from the First World War and a couple who had served in the second. Tom's grave was situated near that of an aircraft-woman who had died on active service, his headstone stark white against the sun, the message engraved on it beneath his name simply saying, 'Beloved.'

I stood, head bowed, reading that inscription, wondering how many times Nadia had stood here too. The rose bush on Tom's grave matched those of the others around it. 'Did you know that they plant war graves with seeds and flowers from the person's homeland? I taught that to a class of mine. They bring maples from Canada and shrubs from Nepal.'

'I didn't. What a lovely idea.'

I raised my face to the sun. 'It is, isn't it?'

A small but beautiful detail. Life was full of them. I'd planted roses on Ben's grave too, along with rosemary for remembrance and heather from the moors he loved to walk. I wondered what Ben would make of this, me being here at Tom's grave. The man Nadia had loved so much. The man in the photograph she'd given him and which Ben had sent to the villa on her instructions – the last thing he ever did. Maybe here we'd start to find some answers. Or at least some inspiration.

I turned to Josh. 'You said you have a friend who might be able to help find out more about how Tom died?'

'He's a friend of David's. He worries about you, you know, David. He thinks this is all too much for you, although I think the same about him. He's already had two heart attacks, and the doctors have told him to take it easy.'

'I'm sorry. I didn't realise. The last thing he needs is me poking around in his past.'

'Not at all. He enjoys showing you his photos and telling you his stories. You remind him so much of her. Of Nadia.'

I gave Tom's grave one last look, touching it lightly. 'A lot of people say that. Which is why I want to find out what happened to Tom. It broke her, you know, although she would never admit it. She loved him until the day she died, and yet she would never talk about any of it.'

Josh said nothing until we were wandering back through the trees that provided some blessed shade. He stopped under a particularly gorgeous one, ablaze with flame-red flowers. 'Strange, isn't it, that you both lost the men you loved like that?'

'Like what?'

'In a way that's somehow connected although I still think we're missing something. An element. There's more to it.'

I stared at him. 'What do you mean?'

I could see him treading carefully, framing his words. 'I've been thinking about what you said – that you didn't really believe it was simply a hit-and-run, and I agree. But there's not a lot of hard evidence for that. Is there anything you can think of that struck you as odd that day? Maybe something else Ben did that was out of character?'

The shade we were standing in seemed to deepen. Or maybe that was the sudden, cold sense that we were being watched. I glanced over his shoulder. No one in sight. We were quite alone in this cemetery apart from the gardener we'd passed on the way in, an old guy who even now was probably napping in a shady corner somewhere. I'd had the same feeling that day at Nadia's cottage but for a different reason.

'There was something, now that you mention it. Nadia's security system. The place was like a fortress. Thank goodness Ben had the codes or we'd have had the police out demanding to know why all the alarms were going off. It seemed strange that a little old lady living in a cottage in the middle of nowhere would need a system like that.'

'Maybe she was scared of being burgled.'

'Nadia? She was scared of nothing. Although we did find a pistol hidden in a drawer. I handed that over to the police, of course. It looked like her old service pistol. That was Nadia all over. Didn't give a fig, as she would say, for rules and regulations.'

Josh looked at me more keenly. 'Had you noticed any of these security arrangements before?'

'Come to think of it, no. But then, she was always there when I was so she had no need to set the alarm, although I don't recall us having one when I was a child.'

'So she could have installed it recently, which takes us back to why. Can you think of any other reason why someone might want to hurt Ben? Anything at all?'

Those red flowers really were dazzling. So bright they almost hurt my eyes. 'No,' I mumbled. 'I can't. I've thought about it a lot and there's no one I know of who would have a reason to kill Ben. He wasn't even that kind of solicitor. He was just a good person who helped other people.'

'Then don't you think you owe it to him to at least consider all possibilities?'

I squinted at Josh, taking in the sunlight casting a halo effect around his head, reflecting off his eyes so they appeared more gold than green. Gold. It was everywhere. In his mind. His eyes. Perhaps his heart. Time would tell. And I had plenty of that. 'Yes, yes of course I do,' I said.

'Good. Then let's keep on going until we get some answers.'

Beyond him, I could see a sprinkler start up, the gardener ambling away from it, letting the grass soak up the life-giving water so that the dead could slumber under a soft, green carpet rather than arid dust. Most of me wanted to trust Josh. A tiny part didn't. A leftover, maybe, from all that had happened? Or a warning from the instincts I was learning to trust?

43

Dr Bakir lived in a villa not too far from Nadia's. Or, I suppose, not too far from mine. I was still not used to the idea that I owned Eden now. Ben's death had obliterated everything, including all our plans, and I had no idea what I wanted to do with the place. If I wanted to do anything.

Dr Bakir rose to greet us as his houseboy showed us into his study. He was a sprightly looking man in what appeared to be his early sixties, although I knew he had to be at least a decade older if he'd known David since both were young men.

'Please, do sit down,' he said, his English barely accented. 'Would you care for some tea?'

'Thank you. That would be lovely.'

He settled into his high-backed chair once more, eyes twinkling. 'Well now, I've heard a great deal about you, Josh. It's good to meet you at last. And who is this?'

'Allow me to introduce Sophie, a relative of Nadia's.'

Dr Bakir's face lit up. 'I can see the resemblance. Welcome, my dear. Nadia was a cherished friend.'

'Thank you. That's the reason I— we are here. I wanted to ask you about Tom, Nadia's... partner.' It sounded odd calling him that, but I had no idea what else to say. 'Lover' sounded awkward, 'boyfriend' too trivial.

'Tom? David's uncle?' Dr Bakir looked quizzically at Josh.

'That's right. I know that your father was Nadia's personal doctor, and I believe he helped when she brought Tom back to Cairo. From what I understand, he tried to save him, but there was nothing anyone could do.'

The doctor took off his spectacles and polished them on the corner of his sleeve. 'I wasn't alive then, you understand. I was born long after the war. My mother was my father's second wife, you see, so he was older when I came along but so young in spirit. He played with me all the time. So did Nadia while she was here. Wonderful people. My father inspired me to become a doctor too. I have kept all his old surgery records. There might be something in there.'

'Really? Could you take a look? That would be a big help,' said Josh.

'Of course. They're right here, in this filing cabinet. You enjoy your tea while I go through the files.'

I felt a surge of hope in my chest. A clue, perhaps, that might unravel the past. Although Josh thought Tom's death was linked to Ben's, I still wasn't convinced. It would be wonderful, though, to know a little more about what had really happened to Tom. Out here, in what I thought of as her city, I felt closer than ever to Nadia. Maybe, just maybe, I should hang on to her legacy. I had the feeling that whatever the doctor found might help sway me either way.

'Here we are,' he said, pulling a folder from the filing cabinet before sitting at his desk once more to go through it. I watched his slender fingers turn the pages over one at a time; his frown as he studied their contents. Dr Bakir evidently liked to be thorough. At length, he looked up. 'As you say, my father tried to save Tom, but his injuries were too great. He had to attend to him in great secrecy as their mission was a clandestine one. They couldn't risk taking him to a hospital, so Nadia nursed him at the villa. He died there, three days after they returned from Tunisia.'

Nadia had never told me any of this, but it explained a lot. The way she would clam up when I tried to ask her about Cairo and the war. Her refusal to talk about Tom and what really happened. Now I knew, and how my heart ached for her, desperately trying to save him, knowing she had to keep it a secret all the while.

Josh leaned forward. 'So they couldn't take him to a hospital for an autopsy either or there would have been too many questions. That figures.'

I glanced at the file on his desk. 'May I see that?'

'I'm not sure you should. There are some graphic photographs in here.'

I reached out my hand, steeling myself. 'I can handle it.'

Dr Bakir looked doubtful. 'If you're sure.'

The photographs were remarkably clear given their age. I could see Tom's awful wounds in detail, but what I focused on was the shot of his face, his eyes closed. He looked as if he were merely asleep, just as Ben had done. Someone, Nadia probably, had washed his face and combed his hair. I never got the chance to do that for Ben. It still hurt.

I handed the file to Josh, grasping for my cup once more and gulping the tea down. If only I could gulp down the memories too. They rose in front of me, unbidden, although right now they'd been triggered by what was in that file. Simply being here triggered so many of them, not only of Ben but of Nadia too. What the hell was I doing here anyway? This was a wild goose chase. We were running after mirages just as people did in the desert.

Josh held out his hand for the file. 'May I see that?' He studied it for a few moments. 'It says here he was shot twice at close range, which indicates it wasn't crossfire. Whoever shot

Tom was only a few feet from him which suggests it could have been one of his own team. My money's still on Casanoff.'

'So you're saying it could have been murder?'

'Possibly. We can't rule out an accident. All kinds of things happen in these situations, although it's odd there's no mention of anyone else injured in this incident, is there, Doctor?'

Dr Bakir shook his head. 'There would be a note in the file to cross-reference. Of course, Nadia might have brought Tom here and another person elsewhere, although, given that this was a clandestine mission, that would have been highly unlikely, and my father would have made a note. He was scrupulous like that.'

As Dr Bakir no doubt was. He exuded it from every fibre of his immaculate appearance to the precision with which he spoke.

I glanced at Josh. 'And you think the gold was the reason he was murdered.'

I just caught the imperceptible shake of his head.

Dr Bakir sat back in his chair. 'You're talking about Rommel's gold, I take it? My father told me something about that. He also said that Nadia had managed to salvage some, but she left it behind, believing it was cursed.'

Beside me, Josh still appeared calm, although I felt rather than saw him stiffen. 'She left it behind? Do you know where?'

The doctor smiled and spread his hands. 'If I did, I would tell you.' He cleared his throat. 'There is, however, something I *can* tell you. It's in a note at the end of the file. Nadia had a breakdown after Tom died and shut herself away in the villa. She wouldn't see anyone. When she left for the UK, it was without saying goodbye. It was probably all too much for her, poor woman. If that gold is anywhere, it's most likely there.'

'I see,' said Josh, getting to his feet. 'Well, thank you for your time, Doctor. May I borrow this file?'

'Of course, but please remember to bring it back to me. My father's records are precious.'

'You have my word. Thank you again.'

It was only when we were back in the taxi that Josh turned to me and murmured, 'Like I said, there's something missing here. None of it adds up.'

Our eyes met. 'What do you think is going on?'

He hesitated and I could see him holding back. For the second time, I felt that twinge of mistrust. Was Josh really all he seemed? Then he smiled.

'That's for us to find out.'

44

Josh was staring at his screen, as he had been for hours, painstakingly trawling through archives and historical sites, trying to find out more about Nadia and her clandestine mission. 'It's very hard to find Second World War service records for agents. We don't even know for sure which agency she worked for, although it was probably SOE. They only declassified some records in 2015, and others were burned.'

'That's what happened in Cairo too,' David piped up from his peacock chair. 'Whole damn thing went up during the '52 riots. Some people took it as an opportunity to knock a few years off their age.' He chortled.

I glanced at Josh. We had David right here, a human resource. His memories might be blurred at times, but he was still sharp enough. 'Did your father ever say anything to you about the way Tom died?'

David looked at me, his face suddenly sober. 'Only that he was shot during some damn fool mission. That was the way my father always spoke about Tom. I think it was jealousy, partly. And guilt. He couldn't go to war because of his health. He'd had scarlet fever as a boy and it left him with a weakened heart. Didn't stop him stealing Tom's girl though.'

There was a harshness in his tone that startled me, given he was talking about his mother.

'I think deep down she regretted it,' he continued. 'She never said as much, but I knew and so did my father. He could never live up to Tom. They were chalk and cheese.'

Josh practically leaped from his seat. 'Cheese. That's it.'

'That's what?'

He started clicking furiously through his open tabs. 'I saw it somewhere. Here we go. Agent Cheese was a double agent who worked for British Intelligence as well as the Nazis. He basically ran a scam that fooled the Germans, inventing dozens of agents who sent false information that even found its way to Hitler.'

'He sounds fabulous, but what does all this have to do with Tom?'

'Remember Casanoff, the double agent? He worked with Cheese.'

'So what if he did?'

'According to this, Cheese was one of our finest agents, but he was arrested in 1941 and imprisoned until 1943. His handlers continued to run his organisation in his absence. One of the main players in that was Casanoff.'

'What are you trying to say? That Casanoff is no longer our prime suspect for shooting Tom?'

'We can't rule him out, but Cheese's organisation ran successfully throughout the war, even when he was in prison. If it was Casanoff running it in his absence, it's unlikely he would kill a fellow agent like Tom. There's no mention of any dirty dealings in the organisation. Of course, anything could have happened and often did. I think we need to keep him in the frame while looking at other possibilities.'

'Why are you so interested in who killed Tom?' asked

David. 'Nadia would never talk about it. Sometimes it's better to let sleeping dogs lie.'

'I agree, but not in this case. You see, I think whoever killed Tom is connected in some way to Ben's death.'

David looked at me. 'Your fiancé?'

'Yes,' I whispered.

'But that's ridiculous. What on earth can something that happened during the war have to do with the death of a man now?'

I could feel the pressure building again around and above my eyes. Soon that band would begin to tighten across my forehead. In many ways, it was ridiculous. In others, not so much. There was enough in what Josh had said to fuel the doubts I already had. And yet we were talking about Ben. My Ben. 'Just tell him,' I murmured. 'Tell him what you told me.'

Josh pulled his chair closer to David's. 'I think that whoever killed Tom did so because of Rommel's gold. That gold disappeared, as you know, and many people believe it was thrown overboard to hide it until it could be reclaimed. I'm not so sure that's what happened, or at least not where people believe. You see, there were two sets of coordinates, fake ones to throw people off and the real ones. I think those coordinates were written on the back of the photograph of Tom that was sent to the villa. Or half of them at least.'

David rubbed his chin, looking bemused. 'You're saying that someone knew about this gold and the photograph and waited all this time to take it?'

'I think someone found out about the photograph only recently, most likely after Nadia died. They probably already knew about the gold. It's worth over forty million pounds in today's money, don't forget.'

'Plenty of people know about Rommel's gold,' I said. 'It's all over the internet. But who would know about the photograph? It's not mentioned anywhere, as far as I know.'

Josh nodded. 'Correct. I've searched too and it's nowhere to be found, which means someone was either told about it or found something like a diary or letter which mentioned it. And who would keep a diary or write a letter like that?'

'The person who wrote those coordinates on the back of the photograph?'

'That's the most likely explanation, which means it had to be someone who was there at the time. So that's where we look again, at all the others on that mission. And we don't rule anyone out.'

'Not even Nadia?'

'Not even Nadia.'

45

12 JANUARY 1943, ALGIERS, ALGERIA

NADIA

The jeep roared up to the plane as we landed, a streak of dust across the desert airstrip, its driver leaping out as we descended the steps.

'Welcome to Algeria. Hop in.'

There was just about room for all five of us with Colette and me sharing the front seat, sunglasses and scarves doing little to stave off the sand that lacerated our skin. At last we reached a metalled road that took us to the outskirts of Algiers, where our driver deposited us at a nondescript house in a quiet backstreet. As he drove off, the door opened and a man dressed like our driver, in civvies, appeared.

'Do come in,' he enunciated in the kind of tone that had established an entire empire.

We followed him through into the customary courtyard where a servant appeared with a tray of tea.

'Make yourselves comfortable. Your next transport will be here shortly.'

I knew better than to ask any questions. No names, no questions. That was the pack drill. Besides, there was no need. The man bristled with that peculiarly British combination of efficiency and eccentricity, from the top of his neatly combed head to the tips of his waxed moustache. The fact he even bothered to wax his moustache out here spoke volumes.

'You got here OK. Great.'

We all looked up as another man entered, this time a far more familiar figure. 'Jim. What the hell are you doing here?'

He glanced at Colette. 'I'm here to oversee this mission. From now on, please address me only as "sir".'

She flushed, more in anger than embarrassment. 'Of course. Sir.'

The edge she added on that last word could have cut through a thousand sheets of paper. He affected not to notice.

'I'll be acting as your communications liaison. Any and all messages must come directly to me. You will shortly be transported to the coast from where you will board a submarine that will take you to Tunisia. When you arrive, you will be taken directly to Agency Africa's contact there. If you need to get a message to me, you send it through him. Is that understood?'

We nodded as one and chorused, 'Yes, sir.'

'Very good. Your transport will be here in around twenty minutes. I suggest you use that time for your personal needs. You'll be on the submarine for several hours, and the facilities on it are basic at best. Hakim will show you the way.'

I took him at his word, rising at the same time as Colette to follow the servant into the rooms beyond the courtyard. He left us with a bow outside a door which led into a plain but functional room containing a squat toilet. 'At least it's indoors,' I muttered.

Colette wrinkled her nose. 'You go first.'

I splashed water on my face and arms at the basin afterwards, trying to wash away the sand, which seemed to have become ingrained in my flesh. Colette joined me, pulling her lipstick from her pocket and reapplying it with fierce concentration.

'What is it with you two?' I asked.

She smacked her lips together. 'I don't know what you mean.'

'Oh come now. You and Jim. There's more to it than teacher and star pupil. Or officer and agent. I can see that. You looked upset when he rebuked you.'

Her smile was bright, bleak and as beautiful as she was. 'Not at all. I overstepped the mark, that's all. He was quite right to say something. We're on a covert mission. Silly mistakes could cost us our lives.'

'I agree, but we're hardly out in the field yet.'

She held out her lipstick. 'Want some?'

I got it. Subject closed. At least for the moment. I wasn't giving up on this one. There was more to it. I knew that in my gut. I hadn't forgotten that Colette had a daughter, one that would be tantalisingly close to her once we were in Tunisia. The lure of seeing Céline might prove too much. I knew it would for me, if Alexander were alive. I wouldn't be able to keep away from him. I still held him at night, in my dreams. Telling him stories. Singing him songs. As for Jim, I needed to know where he fitted into the picture. I was putting my life on the line here. We all were. There was no room for distractions, romantic or otherwise.

As we rejoined the men in the courtyard, I noticed one was missing.

'Where's Freddie?'

'He's staying here with me,' said Jim. 'I need him for comms. It's just you women and the two other guys going in.'

I glanced at Tom, and our eyes held for half a second too long until I tore mine away. So much for no distractions. And here was a big one.

I kept my gaze averted until the British officer reappeared and cheerily announced, 'Transport's here.'

We got to our feet, shouldering our backpacks, Tom's arm brushing mine on our way to the door. No distractions. But the jolt that shot down my arm was most certainly distracting. I squared my shoulders. Once we were in Tunis, we would be apart. It would be easier to focus solely on the mission. On saving other people's lives, even though, at times, it felt as if my own ended long ago, the day we lowered my child into the ground. He was my last link to my old life. To Andrzej. To hope. Now I no longer cared if I lived or died. Or at least I hadn't, until I met Tom.

46

The sun was sinking below the horizon when the next transport dropped us at a remote beach a few miles along the coast, its last rays picking out the boats waiting for us on the shore. The two men standing beside them were dressed in plain jerseys and trousers, their arms folded. They didn't so much as move a muscle as we approached. When we were close enough, I could see they both had that thousand-mile stare peculiar to men who have spent a long time at sea, their eyes washed as blue as the water that had become their home.

The one nearest to us spoke up. 'You two ladies and you, sir, come with me. The rest of you get into the other boat.'

We did as we were told, Tom taking the stern seat behind Colette and me, inches away from my back. I kept it ramrod straight as we heaved off the shore and out into the open water, Tom and the other man at the oars, keeping pace with the boat alongside. Beyond the curve of the bay, I could make out a shape poking from the water, the conning tower of a submarine. We paddled right up alongside it, sailors reaching down to help us up and along the deck to the hatch.

Here, another sailor was offering a steadying hand. 'Mind your head as you go down.'

We descended one by one into the cramped confines of the submarine, and I saw what he meant. The ceiling was so low it brushed the top of my head, never mind Tom's. The air was dank down here, fetid and laced with a heady mixture of diesel fumes and cigarette smoke, despite the fresh air from the open hatch.

An officer stepped forward the moment my feet left the lowest rung of the ladder and saluted. 'Lieutenant Commander Linton. Delighted you made it. I'll be taking you back to Cap Serrat.' We were all here now, filling up the cramped space, clustering around the foot of the ladder. 'I'm afraid we don't have a lot of room here. If you come with me, I'll take you to the wardroom, where you'll be more comfortable.'

We followed him in single file along narrow corridors and through bulkhead doors, the commander pausing to point out the oxygen tubes and masks we would need in case of emergency, then leading us on past curtained-off bunks and doors – through which I glimpsed tables surrounded by yet more bunks – to the wardroom with its polished wooden table.

'I'll have someone bring you some tea,' he said.

More tea. The British didn't just fight on tea, they sailed on it too.

We clustered around the table, Colette next to me. I noticed she was unnaturally quiet. 'Are you alright?' I whispered.

'I'm fine,' she muttered. 'Just a little claustrophobic.'

She seemed to relax a bit when a rating brought us tea along with biscuits. We fell on them hungrily, my stomach reminding me it had been hours since we'd eaten.

The commander reappeared as we were polishing off the last of the biscuits. 'We'll be diving in a few minutes. Our batteries are fully charged, but we're still going to take it slowly along the coast, just in case.'

'Just in case of what?' asked Colette. I could feel her leg jiggling against mine.

'Enemy U-boats and E-boats. Don't worry – I've been in command of this sub for ten months and we have yet to engage. If anything happens, you muster at the points I showed you. We should reach Cap Serrat in around six hours. Now if you will excuse me, I'm needed on the bridge.'

Six hours under the sea. I could see Colette's fists clenched in her lap. 'Why don't you take one of those bunks?' I murmured. 'Get some rest?'

'There's no way I could rest. I might fall asleep and miss an alarm call.'

'Not if I come with you. I can take the next bunk. Come on – there are some in the next mess.'

I could sense Tom listening in, although he was apparently chatting amiably to Nico. Colette was like a coiled spring. It was far better I get her somewhere on her own.

As we rose from the table, I caught Tom's raised eyebrow. I nodded to indicate I had things under control, then ushered Colette out the door and into the next mess, where bunks were slotted into the walls around the table there. I pulled a couple down. 'You take this one. I'll be right here, in the one next to you.'

She climbed up and pulled the rough blanket over her. I settled myself in the next one, staring up at the ceiling a few inches from my face. I didn't blame her for feeling claustrophobic. It was like being in a sardine can under the sea, people and equipment everywhere, with scarcely enough room to manoeuvre, let alone breathe. I half-hoped Colette had fallen asleep, but then her voice floated from the next bunk.

'How watertight do you think those hatches are?'

'Very. These subs are extremely safe.'

She laughed softly. 'That's what Jim said. I didn't believe him either.'

Truth be told, submariners had just about the most dangerous job in this war, but I wasn't going to tell her that. I'd seen the reports and the odds weren't good. Some subs had gone down due to enemy action, others because they'd sprung a leak or malfunctioned in some other way. If you thought about it, we were in a tiny metal tube under a vast sea which was teeming with enemy boats and subs. But I wasn't going to think about it, and I wasn't going to let her either.

'Tell me about you and Jim,' I said.

'There's nothing to tell.'

'You said that before and I didn't believe you then either.'

I heard her exhale, almost as if it was a relief to let go of something she'd been holding too close. 'Very well. I'll tell you. I met Jim before the war. He was stationed at the embassy in Tunis, officially as a diplomatic officer.'

'And unofficially?'

'Unofficially, the United States government already had intelligence agents in its embassies, as most governments do. When America joined the war, Jim set up the OSS in North Africa.'

'You said you met him before the war?'

'Yes.'

'How? Where did you two meet?'

A pause. 'At an official dinner at the embassy. I went with my uncle and aunt. My uncle is a prominent businessman in Tunis. Jim was at that dinner, and we became friends.'

'Friends?'

'Alright, more than friends.'

Now we were getting somewhere. 'You were lovers?'

A longer pause. 'We still are. Jim recruited me to protect me. It was the only way he could keep me safe.'

Something here wasn't quite right. 'What do you mean, to protect you? Surely turning you into an active agent puts you in constant danger? And what about your husband? Didn't he mind about Jim?'

When she finally spoke again, her voice sounded far away, as if she was recounting a dream. 'I never had a husband. I lied to you. I'm sorry.'

'So Jim...?'

'Is Céline's father, yes. He only found out after I had her. He was posted back to the United States before I discovered I was pregnant. By the time I saw him again, she was nine months old. He's married, you see, to a woman back home. They don't have any children. They can't have them. And he swears to me they don't have relations either. That might be true. It may not. You know what men are like. In any event, she's Catholic and will never give him a divorce.'

Another one who was married. Although Tom's circumstances were not the same. 'I'm sorry.'

'Don't be. He's the best thing that ever happened to me, second only to Céline, but you see now how it's the only way we can be with one another. How he can be close enough to make sure I'm alright. And why he must act the way he does to keep anyone from finding out the truth. Céline is safe with my parents in Djerba, or she was until the Germans invaded. I'm doing this for her too. I want her to be proud of me, to know that I fought for the freedom of our country.'

'Don't you also want to get her out?'

The silence was now pregnant.

'Oh my God. You already have a plan, don't you?'

A pause, one so long I wondered if she'd fallen asleep, and then a soft exhale. 'Yes, I do. A secret one. Not even Jim knows about it. Please don't tell him. He thinks it's too risky to try and extract her now. But I can't tell you anything, just in case... you know...'

I did know. In case I was captured and revealed anything under torture. I'd have done the same in her shoes. Now we both had our secret plans – Colette's to rescue her daughter, mine to kill Vulke. 'I understand.'

The trouble was, I understood only too well. The longing to be with someone, knowing it was the wrong thing to do. The desire to fight for freedom and to vanquish the enemy, all the while knowing that the biggest enemy was your own heart, betraying you over and over, leading you into the most dangerous territory of all. The place where you lost yourself and even your mind in the name of love. A place I never wanted to visit again. I knew now it was impossible. I could never be with Tom. It would be the end of us both.

47

I must have dozed off listening to the constant drip-drip of water that accompanied the hum of the sub's batteries. Next thing I knew, a change in motion jolted me awake. The sub was shuddering, and my head was pressed against the back of the bunk. I peered out from behind its curtains to see that the table, the floor, everything was tilting. I could hear someone banging on the door of the wardroom and then Tom's voice.

'We're surfacing.'

Colette and I scrambled from our bunks, following the others back along the corridors, thanking the commander before climbing the ladder once more, out through the hatch into blessed fresh air, hands helping us along the deck and towards the small, inflatable boats that bobbed alongside, just visible in the moonlight. Two more men this time, dressed in the same jerseys.

'SBS,' muttered the sailor who was handing me down to them. 'Special Boat Section.'

I glanced at the man taking up oars, Tom rowing in tandem with him again. He certainly looked tough enough to be one of the infamous commandos. He also had that glint in his eye. I'd met a couple of these types before, out in the desert. Men who acted as if they had nothing to lose except their sanity and even that was called into question. I watched him now, hauling us smoothly across the water towards the beach as if this was merely a day out on a rowing lake, knowing that these waters were awash with enemy patrols and that we were close now to the German front lines. So close, in fact, that this post was practically on top of it.

We had to wade the last few yards onto shore, shoeless, hoicking our trousers above our ankles, splashing up onto the beach, which appeared to be empty, its sands swept periodically by the light from the lighthouse on the hill above. The two pulled their boats up after us and deflated them before signalling we should follow them across the sand and along a winding path that took us up the hill, through scrub and trees, slipping on the sandy soil as we trudged, grimly silent, until at last we crested the final ridge to see the lighthouse right in front of us.

'In here,' said one, and we followed him through a courtyard and up a couple of steps to a door that led to what appeared to be an office. 'Wait here.'

Moments later, he returned with another man, a tall, dapper type who reminded me of the one who'd greeted us in Algiers, except this one had a name. 'Lieutenant Commander Francis Brooks. Glad to have you with us. How was your journey?'

The two SBS men had melted away.

Tom glanced around our small group. 'Very good, sir. I take it this is one of our posts?'

'It is indeed. There are just a couple of us here at the moment, including an OSS observer. The others are holding the line a few miles away. Now, why don't you get out of those wet things and join me for some refreshments? We have excellent coffee.'

Music to my ears.

Over coffee, Lieutenant Commander Brooks outlined the next stage for us. 'The road from here to Tunis is extremely dangerous. The Germans, as you know, have occupied the city, and their front line extends from it towards us. As well as patrolling the main roads in and out, they stop and search all vehicles at roadblocks. We do, however, have a plan.'

Tom smiled. 'I'm sure you do, sir.'

I sipped my coffee. Brooks was right. It was excellent – strong, hot and aromatic. Just the way I liked it. I kept my gaze on Brooks, determined not to look at Tom. Since my conversation with Colette, I was more acutely aware of him than ever. And even more aware that it could never be.

'We're going to deliver you by truck hidden in barrels of oats,' Brooks went on. 'As you were briefed, there's a merchant in Tunis who is now the outpost for Agency Africa there. He will receive you and get you safely to the royal palace. You will both be staying there under the protection of the Bey.' He glanced at Colette and me before turning to Tom. 'You men will remain at the merchant's mansion. He's a wealthy man and has plenty of room to hide you until the time is right.'

Nico cut in, calm and reasonable as ever. 'Can't we do our bit recceing the place?'

'I'm afraid not. You'd stand out immediately. The Germans have made accurate lists of members of the Vichy government, along with other foreign residents. The two ladies here have cover stories that stand up, but there's nothing that would work for you chaps, I'm sorry to say.'

Of course the Germans had made lists. They'd stormed into Poland waving them. Those bastard Krauts and their damn lists. I gulped back my anger. 'I gather I'm to liaise between this merchant and everyone else?'

Brooks nodded. 'You're the point of communication, yes. You have a watertight role with your job at the Red Cross. Any time you need to deliver or collect a message, you can visit the merchant under that guise.'

I looked round the table. 'What if a message is urgent? How will the others be able to contact me?'

'The merchant has a boy,' said Brooks. 'The son of a neighbour, I believe. He will send him at once if anything happens.'

'How old is this boy?'

'I believe he's ten.'

Ten. A mere child. A little boy, as Alexander had been. As Alexander might have become. What kind of a world was this where we sent children into war? Because that was what this was. The Germans would not hesitate to shoot a child, just as they would a man or a woman. Before they did, they would make sure they extracted everything they needed by whatever means they chose. It was why we kept our secrets to ourselves, so as not to place a burden on each other. Secrets that included Colette's own child, little Céline.

I could feel Colette's eyes on me as I lowered my own, blinking back the tears. No. Not again. I would not see another child hurt in the name of this war. Alexander had died because we had to flee home and country. I knew what it was to hold my baby in my arms before I had to bury him, my heart breaking more and more with each sod of earth that hit his tiny coffin, my soul leaving my body to join his as I gasped his name. I refused to let another mother suffer as I had. To see a father broken and a family torn apart. I would protect this boy with my life, as I would Colette's daughter, come what may.

I felt her hand slip into mine under the table in a silent show of empathy. She knew. As I knew. Her secret was now my secret, her child mine to save too.

48

PRESENT DAY, CAIRO, EGYPT

SOPHIE

The villa looked even more forlorn in the twilight, the dust motes no longer dancing in the sun but lying as a thick film over everything, a veil between us and the past. I stood in the gloom, trying to conjure up the figures I'd seen whirling around the ballroom, to hear the music once more. To see Ben. Even the piano appeared lifeless, its lid creaking as I lifted it, the keys sending out notes that jarred. I might never have had those lessons, but even I knew when a piano was out of tune, just like my heart.

They were gone, those ghosts who had waltzed and swirled around me. Now this was just an empty, broken-down building, its walls echoing with nothing but memories. *Where are you, Ben?* I cried in my head. There was no answer. Of course there wasn't. It had all been in my mind.

'Someone's been in here,' said Josh. 'Look. This dust has been disturbed.'

I followed his gaze, looking at the floor by the windows.

Sure enough, the surface was shiny in comparison to the floorboards nearest to us, the edges of the area scuffed as if someone had wiped away the dust.

'Maybe that's where I fainted?'

Josh shook his head. 'You fainted over there, by that chair, see?'

I looked where he was pointing. The chair was still there, on the other side of the room from the windows, the floor shiny here in places too where I'd fallen and where we had all trodden. It was a different kind of shiny though. Less deliberate.

I walked over to the other area and sank onto my haunches, examining it. 'You're right. Someone has definitely wiped this area clean. I wonder why?'

Josh squatted beside me. 'Looking for something, I suspect. Why else would you wipe just one area and leave the rest? Whoever it was thought they knew where to look as well. Wait a second...' He pulled a penknife from his pocket and inserted it at the edge of one of the floorboards, trying to prise it up.

It didn't budge.

'They tried that too. Look at the edges here and here.'

I could see where someone had inserted a knife just as he had, slicing through the wax sealant between the floorboards. 'What do you think they were looking for?'

'That's anyone's guess. More importantly, who was it? If we work that out, we might have a clearer idea what they were after. It wasn't opportunists or kids. They would have wrecked the place and made a lot more mess. This was someone who came straight to where they thought they should be looking. They didn't break any of the locks I put on the place, and I haven't noticed anything else disturbed.'

I looked around. He was right. There was no sign of smashed windows or forced entry. 'Should we call the police?'

'Not the best idea. They don't exactly have a great reputation here. I think we should try to find out how they got in and make sure they can't do it again. My guess is they heard us coming and made a run for it.'

'Do you think they'll come back?'

Josh stood, holding out his hand to me. 'They might because I don't think they found what they were looking for. Come on – let's check the rest of the house.'

We went from room to room, using our phones as torches as the light grew dimmer, until mine finally gave up the ghost. I would have to do something about the electricity supply. About everything, in fact. The library was undisturbed, exactly as we had left it, although even this golden room appeared sadder and more faded with the sunlight now gone, the book spines no longer reflecting it, the cushions simply tatty relics of a bygone age. It was as if something – or more likely someone – had sucked the soul out of the place, tarnishing it with their presence.

'Come on,' said Josh. 'Let's look upstairs.'

So far, we'd only managed to explore the ground floor, and the place was bigger than I had first thought, the main staircase leading up to a landing that branched off into two wings which contained six bedrooms in total, along with a couple of bathrooms and what appeared to be a storage cupboard. We checked every single one. The bedrooms were even more desolate than the salons downstairs, what had once been curtains hanging, torn and tattered, framing windows that were opaque with dust and grime.

The master bedroom contained a four poster, its drapes also shredded. I took a fold of one between my fingers, feeling the fine silk, seeing the threads that had been ripped. 'This looks deliberate,' I said. 'As if someone slashed them. I don't think they just fell apart.'

Josh moved from the window where he'd been gazing out at

the garden below. 'You're right, although I don't think this is recent. See, here, where the material is ripped? The threads in between are disintegrating. That doesn't happen overnight.'

A thought struck me. 'Do you think this was Nadia's room? Maybe not when they were all living here but after, when she bought the place?'

'It might have been. Why?'

'She had these two pet mongooses she'd rescued. She used to tell me stories about them – how they would climb up the curtains and shred them to bits. Apparently, the butler insisted they had to live in the summer house, although he would feed them for her when they were away. Kochanie and Malenka. Those were their names. They meant "honey" and "little one" in Polish. I bet she sneaked them back in here. That would be so like Nadia.'

I could see it now, Nadia lounging on the bed, probably a cocktail in hand, while her pets ran around wrecking the place as she laughed her head off. She did that too when I was naughty as a kid, always telling my parents to let me be. Not that they were great disciplinarians. Nadia certainly wasn't. After I came to live with her, I was pretty much a free-range kid. Funnily enough, I turned out to be rather straight-laced. I think that was the only thing I ever did that disappointed Nadia.

Josh let the silk fall from his hand. 'She really was special to you, wasn't she?'

'Special in so many ways. She took me in, after all, when my parents died. She looked after me as if I was her own. I always knew she'd suffered a great heartbreak, but she did her best to never let that show. I can't bear to think of her all alone here, shut away, refusing to see anyone.'

'I can empathise.'

The air was charged again. I could feel it. The unsaid filling the space between us with impossible questions. I looked away, glancing down at the bedside table. One of the drawers underneath it was partly open. I pulled at it and it juddered on its runners before jamming fast. I reached inside, feeling around for whatever was blocking it. 'There's a false top,' I murmured as I hooked my fingers around a notch in it, pulling it down. The drawer opened easily now, revealing a notebook that had been hidden above the false top along with a pen that rolled forward from where it had been lodged at the back.

'Look at this,' I breathed. It was an ordinary, lined notebook. The kind your grandmother might have used to write recipes. The cover was a plain blue, the spine cracked where it had been glued back together. Same writing as in her children's story-book. Nadia's hand hadn't changed in the intervening years. She wrote boldly, with thick strokes of her fountain pen, the letters sloping to the right, racing across the pages as if she was afraid she might run out of either time or room. That was how she lived too. I suppose that's how you learn to be when you've gone through the things she had, although I thought that was how she was anyway. Living every moment as if it might be her last.

In places, she appeared to have been writing so fast the letters seemed jumbled up or malformed. I could only imagine what might have been happening when she made her notes; the pressure she must have been under. There was one entry right at the very beginning that caught my eye: 'Tom Molyneux?'

'What's in it?' asked Josh, peering over my shoulder.

'I think this was Nadia's notebook. It looks like it might actually have some clues in it, although I can barely read any of it in this light. Look, she mentions Tom here.'

Josh shone his phone torch at the notebook, but that only made it all the harder to read, bleaching out the faded ink and bouncing back off the pages. There was another sentence, though, that leaped out at me. A sentence she had underlined three times. I ran my finger under it. 'What do you think this means?'

'I've no idea. It looks German.'

I read it out loud:

'Vulke must die.'

49

I tucked the notebook in my bag, following close behind Josh.

'Hold on to me,' he commanded at the top of the stairs.

Looking down, all I could see was the faint grey that filtered through the windows in the front hall. So I did as I was told, clutching at Josh's sweatshirt, taking one step after another, my eyes fixed on the circle of light cast by his torch, wondering if the stairs had creaked this much on the way up. When we reached the front door, Josh touched my arm. 'Stay here for a second. I think I know where they might have got in.'

I waited, my heart thumping, trying not to start at every tiny sound, telling myself not to be so stupid, that this was Nadia's house. That it was, after all, just a house. My house.

As my eyes grew more accustomed to the gloom, I thought I could make out more shapes. Had they always been there? Of course they had. That was the hallstand. That was the chest I'd admired the first day I'd visited. It was just furniture. Nothing sinister. Not really. Where the hell was Josh?

Bang, bang.

Oh my God, what was that?

Another couple of bangs. Coming from the rear of the

house where the kitchen was. I reached behind me, my fingers sliding around the door handle, wondering if I should call out, get help. Then something loomed out of the darkness, coming straight for me. A blast of light, the bulk of someone behind it.

'It's OK. Found it.'

'Josh! You made me jump.'

He laughed. 'Sorry. Didn't mean to scare you. They got in through the kitchen door. They must have jemmied the new lock.'

'You're kidding.'

'This is Cairo. Anything can happen here. Don't worry, I've hammered a couple of boards across it. That'll have to do until I can get back here in the morning and fit some bolts. I think my theory was right though. They heard us coming and went out that way too, probably over the back wall. At least they didn't get time to go through the rest of the house.'

I opened the front door and stepped out into the evening air, the scent of jasmine filling my nostrils. Funny. I couldn't remember seeing any. There was another aroma too, that of musk roses. 'I'll come back with you tomorrow. I'd like to try and cut back some of this mess. That will help with security too.'

As Josh checked the chain was secure on the gate, I gazed back at the house, imagining them all here, living hard in between their daring missions, doing all the things Nadia told me about and probably a lot more besides. I could almost see the lanterns she'd described hanging from the trees, lit up for their parties, the music flowing out from the ballroom into the garden, just as it was now.

'Josh, do you hear that?'

'What?'

'That. The music.'

I stood stock-still, every muscle in me straining, listening. It wasn't my imagination. I could definitely hear it. '"In The Mood",' I whispered. 'Nadia used to play it for me.'

Josh stood there beside me, listening too. Then he dropped an arm around my shoulders. 'Come on. It's been a long day.'

He was steering me back down the overgrown alleyway, through the gate and towards the road, and all I wanted to do was run back, into the ballroom, to see them again, all of them dancing, Nadia and Tom, the glittering couples who had glided across that floor in each other's arms, laughing and whirling. At the centre of them, my Ben. No, not my Ben. Another mirage. I stumbled as a briar tugged at my ankle, and Josh swiftly righted me.

'Are you OK?'

'Yes, yes I am.'

I could feel the tears running down my face, dripping off my chin, unchecked, a great gush of pain without end. Did it ever stop for Nadia? Did she ever get over Tom? But I knew the answer to that – just as I knew that the cracks in my own heart would never quite mend.

50

From outside my hotel room, the sounds of Cairo drifted up. There was the endless muffled din of the traffic, along with the low hum of human life that never seemed to sleep here. This side of the island was noisier than the area where David and Josh had their apartment and where the villa was situated, but none of it disturbed me. I was engrossed in Nadia's notebook, trying to make sense of what were mainly records of the missions they'd carried out rather than personal memories. They were fascinating all the same.

The Germans had never occupied Cairo, so it had been safe enough to keep these notes here, although it was a different story out in the field, where she had evidently been. They certainly made for eye-opening reading. Once I was used to her handwriting again, the words were easy enough to decipher, but making sense of it all was another story. I stared at a sketched map of what appeared to be Tunis, with something labelled 'palace' at the northern edge and several shaded shapes labelled 'possible target areas'. Who or what had been the target?

On the next page, there was a list of street names, some starred. Beneath that, another list of what appeared to be hotels and bars, again some starred once or twice, all of it meaningless to me. I pulled out my laptop and tapped some of the names into Google Maps. Sure enough, one or two were still there, although others had changed since independence in 1956. The hotels and restaurants were mostly long gone, but three remained: Café Bleue, overlooking the Mediterranean at Sidi Bou Said; the Majestic Hotel in Tunis; and the Grand Hotel there too. There didn't seem to be any connection between them other than that they were all long established and had been there when Nadia made her notes.

I flipped through the pages, trying to find a date. There were none. Perhaps that was caution on her part, making sure that if anyone found her notebook, they would have no idea when her plans were to be carried out. And plans they were, that was evident. There were yet more lists of people, along with copious notes about some of them.

A Madame Rivaud was, according to this, garrulous and given to gossip, easy to pump for information and entirely indiscreet. Her husband, on the other hand, was a far tougher prospect. Nadia had put a large question mark by his name. Charles Rivaud sounded completely cold-blooded if her observations were anything to go by, apparently turning a blind eye to his wife's affair with a Colonel Rauff while he also did business with him.

Rauff. That name rang a bell.

I flicked forward a couple of pages and then a few more. An entire section of the notebook was devoted to him. He was, by Nadia's account, a total and complete bastard. I scrolled through pages detailing his cruelty. It was too much to stomach.

I rubbed the bridge of my nose, trying to ease out the pressure. I had to take a break. There was only so much of this I could take. God knows what Nadia must have thought. What she had to endure. It was obvious from these notes that she'd spent quite some time in Tunis on that mission. I wondered what else she hadn't told me, what secrets she'd held back. Like exactly how Tom had died. And why.

I'd always believed she couldn't bear to speak of him, but now I was beginning to think she might have another reason for staying silent. I knew she'd done something hush-hush in the war but never knew quite what. From what we'd discovered, it seemed she was almost certainly a fully-fledged spy working with SOE. It didn't surprise me one bit. Nadia loved an adventure. She was bright, witty and sophisticated, and she had the ability to fit in anywhere. What more could you want from someone working undercover back then in a place like Cairo or Tunis?

I'd no doubt Tom had been at it too. They'd been on that mission together, after all, when he was killed. Josh was doing his best to find those records, although, even with his skills, it was no easy task.

Josh. Now there was another enigma. At times, I could feel a pull so strong I had to almost physically resist it. At others, I was fighting back tears over Ben, all too aware that Josh, in his own way, had lost someone too.

We were a right pair. Two scarred people searching for answers, both of us looking to the past to find them. Was that such a bad thing? Maybe not. Josh was convinced there was a link between Ben's death and Tom's, and the more I thought about it, the more I had to agree with him. At the centre of it all, Rommel's gold. The fabled treasure which now lay at the bottom of the sea and for which my Ben had died, according to Josh.

Mind you, how well did I really know Josh? He'd appeared out of nowhere when I nearly got run over and again when I fainted at the villa. Granted, he was working for David, but even so... was it a coincidence? Or had he been following me?

No. No way. I couldn't imagine Josh doing that. Although perhaps it was more that I didn't want to imagine Josh doing that. He'd told me he'd been something in the intelligence services, after all. He was trained to do that kind of thing. His story of writing a book might just be a smokescreen.

I rubbed the back of my neck. My head was pounding. Reading Nadia's notebook was making me suspicious of everyone and everything.

On impulse, I picked up my phone and tapped out a message:

'Been meaning to ask – what were you doing near my hotel that day?'

The moment I hit 'send', I wished I hadn't.

Moments later, my phone pinged. Josh must still have been awake too. 'Went to talk to Mohammed – David knows him. He works at your hotel. Going to talk to him again tomorrow. I think he could help us.'

Mohammed. The old man who had known Nadia. Who had held my hand with such tenderness, dissolving into tears at her memory, and who, along with his grandson, had helped me find the villa. Josh must have spoken to him just a few hours before I did. Why? For his book? Or something else? Now he wanted to talk to him again. Here we both were, in Cairo at the same time, both of us following separate trails that intertwined, leading us inexorably towards each other and into the past. Fate or coincidence? I had no idea anymore. All I knew was that things were never what they seemed and nor were people. Not even Nadia. And maybe not Josh.

Breakfast at my hotel was a sumptuous affair, a buffet laden with all kinds of fruits, pastries, yoghurt and even a full English cooked to order. It made a change from the slice of toast I allowed myself back home, when I remembered. I toyed with my croissant, crumbling it between my fingers as Josh talked, telling me all about the long conversation he'd just had with Mohammed. A conversation that had taken place while I was still asleep. By accident or design? I had no idea.

'As I suspected,' said Josh, 'Mohammed was a spy, like many of the hotel and bar staff in this city. Some worked for the Germans and even the Russians, others for the Allies. Luckily, he was on our side, which is how he came to know Nadia.'

'He worked for her?'

Josh reached for the pot. 'More coffee? He didn't work for her as such. He passed on information, which she, in turn, passed to Dudley Clarke.'

I stirred my coffee. 'Why Dudley?'

'Because, as he told me, she was working for Polish intelligence, Agency Africa, under the guise of running the Red

Cross. They worked with SOE and the OSS as a joint operation.'

'I see.'

'SOE in Cairo was a mess, to put it politely. There were all kinds of leaks and betrayals, some inadvertent and some not. That's why the faction in the villa decided to go it alone, especially after they discovered they had a rat among them. Dudley was the one reliable conduit they had to the powers that be in London, while Jim was their connection to OSS and Washington. Mohammed here gave them juicy titbits he picked up while eavesdropping on conversations or watching the comings and goings. You have to remember that absolutely everybody was in Cairo at that time. The Germans, the Italians. The Russians and the various legations who supported one side or the other. The British. Us.'

I sat back and surveyed the breakfast lounge, taking in the cadences of the multiple languages, the rise and fall of at least a half-dozen tongues. Then, as now, Cairo had been a melting pot. Or rather a cauldron of spies. 'OK, I get all that, but how come Mohammed knows so much? It sounds as if he just passed stuff on. It's not like Nadia or the others told him anything in return.'

A glint of triumph lit Josh's eyes. 'Oh but they did. Or rather, she did. After she got back here, to Cairo, she didn't know which way to turn. Mohammed didn't just pass on information to her. He helped her in all kinds of ways. He was born here. He knows the city. Nadia trusted him with secrets she couldn't tell anyone else, not until she was sure the rat had died along with Tom.'

'He told you that?'

'He did.'

'What about her secrets? Are they to do with this gold?'

Josh's eyes held mine. 'I think he should be the one to tell you.'

'Then let's go talk to him again.'

We found the old man tending to the plants in the sun lounge that led out to the hotel pool. His face broke into that glorious smile when he caught sight of me. He plucked a flower from one of the pots and brought it to me, placing it in my hand with a little bow.

Josh said something to him in Arabic. I recognised my name and Nadia's. He then turned to me. 'I told him you have some questions for him. About Nadia.'

Mohammed's gaze flitted from my face to Josh's and back again. He held out his hands, palms uplifted as if to say he would give us what we could.

'Please,' I said, gesturing to one of the rattan chairs set around glass tables in the lounge and smiling encouragement.

Mohammed shifted from one foot to the other, his eyes scanning the lounge. There was just one other guest there, a man with his nose in a book sitting some distance away, wearing a red baseball cap. Still, Mohammed seemed to think it inappropriate. Looking ill at ease, he took a seat, his hands folded in his lap. Josh leaned forward, speaking Arabic to him in the softest of tones.

I watched Mohammed's face as he listened, at first shut down and then growing more animated as he answered Josh's questions, occasionally darting me a look. In his glance, I saw a need for approval, as if he was looking at Nadia, seeking her blessing. I guess I was the closest he had to her. The old man wasn't senile. He knew I wasn't actually Nadia, and yet he treated me with the same love he would have shown her.

I glanced over at the corner to look at the other man again – something about him was nagging at me. But he was no longer there. I must have been too busy watching Mohammed to notice him leave. Not that it mattered. Still, I couldn't shake off the sense that it did.

After a while, Josh sat back. 'He says that Nadia brought

some of the gold back with her. Special gold. She hid it at the villa.'

'Why would she do that? Why not take it with her to England?'

He turned again to Mohammed, who became even more animated, his eyes wide with what looked like fear.

'According to Mohammed, the gold was definitely cursed. Nadia felt obliged to keep it safe and couldn't risk hiding it where someone might find it, but she hated having it so close. She believed that Tom died because of it, because of the curse. That's why she finally left the villa. She didn't believe in the curse at first, but it began to haunt her, along with the memories. Eventually, she couldn't bear to be there anymore.'

'I don't believe it,' I whispered. 'She loved Eden. She always told me it's where she was happiest.'

'I'm sure it was. Think about it though, Sophie. When she got back there from Tunisia, it was very different. Tom died in her arms in that villa. He was gone, and so were some of her friends. The group that had lived there was disbanded. No wonder she had a breakdown all alone in that house with nothing but those memories.'

Memories and ghosts.

A thought struck me. 'Wait though. It was after she got back that she bought the place. Nadia lost everything when they fled Poland. I always wondered how she managed to do that.'

Josh looked from me to Mohammed. 'Good point. Perhaps Mohammed knows more.'

He grew even more animated this time, almost angry, waving his hands as he spoke.

In spite of his onslaught, Josh's face lit up. 'He says he told her not to do it, but she was adamant. She wanted the place, whatever it took. Even though she hated it, she loved it too. It was to be a monument to Tom, to everything they'd shared. To the life they'd had there. So she sold some of the gold to buy it.'

'The cursed gold?'

'Yes.'

'What happened to the rest of it?'

'As far as he knows, it's still there somewhere. At the villa.'

'Ask him if anyone else knows about this.'

I didn't need Josh to translate Mohammed's vehement denial.

'Well, obviously someone does, and that someone has gone looking. Whoever it was, they must have only just found out about it, or they would have been there long ago, trying to dig up that floor.'

'I agree,' said Josh, his brows knitted together. 'And we disturbed them in the act, or there would have been a lot more damage. They'd only just started on that floor when they heard us coming.'

Bony, long-dead fingers clutched the base of my skull. I could feel my head filling with static, growing fuzzy, just as it had in that ballroom as I'd seen those faces dancing towards me, white noise rushing through my ears. They were trying to tell me something, but what? It was like trying to decode a radio signal from the dead.

I shut my eyes and pressed my fingers against my temples. A fractured whisper across the years. It sounded like, 'It's there.' A chorus of voices agreeing. Then nothing but silence.

'Where?' I muttered. 'Where is it?'

'Sophie, are you OK? Sophie, speak to me.'

Still that silence, so loud now I could hear it. That was all I was getting.

'I can't hear them,' I whispered. 'They've gone again.'

52

Back on the bridge near my hotel, I tried to breathe in some fresh air and dispel the fuzziness that remained. No glances this time. Not with Josh walking alongside me. I stopped to lean on the balustrade and gaze out over the Nile, just as I'd seen those couples doing that first evening.

'You think I'm crazy, don't you?'

Clouds reached feathery fingers across an otherwise cerulean sky. Below us, the water was a darker blue, the reflections of the grand hotels and skyscrapers that lined it shimmering mirages.

Josh gestured to the river below. 'The Nile separates into two other rivers beyond Cairo called the Rosetta and the Damietta. They form the Nile Delta and eventually flow into the Mediterranean.'

The Mediterranean. The sea beside which Nadia had lain her baby son to rest. 'You didn't answer my question,' I said.

I'd never noticed that crease in Josh's cheek before. Not so much a dimple as an underline of his smile. 'No, I don't think you're crazy. Not at all. You forget I've spent a lot of time out here and in other places where people believe in things some Westerners might consider crazy. But I don't.'

'"There are more things in heaven and earth, Horatio..."' I murmured.

'*Hamlet*. Although I prefer *Romeo and Juliet*.'

'You do?'

He laughed. 'Don't look so shocked. How can you beat a story where everyone dies for love?'

I carried on staring at that blue, blue water, feeling the tears gather and forcing them back. The words rose unbidden, spilling out from my lips.

'"My bounty is as boundless as the sea, / My love as deep; the more I give to thee, / The more I have, for both are infinite."'

'That's beautiful,' he murmured.

I swiped a stray, treacherous tear from my cheek. 'Juliet. Act Two, Scene Two.'

'I'm impressed.'

He was standing so close. Too close. 'I teach it, don't forget. That's my job. I'm an English teacher. The kids always roll their eyes when I tell them we're doing *Romeo and Juliet*, but by the time we've finished, they love it as much as I do.'

'I bet they do.'

I could hear the thrumming of the city's pulse, the unstoppable flow of the river below, the birds calling as they soared. Surrounding us, though, was a silence so complete I hardly dared breathe in case I might break its fragile bubble. I knew in that instant something between us had shifted. We were on a path to a place I knew. One I had never seen before. The inevitable destination for a journey that had started long ago.

'We need to find it,' I murmured. 'The gold. For Nadia.'

'And when we do?'

No if. I liked that.

I turned to face him. 'We'll decide that when we find it. Too many people have died for this gold, including Tom and Ben. Maybe it's time to somehow break the curse.'

He was looking at me in total seriousness. Not a trace of a smile. 'So you believe me now?'

The flush stole up my neck, creeping towards my cheeks. He'd known all along. Known I didn't quite buy his story about the gold being cursed. Until now. 'I do.'

'What changed?'

'It's hard to explain... let's just say I heard something.'

His eyes appeared greener than ever as a smile played around his lips. 'And how do you propose to break the curse?'

'I have no idea. Will you try to do it with me?'

His fingers slid through mine. 'You know I will.'

Of course I did. We were on that path together, come what may, united in our quest.

53

The music washed over and through me, finding those places I thought had died along with Ben, the hidden crevices of pain, the ache of a heart beating to the same rhythm. 'Dido's Lament'.

'Remember me... remember me...'

How could I ever forget him? The truth was that I couldn't. I didn't want to. And the more we unearthed about Nadia and the gold, and the closer I got to Josh, the more it felt as if I was digging up the recent past too. Except that I had never laid Ben to rest. Not really. Not while there were so many unresolved question marks hanging over his death. All I knew was that I couldn't stand to hear this music a moment longer.

'Do you mind if we listen to something else?'

David stood and removed the record from his ancient record player, rifling through his vinyl collection until he pulled out a faded album cover. 'How about this? Glenn Miller. Belonged to my father.'

He placed it carefully on the turntable, sitting back with a grunt of satisfaction as 'We'll Meet Again' soared out, transporting us all back to the war. Nadia's war. And Tom's. When it came to 'In the Mood', Josh got to his feet and held out his hand.

I had no choice but to let him pull me close, one hand at my waist, the other clasping my hand as we glided around the apartment while David smiled beatifically, eyes half-closed, swaying in time to the music. I gazed somewhere over Josh's shoulder, not knowing where to look. His hand on my waist was warm, his touch light but impossible to ignore.

'I'm sorry. I'm not much of a dancer,' I mumbled.

'You're doing fine.'

As I turned with him, I saw David had fallen into a doze, chin resting on his chest, lulled by the music. Bless him. He must have heard this over and over as a child too. Perhaps Nadia had even played it to him.

When it ended, Josh returned me to my seat with a gallant bow. 'You said Nadia used to play "In the Mood" for you.'

'She did. Sometimes she would get this look on her face as if she was dancing to it in Tom's arms again. At least, that's what I liked to think.'

'It's a lovely thought. Maybe she is, somewhere.'

I smiled. 'Maybe.'

Ben was no dancer. The most we managed was an awkward jiggle together at a friend's wedding. He was a great speaker though, often called upon to be best man. I guess it was what made him such a great lawyer, that facility with words, the love of language we shared. Josh said more with his body, as he had just now. It had been so easy to fall into his rhythm. Far too easy.

He was good at reading me too. He was watching my face now. 'Something wrong?'

'No. It's just... I wonder if I should take another look at Nadia's notebook. See if there's anything in there about the gold.'

'I thought you'd already been right through it.'

'I have, but I might have missed something. You never know.'

He had his head cocked to one side, studying me. Or so it felt. 'You like to be thorough, don't you? You're right. There might be something in there.'

David let out a deep snore, which jerked him awake. 'Something in what?'

He might be getting on, but he was no slouch.

'I found an old notebook of Nadia's. It contains records of her missions. We were wondering if there was a clue in there as to the location of the gold she brought back.'

David snorted. 'I very much doubt it. She was a cautious woman, Nadia. She would never write something like that down. It's what they were taught, you see. If it was on paper, the enemy could use it against you. That's why all messages were encoded. If you think about it, that's how we won the war.'

I stared at him. Encoded. Of course. I clasped David's face between my hands and dropped a kiss on his forehead. 'You're a genius.'

He smiled up at me, befuddled. 'No one has ever called me that before.'

In that moment, I saw the little boy who had spent his whole life trying to fight his way out from under the blanket of shame his parents had cast over him. A blanket not even his wife could help lift. Inside the broken man who idled away his hours in a corner café was a light that had never been allowed to shine. I saw it in the kids I taught all the time.

'You'd better believe it,' I said. 'You've just solved a puzzle not even Josh here could crack.'

Now, at last, we might discover what had happened in Tunisia.

54

13 JANUARY 1943, TUNIS, TUNISIA

NADIA

I thought the submarine was bad. The oat barrel was far worse. I was buried in it up to my neck for hours as we rattled along the road to Tunis on the back of a truck, every bump sending the barrels crashing together. Each time I prayed mine wouldn't tip over and start rolling all over the place like some of the others. By sheer willpower, or maybe a small miracle, my barrel stayed upright, although at every roadblock and stop I prayed even harder.

We were under strict instructions to immediately sink under the oats as far as possible at our driver's signal, a sharp rap on the back of his cab. Luckily, it never came, but I was still poised, ready to do so, when we reached our final stop, every muscle shaking with the effort of holding still. I waited, holding my breath, listening hard. Was that someone prising open the lid of the barrel? I was already sinking down as silently as I could when I heard a voice. 'It's alright. You're safe here.'

Then another voice, one I recognised. 'Let me help you out.'

Tom, covered in dust from the oats and with the odd one

still sticking to his hair, reached in and hoisted me out of the barrel. For a second, I was suspended in the air, his hands gripping me warm and sure, then he was setting me on the ground, more dust flying from me and floating to the floor. I looked around. We were in what appeared to be a warehouse, its doors bolted firmly behind the truck. The others were emerging from their barrels too, Colette hopping out unaided to land with impossible elegance.

'Well, that was quite a ride,' she exclaimed, slapping the dust from her thighs.

'You can say that again,' muttered Nico, for once looking more than a little dishevelled.

Our driver was nowhere to be seen.

A door opened at the far end of the warehouse, revealing an impressive figure, his lion's mane of salt-and-pepper hair matching his beard, the yellow star stitched to his jacket pocket all too visible against the fine suiting. 'My name is Lucien. Welcome,' he cried, arms flung wide as if to embrace us all.

Colette's eyes lit up. 'Uncle!'

He stared at her for a second as if he couldn't believe what he was seeing. Then he strode over and wrapped her in an embrace, dropping a kiss on each cheek before holding her at arm's length to take another look at her face, making sure she was quite real. 'My child. But what are you doing here?'

She smiled up at him. 'Later, Uncle. I will explain.'

I stared at them, my curiosity piqued, aware that answers, if there were any, would come in good time. For now, it was best to know as little as possible, especially with Rauff and his henchmen only too ready and willing to torture anyone they suspected of being a spy.

The older man patted Colette's shoulder. 'Yes, of course. We must hurry. Please, all of you, come with me. It will be nightfall soon, and then the Germans start banging on the doors. They get drunk, you know, and start shouting out that they want women. We must get you two ladies out of here before then.'

I gaped at him. 'They do this? But what about their officers? Surely they try to control their men.'

He shrugged. 'These men are not so easy to control. They know that they're losing this war. The Italians were better, but the Germans are in charge now. It's not just these drunkards we have to worry about either. It's your people. The Allies bomb us every single night so that we cannot sleep. We know that they're fighting the enemy, but, at times, it does feel as if we are – how do you say? – collateral damage. So many people have died because of bombs intended for the occupiers.'

His French was perfect, his manner that of a gentleman. I had to avert my eyes from the yellow star that blared from his chest like an abomination.

He pointed to it. 'The Germans force us to wear this now. Even the French couldn't manage that. The Bey does his best to protect us, but every day those Nazis take more and more, including our young men. And our women.'

'Have they tried to take your house, Uncle?' asked Colette.

'Yes, but the Bey has taken it under his personal protection, putting it in his name. We have a legal document that says it remains mine and always will, but the Germans don't know that.'

We were standing in what looked to be his office, paperwork piled neatly on a desk beside a telephone.

He gestured to it. 'When that phone rings, it will be your driver with instructions. You gentlemen will be staying here. We have prepared beds for you in the stables. You ladies will be going on to the palace. Until then, you are my honoured guests. My wife has prepared some food for you all. Please, this way.'

The mansion was as beautiful as any I had seen, built around courtyards in the Arab tradition, its arches, pillars and walls decorated with paint and inscriptions. I spied one above the door opposite us in the main courtyard as we entered, carved in Hebrew.

Lucien saw me looking and walked over to it, tracing the words as he read aloud. 'Blessed shall you be in your comings, and blessed shall you be in your goings. Through this portal, pain shall not come. Not to the elderly, and not to the child, and not to the youngster. May it be His will. Amen.'

As his voice died away, so did the breeze that stirred the air, leaving a stillness so complete it seemed all the more obscene when it was broken by the sound of someone battering on the main door. The hammering grew louder and more insistent. Whoever it was, they weren't going away.

A shout in German, followed by another that sounded like an order. Then the unmistakable blast of a Luger. They were firing at the lock.

55

'This way.'

A manservant had come running at the sound of the knocking. Lucien signalled to him to stall them as he led us back the way we'd come, towards the rear of the mansion, on through room after room until we emerged into the final courtyard, the back wall of which formed the stable block. Fine Arab heads poked over the stable doors to see what we were up to as we passed, Lucien stroking the nose of one and patting the neck of another. At the penultimate stable, he stopped and unbolted the door. A pretty grey mare looked up from the hay she was chomping.

'Don't worry. This one is very gentle. Walk slowly in single file so you don't startle her.'

We did as we were told, moving past the mare and through a door set into a false wall at the back of the stable, which opened into a tiny vestibule. Steps led up to a hatch, above which more steps led to a vast hayloft that extended across the entire stable block. Instead of bales of hay, however, it housed several sleeping mats at the far end, along with jerrycans of water and washbowls.

'Stay here,' Lucien instructed. 'Keep as quiet as you can. I'll be back.'

With that, he descended the steps, leaving us to look at one another.

'Do you think we were followed?' I whispered.

'Who knows?' murmured Tom. 'Hopefully not and it's just a random raid.'

Although there had been nothing random about the way they'd shot at the door. If it was the SS, we could only hope Lucien's rambling mansion would keep us safe. Even ordinary German troops were brutal enough, and they would hand us over to Rauff's lot eventually.

My eyes met Tom's, and I saw reflected in his eyes the same thoughts that were running around my head. Had someone betrayed us? Would we get out of this alive? The thoughts that were a constant on every mission. We all stood, still as statues, listening out for the slightest sound.

The minutes seemed to tick by in tandem with my heartbeat. *Tick, tick, tick.* Speeding up as I thought I heard something, slowing once more when I told myself to breathe deep. A slam from somewhere out in the courtyard sent it into overdrive. They were here, marching in our direction, the sound of their boots ringing out on the tiles. The horses were whinnying, sensing the danger, then came the clatter of hooves on a stable door. One must have reared in fright. Someone, the commander no doubt, was barking out orders and questions. In response, I could hear Lucien's soft, soothing tones.

Colette was standing so rigid I feared she might snap in two.

'He'll be alright. He knows what to do,' I murmured.

She stared back at me, her eyes stricken.

All at once, I heard the rasp of the bolt on the stable door below us being drawn. The sweet mare snickered. *Please, please don't hurt her,* I begged silently.

Lucien's voice again, closer now, telling them to see for

themselves that there were just horses here. A double bluff. Genius or insanity. Another voice ordered his men out. Then came the sound of the bolt sliding back into place. It had worked.

We waited for what seemed an age until Lucien reappeared. 'They've gone.'

'Do you think someone tipped them off we were here?' I asked.

'I have just seen our neighbours out in the street. They tried to warn us, but it happened too fast. The Germans drove up in their jeep and were shooting at the door before they knew it. This is a close community. We all live together in harmony, Arabs and Jews. Our neighbours are good people, and they would never do anything to harm us. If someone tipped them off, it wasn't one of them.'

'Which means,' I said, 'that our rat might still be out there somewhere.'

Somewhere far too close.

'We must move you,' said Lucien. 'I have another place the Germans don't know about, a factory on the other side of the city. On paper, it's owned by an Arab friend. We need to make sure they've really gone before I take you there. You ladies, come with me now and we will get you to Bey's palace.'

Tom stepped forward. 'You two are our eyes and ears on the ground. As soon as you have some intel we can act upon, we can make our next plan. Rauff's routines. Regular haunts. That kind of thing.'

'Roger that,' I quipped. Anything to stop my heart feeling this heavy. What in heaven's name was wrong with me? We had a job to do. The men would be fine.

Colette was already following Lucien down the stairs, talking to him in a low voice.

I held out my hand. 'Be seeing you then.'

His fingers closed around mine. 'Be careful,' he murmured. The rest was written in his eyes.

56

19 JANUARY 1943, PALACE OF THE BEY, TUNIS, TUNISIA

We'd been here nearly a week and still the palace took my breath away, especially this evening with every corner illuminated by lanterns, partygoers flitting through it like multicoloured moths in their finery on their way to be presented to the Bey. The palace was built, just like Lucien's mansion, around a central courtyard, its elaborate arches framing the fountain that flowed as tradition dictated, the sound of it drowned out by the musicians who greeted us as we were led through to a reception room divided by pillars. Chairs were set around the edge of the room, some of them occupied by the wives of the Vichy officials and businessmen who were the invited guests, every one of them bourgeois to the bone.

The women gathered in clusters, their painted mouths pinched with the effort of holding back their thoughts while the men talked shop, as bored as their spouses. It was this boredom that had no doubt led our targets to their dalliances with Colonel Rauff. Certainly, he represented something more interesting than the self-important rodents they'd married, although I would have found the very idea repugnant. We were looking for a Madame Darlan and a Madame Rivaud. Apparently, they knew about one another but, being French, they simply pretended not to know or care of their shared place in Rauff's bed.

I had no doubt he had others too. His reputation, after all, preceded him. But it was these two who offered a way in. I scanned the room, my gaze alighting on Colette talking animatedly to a woman who was pretty enough in a provincial way, her hair just a little too brassy, her dress not quite à la mode. If my guess was correct, this was Madame Rivaud, wife of the businessman Charles Rivaud, who had his fat fingers in several pies, all of which he liked to serve up to the Germans. I drifted over as casually as I could, affecting surprise when I drew closer.

'My dear, how lovely to see you. What are you doing here?'

Colette's eyes widened. 'I don't believe it! I could ask you the same.' She turned to the woman next to her, who was patting those brassy curls, clearly dying to be introduced. 'This is my good friend Nadia. She's here on behalf of the Red Cross. Nadia, this is Madame Rivaud. Her husband is in import-export here.'

Madame Rivaud tittered. 'It's Simone, please. I'm so happy to meet you. I have to say things were a little dull until Colette here showed up.'

I followed her gaze, taking in the stout man who stood at the centre of a group of men, his shoulders thrust back, holding court. He clearly fancied himself on a par with the Bey, who was engaged in conversation several feet from him. 'Is that your husband?' I asked, although I already knew the answer.

She rolled her eyes. 'How did you guess?'

I rather liked Simone's frankness, if not her choices in men. Her husband looked to be even more of a crashing bore than most. It was no wonder she was searching for excitement, although she was finding it in all the wrong places, if indeed an encounter with Rauff could be considered exciting.

I heard her suppress a tiny gasp as her eyes drifted over my shoulder.

'Care for another drink?' I asked as I spun on my heel to catch the waiter passing with his tray, getting an excellent view of whatever was behind me in the process. What was behind me was Rauff, along with a couple of his men. He needed no introduction. His eyes were as hard as a scarab beetle's, even at this distance, his mouth twisted in a smirk as he advanced upon the Bey. The Bey was no slouch when it came to politics. He'd already clocked Rauff and was conferring with his aide who suddenly clapped his hands, bringing the room – and Rauff – to a hushed standstill.

'His Majesty wishes to say a few words of greeting.'

The colour rose in Rauff's cheeks, but there was little he could do or say. It wasn't exactly a snub, but it wasn't a warm welcome either. The Bey had seen him coming, in all senses. And his words weren't exactly effusive as he reiterated Tunisian neutrality and then introduced his new Prime Minister, a man the Germans had described as 'half-American' to the throng. This was the first time I had clapped eyes on the Bey, although we were living under his vast roof, and I was impressed. He was holding his own against the Nazi occupiers, a dignified figure in his white robes, a red fez on his head.

He must have been around sixty, but his face and posture were youthful, his close-clipped beard and splendid moustache accentuating his regal air. He wasn't tall, but what he lacked in stature, he made up for in charisma. Above all, it was apparent he wouldn't stand for any nonsense. He had already stood up to the French, insisting Tunisians be given roles as civil servants and establishing a legislative council. Now here he was standing up to the Germans too. It was an impressive sight.

Rauff half-extended his hand and then thought better of it, resorting to a stiff little bow instead. The Bey simply stood, his expression impassive, although I was sure the embers of hatred were smouldering underneath that ice-cool surface. He was far too astute to let that show, however, preferring to convey his true feelings through his silence, his eyes never leaving Rauff's face. And then, slowly but surely, he turned his back on the German colonel, leaving Rauff staring after him with murder in his eyes.

57

I was dying to applaud the Bey, but etiquette and prudence dictated otherwise. Instead, I savoured the moment before turning back to Simone. 'Who is that?' I asked innocently.

The flush on her neck was a dead giveaway. I could only hope for her sake that her husband was too busy blowing his own trumpet to notice it.

'That? Oh, I believe that is Colonel Rauff.'

She believed. God help her. I had no doubt she knew every inch of the body he'd squeezed into that uniform, his slack cheeks giving away his fondness for food and wine even if his belly was concealed by a well-cut jacket. You had to hand it to the Nazis. They dressed in style. A coating of civility that belied the vicious bastards they were underneath. 'Colonel.' Simone's husband beckoned to Rauff to join their group. A moment later, he turned and gestured to his wife. I glanced at Simone, her face frozen into a social smile. Did he know after all? There was nothing in his demeanour to suggest it. He was chatting away to the colonel, all charm. This had to be a business conversation then. I wondered what exactly M. Rivaud was supplying to the Nazis. I had thought that supply might include his wife, but I may have misjudged Rivaud. He looked like a man who would jealously guard all his possessions, including his wife, if only to preserve face. Not that he needed to. He was one of the most confident men I had ever seen, exuding the power that comes with great wealth. She, on the other hand, appeared ill at ease as she stood on the other side of her husband from the colonel, that silly smile still plastered to her face.

'Don't look now but here comes the other one,' muttered Colette in my ear. I watched as a taller, more patrician-looking woman joined the group, along with a man who matched her in build although not in height, a whippet to her saluki. If I'd had to draw a French civil servant, this would have been him, with his bald pate and spectacles perched primly on a nose that looked as if it enjoyed poking in corners. Rauff seemed entirely relaxed at having his two mistresses stand a few feet from one another along with their husbands. But then, this was a man who routinely gassed entire families without a second thought. Where his conscience should have been, there was just a gaping well of evil that knew no bounds.

I smiled at Colette, acting as if we were simply engaged in chit-chat. 'Simone, she's easy. The other one might prove a little more difficult to get to know.'

'I agree. I think perhaps we should take one at a time. We've already made inroads with Simone, so let's work on the other one, Madame Darlan. From what I've heard, she enjoys a game of baccarat.'

'Surprise me.'

Colette sniggered. 'I know. Of the two, she's the bigger snob, so I think we should play on that.'

'Give her the full countess treatment?'

'Along with a few references to my royal connections.'

'Perfect.'

'Let's go.'

Rauff was on the move, his conversations concluded. The group that had surrounded him was breaking up. This was our chance. Monsieur Darlan was thrusting out his chest, strutting in the direction of someone he no doubt considered worth his while. The Rivauds were nowhere to be seen.

In a swift pincer movement, we descended on Madame Darlan. 'Lovely party, isn't it?'

Her eyes grazed me from top to bottom. 'If you can call it that.'

'I don't believe we've been introduced. I am Countess Nadia Pulaska.'

'Oh. Ah. *Enchanté*. Madame Antoinette Darlan.'

She raised an eyebrow at Colette, clearly ranking her as some lowly native.

Colette smiled sweetly and extended her hand. 'Colette. I live here at the palace.'

I could see Madame Darlan trying to work that one out. Was she a concubine? Possibly a favourite of the Bey? Or something more mundane? The Frenchwoman erred on the side of caution. '*Enchanté*.'

She still managed to lace that one word with vinegar.

Colette smiled all the more broadly. 'I understand you enjoy a game of baccarat. Perhaps you would care to join us some time, here at the palace.'

Madame Darlan's mouth formed a moue of surprise. 'How did you know that?'

Colette giggled girlishly. 'You'd be surprised at what I know. The walls have ears, even in a palace. We ladies talk, but I'm sure you knew that already. How about tomorrow? We could enjoy the hammam before a game or two.'

I thought Madame Darlan might throw a fit of the vapours at the very idea of the hammam. The lure of a private invitation to the palace, however, was hard to resist. 'That would be marvellous,' she managed through compressed lips.

'Excellent. Come after the afternoon prayers. We can relax and get to know one another.'

Madame Darlan looked as if she would rather let an asp strike her, but, smart social climber that she was, she knew how to play the game. 'I look forward to it.'

'Not as much as I do,' murmured Colette as we watched her make her escape across the room. 'It won't just be her body that gets stripped bare in that steam room.'

I watched as Madame Darlan reached Rauff's side. He stood with another group of people, but she briefly brushed his hand with her own – so briefly that no one would have noticed unless they were looking out for it, just as I was. Of the two, Madame Darlan seemed the more dangerous, as well as the more ruthless. She might be a tougher nut to crack, but crack her we would. All part of the plan.

I gazed at Rauff's head, lining up a gun in my mind, imagining it exploding. A far quicker death than he'd allowed any of his victims. Including my husband.

Rauff turned his head to speak to the man beside him, and that was when I saw him, the lone wolf at the edge of the group, dressed like Rauff in the black tunic and trousers of the SS.

Vulke.

He was here.

58

By the time we'd made it across the room, Vulke had evaporated like the evil djinn he was – a demon in human form according to Arabic lore. They had it about right.

'Do you think he saw you?' murmured Colette.

'I don't think so. If he'd seen either of us, I'm pretty sure we'd know about it.'

Colette's hand was on her throat, remembering. The body always remembers, even if the mind tries to blank something out.

'Come on,' I said. 'Let's get out of here. See if we can find him.'

Someone spoke from behind us as we sidled towards the archway that led from the salon. 'Leaving so soon?' His French was heavily accented. Even without the accent, I would have known who it was. There was something about it, a flatness of tone underpinned by expectation. This was a man used to getting his own way.

'Walther Rauff,' he said as he moved to block the archway. 'I am in command of the SS here in Tunisia.'

I'd always thought I'd know what to say when I finally met

him, this man who was responsible for the murder of so many innocents, including my Andrzej. But when it came to it, my throat closed, constricting the words I so wanted to say. Words that would no doubt have got us killed.

Beside me, Colette was similarly silent, although I imagined for different reasons. She at least had a cool head on her. I was still struggling to remain composed when a familiar figure interjected herself between us.

'Walther, there you are. I see you've met my friends, Nadia and Colette.'

His social smile turned into a leer. Whatever was going on between them, Simone evidently had Rauff dangling on the end of a very alluring string. Interesting. I might revise my opinion of the two mistresses. It took a wily woman to play dumb while getting exactly what she wanted. *Chapeau*, Simone. Rauff was putty in her hands.

He clipped his heels together and executed a little bow, smaller than the one he'd offered the Bey. 'I have indeed. It was good to meet you, ladies.'

With that, he walked away, shooting a last glance back at Simone. That was all the proof I needed.

'Looks like she's got him right where she wants him,' I murmured as we seized our chance to slip through the archway and on towards the courtyard, walking at a sedate pace so as not to arouse suspicion and casting glances all around from under our lashes.

The merest flicker of movement caught my eye, a shadow that could be the edge of a black jacket.

'Over there,' I hissed, tugging Colette towards the fountain framed by its own pillars, which were wide enough to slide behind. From there, I peered out, scanning the courtyard.

Everyone else was still in the salon or had already left. The musicians had long ago ceased to play. There was just the sound of the water rising and falling, tumbling into its wide basin, the oasis of life, along with our breathing. No, not just our breathing. The unmistakable sound of a shoe treading on marble as softly as it could. Not softly enough, though, to escape what my mother always called my 'bat ears'. Those ears had served me well when Vulke struck before. They served me again now.

He appeared from the far side of the courtyard, padding back through another archway like the animal he was, a beast on the hunt for its prey, sniffing the air as he went, eyes flicking everywhere. When he drew level with our hiding place, he paused, taking in the fountain. I could feel Colette's breath on the back of my neck as we stood stock-still, my fingers on my thigh, reaching for the gun strapped to it. Not the ideal place to take him out, but needs must. At least I wouldn't miss this time. I could see the bulge of his gun in its holster. There was probably another strapped to his thigh too and a knife at his ankle. These bastards liked to come well equipped.

He glanced away, towards the salon. This was it. My chance. I raised my pistol, aiming it for his heart. Or where most people had one. A clear line of sight. My finger squeezed the trigger. But someone else glided into view. Oh God, no. A servant emerging from the salon, bearing a tray. Vulke clocked him too. The servant was passing in front of him now, head lowered respectfully. He was past. And so was the moment. Vulke was now walking the way he'd come, back into the main salon, no doubt to report to his master. I wanted to scream in frustration.

'Let's get out of here,' I whispered.

We proceeded as quickly as we could to the other end of the palace, through a maze of more courtyards to the women's quarters, only speaking once we were safely in Colette's room – a spacious chamber even bigger than mine, with those ornate arches framing the windows, the bed set into an alcove beneath another arch, and a low silver table in the centre of the room, the lamp on top of it sending out a soft light.

'Let's wait here until we're sure everyone has left,' Colette murmured. 'The reception was due to end half an hour ago so it won't be long. After that, it should be safe enough to go back out.'

'I'm not so concerned about my own safety,' I growled. 'It's Vulke who should be worried.'

'All in good time,' Colette soothed. 'I understand how you feel about Vulke, but we must first make a plan and then follow it. Let's see what we can get out of Madame Darlan and then work the other one. Don't you worry. We'll get them both, in the end. Rauff and Vulke.'

'Vulke's mine. I want him to know, in his dying seconds, exactly who killed him and why. I want Andrzej's name to be the last word he ever hears.'

'Is that what you were going to do back there? Stand over the man while he died?'

'Yes.'

Colette shook her head. 'Then you're crazy. The whole place would have come running the moment they heard a gunshot. There are guards everywhere. We would both have been arrested. Rauff would have insisted on it, and the Bey would have had no choice. You might have a death wish, but I don't, so if that's the way you feel, then I'm out of here.'

I stared at her, the thudding of my heart slowing as her words penetrated my brain. She was right of course. I'd been acting on animal instinct. On a carnal desire for revenge. A desire that would get one or many of us killed if I let it control me. I had to think more rationally. To focus on saving the living rather than avenging the dead.

One time, a boar had picked up my scent and charged, much as Vulke might have done. We'd only escaped by shinning up a tree. Those beasts could kill. These Nazi beasts could torture and then kill, as they had Andrzej and so many others. Slow down I would. Until I got my chance. Then I would move so fast Vulke wouldn't even see me coming until it was too late.

'I'm sorry,' I said. 'You're right. We'll stick to the plan, I promise.'

Until the plan no longer worked for me.

Or Vulke.

59

PRESENT DAY, CAIRO, EGYPT

SOPHIE

Josh ran his hands through his hair, grimacing at the notebook in front of him, hunched over the narrow desk in my hotel room while I sat on the bed, turning the pages of Nadia's storybook, which I'd taken with me the day I'd discovered it.

I glanced up at his grunt of exasperation.

'If there is a code in here, I can't crack it.'

Disappointment flooded through me, washing away the hope that had been bubbling up since the night before. It wasn't the only thing that had kept me awake into the small hours though. 'In the Mood' was running through my head on repeat. On my waist, the imprint of Josh's hand lingered, a warmth that spread across my belly and on up to my heart.

We'd glided together across that floor just as Nadia had done with Tom, at least in my mind. I wasn't kidding when I told him I wasn't much of a dancer, but he somehow made me feel like one, guiding me, surprisingly light on his feet for such a tall guy. Those feet were tapping now in frustration as he tried one thing after another, scribbling down various permutations while I sat watching him, twisting my hands.

'Maybe there isn't a code after all. It could just be her notes and records. As simple as that.'

Josh set his pen down with a sigh, the sheet of paper in front of him covered in his scribbled attempts. 'Maybe. But I don't think so. Nadia was so precise. She documented everything. She made sure to write only half of the coordinates on the back of the photograph and the other half in her notebook. Why wouldn't she leave a record somewhere of what she'd done with the gold?'

'Because she didn't want anyone to find it?'

He rubbed his eyes. 'That's just it. Why hide it and then simply leave it there? Nadia knew she was leaving you the villa. Why not leave you the gold as well? It's not like she could take it with her, and it obviously meant something or she wouldn't have kept it in the first place. Yes she may have thought it was cursed, but she still hung on to it. It doesn't make sense.'

'All true, although I doubt Nadia thought that far ahead when she hid the gold.'

'No, but she could have told you about it when she knew she was dying. It wasn't a sudden death, was it?'

'She had cancer,' I said quietly, remembering her stoic acceptance of it, her refusal to feel sorry for herself or to let anyone else pity her. 'I've had a long and lovely life,' she would say. Long maybe, but lovely? When she'd lost not one but two loves of that life along with her only child? 'I visited her a lot over those months, although towards the end, she didn't really have the energy to talk. What I hated was watching her grow so thin. She literally wasted away. I always thought of Nadia as full of life and energy. That's how I still like to think of her.'

'Of course you do. She was an amazing woman. That's why I'm not giving up on this. I have a feeling Nadia wouldn't want you to either. I just know in my gut that gold is the key to everything.'

'In that case, we'd better continue. Want me to take a look? You've been staring at those pages for hours. Give yourself a break.'

He yawned, stretching as he handed me the notebook. 'Knock yourself out. How are you getting on with that storybook?'

'It's lovely, but it's just stories and sketches. I can imagine Nadia writing them back at the villa, on her own.'

'Maybe we should go back there. If nothing else, to check on the place. And get a fresh perspective.'

I grabbed my bag and stuffed both books back in it. A fresh perspective was exactly what we needed. Besides, it was getting a little claustrophobic in here, with me on my bed and Josh inches away. 'Good idea. Let's go.'

He looked at me, startled. 'Whoa. What's the rush?'

'No rush,' I squeaked, instantly hating myself for that, for the fact the thought had even crossed my mind. A thought that made me feel like a traitor, stirring up the thrill of a possibility, or even a promise, I could no longer ignore.

60

The light in the library was once more inviting, its gilded warmth offering us the perfect place to work. I chose one of the armchairs, giving it a good bashing before settling down with the notebook while Josh roamed the shelves, looking for anything else that might help. I could imagine Nadia in this room, perhaps writing her stories at the desk under the window. I glanced over at it, bathed in sunlight. As I did so, a flash of movement caught my eye.

'Josh, there's a kid running round out there in the courtyard. Look.'

He peered through the window. 'Where? I don't see anything.'

'Right there. By the old fountain. A little boy. Wait a minute...' I looked down at the storybook laid on the table beside my armchair, staring at the cover. 'It's him. The same boy,' I whispered.

Josh was looking at me as if I'd lost it. 'Sophie, there's nothing there.'

I took a breath. Looked away and looked back. The boy was looking right at me, smiling and waving as he perched on the fountain's edge, and then a little girl ran up to him. There was something about her cheeky smile that struck a chord. It wasn't just that she was the other child from Nadia's drawing. There was something else, something closer to home. 'I... You're right. Never mind. Trick of the light.'

He was still staring at me, brow puckered. 'Wait a minute... back in the ballroom that day, you were talking about people, but there was no one there either. The music you said you heard. You see things, don't you? And hear them?'

I dropped my head. 'Now you really do think I'm nuts.'

'Not at all. If there's one thing I've learned in life, it's that nothing is certain. *Hamlet*, remember? "There are more things in heaven and earth", as we both know.'

I raised my head. 'I remember.'

'So no, I don't think you're nuts at all. I think you're very special.'

At that exact moment, a book fell off the shelf beside Josh and landed at his feet. A red leather-bound book. *The Complete Works of Shakespeare*. As it landed, it fell open at the same page, *Romeo and Juliet*, Act Three, Scene Five. But then it would do. Or maybe not. If Josh could take a leap of faith, then so could I. I gazed at the page again, taking in every line, rereading them over and over, an idea forming.

Romeo and Juliet. Tom's favourite play, according to Nadia. The play I'd taught over and over, along with all its context and controversies, including the theory that Francis Bacon had written it rather than Shakespeare, interweaving all kinds of hidden messages within the poetry.

Bacon. The man who loved symbols and codes so much he'd invented his own. Of course.

'I've got it,' I cried, grabbing a pen and piece of paper from my bag, along with Nadia's notebook, then frantically scribbling down what I saw. And once I *had* seen it, it was easy.

I waved my piece of paper at Josh in triumph. 'She used

Bacon's Cipher. Francis Bacon. Some people believe it was he who wrote Shakespeare's plays and inserted code into them. Only it's not really a code – it's steganography, hiding a message within a message. Look, here, how some of the letters are different? That's the Baconian code.'

I could see the light dawning in his eyes. 'So what does it say?'

'See here? It says to go where life flows. And here – this looks to me like another set of coordinates. Or rather, half a set.'

'"To go where life flows..." What does that mean?'

I grinned at him. 'It means the fountain in the courtyard. That courtyard right outside this window. A fountain in an Islamic garden signifies life. I bet you anything the gold is buried there somewhere.'

'Then what are we waiting for?'

61

20 JANUARY 1943, PALACE OF THE BEY, TUNIS, TUNISIA

NADIA

The women's hammam consisted of a series of rooms, starting with the hot relaxation room, or *beit skoon*. I noticed Antoinette dabbing at her forehead with the corner of her *fouta*, the traditional garment she kept wrapped tightly around her, the sweat already pouring from her brow. Good. By the time we'd finished, she'd do a lot more than sweat.

'Have you not visited a hammam before?'

She glanced at me and then hurriedly looked away. For a Frenchwoman, Antoinette was astonishingly prudish. There was no one else here so I'd deliberately dispensed with my *fouta,* as had Colette. Nothing like disarming someone with your naked flesh. I stretched my legs in front of me, luxuriating in the heat that penetrated each muscle and tendon, liquefying them. The tiles under my buttocks were warm, the sweat trickling down between my breasts. Colette had her head tilted back, eyes closed, although I knew she was taking in everything. Time to turn up the heat.

'Shall we move on?' I murmured. The next room was even

hotter. If Antoinette was uncomfortable now, she was going to hate this even more.

Sure enough, she began to shift around within a few minutes of us settling on the next bench, her face now puce and her hair plastered to her brow. We were only supposed to stay in here just as long as it took to sweat out every last bit of stress and dirt before moving on to wash it all off, but a little pressure never hurt. By the time we reached the washroom, Antoinette was finding it hard to breathe. She tried to clutch the basin full of cold water, but her grip kept slipping.

I steadied it for her so she could wash from head to toe, something she achieved while still clutching her *fouta*. 'Are you alright, my dear?'

'Yes, yes. I feel a little faint, that's all.'

My eyes met Colette's over the top of her head. Time for the next step.

In the massage room, a well-built woman was waiting, her meaty arms testament to years spent ironing out the knots in a thousand backs. Alongside her, two assistants, all of them bribed in advance. The assistants got to work on Colette and me, scrubbing us all over so that our skin practically peeled away before subjecting us to a vigorous massage. I kept one eye on Antoinette the whole time. She was hating this, I could see it. She hesitated when her masseuse indicated she should take off her *fouta,* only giving in when it became apparent she had no other option. As soon as she did so, I saw why she'd been so reluctant.

The welts across her back were clearly visible, livid against her lily-white skin. There were bruises too, all over her buttocks and upper arms, which looked to be fresher than the welts, perhaps a few days old.

The moment she'd dropped her *fouta* to the floor, she lay down with her eyes tightly closed, just as a child does when they believe you can't see them if they can't see you. My stomach contracted, repulsion and pity fighting one another. She'd made her choices. This had to be either her husband's doing or Rauff's. Perhaps both. The thought was so obscene, I pushed it away. For now. Information was power, and now that we knew someone's predilection, we might be able to use it later to gain leverage.

Colette twisted her head so we were gazing at one another. I arched an eyebrow towards Antoinette. She blinked to indicate she'd seen it too. Our bribes had bought silence. Anything that happened in this hammam stayed here.

As we moved on to the final relaxation room, I rehearsed what I was about to say.

'Enjoy that?' I murmured as Antoinette sank onto the bench beside us, her limbs a little looser, her face too. Her masseuse had worked around the bruises and welts, using all her skill. Even so, I'd heard Antoinette muffle a gasp once or twice. Maybe she even liked the pain.

'You know what, I did.' She smiled, transforming that stern face into one that was altogether more youthful and alive. 'I don't think I've ever had a massage quite like that before.'

Colette let out a contented sigh. 'I love it. That feeling afterwards. It's just like great lovemaking.'

A tiny pause. I wondered if she'd gone too far. And then Antoinette, too, sighed. 'I wouldn't know,' she said.

'Is your husband not all that good in that department?'

Colette's tone was teasing now. That was how we'd agreed to play it – light-hearted chatter among girls.

The silence that followed was longer than the last one. 'Not really. But I have a lover, you know.'

I gave her a conspiratorial smile. 'You do?'

She was bursting to tell. Of course she was. In my experience, any woman conducting an illicit affair felt deeply lonely within it and longed to share, even with relative strangers, as we were. 'Yes, although it's a little complicated.'

She was the centre of our attention now. The attention she craved. 'How so?'

'Promise you won't say anything to anyone?'

'Of course not,' we chorused.

The smug smile on her face said it all. 'He's someone important here, you see. A German officer. In fact, he's in charge of the entire SS in this country. Rommel himself put him in charge.'

I had to push my smile wider. 'My goodness. That does sound glamorous.'

She simpered. 'I know. I suppose some people might disapprove, but after all, the Nazis talk a lot of sense. At least, that's what my husband says, and I agree. Those ghastly people should not be allowed to breed, let alone live. They're all cheats and liars, you know, stealing from the rest of us. Walther – that's his name – he says we must get rid of all the inferior races and ensure a pure, Aryan nation.'

I gaped at her, hurriedly rearranging my expression into one of understanding. She was hardly the Aryan ideal with her dark, almost black hair and aquiline nose. In fact, she could easily have been mistaken for a Jew. I wondered if that was part of the attraction, if Rauff enjoyed beating her because of the way she looked. 'I see. He sounds like an interesting man, your Walther.'

'Oh he is. And so intelligent. He knows all about world politics and how these things really work. He tries to teach me, but I really have little interest in that kind of thing.'

My glance slid sideways and met Colette's. I suspected his teaching methods might prove unorthodox. 'Is that what you two talk about? Politics?'

A titter. 'We don't really do much talking, if you know what I mean. He shows me. That's what he says. He's showing me the error of my ways and says I should be grateful to him.'

A fiery lump of fury was threatening to burst from my

throat. I had to swallow it back before I could speak again. 'Are you? Grateful?'

'Oh yes. It hurts, you know, but I have to learn. That's what Walther says. What my husband says too.'

'Your husband also shows you the "error of your ways"?' I couldn't quite disguise the contempt in my voice.

She threw me a worried glance. 'I do what my husband tells me. That's the role of a good wife and mother. I am there to support him in any way I can.'

Colette examined her nails, pretending to lose interest. 'Men, eh?'

Antoinette bridled. 'My husband is a good man too. We are a team. That's what he says. Walther can help him in his work and so help us as a family. I do my duty. Isn't that the role of every good woman, to support men?'

'Of course it is,' I soothed. 'It sounds as if you have everyone's best interests at heart. I should like to meet him, your Walther. He sounds remarkable.'

She looked like the cat who'd not only got the cream but the entire dairy too. 'He is. In fact, I'm going to see him after this. My skin will be all lovely and soft for him.'

All lovely and soft so he could mark it again. 'Don't let us keep you if you have an appointment. We can play baccarat another time.'

And there would be another time, plenty of them. First, though, we had to follow Antoinette to her assignation. It shouldn't be too hard. She was evidently not overburdened with brains. Or a conscience.

As I rose from the bench, so did Colette, signalling that our time in the hammam was over. Our time on Rauff's trail, however, was just gathering pace.

62

Antoinette reappeared fully dressed, complete with the mask of politesse that hid her true self. For a moment back there, in the hammam, I'd almost felt sorry for her. That quickly dissipated in the face of her haughty sneer.

'We can summon you a velo,' said Colette.

'No need. I'll just go and hail one in the street.'

Her smile was practiced. Evasive.

'We'll come with you then,' I said, looping my arm through hers. 'Can't have you in the street on your own. That simply wouldn't do.'

She had no choice but to grit her teeth and let us accompany her out of the women's gate, past the guard who stood to attention and on into the dusty street beyond. Velos, the bicycle-drawn buggies that served as taxis here, were not easy to come by since the occupation. We had to walk down the street to the next corner before we spotted one, and I hailed it.

Antoinette climbed in and instructed the driver. 'La Cathédrale.'

I was fairly certain that wasn't her final destination. For one thing, Antoinette didn't look the praying sort, and for another, she'd already told us she was off to meet Rauff. Unless the pair of them wanted to make a joint confession, my guess was that her real destination was somewhere nearby.

We watched the velo disappear in a cloud of dust. 'We have to follow her.'

'Are you sure that's a good idea?'

'Who cares?'

At that moment, another velo came around the corner. I practically threw myself under it. 'Follow that velo,' I commanded, indicating the cloud of dust ahead that was diminishing by the minute. 'And hurry.'

The driver looked at us without a trace of surprise. Since the occupation, the local people had become more fatalistic than ever. Our driver, though, seemed to enjoy the chase, pedalling like fury but instinctively keeping back just enough so that Antoinette wouldn't spot us.

We followed Antoinette all the way to the Majestic Hotel, where her velo halted outside the main entrance. The Majestic occupied a corner of the Avenue de Paris, the German officers entering and exiting its colonial magnificence an indication that it had been requisitioned by the enemy. Our false papers might be expertly forged, but I still didn't want to risk trying them out in a hive swarming with Nazis.

'Go around the corner and stop,' I instructed our driver, handing him a handsome tip along with our fare as we alighted.

The driver jerked his head towards the hotel. 'Bad people.'

'Very bad people.'

He grinned at us both, exposing the gaps where his teeth had been, and then spat at the hotel, saluting us as he pedalled off.

On the other side of the avenue was a café.

'Shall we sit it out in there and see if they leave? She might just be meeting him here.'

Colette looked dubious. 'She might, although with all those rooms, I imagine they'll be quite some time.'

'How long does it take to whip the life out of someone?'

From behind us, the measured footsteps of someone who was used to marching. An officer dressed in the olive-green uniform of the Afrika Korps strode past us then stopped and turned. 'Do you ladies need some help?'

I simpered in an approximation of a good Vichy wife like Antoinette. 'Thank you but we are just a little late to meet our husbands. We were trying to think of a good excuse.'

At that, he threw back his head and laughed. 'Spent too long in the medina, did you?'

'Something like that.'

'Your secret is safe with me, and tell your husbands they are very lucky men.'

Colette smiled coquettishly. 'We will.'

The second he disappeared around the corner, we turned as one and walked back the other way. A few seconds more and he might have thought better of his gallantry, wondering why two women were wandering around so close to what were now officers' quarters. At best, he might have suspected us of prostitution. At worst, spying. Either way, the outcome would not have been good. I could feel my pistol pressing against my thigh in its holster as we strode towards the central park, in the opposite direction to the hotel. Rauff would have to wait. But not for too long.

I felt a familiar tightening in my stomach then, my instincts screaming at me. All at once, I bent and pretended to adjust my shoe.

'What are you doing?' Colette hissed as she bent down too, apparently trying to help me.

'I think we're being followed. There's a man by that fruit stand on the opposite side of the street. He stopped when we did. I can't get a good look at him without making it obvious. See if you can.'

I stood, holding out my arm as if to help Colette, swivelling as I did so to brush imaginary dust from her coat. That was all it took. A few seconds, no more. But in that time I got a clear enough look at him to be absolutely sure.

It was Vulke on our tail.

PRESENT DAY, CAIRO, EGYPT

SOPHIE

The fountain, like the rest of the courtyard, was crumbling, the tiles that adorned its basin cracked and worn. The fountain itself was ceramic and rose in tiers, each separated by its own smaller basin. Water had long ago ceased to flow from it, but this was still the place of life in the garden, even if that life, like Nadia's, had changed form. I could feel her with us as we started to examine the base, the most logical place to start, although there was no sign of the little boy.

'There's no way she buried it under this unless this fountain was put in after she did so,' said Josh. 'Look at it. The base is at least six inches thick and solid stone. I think we're wasting our time.'

He was right. Unless she had a jackhammer to hand, Nadia could not possibly have got through this lot. So much for Baconian codes. I stared mutely at the surrounding jungle, the mass of shrubs and weeds I had still to clear. 'Wait. This isn't the only source of water in the garden.' I pointed towards the summer house. 'I'm sure I saw a tap over there.'

Sure enough, there was a brass tap affixed to a post, aged with verdigris and so stiff I couldn't budge it.

'Remember I told you her pet mongooses lived in this summer house? Apparently the butler refused to have them in the house after they ripped up her room.'

'I don't blame him,' said Josh. 'We've seen the evidence, after all. Here, let me have a go.'

The tap squealed under his grip, finally turning a few inches, although not a drop of water came out.

'Let's take a look in the summer house. There might be some tools in there.'

The summer house was as unloved as the rest of the place, stacked with rotting garden furniture, carboard boxes and empty bottles. I picked one up, peering at the label. 'Veuve Clicquot. Nice. This was probably left over from one of their parties.'

Josh ferreted behind the broken furniture, sending up more clouds of dust. I ran my finger down the champagne bottle, leaving a clean line where dust had settled on it too. How long had it been here? And why hadn't Nadia thrown it away years ago? Then again, her house in London had been cluttered with her treasures, objects she'd picked up on her travels, along with photographs and, of course, books everywhere.

With a cry of triumph, Josh hauled a spade out from behind a pile of deck chairs. 'Here we go.'

Back outside, he drove it into the ground about a foot from the tap, then pulled it out and did the same three more times, forming the outline of a square. The grass here was lusher, possibly thanks to the water supply.

Sure enough, as Josh dug up the square sod of earth, we could see the pipe below, the earth around it dark with moisture. He dropped to his knees and started to scrabble in the hole he'd made with his fingertips, carefully scraping through the earth before sitting back with a sigh. 'Nothing.'

We tried several more spots around the tap, Josh digging out the holes while I sifted through them, my fingers eagerly reaching through the soil, feeling for a bag, a box, anything that might have contained the gold.

'We don't even know what we're looking for,' I said, swiping my hair back from my face. It was cooler here in the shade of the summer house, but even so, the sweat was trickling from my brow and down the back of my neck. 'All we know is that she brought back some of this gold. Maybe. We don't know how much or what it is. It could be gold bars or coins or even jewellery.'

'Wait,' muttered Josh. 'I think I can feel something.'

I held my breath, watching as he dug around some more, moving with care so as not to break anything he might find.

At last, he began to tug on something, shovelling the dirt aside with his other hand to help loosen it. A few more seconds and he had it in his hand – an earthenware pot with a lid resembling the canopic jars found in Egyptian tombs. He handed it to me. 'You do the honours.'

I prised the lid open as carefully as I could. A silk pouch was stuffed inside, tied with a drawstring. I undid the drawstring with trembling fingers and let the silk folds fall away to reveal several heavy, intertwined gold necklaces, a couple of rings, one of which was almost the twin of my engagement ring, and five crescent-shaped gold earrings along with a fine, gold ribbon bracelet set with what appeared to be a carnelian. The longest necklace was made up of various beads and pendants, some of which looked like goddesses. Another consisted of four gold chains from which dangled coins and what looked to be charms, including a bull's head. I stared at the hoard, mesmerised. It seemed to have come from another world.

'Is this really it?' I whispered. 'Dido's gold?'

Josh opened his mouth to speak at the exact second I heard it. The click of a gun.

64

I didn't recognise him at first. But then it dawned on me. The man reading a book back at the hotel as we'd spoken to Mohammed. At least, that was what he'd pretended to be doing. It had struck me then that it was odd he was wearing his red baseball cap indoors. He was still wearing it now. A red baseball cap. Oh my God. It came to me in that moment. The witness had described the driver speeding from the scene of the crash as wearing one. Could this be him?

Close up, I could see he was in his late thirties or early forties. Medium height. Nothing distinguishable about him.

'So sorry to interrupt,' he said, 'but I believe that's mine.'

A Brit, although his voice sounded put on, as if he was posher than he actually was. A gentleman thief.

He waved his gun at my hand, indicating the gold I was clutching even tighter now. 'Be a good girl and hand it over. And you – put that spade down.'

Girl? I glared at him. Was that gun even real? 'Who the hell are you?'

Josh laid the spade on the ground and then held up his hands. 'Do as he says, Sophie.'

'You what? No way.'

Josh made a tiny motion with his head, barely a shake.

The gunman leered, exposing his gums. 'You heard the man. He's smart. So why don't you listen to him and give the gold to me?'

A tremor rippled from my ankles, through my legs and on up so it rattled my ribcage. I gritted my teeth, willing my arms not to shake too. My calves were starting to cramp. I'd been kneeling for far too long, next to the hole we'd dug out together. Beside me, Josh was still crouched, apparently at ease, although I could sense his mind working at double speed.

The gunman must have sensed it too because he took a step towards us. 'Try any funny business and she's dead.'

I lifted my eyes, determined to stare him down. He had a thin, ferrety face. Weak mouth. Rats' eyes, shining bright with greed. 'Who are you?' I croaked.

He ignored me, swooping down to snatch the gold from my grasp and tuck it into the bag strapped across his body. 'Thank you,' he sneered. 'Nice doing business with you.'

At that moment, Josh sprang to his feet with a roar, slamming the man in the chest with his elbow while chopping at his wrist with his other hand so the gun flew from his grip, landing a few feet away. Both men dived for it, kicking and grappling, rolling over and over. I grabbed the spade, but they were moving too fast.

Another split second and Josh rolled free. This was my chance.

As I brought the spade up, the man flung himself forward, his fingers closing around the gun. He threw himself onto his back, pointing the gun straight at me. 'Drop it,' he snarled.

I let the spade fall to the ground.

Keeping his gun trained on us both, he edged backward towards the gate. A few more seconds and he was through it. I heard the gate clang behind him even as Josh raced over to it. As

I sprinted after him, I heard him shouting something in Arabic, but it was no use. The man had vanished into thin air.

We ran all the way to the main road, scouring it for a sighting of him, asking anyone and everyone if they'd seen a man in a red baseball cap. His mousey brown hair was as indistinguishable as the rest of him, but I would recognise that ferrety face anywhere.

'Josh – the red baseball cap. The witness said the driver of the car speeding away from where Ben was hit was wearing one. Should we call the police?' I gasped as we finally turned and headed back to the villa.

'And tell them what? That we dug up this treasure and a man stole it at gunpoint? A man who was wearing a baseball cap that millions of other people on this planet wear? They'd probably arrest us for some invented by-law.'

'Millions of people didn't kill Ben.'

'I know, but the police here won't care.'

I stared at Josh. 'So that's it? We're not even going to try?'

He stopped in his tracks and took me by the shoulders. 'Listen to me, Sophie. Remember the police in England and how they handled Ben's death? I promise you that the police here are a hundred times worse. If anything, they'll make it harder to find this guy.'

'Then *we* have to.'

'Damn right we do, and the first place we're going to start is back at your hotel.'

'He won't go back there, will he?'

A muscle was working in Josh's cheek. Other than that, he appeared deadly calm. 'He might, he might not, but we have a secret weapon, don't forget.'

'We do?'

'Yes, we do. The same weapon Nadia had. Mohammed.'

65

20 JANUARY 1943, TUNIS, TUNISIA

NADIA

There was a café a few yards further along the street. I grabbed Colette by the arm. 'In here.'

We strode straight through the tables – mostly occupied by what appeared to be Vichy wives – and past the counter, ignoring the stares, pushing open the kitchen door and carrying on until we exited through the back door into a narrow passage full of rubbish, stepping over old oil cans and sacks of rotting vegetables until we reached the road.

Emerging onto it, I could see it was the boulevard that ran parallel to the one that housed the Majestic. We turned north, staying close to the shops and cafés that lined it and provided a modicum of cover. Not a velo in sight. Any moment now, Vulke would realise where we'd gone, if he hadn't already.

I scanned the road ahead. 'What about that van?'

Colette glanced at me and then raised her hand to flag it down, assailing the driver with a stream of words I didn't understand. Whatever she said, it worked.

'He says he'll take us.'

I returned the driver's smile. 'Great.'

As we jumped in, I looked back. There he was, emerging from the passage. Too late. We were already roaring away, the van's engine squealing in protest as the driver kept his foot to the floor, taking a left then a right, navigating the backstreets and then on up a boulevard, putting as much distance as he could between us and Vulke.

'I think we can forget about Vulke not recognising us,' I murmured. 'He obviously knows who we are, although if he'd wanted to kill us, he'd have done so already.'

'So what do you think he wants?'

'I don't know. More importantly, how did he know that we'd be here right now, in this area? First the palace and now this. Someone has blown our cover. I'm betting it's the same someone who's been leaking other intelligence. He was following us before Antoinette met with Rauff, so it can't have been her. Besides, I don't think she's made us. Of course, it could be someone at the palace.'

Colette frowned. 'I doubt it. We've been so careful. Only the Bey knows why we're really here, and he hates the Germans as much as we do.'

'Well then,' I said. 'That narrows it down to those of us who were there when we planned this.' I cast my mind back to that steamy bathroom. 'Unless someone there accidentally let it slip.'

'Everyone knew it was a top-secret meeting. You'd have to be an idiot to blab, and none of us are that stupid. If someone passed on information, they meant to do it.'

One look at Colette's set expression and I knew she was right. Which meant we were back to our rat and the fact that it had to be one of us. Perhaps even someone who was here now. I could sense Colette beside me thinking the same. Our eyes met.

'I know it's not you,' I said. 'He nearly killed you, after all, when he was trying to get to me.'

Colette slid me a sly smile. 'Likewise. I've learned to trust my instincts. They've kept me alive so far.'

'And what do they tell you about me?'

She playfully punched my arm. 'That you're not bad for an uptight aristocrat.'

'You think I'm uptight?'

'Far from it. I was joking. I waved you off that night, remember? When you spent an awfully long time on that walk of yours.'

I grinned. Ah yes, our walk under the stars, alone beyond the Great Pyramid, sheltered by the sand dunes that had held us in their embrace. I could almost feel Tom's arms around me now, his mouth insistent on mine.

'You're blushing.' Colette jabbed me in the ribs, breaking my reverie.

'I am not.'

'Oh but you are.'

All at once, a car shot across the street in front of us and screeched to a halt, forcing our driver to slam on his brakes. In that instant, I recognised the figure that leaped from the vehicle and strode towards us, pistol raised.

'It's Vulke.'

'What do we do?'

I pulled my gun from its holster once more. 'We fight.'

66

I slammed open the van door, dropping to a crouch behind it, Colette doing the same on the other side, her gun in her hand too. The driver stared at us in panic, eyes wide with fright. Vulke raised his pistol and took aim.

'Get down!' I screamed.

Whether he understood my words or not, the driver reacted, throwing himself across the front seats as Vulke fired again and again, shattering the windscreen. I heard another screech of tyres and looked over my shoulder. 'There's more of them. We have to get out of here.'

The traffic had stopped behind and in front of us, horse-drawn carts, vans and the odd car forming an obstacle course between us and the German staff car that had halted behind them, an SS officer and a couple of his henchmen piling out.

'Most of these drivers are Germans,' muttered Colette. 'They stole all the private cars. We have to go.'

There was nowhere to run. To the right of us, shops. To the left, on the opposite side of the boulevard, I caught a glimpse of green. 'Follow me,' I hissed, raising my gun and firing back as we broke cover and darted across the road, through the oncoming traffic to hoots and shouts, and into the park beyond.

We pounded on, sprinting along winding pathways and then plunging off them through a wooded expanse, thrusting branches aside with care so as not to break them and betray our whereabouts, all the while listening out for our pursuers. For Vulke.

At last, we emerged from the trees onto a grassy expanse that rose to a hillock, peppered with saplings and shrubs. There was little to no cover here. We were totally exposed.

A shout from somewhere in the woods. They were right behind us.

'Up here,' Colette gasped, pointing to a cupola I could just see at the top of the hill. We skirted it, scrambling up the far side between the shrubs, keeping low, until finally we crested it to see a domed pavilion set on a ridge overlooking the park below. Four domes covered the corners of the building, with a larger dome soaring over the central, square-shaped room. I gazed up the delicate tracery that adorned the arches, almost Spanish in style, the whole supported by pillars while the side walls were open. From here we could see right across the park with its lawns and forested areas, tents set out in neat rows on the open grass. The Germans had taken this too.

A movement at the edge of the woods below had me reaching for my weapon.

'There they are. You see them?'

Colette's mouth was a grim line. 'I do.'

If they climbed the hill after us, we could easily take them out. The cupola gave us excellent cover, and we had the advantage.

We watched as they stopped at the foot of the ascent to the cupola, conferring. There were two of them besides Vulke. The officer must have stayed with his car. My fingers itched to pull the trigger. Patience. That was the name of this game.

Vulke looked up, scouting out the hill.

'Come on, you bastard,' I muttered. 'Let's have you.'

This was our chance. Without meaning to, we'd led Vulke into the perfect trap.

Beside me, Colette stood, nostrils flared, looking every bit as eager as I was to finish them off.

They stood for a couple more minutes, and then one of them pointed back towards the main road from which we had come. More discussion. Both of us glaring down at them, watching and waiting. Vulke looked up at us once more. Even from this distance, I could feel his eyes burning into us, or so it felt. Then he turned, said something to the others and headed back the way they had come, leaving us staring after them, frustration like a gut punch, choking up my gullet. We'd missed our chance.

67

PRESENT DAY, CAIRO, EGYPT

SOPHIE

Mohammed stared at us, aghast, his hand shaking as he folded it over mine. He had no idea who the man was.

Josh turned to the concierge. 'And you've never seen this man before either?'

'No. I've gone right through the hotel records. There were only three single European men staying here in the past week. Two checked out a few days ago, and the third is still here, but he is a regular guest. He doesn't match your description.'

I patted Mohammed's hand. 'It's alright. We're OK.'

The old man didn't look convinced. He muttered something, fury filling his face.

'He said that he will contact all his friends across the city,' said the concierge for my benefit. 'My grandfather has a network of people he knows from the old days. Many of them, like him, are still working in hotels and bars and the like.'

'I know.' I smiled at Mohammed. 'I understand that's how he helped Nadia after Tom died. Apparently, your grandfather knows everyone.'

Mohammed nodded at the mention of Nadia's name. 'Yes, yes. I help you.'

'In the meantime,' said Josh, 'we should go check on your room. Make sure he hasn't got in there too.'

Upstairs, my room appeared undisturbed.

'Are you sure we shouldn't call the police?'

'Perfectly sure. Let Mohammed do what he can. I think we should go and talk to David too. He's well connected in this city. He'll know what's best.'

As it turned out, David had already heard what had happened, thanks to Hassan. 'He told me you were running after some gunman down the street.'

'Not just some gunman. The man who held us up and stole Nadia's gold.'

David's eyes narrowed. 'Her gold? Good Lord. Where on earth did you find that? I thought she'd used it all up long ago when she bought the villa.'

'Not quite all of it. She buried the rest in the garden. Sophie worked out where it was from Nadia's old notebook. It turns out she used some sort of cipher.'

'A Baconian code,' I blurted out.

David gazed at me as if seeing me for the first time. 'Well I never. You're a chip off the old block, Sophie, working that one out.'

I felt my heart expand, like a flower unfurling in the sunlight. It was a warm feeling, being likened to Nadia, even if there was no way I could ever be half the woman she'd been. 'I doubt Nadia would have got caught out like that though.'

'It's my fault,' said Josh. 'I should have noticed he was tailing us. I was far too focused on finding the gold to even think someone might have followed us there.'

'What's done is done,' said David. 'What you need now is a plan.' He seemed, if anything, rejuvenated by what had happened. 'I have a few old friends in my pocket too. I'll make some calls. Wait here.'

While David disappeared into his study, Josh and I wandered out onto the balcony. I slumped onto one of the chairs set between pots of plants. 'I can't believe it. Any of it. Where the hell did he spring from? How did he know what we were doing?'

'Good question,' muttered Josh.

The man who appeared at the apartment was around David's age, his white hair curling around a cherubic face. He didn't look like a spy, but that was what he was, or rather, as David put it, 'My old friend Henry was stationed within the British embassy here.'

His handshake was firmer than I had expected, his gaze soft and inviting. Henry was clearly a master of his craft and quickly extracted everything I could tell him.

'Let me get this straight,' he said in a voice so gentle it would have persuaded a Trappist monk to talk. 'You caught a glimpse of this man at the hotel when you were discussing the gold and you are absolutely sure it's the same man who held you at gunpoint?'

'Correct.'

'How can you be so sure? You saw him for, what, perhaps a minute or so?'

I gaped at him. 'I-I know it was him. He was wearing a red baseball cap, just as he was when I saw him at the hotel. I thought at the time it was weird he was wearing it while he was indoors, but I suppose some people do. He has this narrow face and nose. Beady eyes, like a rat. And he was wearing the same clothes, I'm sure of it. A blue T-shirt and jeans.'

'Fair enough. You also think he might have followed you from England?'

'That's my gut feeling,' Josh butted in. 'It's too much of a coincidence that Sophie's fiancé, Ben, was killed in a hit-and-run and someone wearing a red baseball cap was witnessed fleeing the scene. That was just before Ben posted a photograph to the villa with a possible connection to this gold, and then another man in a red baseball cap turns up just as we dig some of it up to steal it from us. It has to be one and the same man or, at the very least, an accomplice.'

Henry accepted another of the melt-in-your-mouth butter cookies David had produced. 'Indeed. It does seem a little unlikely that a random stranger would pop up here with a gun.'

'Not just any old gun,' said Josh. 'A Glock 19. Then there was the way he moved. The guy has been trained in hand-to-hand combat. All of that adds up to some kind of military background and probably special forces.'

Henry chewed that one over. 'I agree. The important thing now is to try to think one step ahead of him. What will he do with this gold? How will he get it out of the country? It's not easy trying to march through airport security here with a bag full of antiquities. The authorities are very hot on that kind of thing.'

'Wait a moment,' I said, drawing the notebook from my pocket. 'There are coordinates in here. There are also coordinates on the back of the photograph Ben posted to the villa. Neither is a full set but, put together, we think they might lead us to where they dumped Rommel's gold during the war, which is a much bigger haul than the jewellery we dug up at the villa.'

Henry dabbed at his lips with his handkerchief. 'Rommel's

gold, eh? I've heard the stories, although I must say, I've never quite believed them. Now I understand your aunt had something to do with it?'

'My great-aunt Nadia, yes. She served here during the war, as a spy. She was sent to Tunisia on a mission. According to what you told me, Josh, the gold was stolen from the Jewish people there by this Colonel Rauff, who smuggled it out of the country on a boat. Nadia tried to stop him, along with her comrades. That's when her great love, Tom, was shot. She managed to save some of the gold jewellery that belonged to her friend's family while saving the life of Josh's grandma, Céline. Nadia brought that jewellery back here, to Cairo, along with Tom, who sadly succumbed to his injuries. She buried the jewellery at the villa where he died. I believe she intended me to find it. That's why she asked Ben to post the photograph here in the first place. We'd just found it when the man in the red baseball cap took it from us at gunpoint.'

'I see,' murmured Henry. 'A complicated story and a tragic one.'

'It is,' said Josh. 'Look, I'm sure you still have some useful contacts. Is there any chance you could ask them to circulate a description of this man? Find out if anyone recognises who it might be?'

'It's a long shot,' said Henry. 'I shall certainly give it a go.'

'Thank you.' I was still holding the notebook in my hand, stroking its worn edges. 'You know what you said about thinking one step ahead of him? Well, don't you think his best option is to get the gold out of the country on board a boat, just like Rauff did?'

At that moment, Josh's phone rang. He answered, listening intently for a couple of minutes before ending the call with a heartfelt *choukran*. 'That was the concierge at your hotel. He says Mohammed has heard back from an old friend at the

Marriott. A man fitting the description just checked out and ordered a cab to take him to the yacht club in Alexandria.'

The look in Josh's eyes mirrored my surge of excitement.

'Oh my God. I was right. That's our guy.'

69

2 FEBRUARY 1943, TUNIS, TUNISIA

NADIA

Simone Rivaud giggled as she raised her third martini to her mouth. 'It's such fun being here with you both.'

Colette clinked her glass against Simone's conspiratorially. 'Tell us more about this man of yours. How delicious, having a secret lover!'

Simone lowered her eyes, calculating the risk, her mind already too blurred to do so with any accuracy. 'Promise you won't tell?'

Colette placed her finger on her lips while I shook my head emphatically. 'Good heavens, no.'

Simone smirked and I noticed her lipstick was slightly smeared. Good. Another cocktail or two and we'd have everything we wanted.

'He's a very important man, you see,' she whispered theatrically. 'In fact...' She looked over her shoulder to see if anyone was listening. At this time of day, the bar was all but empty, the occupants of the Grand Hotel no doubt engaged in more pressing affairs, the only other occupants of the tables bored French wives just like Simone. 'He's in charge of Tunisia.'

I took a tiny sip of my sidecar. The day was drawing in, and with it, the air in the courtyard was cooling. Simone, though, was fired up now, desperate to spill the beans on her illicit affair. 'He's in charge of Tunisia? How thrilling.'

Another giggle, a little more high-pitched this time. 'Well, of course, not like the resident-general. I mean that he's in charge of the SS here.'

Colette arched an eyebrow. 'Heavens. Doesn't that worry you?'

Simone winked. 'Not at all. He's an absolute lamb when he's with me.'

An image sprang to mind of the welts and bruises on Antoinette's torso. Perhaps he was a lamb with Simone and a beast with her, although I doubted it. 'Oooh. He's a romantic then?'

She titled her head girlishly. 'So romantic. He calls me his *Schatzi*. That means his jewel or treasure. I make him work for it, you see. He doesn't get everything he wants from me, and that makes him all the more eager. I've told him – nothing else until he leaves his wife. He's going to, you know. Once Hitler has won the war. In the meantime, we just talk and cuddle. Nothing more. I think the poor man is lonely.'

'Adorable,' murmured Colette.

'Although...' Simone leaned forward now, lowering her voice once more. 'He does have some actual treasure. He told me. It's worth over twenty million. He calls it a tax on the Jews. They had to give him their gold in exchange for their lives. Personally, I think that's quite a fair deal, don't you? It's why I'm going to leave Charles for him. He can afford me.'

Mercifully, she was too busy taking another slurp of her drink to notice Colette's face darken. As she drained it, I summoned the waiter. 'Another for madame, if you will.'

'Excuse me one moment,' muttered Colette. 'I must go and powder my nose.'

I watched her back, stiff with contempt, as she disappeared through the doors into the interior of the hotel.

Simone lit up a cigarette. 'Is she a native, your friend?'

'Colette? She's part French and part Tunisian.'

A wild guess, but I wasn't going to let this woman get away with her prejudice.

'Oh, I see. Well, that helps, I suppose, although frankly I do find most of the local people to be paysans.'

Peasants. Nice. My initial warmth towards Simone had all but evaporated. As the drink dissolved her social layers, it revealed a vacuous snob. But then, what else did I expect from the wife of a man who was only too happy to do business with the Nazis while his wife serviced one of them?

'Tell me, do you ever meet your man here?' I asked, changing the subject back to Rauff.

She looked at me as if I were mad. 'Here? Of course not. This place is far too full of people I might know.'

'I see.'

She must have heard the frost in my tone because she quickly backtracked. Simone might be stupid, but she wasn't that stupid. She realised we could be of use to her, if only to allow her to unburden herself. 'We meet at the Majestic. Much safer. It's been requisitioned, you know, so it's only other German officers, and as Walti is in charge of them, they can't say anything now, can they?'

The titter was one of triumph this time. If only she knew he took Antoinette there too. Perhaps she did and didn't care. I wouldn't put it past her. Simone was evidently as callous as she was stupid, with the attendant morals of an alley cat. Except that I liked cats. 'I suppose not. That must be rather fun, sneaking off to a hotel like that. Surely your husband must suspect something?'

Simone pouted, that smear of lipstick only appearing all the more prominent. 'We don't "sneak off". My husband is never here. He's in Morocco at the moment, visiting his factories there. He cares only about his business, and so long as that's fine, then everything else is too, although he would be furious if he thought anyone was even looking at me. I am one of his possessions, after all. Besides, as I told you, Walti and I don't actually make love. Everything but. A woman has her needs, after all, and Walti fulfils mine.'

I had to force myself not to gag on my drink. The very thought was too much. 'You lucky thing. How often does he fulfil you, as it were? Just between us girls?'

'Every Friday, if we can manage it. Sometimes more. Poor Walti has to go away for work now and then, but otherwise, as often as we can.'

'My, my. You are a lucky woman.' My mind was working rapidly, calculating. If he was meeting Simone on Fridays and at other times and Antoinette at least once, there had to be some kind of pattern to it, otherwise he risked them running into one another. These women might pretend to be sophisticated about it, but I'd have bet anything they'd scratch one another's eyes out if it came to it. 'How on earth does he find the time with all his important work?'

Simone stubbed out her cigarette and immediately lit another. 'He's very organised. We always meet at the same time – noon on Fridays. That's his lunch hour, you see. Although he has adopted the French habit of a longer lunch, if you get my drift. If he can manage another time, he sends a boy with a message. If my husband is around for some reason, I do the same. It wouldn't do to disrupt Charles' business, but Walti and I, we're in love. You know how it is.'

I had to take a slug from my water glass to stop myself gagging again. It was also to hide the twitch of triumph now pulling at my own lips. We had it. We had his routine, which meant we could now plan around it. Little did Simone know she had just handed her Walti his death sentence.

I patted my mouth with my napkin. 'Oh I do. I certainly do.'

It looked like any other office in any other factory, one window overlooking the factory floor and the storage area beyond where more barrels of oats sat waiting to be turned into oatmeal. I had my Red Cross credentials while Colette carried a clipboard, supposedly to inspect the place.

'Come,' said Lucien. 'Let me show you around.'

The secretary carried on typing as we marched behind him down the steel stairs and between the conveyor belts, where local women picked over the oats, selecting and rejecting those that did not make the grade. We wove our way through towards the barrels at the far end, Lucien keeping up a monologue all the while, pointing to one part of the operation here and another there until at last we were standing among the barrels in front of a heavy steel door.

'This is another storage area,' he announced.

More stairs leading down, stone ones this time. At the bottom of them, a cavernous room that led to another and another. As we entered the final room lined with wooden crates, a familiar voice said, 'Hello.'

There they were, the two of them, sitting as they might in

the garden room back at the villa, whiling away the time with a game of cards, a few bottles of beer to hand.

'My darlings,' cried Nico. 'How marvellous to see you. I must say, gazing at this ugly mug all day does leave you longing for a pretty face.'

'Speak for yourself, Nico,' said Tom. 'Some of us are here on a mission.'

'So? Are you telling me we can't have a little fun along the way?'

I took the chair Tom was offering while Colette sat next to Nico.

'If you will excuse me,' said Lucien, 'I'll wait for you in the next room. It will look a little strange if I reappear without you, but please, take as long as you need.'

'No, Uncle, stay,' urged Colette, turning to the rest of us. 'Lucien is my mother's brother as well as the representative here for Agency Africa. He knows more about the Nazis and what they are up to here than any of us. We need him.'

'Indeed we do,' said Tom. 'Please do join us, Lucien. Now, Nadia, if you would be kind enough to brief us on what you two have discovered.'

'We have information about Rauff's routine,' I said. 'At least, the one that involves his mistresses. He meets a woman called Simone Rivaud every Friday between noon and around 1.30 p.m. at the Majestic Hotel.'

'The Majestic has been requisitioned,' added Colette. 'Rauff has a room there where he also brings his other mistress, Antoinette Darlan.'

'Quite a player, this Rauff,' said Nico.

'To look at him, you'd never imagine it,' I said. 'Colette and I followed Antoinette there when she went to meet him just after five in the afternoon. We're sure of Simone's timetable with him, and I suspect he keeps Antoinette to the same time too.'

'Midday is trickier,' said Tom. 'There will be far more

people around. Late afternoon would work better. If he's with this Antoinette for an hour or so, that gives us a window, although it might coincide with the call to prayer, which means more people coming and going.'

'It also means Rauff is less likely to go anywhere afterwards,' I said. 'He sees Simone during his lunch break and then has to return to whatever he was doing. When Antoinette visits, he probably has a shower afterwards and then goes for dinner. It's the end of his day, after all, unless he's off on a raid somewhere.'

Tom's eyes met mine. 'Good point.'

'There is just one more thing,' I added. 'Vulke followed us outside the Majestic. I have no idea how he knew we were there, but he did, and it's evident he now knows exactly who we are. I'm sure he's also told Rauff.'

'Great. You're telling me you're compromised? Which means any op we now try to pull off is also compromised. Why the hell didn't you tell me this before?'

I met Tom's furious glare with one of my own. 'Not necessarily. Colette and I can easily disguise ourselves as local women. All it takes is a safseri, those long veils with which they cover themselves from head to toe. There is no way anyone, let alone Vulke, will guess who we are under one of those.'

'She's right,' said Colette, looking at her uncle. 'I'm sure my aunt has some spare?'

Lucien nodded. 'I'm sure she does. I will ask.'

Tom was still looking at me in that way he had, the one that suggested so much more than he was saying. I could tell what he was thinking because I was thinking the same. We still had a rat scuttling among us, although I was pretty much certain it was no one in this room. I knew it wasn't Tom or Colette. My instincts told me it wasn't Nico either. For one thing, Tom trusted him implicitly, and for another, I'd seen his file. That left Lucien. Anyone Słowikowski considered a comrade was OK in my book. Then again, could you ever be really sure about anyone? Impossible to say. Impossible, too, to plan anything without taking that risk, but we had no other option. There was too much at stake.

Nico reached for a map, opening it up and spreading it out on the table. 'This is the Majestic Hotel here. It sits on the corner of two boulevards. It's not going to be easy to get close enough to assassinate Rauff without being spotted and to then get away.'

I peered at the map. 'Do we know where Rauff's office is?'

'He is based at the hotel,' said Lucien, 'although he lives elsewhere, in a villa which is heavily guarded.'

'He brings his women to his headquarters? Just shows the arrogance of the man.'

'Arrogance is good,' murmured Colette. 'It's a weakness we can play on. He hates not getting what he wants. All men like that do.'

'Wait,' I said. 'There's a much simpler way. One that doesn't rely on getting the time right but on human nature.'

The men looked nonplussed, but Colette's eyes lit up. 'We play it like Simone. She's the bait.'

'We do. You think Rauff would fall for it?'

'I'm sure he would.'

Tom threw up his hands. 'Would you two care to enlighten the rest of us?'

I shared a smile with Colette. 'Absolutely. Simone, one of his mistresses, told us she doesn't give him everything he wants and that makes him putty in her hands. She's playing him, in other words. Unlike the other one, Antoinette. You should have seen her. Covered in welts and bruises. You'd have thought it would be the other way round with those two. As it turns out, Simone is by far the tougher.'

'But if she should suddenly decide to succumb,' said Colette, 'then Rauff would find that irresistible. She's a conquest, after all. And there's nothing the Germans like more than conquering. We just have to make sure the planned rendezvous is a long way from the hotel.'

'It all sounds very plausible,' drawled Nico, 'but how on earth are you going to persuade this Simone to play ball?'

'She has a jealous husband. A businessman who has dealings with the Nazis but is in Morocco right now. Rauff needs to keep him onside. We could get her out of the way while we send Rauff a message telling him that her husband is coming home early because he's suspicious and they need to meet on Thursday instead of Friday, in a different place. One where we can easily ambush him.'

'And you think Rauff would actually turn up?'

'He would if she makes it clear he'll get what he wants this time.'

Tom's eyes held mine. 'Yes, that would probably work.'

My mind skittered back to the day at the beach, lying in his arms on the sand, telling him I just wasn't ready. Tom, of course, had behaved like the perfect gentleman, even though the desire was naked on his face. I doubted Rauff was as patient.

'Simone hinted he's been pushing her for more. We know he's a sadistic bully, and that type always thinks they're entitled. Rauff won't be able to resist claiming his prize.'

'I agree,' said Colette. 'Although we need to get Simone well out of the way. Somewhere out of the city.'

Lucien clapped his hands together. 'This is genius! My dear Colette, Nadia, you are to be congratulated. Only a woman could come up with a plan like this.'

'You know what?' Tom grinned. 'You're right. It is genius. Let's get to work.'

71

PRESENT DAY, CAIRO, EGYPT

SOPHIE

The yacht club was perched on the edge of the Mediterranean, overlooking the port of Alexandria with its citadel guarding the entrance to the eastern harbour. Our cab deposited us by a green gate that led into the clubhouse. Instead of going in, Josh headed back along the promenade, past the anglers and people sipping a sundowner outside a bar. A wooden jetty doglegged out into the harbour where boats large and small were moored. Josh stopped by the harbour wall, his baseball cap pulled low, pretending to admire the view. Across the water, Alexandria glittered in the setting sun, its domes arcing across the skyline, silhouetted against the light.

'Come here,' he muttered. 'Act like we're tourists.'

I was wearing an old T-shirt of Josh's that hung almost to my knees over my mud-stained shorts as an attempt at a disguise, but even though I had my sunglasses on, it wouldn't be hard to recognise us. 'If he's here, won't he just spot us anyway?'

'I'm banking on him being too busy getting ready to go to sea,' murmured Josh, his mouth perilously close to mine. I could feel the rough graze of his stubble against my cheek as he bent his head, acting as if we were deep in conversation while surreptitiously scanning the port over my shoulder. He smelled of earth and sweat overlaid with soap. Masculine smells that stirred memories along with something else. A sense of coming home.

'Over there,' Josh hissed. 'There's a dinghy approaching one of the yachts. I can only see one person in it. Wait until he gets closer.'

All of a sudden, he dropped his mouth onto mine, bending at the knees as he kissed me. 'Sorry,' he murmured against my mouth. 'He picked up speed. Didn't want him to make us.'

'Th-that's quite alright,' I stuttered.

'OK. He's on board. That's a nice yacht he's got there. Top of the range Sundancer. That thing can do forty knots at full speed. Let's give him two minutes and then we go after him.'

I didn't have time to ask how we were supposed to do that. Josh was already grasping my hand, guiding me along the jetty as if we were just another couple admiring the sunset, stopping when we drew level with a dinghy tied to it.

'Hop in.'

Moments later, we were pulling away from the jetty, Josh rowing in strong, even strokes, heading across the harbour towards a boat that floated at anchor a good hundred feet from the one our man had boarded. He brought the dinghy in on the opposite side so that the boat acted as a screen between us and our target, shipping his oars to leave us to rock on the swell. The sun was scattering its last glimmers across the water, casting a golden glow across the ripples that drifted towards the shore.

'What do we do now?' I whispered.

'We wait.'

When the sun finally slipped below the horizon, we set off once more, Josh pulling slower this time so that we didn't make a splash.

I gazed up at the sleek hull of the racing yacht as we stealthily approached. The boat was around fifty to sixty feet in length and clearly built for speed. Lights glowed from the portholes down below. His dinghy was tied to the stern, rising and falling in a gentle rhythm. A stepladder ran up the stern and onto the deck.

'Hold her steady,' Josh hissed as he grabbed the rope and tied our dinghy next to the other one before extending a hand to me. 'Come on.'

Holding his finger to his lips, he headed towards the bridge, moving as softly as a leopard stalking its prey. Padding as quietly as I could in his footsteps, I noticed something sticking from his belt. A gun. Shit. This was serious. Of course it was serious. Blind panic blared, red, across my vision.

We were standing at the top of the steps that led below. I could smell coffee being brewed. Hear the sounds of someone moving around, opening and shutting cupboards. Such ordinary, domestic sounds. This could not be happening.

Josh held up a hand, signalling I should stay where I was. The next moment, he'd disappeared down the steps. There was no way I was letting him do this on his own.

But as I put my foot on the first step, I heard a roar of rage. Then another sound. One that stopped me in my tracks.

The sound of a gun going off.

72

He was sprawled on the floor between a leather sofa and the doorway at the far end of the saloon, a dark stain spreading across his shoulder. I clapped my hand to my mouth. No, no, no, no. This wasn't happening. The man waved his gun at me, his head bare now, mousey hair sticking up in tufts. 'You. Sit there or you're next.'

It took all I had not to scream, but I knew that would only enrage him more. My legs started to shake uncontrollably as I staggered towards the sofa, my eyes darting to Josh as I sank onto it. Was he alive? Please God, let him be alive. There was so much blood seeping into the carpet now. I wanted to gather him up in my arms, to stop the bleeding.

'Hands out, wrists together.'

The man wrapped a cable tie around my wrists and pulled it tight, then did the same to my ankles. He moved with such efficiency I just knew he had to be a pro. I glanced at Josh again, biting back a gasp as I saw him twitch, looking up at the man to cover it. 'That hurts.'

'It'll hurt a lot more if you don't shut up,' he snarled.

Out the corner of my eye, I saw Josh twitch again, the

nearest foot to me jerking as he regained consciousness. I had to keep this creep talking. Give Josh half a chance.

Too late. Josh let out a groan, and the guy swung round, gun trained on him. 'Sit up,' he snapped, aiming a kick at Josh's side.

'Don't hurt him!' I cried.

'And you, shut up or I'll shut you up.'

My eyes bored into his back. If it was possible to hate someone to death, I'd have killed him on the spot.

Josh was moving his head from side to side now, raising one arm to feel the back of it, trying to move the other and letting out an involuntary yelp of pain. The hand he'd put to his shoulder was covered in blood, as was his T-shirt.

The man gave him another kick. 'Sit up.'

Somehow, Josh managed to struggle up, leaning back against the sofa behind him, his breath coming in short pants. Sweat beaded on his forehead, in contrast to the pallor of his skin, and blood still seeped from his shoulder wound. He wasn't going to last long without medical attention. 'He's bleeding out,' I said. 'Let me at least put a compress on that.'

The man's eyes flicked to me and then back to Josh. 'You want to save him? That's sweet. OK, darlin', have a go, but no funny business.'

I swallowed my retort. That *darlin'* along with his accent was a dead giveaway that he was no longer playing gentleman thief. He was a Londoner. It was the kind of mockney accent a nice middle-class boy adopts when he wants to sound streetwise.

'I can't do it unless you untie my hands,' I said.

I watched the emotions play across his face. Part of him wanted to just finish us both off. The other, saner part needed us alive. But for what?

Thankfully, the saner part prevailed. He took a knife from the galley and sliced it through the cable tie at my wrists, taking another from his pocket and using it to tie Josh's ankles before standing over me with his gun aimed at my head. 'Go on then. Do your first aid bit.'

'I can't without something to use as a compress. Do you have a towel?'

He stared at me, one corner of his mouth curled in a sneer. Then he backed towards the bathroom, grabbing a towel from the rail before handing it to me. I took it from him and folded it into a neat square before shuffling over to Josh and up onto my knees. 'I'm sorry,' I murmured. 'This is going to hurt.'

Josh grimaced as I pressed down firmly, covering the wound with the towel, trying to remember everything I'd learned in first aid class what felt like a lifetime ago. I dimly recalled that firm pressure should stop the bleeding and that was the most important thing, so I kept it up even when my arm started trembling with fatigue.

'Don't worry about me,' muttered Josh. 'Look after yourself.'

His skin was growing clammy. I placed my free hand on his forehead. It was cool. For now. He was going into shock. We probably had around twenty-four hours before infection started to set in. There was no way my first aid training would help me extract a bullet. It might look easy in the movies, but this was all too real.

I looked over my shoulder at the bottles arranged in a rack next to the galley. 'Pass me that vodka.'

'Pass me that vodka *please*.'

I hadn't thought I could hate this guy any more than I already did. 'Could you just do it? Unless you want him to die of sepsis.'

He glared at me for a moment but did as I asked.

'And another towel. Better still, some cotton wool if there is any.'

The glare deepened into a scowl, but the bit about Josh dying must have got to him. I was right – for some reason, he needed us alive. For now.

He rummaged in the bathroom, keeping a firm eye on us through the open door, then returned with a wad of cotton wool and another towel. 'There you go.'

I poured the vodka onto the cotton wool. 'I need scissors too.'

'No way.'

'I have to cut off his T-shirt to clean the wound.'

'For fuck's sake. I'll do it.'

He squatted beside me with the scissors, and for half a second I thought of snatching them and ramming them into his heart. If he had one. But he was twice my size and it would have only set him off, so I simply watched as he snipped away at Josh's T-shirt until all but a patch of material that had stuck to the wound fell free. I looked at that patch, weighing it up. There was nothing else for it. As fast as I could, I ripped it away. Josh let out a blood-curdling yell and then fell silent, his head dropping forward. I thought he must have fainted, but a few seconds later, he raised it again, his eyes dull with pain.

'I'm so sorry,' I whispered as I applied the vodka-soaked wad of cotton to the wound, reaching for his fingers with my other hand and holding them between mine. His hand was shaking. Shock probably. I wiped away the sweat on his brow. 'Hang in there, Josh. For me.'

'Very touching.'

I stared up at the gunman. 'What's your name?'

He gazed back at me, unblinking. 'Falcon will do.'

'What the fuck do you want from us?'

He sniggered. 'Not very ladylike, darlin'. As it happens, I need you to help me find something.'

I kept my face blank. 'What?'

'Oh I think you know, sweetheart. In fact, I'm pretty sure it's something you want to find too. Does Rommel's gold ring any bells?'

73

2 FEBRUARY 1943, TUNIS, TUNISIA

NADIA

'There is just one more thing,' I said. 'Simone told us that Rauff has a vast quantity of gold he stole from the people here. I think we need to find out where he's keeping that before we finish him off so we can return it to its rightful owners. Otherwise, it will be lost forever.'

'He took it from the Jewish people on the island of Djerba, where we come from,' Lucien growled. 'He demanded it as a tax on their lives to pay for their clothing and forced labour. He said if they didn't pay up, he would kill all the young men and he gave them two days to find twenty million in gold, to be paid every month. The elders gathered together and collected from each family, including ours.' He looked at Colette. 'He took your mother's dowry.'

Colette's face was set. 'So I heard. My mother's dowry was her collection of gold and silver jewellery. It's been passed down her family through the centuries. Some people say it's Queen Dido's jewellery, but who knows? One thing I do believe is that it's cursed.'

'Cursed?'

Colette's eyes flashed. 'My mother is from a very old family who have always been courtiers in one way or another. It's why the Bey was happy to have us at the palace, apart from helping the Allies. The jewellery was given to one of her ancestors for safekeeping by Dido before she killed herself, or so the story goes. Apparently she cursed anyone who might try to take it. I remember once, a boy, a friend of my brother, stole a ring from the collection. He died not long after in a freak accident and his father returned the ring, saying there was something evil about it.'

Icy fingers stroked the back of my neck and trailed on down my spine. I didn't believe in this kind of thing. And yet... there was something so compelling in Colette's tone I could not help but believe her. 'Rauff now has this ring?'

'I believe so, along with the rest of my mother's jewellery. For us, and for most of the other people on Djerba, that's our entire wealth gone, stolen in exchange for their lives.'

'Then we must get it back for you.'

She spread her palms. 'How?'

'From Rauff. We'll find out where it is before we kill him.'

Colette glanced at me then looked away, biting her lip. 'That's not going to be easy,' she muttered.

Tom held up a hand. 'Let's take this one step at a time. The first stage is to entice this Simone somewhere out of the city. Close enough that you can get there easily without being stopped by Rauff's troops but where you can be gone for the whole day. Any suggestions?'

'How about Sidi Bou Said?' said Colette. 'It's a pretty seaside village around twenty kilometres, so not far.'

'Sounds good,' I said. 'Now, where do we tell Rauff to meet her? Somewhere that hasn't been requisitioned but still sounds as if it's a place she might suggest for a rendezvous.'

Lucien looked thoughtful. 'Why not suggest a private residence rather than another hotel? That would be more discreet. I know of one you can use. A villa that belongs to a Frenchman who also works for Agency Africa. He departed for Algiers when the Germans arrived, but he gave me his keys. We could say in the note that it belongs to a friend of hers who is away. It's in the French district, so it won't look suspicious. Send a key with the note. That will reassure him. He's bound to check the place out beforehand, but it all adds up.'

'That's a brilliant idea,' said Tom. 'And we can be waiting for him inside.'

'Exactly.'

'What do we do with Simone afterwards?' I asked. 'She's not going to be happy when she hears about Rauff.'

Nico rolled his eyes. 'Why don't we just kill her too?'

Tom shot him a look. 'I don't think that's necessary.'

'I also don't think we need to stoop to their level,' I snapped. Simone might be as manipulative as she was ignorant, but I had no doubt life had shaped her that way. She had to put up with the sneers and gossip of the petit bourgeoisie who clearly thought themselves a cut above her while somehow surviving a life with that husband of hers.

No doubt he had married her for her looks, as rich, ugly men who want attractive children do, although he didn't seem too bothered about her breeding potential. Perhaps she had none. That might explain the coolness between them. Whatever the reasons behind her callous stupidity, she did not deserve to die like an animal, as the Nazis would have ensured she did.

I looked round the table. 'Do you think he's going to fall for it? We're asking him to change his routine, which is not something Rauff will like, and go out of his way just to meet Simone.'

Nico smirked. 'Trust me, if he thinks he's going to get what he wants, he'd cross the Sahara on his hands and knees.'

I arched an eyebrow at Tom. 'Oh really?'

He gazed back at me, sending white-hot darts of desire shooting through me. 'Absolutely.'

'Good to know,' I murmured. 'I suggest we move sooner rather than later. It's Tuesday today, so why don't Colette and I arrange to meet Simone tomorrow and invite her out for the day as a big surprise? That way, we can get a note to Rauff first thing on Thursday, supposedly from her, telling him that her husband is on his way back and they need to meet that day instead for some very special fun.'

Tom frowned. 'You're leaving everything very last minute.'

'That's the idea. We don't want to leave either of them time to think. If we play on the fact her husband is getting suspicious, which is why he's coming back early, it won't seem all that odd. It will also focus Rauff's mind. This might be his last chance to get what he wants. Besides, as you said, he won't be worrying about the details. He'll be focusing on what lies ahead, so to speak.'

'Not just that,' said Colette, 'he trusts Simone. He's been seeing her for a while now, and he knows her husband. He has absolutely no reason to think this is anything other than him getting what he wants at last.'

'We'll have to make the note to him convincing,' I added. 'What is it he calls her? His *Schatzi*? We can sign off with that.'

'I'm pretty good at forging handwriting,' added Colette. 'We tricked her into giving us a sample of hers, although all those Frenchwomen write in the same way.'

Tom burst out laughing. 'I'm glad I never met you two when I was a callow youth. You'd have run rings around me.'

'Who says we can't now?' I muttered under my breath, so softly I thought he hadn't heard. Then I looked up and caught the glint in his eye. A glint that no doubt matched my own. He was up for the challenge. I had better make this good.

74

3 FEBRUARY 1943, TUNIS, TUNISIA

Simone flushed with excitement. 'You really mean it? We can have an excursion outside the city? My dears, I can't tell you how much I have longed for something like this. I feel so cooped up here.'

She seemed so happy I almost felt sorry for her. Almost. 'We thought we'd take you to Sidi Bou Said. Have a whole day away from here.'

'You'll love it,' chimed in Colette. 'It's the prettiest fishing village, right on the edge of the Mediterranean. The houses are all blue and white to reflect the sea. We can take in some fresh air and have a walk on the beach.'

Simone wrinkled her nose. 'I'm not so sure about sand, but I do love the sea air. Perhaps a promenade through the streets?'

'Whatever you wish,' I said. 'We simply want you to have a good time.'

She lit up. 'You said Thursday?'

'Yes.'

'That's tomorrow.'

'I know, but we wanted it to be a surprise for you.' I could see her vacillating. 'Of course, if you have something better to do, that's fine, but we'll miss you.'

That did the trick. I knew that Simone passed her days in mind-numbing loneliness, ostracised by the other wives and with precious little to do other than wait for her husband to return or Rauff to summon her.

'No, no. I do want to come. Very much. When and where shall we meet?'

'Why don't we come and collect you at nine? That way we can make the most of our day. We can arrange a car from the palace. Write your address down here.'

The car was another touch. There was no way Simone would turn down the chance to travel in a car with the royal insignia. I handed her a pen and piece of paper torn from my notebook, pocketing both when she'd finished. 'It's twenty kilometres or so to Sidi Bou Said from the city, which gives us plenty of time to get there for a coffee and a stroll before lunch. There's just one thing – please don't tell any of the other wives. This is a special privilege, you see, organised by the Bey himself. We wouldn't want word to get out and cause him any trouble.'

Simone put her finger to her lips. 'You have my word on that.'

'Wonderful. We'll see you in the morning then.'

Simone picked up her dainty bag. 'I'm so looking forward to it.'

We watched her exit the café, one carefully chosen so it was nowhere near the Majestic or the palace. Our route there had been circuitous, involving several double-backs and pauses for surveillance. It was only when we were satisfied we weren't being followed that we'd entered the café Lucien had suggested to us, a neighbourhood place near his factory that served excellent coffee along with Tunisian orange cake.

'I make sure they get supplies,' he explained. 'Even so, they're struggling. The Germans take all the food, and so local people are left waiting for hours outside shops just to get things like bread. They bake their own at this café, along with making their own cakes. They often run out by lunchtime, so make sure you go early.'

I looked at my watch. It was half past eleven. Less than twenty-four hours to get everything set up. At least the first piece was in place. Simone was primed and ready. There was just one thing that worried me. 'What if she tells Rauff?'

Colette picked the last crumbs from her plate. 'She won't.'

'How can you be so sure? If she tells Rauff and we then send him a message in the morning purporting to be from her, he's bound to start smelling a rat.'

'She knows that if she tells Rauff she's off for a day out with some new friends, he'll stop it happening. Rauff is SS. A control freak by nature. He'd want to know every detail about us and our plans. She's not stupid, at least not about that.'

'True. In any case, we'd better report back.'

The factory was around five minutes away on foot, but it took us fifteen as we repeated our security measures, determined to make sure we didn't lead anyone back to Lucien and the men.

We needn't have bothered. As we entered Lucien's office, he put down the phone, looking agitated. 'Ladies, it is good to see you. Mrs Abdelli, I wonder if you would be kind enough to bring us some coffee?'

The minute the secretary left the room, Lucien closed the door. 'That was my contact at the palace. He says the guards have reported plain-clothes Gestapo staking out the gates and the approaches to the palace. I don't think it's a good idea for you to go back there right now. You can come and stay with us at my house as our honoured guests. They've lost interest in us, so you should be safe there.'

I looked at Colette. 'It's Vulke. I know it is. We really are compromised. The question is, does that mean the operation is compromised too?'

Lucien raised an eyebrow. 'Felix Vulke?'

'The same.'

'You mentioned him before, but I didn't realise he had a special interest in you.'

I grimaced. 'Vulke has had a special interest in us since he tried to kill Colette in Cairo, mistaking her for me. Before that, I thought I'd managed to finish him off in Paris but apparently not. It seems Vulke can rise from the dead. Now he's coming after me and, by extension, the rest of us.'

Lucien stroked his beard. 'All the more reason for you to stay with us, at least until after tomorrow's business. We need to plan a swift extraction for you all after the event.'

Colette shook her head. 'I'm not leaving. I'm staying right here.'

Lucien looked aghast. 'You can't, my dear child. It won't be safe. Once you've assassinated Rauff, they'll be hunting down his killers. Vulke knows you're here. You'll be top of his list.'

I smiled. 'Not if we kill him too.'

75

PRESENT DAY, ALEXANDRIA, EGYPT

SOPHIE

'It was you, wasn't it? You killed Ben.'

Falcon drew back his lips, exposing his teeth. They were white and even, just like the war graves in the cemetery in Cairo. I wondered how much he'd paid for them. 'Sorry about that, but the old girl sent me packing, so I had no choice. Unfortunately for your bloke, she didn't realise I'd left a bug in the room. At least, not at first. Old bat must have found it though because the thing went dead but not before I knew all about her little plan with the photograph. All I had to do was watch and wait until you two turned up at her house after she carked it. Soon as I saw him on his way to the postbox, I knew that was my chance and waited up the lane. Unfortunately for him, he moved a bit quicker than I expected and had already managed to post the bloody thing. When I got out the car to, shall we say, ask him a few questions, he starts running and shouting. I had to run him down to shut him up. My mistake. Too late to ask him where he'd posted it when he was already dead, and you can't break open a postbox like that for love nor money. Your old man was what you might call collateral damage.'

My old man? Ben. My love. My future. 'What is it you want from us?' I spat. 'Or are we going to be "collateral damage" too?'

He laughed. 'Feisty, aren't we? Thing is, I worked it out the minute your colleague told me you'd gone to Cairo. Told me the whole sad story, in fact. Amazing what you can discover when you're pretending to tour a primary school as a sad, widowed single dad.'

I gaped at him, aghast. 'You've been stalking me.'

'Let's just say I've been keeping an eye on you. I knew sooner or later you'd lead me to that photograph. I want that along with the other half of the coordinates, and I believe you've got them, otherwise you wouldn't have come chasing out here. I knew you'd do that too. Left an easy enough trail for you to follow. Come on – hand them over.'

I stared him down. 'I don't know what you mean.'

'Oh I think you do. You see, your auntie Nadia also wrote you a letter. One your fiancé was supposed to give you on your wedding day. You'd be surprised what's in it. All very touching, except I got there first.' He squatted down, placing the nozzle of his gun against Josh's temple. 'Now, unless you want your boyfriend here to die too, I suggest you give them to me.'

I felt my limbs turn to jelly, terror flooding through them. 'There's a notebook,' I mumbled. 'In my pocket. The right-hand side. The photograph is tucked in it.'

'Good girl,' he leered.

I flinched as he reached into my pocket. He pulled out the notebook and inspected the photograph, grunting in satisfaction when he saw the numbers on the back. 'Where are the other coordinates?'

'About halfway through. It's in code though. Baconian code.'

He licked his lips. 'Clever little bitch, aren't you? Tell me when to stop.'

He held the notebook in front of me, flicking through the pages until I cried out, 'Stop!'

'OK. What does it say?'

I peered at the page, trying to remember the substitution code, my brain scrambled with fear.

'Hurry up,' snapped Falcon. 'Or I'll have to make you concentrate.'

He placed the gun nozzle once more against Josh's temple.

I took several deep breaths, trying to steady myself. 'Twenty-three... no, twenty-four... 24.0694 degrees east.'

Falcon rose to his feet and grabbed a pen from the galley. 'Say that again.'

I repeated the coordinates and he wrote them down, together with those on the back of the photograph, a grin spreading across his face.

'Good stuff, princess. OK, let's get this show on the road. Move over here.' He pointed at the table leg opposite to where Josh was slumped.

I stared at him and then shuffled over to it.

'Hands together.'

I gritted my teeth as he secured a fresh cable tie around them.

'Now your feet.'

This time, he tied them and then attached the tie to the table leg with another cable tie before doing the same to Josh.

When he reached to pull his hands together, I cried out. 'Don't do that. You'll start the bleeding again.'

He glanced at me, thought about it for a second and then secured Josh's uninjured wrist to the table leg instead. 'Don't do anything stupid,' he growled before heading back up the stairs to the bridge.

I heard the whir and rattle of an electric anchor rising and then Falcon gunning the engine. The yacht rose in the water, its bow pointing out to sea, and we were off. I could see shapes and lights through the porthole as we navigated the harbour and then nothing save inky darkness as we picked up speed, heading out into the open sea, to God only knew where.

76

The boat sped over the water at top speed, its engines screaming. Huddled below in the dark, I felt like screaming too. We'd been at sea for hours, racing over the Mediterranean. Josh needed to see a doctor before that wound got infected, although that was probably the least of our worries. At least it had stopped bleeding. That was the main thing. But he was still slumped against the sofa on the floor, his head lolling to one side, jerking now and then when the pain seared through his consciousness, the cable ties digging into his flesh every time he did.

The saloon was narrow, the built-in sofas lining its sides making it even more of a tight squeeze. The table was fixed to the floor, so there was no way I could shuffle anywhere except, with some difficulty, around to Josh to check his temperature with my cheek, laying it against his to try and gauge if there had been any change. I checked the cotton wadding strapped to his chest too. So far, there were no signs of blood seeping out from under it, although I had no idea how badly he was injured or what exactly the bullet had struck.

He was still unconscious, which meant he had either bled a

lot or hit his head in the fracas. There was plenty of blood now drying out in the carpet, but my money was on the latter, although I couldn't see any bruises. 'Come on, Josh,' I muttered. 'Stay with me. You can do this. For God's sake, Josh. Wake up. Please. Don't you leave me too.'

I thought I saw one of his eyelids quiver and shuffled over to him, placing my cheek on his and checking his temperature yet again. He seemed a little warmer. Maybe less clammy.

'That's nice,' he murmured, his cheek muscles moving under mine.

I pulled my face away. 'You're awake.'

He opened one eye and then the other, blinking at me, confused. 'What's going on?'

'Shhh. You were shot. In your shoulder. You bled a lot, but it seems to have stopped. I also think you may have hit your head. Falcon is up on the bridge. From what I can guess, we're heading out to sea. He has the coordinates. All of them. So we're probably going in the direction of the gold.'

Josh shook his head, trying to take all this in, glancing at the cable ties on his wrist and ankles, then at mine. 'There has to be a way we can get out of this...' His eyes roamed the saloon and into the galley beyond.

'I've already tried,' I whispered. 'Can't reach anything.'

'It's like I said. The guy's a pro.'

We stared at one another. 'Even pros make mistakes.'

Josh managed a half-smile. 'That's what I love about you.'

'What?'

'The fact you never give up.'

'You're not going to either.'

He closed his eyes for a moment, wincing.

'What is it? The pain?'

'Don't worry about me – I'll be OK.'

I faked a smile back. 'Of course you will.'

The truth was, he was looking worse if anything, beads of

sweat now standing out on his forehead while his skin was waxy and bone white. I wasn't sure how much longer he could go on. How much longer we could both go on.

All at once, the whine of the engines stopped. Then there was another sound – the electric whirr and clank of the anchor again. My shoulders stiffened as Falcon reappeared at the top of the steps, his figure a darker shadow against the gloom.

'Happy days,' he announced, slapping his hands together. 'We're here.'

77

I watched the dawn sky turn from mother-of-pearl to pinky gold, burnishing the water as the sun rose. Falcon had half-dragged me up the steps, protesting, then lashed me to a rail with a length of rope. He was busy now manoeuvring the yacht closer to a rocky cliff punctuated by sea caves, dropping the anchor when he was satisfied, its chain unravelling into the depths until it bit. The boat tugged against it as it settled, lolling in the gentle waves.

When he was done, Falcon pulled on the cord holding me to the rail. 'I'll go check on your boyfriend. You stay here.'

I didn't give him the satisfaction of a response. He was enjoying this far too much already. I was worried, though, about Josh. His temperature was definitely higher now. We'd both still been grubby from the garden when we'd set off after Falcon. Some of that dirt might well have transferred into his wound, despite my best efforts. What he really needed was for me to try to clean it once more and re-dress it, but Falcon was adamant. He needed me up on deck for God only knew what reason. All I could do was sit here, tied up to this rail with my wrists and ankles still bound, and hope he didn't do anything to hurt Josh even more.

Ten minutes or so later, he reappeared, dressed in a wetsuit and carrying a mask and oxygen tank. 'Right, darlin', I'm going to untie you now, but I'm warning you – no funny business. Your boyfriend doesn't look too good. I might just be tempted to put him out of his misery, if you get my meaning.'

I scowled at him but managed to keep my mouth shut.

He pulled out a diving knife and sliced through the cord and then the cable ties on my wrists and ankles. As I rubbed them, I thought for half a mad moment of striking out as hard as I could. That was until I remembered the knife. As well as the gun strapped to his thigh. Then there was Josh and his threat. I swallowed, keeping my eyes averted, determined not to let him see what I was thinking. If I could just get hold of that knife or the gun, I'd turn the tables...

Falcon sniggered. 'Don't even try it, love. One move from you and your boyfriend gets it.'

Was I that transparent? Evidently. But then, I'd never been in a situation like this before, while Falcon had seen plenty of action, at least according to Josh. You learned to read people when you were used to making them fear for their lives. Especially when you were a cold, calculating bastard like him. I had no doubt he intended to kill us both when he was done with us. The only reason we were still alive was because he needed us for some reason.

That reason became clearer when he waved his knife at me. 'Move.'

He marched me to the stern. Our dinghy was no longer there. He must have untied it before we departed. He threw his gear into the one that remained. 'Get in.'

I hesitated.

Falcon pulled the gun from his thigh holster. 'I said get in.'

I stepped down into the dinghy, perching on one of the

seats. Falcon cast away then leaped down into the boat to fire up the outboard motor. We shot away from the yacht, heading for the sea caves that yawned like open mouths at the bottom of the cliffs. I forced myself not to glance back at the yacht, wondering if Josh was OK, praying that he was, clutching the edge of the bench seat as we slapped up and down on the waves and keeping my eyes fixed front.

Falcon dropped the engine to a gentle putter as we entered the largest cave, then stopped around fifty feet from the entrance. The water here looked dark and deep, the anchor playing out until it dug into the bottom.

Falcon strapped on his flippers and tank. 'Your job is to stay here and keep watch. Remember, no stupid moves. I have this here, don't forget.' He patted his thigh holster and I could see the diving knife glinting at me from his belt. 'This baby fires even after it's been underwater, and don't imagine I won't use it.'

I gazed at him, speechless. Keep watch? For what? My guess was this was where Falcon believed the gold was located. More fool him. This was probably a recce while he tried to locate the exact spot. Then, no doubt, he'd get both Josh and me to help him bring it up from the seabed. Well, he had a shock coming to him. We weren't even in the right place. The numbers I'd given him were just different enough to seem like the real coordinates, when in fact, the actual site was probably a mile or so down the coast.

The minutes ticked past. I glanced at my watch. He'd been down there nearly an hour. The boat rocked under me as the waves slapped against the cave entrance and curled on through, disappearing into the half-light beyond. I peered into the depths praying that his tanks would malfunction. That he'd never resurface. No such luck. I could see the top of his head emerging, and then he flung his mask into the boat before he hauled himself back over the side. I could see from his face that he'd found nothing. Of course he hadn't. And then another thought struck me. What was he going to do if he didn't find the gold? I might just have made my biggest mistake of all.

Without a word, he jerked the outboard into life once more and we were heading back to the yacht. As we drew alongside, my stomach coiled. Something was wrong.

'Go check on your boyfriend,' snapped Falcon. 'I need to take another look at those coordinates.'

I could hear him slamming around as I descended the steps into the saloon, heart thudding in my ears, terrified of what I might find. I could hardly bear to look at the corner where I'd left Josh. When I did, I blinked and blinked again, unable to believe my eyes.

He'd vanished.

78

3 FEBRUARY 1943, TUNIS, TUNISIA

NADIA

We arrived in the courtyard in another of Lucien's vans, hidden this time behind crates of olive oil. As we emerged from it, I noticed a small boy hovering by the gate. 'Who's that?' I asked.

Lucien glanced over. 'That's Ibrahim, my neighbour's youngest son. He acts as unofficial watchman. The Nazis don't notice him because he's only a little boy. They have no idea he has the swiftest feet in this city, along with the sharpest eyes.'

The little boy I'd sworn to myself I'd look out for. I could see Ibrahim eyeing us up. I waved at him. He grinned and ducked his head shyly. 'When you next speak to him, please tell him we're very grateful for his help.'

Lucien smiled. 'I will. Do you have children?'

I took a deep breath. 'I had a son, yes.'

He studied me for a moment. 'But no longer?'

'He got sick on our journey from Poland and died when we got to Palestine. He's buried there, where he can see the sea.'

Lucien's eyes glowed with a deep compassion. 'May he rest in peace.'

'I pray he does. Just as I pray that those who killed him and his father rest in eternal damnation, Vulke among them.'

We were entering a room off the main courtyard now where a table awaited us laid with all kinds of salads. A smiling woman appeared.

'My wife, Jacqueline.' Behind her, a line of servants brought dishes of couscous and tagine, beef and lamb stews along with an array of breads piled in baskets that they placed before us.

'My goodness,' said Tom. 'What a feast. You are too kind. You really shouldn't have gone to all this trouble.'

'It's no trouble at all,' said Lucien. 'You are here helping to save our country and our people from these invaders. We owe you a great debt.'

Jacqueline waved her hands. 'Eat up, eat up. You must be starving. You poor things cooped up in that cellar all this time. As for you two, you're far too thin. I've told you before, Colette. You need meat on your bones.'

I looked more closely at Colette. Jacqueline had a point. Her face was gaunt, the shadows under her eyes speaking of lack of sleep. 'Are you alright?' I murmured.

She managed a wan smile. 'I'm just tired. I'll be glad when this is over.'

I wish I'd pressed her more closely then, but the truth was, I was as exhausted as she. The strain of worrying that every element of our plan would somehow fall into place was beginning to tell. Then there was the other worry. That of keeping secrets. I knew Colette was determined to get her tiny daughter out of Tunisia, just as I was determined to make sure Vulke only left in his coffin. Two women hellbent on our own missions as well as on the one that would save thousands of lives and inspire thousands more to victory.

Rauff's assassination would not just stop him carrying out his heinous acts; it would be a propaganda coup we Allies desperately needed. The Germans might have their backs to the wall in this war, but it wasn't over by a long chalk. Kill Rauff and we would breathe new life into our fight. It was as simple as that.

Colette excused herself almost as soon as dinner was over, claiming a headache. Her aunt whisked her away upstairs to the chamber she had prepared.

Tom leaned towards me. 'Would you care for a stroll in the courtyard?' he murmured.

We left Nico and Lucien to their cigars, wandering through the corridors and colonnades to the courtyard, which was now bathed in moonlight, the fragrance from the jasmine clambering around its pillars and arches filling the air. We sat, as we had done back in the camp in Egypt, on a bench, only this one was intricately carved, set under the branches of an orange tree. I gazed up through those branches to the stars above, trying to identify the constellations.

'Look, there's the belt of Orion, the hunter. And there's Venus.'

'Planet of love.'

I turned my gaze to Tom. 'Indeed.'

There was no more need for words. We both knew what we wanted to say. Or rather, what we wanted to do. Our lips met at the same moment as our minds, both yearning for more, for the ultimate bliss.

Tom stood and reached for my hand. 'Come.'

I let myself yield as I placed my hand in his, the two of us merging with the shadows cast by the colonnades then sinking to the cool marble floor, where Tom pulled off his shirt to act as my pillow, and I cast aside my skirts to form a bed beneath the both of us. Our limbs twisted and twined as somewhere out there a bird sang – a nightingale this time, not a nightjar, its lovely song rising and falling as we did, reaching its crescendo, singing softer as we lay in one another's arms, fulfilled and yet hungry for more, speaking of love and of longing, of everything we wanted from and for one another. Until, at last, like us it fell silent, while above us the stars continued to shine and the moon to watch over us. Only then did I let go and fall asleep in his arms.

79

4 FEBRUARY 1943, TUNIS, TUNISIA

I woke the next morning wondering where I was. The room was unfamiliar, the bed hard and strange. I could make out the outlines of furniture and ornaments in the light that filtered through the louvered window shutters and the soft yellow safseri hanging behind the door, its silken folds offering protection. And then I remembered. I was here, in Lucien's house, in the room I had crept to a few hours before. The sky was already lightening when I stirred in Tom's arms and heard him murmur into my hair. 'Good morning.'

'Oh my God. Is it dawn already?'

I sat up, running my hands through my hair, twisting to see him lying there in a tangle of our clothes, smiling up at me as he pulled me back down beside him.

'You're the loveliest thing I've ever seen.'

His flesh felt so warm, the heart pulsing beneath it calling out to me. I could no more resist him than I could the urge to breathe. He was that to me too, the oxygen that filled me with life. And love. I knew that now. I'd always known it. Deep in my own heart, I knew Andrzej would approve.

This time, it was quick and urgent, a greed in each of us for the other that cried out for more. We lay again in our tangle, slick with sweat in spite of the cold.

'I'll keep you warm,' murmured Tom as he held me tight, his heart beating beneath mine, his hands cradling me as if I was the most precious thing he had ever held. I inhaled him, his skin, the essence of him, his soul, knowing that we were now joined in a way more holy than any marriage. We had an unbreakable bond forged in a place few knew, a place beyond most imaginings where we lived today, knowing it could all end tomorrow or in an hour. Or even a heartbeat. I listened to his now, hearing the throb of his lifeblood, a pulse that matched mine.

'We have to move,' I murmured. 'Otherwise they'll find us here.'

Tom kissed the top of my head. 'I know.'

With a groan that echoed the one silently reverberating through me, he sat up, handing me my clothes and pulling on his own.

I heard another bird pipe up, this time with sharp, tinkling notes that rose and rose. 'Listen,' I whispered. '"It was the lark, the herald of the morn..."'

He dropped a long, sweet kiss on my lips. 'We'll hear many more nightingales, my love. Along with larks. Now let's snatch a couple more hours' sleep. It's a big day, remember.'

How could I forget?

It was the first thing I remembered when I woke again those few hours later. The feel of him. The smell of him. The sense we belonged to one another. I smiled as I flung open the shutters to greet the sun. It was a brand-new day. A good day. The day we would avenge the many people Rauff had murdered and stop him murdering any more. I should have been alive with excitement, but all I could feel was a creeping sense of dread.

The same, leaden weight in my stomach stayed with me through breakfast as we went over our final plans.

'You have the message?' asked Tom.

'Right here.' I handed over the note we'd prepared, carefully written by Colette to match Simone's handwriting on the address she'd scrawled for us on the page from my notebook.

Charles returns on Friday. I think he knows. I can't wait any longer. Meet me at this address at noon.

Your Schatzi.

It was followed by the address I'd copied down from Lucien, written in block capitals so there could be no mistake. The villa was located in the north of the city, in the French district occupied by the colonial administrators, businessmen and representatives of the Vichy government who loved to lord it over the native Tunisians. Simone's own home wasn't too far away, albeit in an even more exclusive street. Rauff wouldn't bat an eyelid at going into that area. The Vichy French had rolled over happily for the occupying German forces in France and were repeating the exercise here.

Tom read the message through. 'I can't wait any longer?'

'How else was I supposed to put it? She's no poet, don't forget, and she has to be reasonably discreet in case the note falls into the wrong hands.'

He was looking at me, the ghost of a smile playing around his lips. 'I guess it's blatant enough for Rauff.'

'Well, yes, considering he thinks he's on to a good thing anyway. I'm sure he always expected to get what he wanted in the end. He just enjoyed the chase.'

Tom lowered his voice. 'I don't believe in chasing.'

'You don't?' I murmured.

'No. I believe in arriving. In feeling like you've come home.'

To my horror, I could feel a tear pricking, hot, at the corner of my eye. I bent my head quickly, hoping no one would notice.

He felt like he'd come home. That was how I felt too. But it was a home built on quicksand, one that could disappear at any moment. We were about to embark on a dangerous operation. Anything could go wrong. In my experience, it often did. How could I risk my heart again when it had already been smashed to smithereens not once but twice over? I would carry the scars left by Andrzej and Alexander forever. And yet I would also carry their love and the light they had brought into my life too.

None of us really knew what was going to happen next. All we knew was that we had to rid the world of a monster like Rauff, and our best chance was Simone. If Rauff took the bait and we succeeded in assassinating him, then we were one step closer to winning this war. Not quite close enough for me, as I still yearned to take out Vulke too, but it was something I had to hide from Tom at all costs. I knew he, of all people, would do everything he could to stop me, if only to protect me from myself. The thing was, as much as I loved Tom – and I knew I loved him – the desire for justice burned even brighter in my heart.

It was a desire I knew could cost me everything, and yet I still didn't understand how high a price I would have to pay.

8 0

PRESENT DAY, OFF THE COAST OF CRETE, GREECE

I heard a shout from up on deck and thought fast. Falcon had been with me the whole time. There was no way he could have done anything to Josh, which meant Josh had to be here somewhere. I had a last look around the saloon, poking my head into the galley and the staterooms. Empty. The shouting grew louder. Falcon was growing impatient. The last thing I wanted was him coming down here. I headed back up the steps, almost running into him. 'What took you so long? I told you not to try any funny business.'

His eyes were flicking from me to the hatch.

'I didn't. I went to the loo. He's still out cold.'

Falcon shot me a disbelieving look and went to shove me aside when we both heard it. The rattle of the anchor chain. He pulled his gun from its holster. 'You stay here.'

I gave it a couple of seconds before I followed him up to the foredeck, creeping along the opposite side to the one he'd taken, keeping low.

A yell from Falcon. I froze. Then an answering roar. Oh my God, that had to be Josh.

I scuttled forward a few more steps, emerging onto the foredeck in time to see Josh lunge forward and knock the gun from Falcon's hand as he fired it, sending it flying onto the deck, where it landed with a clatter then slid along the sloped deck, over the side and into the sea.

'Josh! He has a knife!' I screamed.

Too late. Falcon was stabbing at Josh, the men rolling over and over, blood flowing again from Josh's wound. Falcon had the advantage and he knew it, aiming for that wound with his fist while he slashed at Josh's throat. The knife was inches from it. Any second now and it would all be over.

I scanned the foredeck – nothing I could use – then ran back to the stern as fast as I could, clutching the side rail as I cast around for something, anything. My eyes lit on the fridge set into the rear seating area, and I hauled it open. Bingo. The fridge was stocked with everything a charter client might want. I grabbed a bottle of champagne and raced back to the foredeck not a moment too soon.

Falcon was kneeling astride Josh, his forearm across his throat, choking the life out of him while the knife was poised above his heart. An animal scream emerged from the depths of me, a howl that brought Falcon's head snapping round just as I slammed the champagne bottle down onto it, force meeting force. He fell sideways, the knife dropping from his fingers, and sprawled on the deck, unconscious. I kicked the knife away from him, sending it skittering over the side too.

'Is he out?' croaked Josh.

'I think so.'

'Give me a hand. We need to get that anchor.'

I helped him stagger to his feet and then over to the anchor now dangling above the water. Together, we hauled it up and onto the deck. I looked at Josh.

'Right, now him,' he gasped, his face grey with the effort.

I did as he asked. Questions could come later.

Josh took him by the shoulders while I grabbed his ankles, and together we dragged him across the deck towards the anchor, leaving a wide streak of blood in his wake. Josh dropped his torso back over the anchor and then reached into his pockets, pulling out a bunch of cable ties. 'Found them below,' he muttered. 'Bastard has a whole stash of them.'

Gritting his teeth, the sweat now pouring from his brow, Josh started to tie Falcon to the anchor. I followed his lead.

'He's coming round,' I muttered.

Falcon's tongue darted from his lips as he licked them, tasting the salt and blood. His eyelids snapped open. He was staring up at me, the veins blood red against the whites of his eyes as he realised what was happening and began to strain with all his might against the cable ties, roaring with rage. At the same moment, Josh slammed his foot down on the windlass switch, sending the anchor hurtling towards the water, dragging Falcon with it, the rattle of the chain drowned out by his shouts. He slid through the gap in the guard rails, over the side, still roaring and screaming.

A splash. I ran to the side, looking over, watching the ripples spread, bubbles rising through them, the anchor chain playing out, all of its weight falling on top of Falcon, ensuring he couldn't escape his watery grave.

When it had stopped rattling across the deck, Josh unbolted it and the last of the chain slithered into the water. He swayed as he stood upright, and I gave him my shoulder to lean on as together we made our way back to the bridge. 'Are you sure you can do this?'

Josh flicked on the battery switch and checked the gear was in neutral before turning the key. 'Absolutely.'

He was breathing heavily, but he was completely calm, checking the instruments and letting the engine run for a few minutes before smoothly turning the boat and arcing away from the cliffs. 'We have enough fuel to get as far as Heraklion. We can refuel there and radio in for help.'

It was starting to sink in. All of it. I felt my legs go from under me and grabbed at the spare seat beside Josh, my fingers slipping from it as white noise filled my ears and the world turned to black.

81

They were all there. Nadia. Tom. Ben. Falcon. Their faces hovering over mine, calling to me.

'Sophie, wake up. Sophie, come on, darling.'

Only that wasn't Ben's voice. I forced my eyes open, shutting them just as fast as the sun blazed, too bright, into them.

'Here, drink this.'

A hand under my head, holding it up. A glass of water to my lips. Wait, this had happened before. I opened my eyes fully this time. 'Josh. What happened?'

'You fainted.'

'I did? I keep doing that. I'm sorry.'

I scrabbled up from the seat I'd been lying on and looked around. The foredeck cabin. We were still on the boat. Of course we were still on the boat. It was all coming back to me. Falcon. Being pulled over the side to his death. Josh. I glanced at him. 'You look really rough.'

He managed a wan smile. 'Thanks a bunch.'

'I mean it. You need a doctor. Where are we?'

'Just about to head into the harbour at Heraklion.'

I looked to my right, seeing the old fort we were passing and then the harbour wall, boats at anchor ahead of us. I could hear the harbourmaster on the radio and Josh's responses, and all the while I was thinking. Falcon killed Ben. He deserved to die. I knew all of that intellectually, and still I could feel the shame and the fear washing over me, threatening to drag me under once more. 'What are we going to tell them? About Falcon?'

Josh kept his eyes on the harbour. 'We're going to say nothing. I've downloaded the CCTV footage to my flash drive and erased it from here so they'll think it was a camera malfunction. I've also sluiced and bleached the deck. As far as the harbourmaster is concerned, we're just here to refuel. He's sending a lighter out to guide us in, and we can use the spare anchor to moor up. Then we head back to Cairo and tell David and Henry what's happened.'

'There's CCTV?'

'Inside and outside the boat, although I've disabled it now. It captured sound too. Falcon confessed to everything. He kidnapped both of us at gunpoint. We were fighting for our lives. We keep that in our back pockets in case we ever need it, but I don't think anyone is going to come looking too hard for him. He obviously used a false identity for starters, so he'll have covered his tracks on that score. He turned off the transponder and GPS, so the charter company will have no idea where we went. I take it he didn't find anything when he dived for the gold?'

'Of course not. I gave him the wrong coordinates. The actual site is about a mile down the coast.'

Josh glanced at me and then burst out laughing. 'Brilliant. I should have known.'

'And what about you? How did you manage to get free?'

'Falcon forgot those saloon tables often have a lever underneath. I managed to snap one off and use the edge of it to saw the cable ties off my wrists. Piece of cake to cut them from my ankles too. Unfortunately, he grabbed the lever off me. I'll give him that, he was good.'

'But you were better.'

Josh shrugged – an awkward, one-sided shrug. The bleeding appeared to have stopped again, but I could see his shoulder was killing him, his left arm hanging uselessly. 'I had more to fight for. That's all it comes down to.'

I opened my mouth to speak, but the blast of a horn interrupted me. The lighter, approaching from the dock. Seconds later, it was alongside and we were following it into the harbour. The moment was lost.

In the flurry of paperwork and refuelling that followed, I kept thinking about those faces bending over me. But the more I thought about it, the more Ben's face and Josh's blended into one.

82

The doctor finished off Josh's stitches. 'These need to come out in ten to fourteen days. You're lucky the bullet went through you without causing major damage. Take the full course of antibiotics and make sure you keep that wound clean. Do you have someone to dress it?'

I raised my hand. 'I can do that.'

The doctor scribbled a prescription and handed it to me. 'Take this to the hospital pharmacy. Change his dressings once a day. If you notice any redness or pus, go straight to a hospital. Where did you say you're going?'

'Malta,' mumbled Josh.

The doctor raised his eyebrows. 'That's a long way. Are you sure you're up to it?'

'Don't worry,' I blurted. 'I can handle the boat.'

He gave me a doubtful look. But then, I wasn't sure he believed our explanation that Josh had accidentally shot himself while cleaning his gun either. Somehow we'd managed to persuade him that it was just a stupid mistake and there was no need to inform the police. 'Very well. The pharmacy is on the second floor.'

The sunlight hit Josh's face as we emerged from the hospital. He still looked deathly pale.

'Why don't we go and get something to eat?' I said. 'You look as if you could do with it.'

To be honest, so could I. My stomach let out a loud rumble and I realised it had been hours since we'd eaten.

Back at the harbour, we found seats at a small café overlooking the water. Its smiling owner brought us plates heaped high with meze, dolmades sitting plumply beside stuffed courgette flowers, olives and tzatziki followed by kleftiko, the lamb so tender it fell from my fork.

As we ate, I could see the colour come back into Josh's cheeks. 'Feeling better?'

He let out a contented sigh. 'Much better, thank you.'

'What time do we head back to Alexandria?'

Josh gazed at the horizon where the sun was beginning to sink down the sky. In another hour or so, it would be dark. 'It's too late to leave today. We were hours in that hospital. It's going to take us around nine and a half hours to get back to Alexandria even at top speed and I don't want to take the boat back across the water by night. The harbourmaster said we can stay one night in harbour and leave in the morning.'

'Great. We can explore Heraklion.'

'We could. Although I have a better idea.'

I caught the gleam in his eye. 'You do?'

'I most certainly do. That champagne bottle didn't break when you hit him across the head. Nice move, by the way. I owe you for that one. I put it back in the fridge. It should be nicely chilled by now.'

I forced myself to keep a straight face. 'Really?'

'Unless you have a better idea?'

So many ideas raced through my mind. Thoughts of Ben. Of Nadia and Tom. Of lost opportunities and second chances. Nadia had mourned Tom for the rest of her life, closing her heart to everyone else. I wasn't going to make the same mistake.

I smiled into Josh's eyes. 'I can't think of anything I would rather do.'

83

4 FEBRUARY 1943, TUNIS, TUNISIA

NADIA

The palace car was waiting for us inside the gates, Lucien's small sentry goggle-eyed at its presence.

'Don't worry,' said Lucien. 'He won't say anything. He's just like all little boys when he sees a car like this.'

The Bey had sent a Rolls-Royce for us, no less, decked out in the royal livery, its chrome bumpers and wheels gleaming in the sun. Our chauffeur was waiting for us, holding the door open.

Tom stepped forward and took my hand between his, dropping a kiss on it. 'Good luck.'

'It's you who needs luck. Your job is far more dangerous.'

'Oh I don't know,' quipped Tom. 'By the sound of it, Simone is quite a number.'

I gazed at him, taking in his eyes, soft in spite of his words, and his mouth, memorising each and every feature as if I might never see it again.

I leaned forward and placed my lips on his, feeling them

soften and embrace me. 'I love you,' I murmured. Somehow it felt important to say it.

'I love you too.'

I could hardly bear to tear my gaze from his. One last kiss and I forced myself to turn away.

Lucien hugged Colette to him. 'Be safe, my child. Remember to go to the Café Bleue when you arrive and let Ahmed know that everything is alright. He is the proprietor and he's also one of our network. If you need anything, let him know.'

'I will, Uncle.'

I followed her into the car and settled back into the leather seats, my gaze holding Tom's until it was no longer possible. As we swooped through the gates and on towards Simone's villa, I chanted a little prayer in my head. 'Please, please keep him safe. Keep them all safe. I couldn't bear to lose him too.'

Colette patted my arm. 'It will be alright. They know what they're doing.'

'Was I speaking aloud?'

'Yes, but don't worry about it. I know how you feel. I spend most of my time praying Céline is safe too.'

In that instant, I felt ashamed. I was so caught up in Tom, in everything that was happening, that I'd quite forgotten Colette's little girl and how much she longed to make sure she was safe. I squeezed the hand that had patted my arm. 'You'll get her out of here. I know you will.'

She looked at me, her eyes brimming. 'I hope so.'

'My God,' I exclaimed. 'Look at the pair of us perfect wrecks. At this rate, Simone will take one look and suddenly remember another engagement.'

As it turned out, Simone was so eager she was already waiting for us on her front steps, a parasol in her hand and a basket on her arm. She gave the car an appreciative glance, sashaying up to it with all the aplomb she could muster, ignoring the driver as he held the door open for her and handing him her parasol as she clambered in.

'My goodness, what are you two wearing? Have you gone native?'

I could almost hear Colette gritting her teeth. 'They're called safseris. The local women wear them for modesty and out of pride. The place where we're going is quite traditional. We brought you one too.'

Simone glanced at the folded safseri Colette was holding out and then patted her hair, gazing regally out of the window. I had no doubt curtains were twitching all around the French enclave, which was exactly what she intended. They might have cold-shouldered her up until now, but they could hardly ignore the Bey's car. Even the most die-hard snob among them would have given her eye teeth to have sat in that Rolls.

With a gratifying snarl of the engine, we were off, swooping out of the city and along the coast road, Simone's endless chatter a background hum to the thoughts replaying in my mind. What if Rauff brought a posse of his SS men with him? Unlikely. This was an assignation he would want to keep private, if only because it was such a risky thing to do. Then there was Charles, Simone's husband. The Nazis needed his food for their troops. Their supply chains were weak. It was one of the reasons they were now on the back foot in this war. Charles was a vital cog in their machine, no matter how much they would like to pretend otherwise. Angering and humiliating him would jeopardise all of that, and Rauff was no fool. He was a heartless killer who prized efficiency above everything.

Colette dug her elbow into my side. Simone was looking at me with expectation on her face.

'I'm sorry,' I said. 'I didn't catch that. The engine, you know.'

In fact, the engine purred like the pedigree animal it was, transporting us in the style to which Simone would love to be accustomed. She might have her husband's money, but you couldn't buy class.

She pouted. 'I was just saying how much I wish Walti could see me now. He's on a special mission today, you know. Something top secret. I'm not supposed to say anything, but I know it's just between us girls.'

She was obviously bursting to tell us. I gave her the prod she needed. 'How thrilling. And what is this special, top-secret mission?'

Simone pretended to hold back for a moment, hoarding her prize. 'He's moving the gold today,' she said in a stage whisper. 'From La Goulette, by boat. There are too many people who would love to get their hands on it, including Hitler himself. If he doesn't move it now, he might lose it forever.'

Her eyes were as round as her mouth, glittering with greed. Any residual pity I might ever have had for her evaporated in that moment. She didn't seem to realise it wasn't his gold in the first place – or care. Simone was already seeing herself on her wretched Walti's arm, parading through the streets of a Berlin that ruled the world, no doubt in a car just like this. She made me want to vomit. More importantly, she was spilling secrets that changed everything.

Colette and I exchanged a look.

'That is quite something,' murmured Colette, gazing out of the car window at the coastline along which we were travelling. 'A boat, you say? How clever.'

There was a note in her voice that sent my nerves tingling.

Simone snickered. 'Isn't it just? It's a fishing boat. No one will suspect that. These boats are out all the time across the Mediterranean.'

I could see a couple now out at sea. 'It must be quite a big fishing boat to go any distance. Is he sure he knows what he's doing?'

Simone puffed out her bosom. 'Of course he does. He's even arranged a diversion so that no one notices it leaving.'

I tried not to look too interested. 'A diversion?'

She spoke as if she was explaining something to a particularly slow child. 'He's ordered some of his men to set limpet mines on one of the naval ships in the port. When it blows, he'll set sail. Too many people are asking questions about the gold, including Rommel. Walti will say he took it to Corsica and hid it there until it could be retrieved and taken to Germany.'

'I see. And what will actually happen to it?'

Simone leaned in, cupping her hand to her mouth. 'He's actually taking it to Crete. There are some sea caves there where they can hide it until everyone has forgotten about it.'

She sat back, basking in the glory of her big secret.

I digested it all in seconds. 'I must say, your Walti is very clever indeed. Can we go and wave him off?'

Simone fanned herself. 'I wish we could, but Walti told me about this in strictest confidence. He'd be furious if he knew I'd told you as well.'

'Of course. You never know, we might see his boat passing from Sidi Bou Said. It is right on the coast.'

She brightened. 'We might. He's leaving from La Goulette so they could even pass right by us. Then I could give him a little wave. He won't see, of course, but he might feel it, you know?'

I doubted Rauff would feel anything apart from triumph at spiriting the gold away from under the noses of his masters, as well as the people he'd stolen it from. 'He might. What time is he departing? We could make sure we're looking out to sea soon after.'

She was looking happier and happier. 'He said around eleven.'

I was firing questions at her now, but Simone was only too pleased to be the centre of attention.

'This fishing boat goes out every day so no one will notice anything unusual, according to Walti. He really is very clever.'

She was enjoying this far too much, vicariously participating in his victory. I wanted to shake her. If she really thought Rauff was going to take her back to Germany with him, she was due for a rude awakening. I had no doubt there was already a Mrs Rauff waiting for him back in the Fatherland and probably a couple more mistresses as well. It was his fatal weakness, after all. Women.

And we were here to deal the killer blow.

84

Café Bleue was situated near the seafront at Sidi Bou Said. I bade the chauffeur to wait for us as we climbed out of the car.

'I don't know about you, but I am absolutely dying for a coffee,' I said, surreptitiously taking a look at my watch. It was nearly ten. We had barely an hour to abort the other plan and go after Rauff.

The moment we entered the café, I suggested the other two sit while I went to the powder room. Colette took my cue, steering Simone to a table at the far end of the café, overlooking the bay, seating her in a chair with her back to the room.

I hurried over to the man who had greeted us. 'I wish to speak to Ahmed. Lucien sent me.'

He opened the flap in the counter. 'In here.'

I followed him into the back office, waiting until he shut the door.

'I am Ahmed. How can I help you?'

'I need to use your telephone. It's urgent.'

He gestured to the one sitting on his desk. 'Please – help yourself. I will be outside.'

I lifted the receiver and dialled the number Lucien had

given me. It rang just the once before he picked it up, his voice unmistakable down the line. 'Yes?'

'The shipment you were expecting is now leaving from La Goulette at 11 a.m.'

A sharp intake of breath. 'Understood. Say no more. Meet us there at the café with the same name as the one you are in now.'

I replaced the receiver, wondering how the hell we were going to manage that. La Goulette was the main port for Tunis. It would take them perhaps fifteen minutes to get there, whereas we were here, up the coast with Simone.

I was working through all the options in my head as I emerged from the office just in time to see the waiter placing our coffee on the table.

'Is your line secure?' I muttered to Ahmed, who was busy polishing glasses while keeping an eye on his domain.

'As far as we know, but you can never be sure.'

'Indeed. I need your help to create a diversion.'

If Rauff could do it, then so could we.

Ahmed carried on polishing glasses. There were five other people in the café besides us. It wasn't going to be easy. 'What kind of a diversion?'

'We need something to happen in the street so my friend and I over there rush out to help, leaving that woman behind. Our car is waiting just down the hill. It would be helpful if we could go in that direction.'

I was speaking as softly as I could, indicating Colette and then Simone without being obvious.

'That shouldn't be too hard. Will you be coming back in afterwards?'

'No. My friend and I will be leaving. That woman will be staying behind, although she doesn't know it yet.'

'Very well. What would you like us to do with her after you've gone?'

I thought for a second. So many tempting options. 'Don't let her go anywhere,' I said. 'Delay her. Keep telling her we'll be back. Above all, don't let her know you have a telephone. If necessary, detain her.'

'As you wish, madame.'

I went over to our table and slid into my chair. 'That coffee smells delicious.'

Moments later, an almighty shriek reverberated through the café, coming from the street outside. A woman was struggling with two men, one of them ripping the bag from her shoulder, the other snatching the one from her hand. 'Oh my God! We must help her. You stay here.'

I was on my feet before Simone could protest. Colette was still in her seat, looking bewildered. 'Come on,' I snapped.

She blinked, apparently coming out of her reverie as she, too, stood. Together, we raced out to see the men running off down the hill towards our car and gave chase while Simone gaped out at us from the café. As soon as we were out of sight, I slowed. The men were ahead of us, and one turned to give us the thumbs up.

'Coast's clear,' I muttered. 'She's still in the café. Let's go.'

We found our chauffeur standing by the car having a cigarette. The moment he saw us, he sprang to attention, grinding it out under his foot before holding the door open for us.

'We need to get to La Goulette urgently,' I said.

He looked confused. 'And the other lady?'

'She's staying here to wait for us. Now, please hurry. The Bey would be most displeased if we missed our rendezvous.'

At the mention of the Bey, the chauffeur leaped back into his seat. Seconds later, we were speeding out of Sidi Bou Said, back along the coast road towards the port of La Goulette. Towards the gold.

Beside me, Colette sat lost in her thoughts.

'Don't worry,' I murmured. 'We'll get your mother's dowry back.'

She looked at me, her eyes raw with pain. 'I don't care about the gold. I care about my daughter.'

'You'll see her again soon. I know you will.'

'You have no idea,' Colette whispered. 'None at all, do you?'

I stared at her, wondering what on earth she was talking about, knowing deep in my soul that something was very, very wrong.

85

We drove like the wind back down the coast road, reaching La Goulette in just twenty-five minutes. The town lined the curve of the bay, stretching back from the port.

'Go through the backstreets,' I instructed the chauffeur. 'We don't want to waste time running into one of their patrols.'

No such luck. As the car turned right at a junction, a soldier stepped out in front of it, hand raised. 'Halt!'

I tried not to glance at my watch. The chauffeur remained impassive, handing over the papers with a resigned air. The soldier took his time inspecting them while his mates looked on, picking their teeth. At last, he handed back the papers. 'You may go.'

Thirty-three minutes since we'd set off. And we still had to find Café Bleue. Forty-one minutes and we finally found it after trying to ask directions from several locals. The first scurried away, the second took one look at the car and was only too eager to help, but it was the third who actually sent us to the right place. Our chauffeur was used to the drill by now, pulling in behind a truck while we piled out and into the café.

They were sitting, waiting for us at a corner table near the back.

I hurried over, pulling my safseri aside so they could see it was me. 'We don't have much time. Simone told us Rauff is staging a diversion. He's attached limpet mines to one of the German ships. When that blows, he's going to slip out of the harbour while everyone's looking the other way. We need to stop him before he does.'

Tom took all this in, his eyes never leaving my face. 'OK. Lucien knows the harbourmaster here. He imports and exports a lot through this port. He has given us these uniforms.' He indicated the tunics and trousers they were wearing along with caps pulled down low over their foreheads. 'They're the ones the forced labourers who carry out the maintenance wear. Here are yours. Put them on. The maintenance truck is waiting outside.'

I diched the safseri and slid into my tunic and trousers in the cramped café toilet. But Colette, standing alongside me, was still staring at the uniform piled at her feet.

'What's the matter? Colette, we need to hurry.'

All of a sudden, she unbolted the toilet door and burst through it, tears streaming down her face. I snatched up our clothes and raced after her, just in time to see Lucien grab her by the arm. 'What is it, *ma petite*? What are you doing?'

She was shaking from head to toe, repeating over and over, 'I'm sorry.'

I could see the hysteria rising in her. Any second now, she would lose it completely.

I raised my hand and slapped her across the face. 'Calm down now, or you'll get us all killed.'

She gaped at me, one hand to her cheek, sanity returning. 'There's another boat,' she gasped out between sobs. 'The same as the one Rauff is taking, only this one actually has the gold on board.'

'Wait, what are you saying? That this is a double bluff? Rauff is using a decoy?'

She nodded, taking in a long, shuddering gulp of air. 'Vulke is on the boat with the gold. And my baby.' Her tears were flowing fast now in between her sobs.

I stared at her, taking all this in, looking at the others, then back to her. 'Where is Vulke's boat leaving from?'

'Here, same as the other.'

'Do you know which end of the port?'

She shook her head. 'I don't know anything else except that he has Céline. Please, you have to find her. I don't care what you do to me. Just please, please get her back from those animals.'

'So it was you all along. You were the rat.'

'I had to do it. You're a mother. You must understand. I did my best to protect you while I did what they asked.'

'I knew there was something wrong, but I trusted you,' whispered Lucien, his face ashen. 'You said you'd heard your mother's dowry was stolen. You couldn't possibly have done so unless the thieves told you. There has been no communication from Djerba in weeks. In the name of God, Colette, what have you done?'

She dropped her head. 'I did it to save Céline.'

'And in doing so, you might have killed all of us.'

'I know.'

I was still trying to accept all this as Tom stood. 'Let's go.'

I grabbed Colette by the arm. 'You're coming with us. I'm not letting you out of my sight.'

I bundled her into the truck and squashed in beside her. The others followed so we were all huddled in the back. She was still sobbing quietly. I didn't even want to look at her.

'The whole thing was an act, wasn't it?' I muttered. 'You and Vulke – you even staged him attacking you.'

'That wasn't staged,' she mumbled. 'It was a warning to me to do what they wanted.'

I stared straight ahead.

'Why do you think you're still alive?' she added. 'Vulke would have killed you long ago, but I got you out of the way, remember? I made sure there was always an escape route. For all of us. But I had to keep them sweet. I suggested Sidi Bou Said today. Then Simone started blabbing. What was I supposed to do?'

I thought back to us running along the street by the Majestic, crossing into the park and on up that hill. Hiding behind the pillar in the palace. In her uncle's stables. She could have given us up at any time, but she hadn't. And yet she'd betrayed us all. To save her child's life. Would I have done the same? I didn't know. All I knew was that I wanted to kill Vulke more than ever. Then I would deal with Colette.

86

PRESENT DAY, ALEXANDRIA, EGYPT

SOPHIE

The lights of Alexandria beckoned to us like a siren, drawing us in to her glittering shores. Josh steered the boat towards the farthest end of the harbour, away from the clubhouse, dropping anchor near two other boats of similar size. 'We'll leave the keys in it. They have no evidence we were ever here, but we need to check this boat over before we leave. Make sure we haven't missed anything.'

While Josh went over the upper decks and bridge with a fine toothcomb, I went below, scouring the saloon, galley and both bathrooms before finishing up in the two staterooms. It was in the second one that I found a bag poking out from under the bed, a small rucksack of the type you might take on a day trip. Inside, there was a change of underwear, a couple of chargers and a toilet bag. Falcon had clearly been fastidious.

I could feel something in the front pocket and unzipped it to reveal a passport with '*Reisepass*' printed on the front. Along with it, a letter addressed to me. The envelope had already been torn open, but I recognised the handwriting on it at once. I could almost see Nadia inscribing the sinuous 'S' of my name on the thick, cream vellum, the same as the letter I drew from it.

My darling Sophie,

I asked Ben to give you this letter on your wedding day because I know that it will not only be the happiest day of your life, but it will also be the day you are formally joined as man and wife to support and love one another. I never had that chance with Tom, as you know. I also know that I will not be able to be there to see you two married. Those damn doctors keep telling me I may last another six months, but I know that's hogwash. This wretched cancer is killing me much faster than that.

It also kills me to know that I cannot be there for you and tell you this in person. I should have done so long ago, but I am an awful coward when it comes to matters of the heart. Or, at least, matters concerning you and your family. Your grandmother, you see, was not just my beloved niece but my greatly loved daughter. Our greatly loved daughter – mine and Tom's. She was born eight and a half months after he died so he never knew he was to have a child. He would have loved that so much.

I know you will probably hate me for not telling you this before, but I felt so guilty that I could not look after her when she was born. I tried, I really did, but at that time I was a lost soul, half out of my mind with grief. Tom's parents rescued me, or at least your grandmother, taking her to live with them and bringing her up as their own. By the time I was well enough to move back to England, she was older and it would have been cruel to uproot her. Sadly, my dear Gaby died not long after she gave birth to your mother, my beloved granddaughter. Then your mother was killed along with your father, and I again found it hard to cope. It felt as if we were truly cursed. Perhaps we were. I tried to hide my despair when I saw you, but children are wise little creatures, and I am sure you must have known.

When you came to live with me, you brought the sunshine back into my life, even at such a dark time. I tried to make up for not being honest with you by treating you as if you were my own, which, of course, you always were. It is why I am leaving you everything I possess, including Eden, my greatest treasure, the place where I spent some of my most golden moments. I hope you spend many long hours exploring the library there, as I did with Tom.

With all my love forever,

Nadia

I read it through twice, tears streaming down my face. 'Oh, Nadia,' I whispered. 'If only you knew.'

I think she did, in her way. In fact, I was sure she did. I was also sure this letter contained some big, fat clues which Falcon, or rather Peter Vulke, had missed, more fool him and which Josh and I had stumbled across anyway.

I stuffed the letter into my pocket and scrambled back up the stairs to where Josh was busy wiping down every single surface with bleach.

'Look at this,' I said, waving the passport. 'Falcon's real name was Vulke. Peter Vulke.'

'Vulke?' Josh took the passport from me, frowning as he peered at the identity information page. 'It's a German passport.'

'Yes. And Vulke was the man Nadia was determined to kill. It says so in her notebook, remember? "Vulke must die."'

'I do remember. We need to take this with us. Did he leave anything else behind?'

'Nothing. I checked absolutely everywhere.'

I'd tell him about the letter later. It had nothing to do with Vulke and everything to do me and with Josh's book.

He smoothed a stray lock of hair back from my face, the scent of bleach wafting from his hands as he did so. 'Well done. It's been a helluva ride, I know. Let's get off this boat. Be careful not to touch the rails.'

He jumped down into the dinghy first, catching the bag from me before reaching up to help me down. Then we were casting off, rowing back towards shore in a wide circle, the lights ever closer as we threaded our way through the other boats at anchor, finally tying up at a jetty some distance from the yacht club. There were no smart cafés here or twinkling lights, just a few fishing nets piled up along with crates and buckets. Josh shouldered Falcon's bag, and we made our way to the cruise terminal further along the port where taxis sat waiting to ferry passengers into town.

'The Steigenberger Hotel,' Josh instructed the driver. We drove along the curve of the bay, the harbour and the yacht now moored in it receding behind us.

The Steigenberger turned out to be a splendid colonial relic overlooking the Mediterranean.

'Let's go in for a drink,' said Josh. 'I could certainly do with one.'

I could feel the adrenaline leaching from me as we walked through the lobby to the bar, where I flopped into a chair at the table Josh selected, too tired to even glance at the drinks list. 'I'll have a gin and tonic.'

He took my hand in his. 'I know you're exhausted, but we have to make this look casual. We'll have a drink and then we'll go outside and take a cab back to Cairo. We're tourists at the end of our day trip. We don't want to attract any attention.'

My hand felt numb in his. 'Got it.'

He let go with a final squeeze. 'Good.'

I tried not to swig down my drink in double-quick time, but all I could think of was getting out of there and putting distance between us and that boat. I could still see Vulke's face, his eyes bulging as he writhed, trying to free himself from the cable ties strapping him to the anchor, his screams ringing in my ears as it dragged him over the side.

'Vulke must die.'

He had.

At least, this one had.

Once we were back in Cairo, I was determined to find out what had happened to the other Vulke, the one Nadia had hated so much. It felt as if the threads of history were drawing together, weaving a tapestry of which we were all a part. I had yet to see the full picture, but at least I now had justice for Ben, a far fairer justice than any I would get in a system that failed the innocent time and again while allowing the guilty to walk free. Falcon. Vulke. Call him what you like, he would never walk anywhere on this earth again.

I raised my glass in a silent toast. To Nadia. And to Ben.

87

4 FEBRUARY 1943, TUNIS, TUNISIA

NADIA

The maintenance truck pulled up at the far end of the port where the fishing boats were moored in front of the warehouses and sheds that housed their catch. Many were already at sea for the day, but there were a few still tied up and one or two in dry dock.

We emerged clutching brooms and equipment, all except for Colette.

'Stay in the truck,' I ordered. 'If they see you, who knows what they might do to Céline?' I handed her my spare gun. 'You might need this.' It was a risk and I knew it, but I couldn't leave her undefended. Besides, I believed her. There had been so many times she could have killed me or let Vulke do it. And she was right – I would have done the same for my child.

Tom shot me a look from under his cap. I could see the anxiety in his eyes. This could all go so horribly wrong. I didn't dare glance at my watch. All I knew was that we had to move quickly.

'Over there,' I murmured, sweeping my broom in the direction of the idling engine I could hear.

A jeep was coming towards us along the dockside, packed full of soldiers, no doubt wanting to know why there was no one in charge of our labour gang. I pulled my gun from my belt.

'Easy,' muttered Tom.

The idling engine was growing louder. Any minute now it would be casting off.

The jeep carried on straight past us. 'We have to go now,' I hissed.

Tom put down his toolbox and began to stride in the direction of the idling boat. I dropped my broom and followed, seeing Nico do the same out the corner of my eye. Lucien was back near the truck, making sure Colette stayed in it. I could see the boat now, a large fishing smack just as Simone had described, with someone standing at its bow. 'He's casting off,' I cried as I started to run towards the boat, hearing Tom's feet pounding right beside me, raising my gun as I ran.

I could see someone else on the bridge, beside the pilot, issuing orders. Then he glanced back at the dock over his shoulder. I recognised him at once. 'That's Rauff.'

At that exact moment, there was the sound of an explosion. The limpet mines going off. In its wake, a scream echoed across the dock. I spun round to see Colette being dragged from the truck, Lucien lying on the ground at her feet. I took aim.

Vulke laughed. 'Shoot me and she dies.'

He had his arm around Colette's throat, his gun pressed against her head, her gun in his other hand, dragging her backward with him as he edged towards another, smaller fishing boat, one so similar to the others still in dock I hadn't even noticed it. Except now there were two men on the deck holding weapons. And another holding a small child who was kicking and wriggling in his grasp, her little face as pink as the dress she was wearing underneath her blue coat.

Vulke hauled Colette round so she was facing the boat now. A guttural cry emerged from her throat as she caught sight of the child.

'Céline,' she croaked. 'Oh God, please, please don't hurt her.'

Vulke shoved the gun harder into the side of her head. 'Tell your friends to lay down their weapons or we might have to.'

Colette's eyes pleaded with us, every bone and muscle in her body trembling at what might happen.

Céline was shrieking now. 'Mama!'

Tom dropped his gun, as did Nico. I gave Vulke one last look and then threw mine down too.

'Very good,' sneered Vulke.

He thrust Colette aside, raising his arm at the same time. I heard her cry out as I dived for my weapon and snatched it up, rolling over and over as I fired, the men on deck firing back. Céline was struggling ever harder. This was no good. Any moment now, a stray bullet could hit her. The man holding her was reaching for his weapon too, letting her go for a split second as he did so.

'Céline, run!' I roared.

I don't know if she even heard me. She was looking only at her mother, desperate to reach her, tiny legs scrabbling as she ran towards the bow of the boat, slipping and sliding. 'Mama, Mama.'

Vulke glanced at the boat, saw what was happening and shouted at his men to hold their fire. Then he grabbed Colette once more. 'Get on that boat now or she dies.'

Céline was clutching the side of the boat, trying to climb up and over it to reach her mama, her chubby fingers and the top of her curly head all that was visible. I knew that once Vulke no longer had any use for them as hostages, he would kill them both. They were his safe passage out of here and across to the Eastern Mediterranean where Germany ruled the waves. I couldn't let that happen. I had to stop him, and this time, I wouldn't miss.

My eyes flicked from Vulke's face to Colette's, making a split-second decision. But as my finger tightened on the trigger, so must have Tom's. And Vulke's. A volley of gunfire exploded, ringing in my ears. Glancing down, I saw Tom lying on the ground and let out a howl of rage that came from the very depths of my soul. I raised my gun again, staring down the barrel of Vulke's, but Colette flung herself in front of him just as he fired, taking the bullet.

The bullet that was meant for me.

88

Shouts from every direction. Nico waving his arms, yelling at the German jeep which was speeding back towards us from the explosion, the soldiers inside it with their weapons at the ready. More yells from the boat. Vulke glancing at the jeep and then the carnage in front of him, sizing up the situation. He couldn't afford to be caught, not with his precious cargo. He knew that, and I knew that. The jeep was getting closer and closer. The boat's captain was now at the bow, casting off, ready to leave without him.

More shouts from the jeep. 'Halt!'

In one bound, Vulke leaped aboard, then he bent down and hoisted Céline high in the air before dropping her overboard, a useless burden now her mother was dead. I could see that in the seconds it took me to run to the dockside – Colette's eyes were fixed and staring, one arm flung out as if to protect someone. Not someone. Me. And Céline.

As I dived into the water, I knew just one thing. I had to save her. For Colette. For all of us.

The water was murky, churning up with the boat moving

above me. The propeller. She could get caught in it. I had to find her. Where the hell was she?

A flash of pink. There. She was over there.

I dived lower, grabbing hold of one little arm, pulling her through the water and wrapping my arms around her as we broke the surface, her head lolling against my shoulder. Oh please God, no.

Nico held out his arms. 'Hand her up to me.'

He pulled off her soaking-wet coat and patted her on the back again and again.

'There's something here, under her dress.'

I gently lifted it to reveal a pouch strapped tight to her tiny body. I removed it as carefully as I could, giving Nico more room to pat her on the chest and back some more. At last, she let out a cough, water spurting from her mouth and nose. I could see the German soldiers running towards us. 'Give her to me.'

At the same time, I glanced inside the pouch to catch a glimpse of gold, the shape of a scarab visible amid coiled chains. I hastily shoved it inside my pocket before the approaching Germans could get any nearer.

Nico saw them too and immediately raised a hand, pointing at the boat, shouting out to them in German. 'They are stealing from the Fuhrer. You must go after them.'

Their captain stared at him as Nico kept repeating it, adding, 'They have taken Rommel's gold.'

Comprehension dawned. The captain barked an order at his men, running back with them to the jeep where he continued to shout commands down the radio as they raced along the dockside, following the boat. Nico took off his jacket and wrapped it around Céline, carrying her towards the truck, away from the sight of her mother's body. 'Go to Tom,' he called out to me over his shoulder. 'I will get help.'

I stumbled to where Tom lay, dropping to my knees beside him, water dripping from me and onto his face. He was chalk white, but his lips were moving. 'Oh my love, my darling, hold on.'

His eyes fluttered open then, looking right into mine. 'Nadia. I love you.'

'I love you too. It's going to be alright. Help is coming.'

'I'm so thirsty, darling. Have you got any water?'

'I'll get you some. Just please, please keep breathing.'

That slow smile, the one that always made my heart twist, and then a groan of pain.

'Where does it hurt?'

Stupid question. I could see the blood seeping from his side, bright red. You would think it was just a scratch, except I knew most of the bleeding was internal.

He was struggling for breath now. I could hear his lungs rattling.

I bent lower, scooping his head up, cradling him in my arms. 'That's it, darling. You keep breathing. In and out. I love you so much. I don't think you even know how much.'

The tiniest sigh from his lips. 'I do. I love you more.'

I was weeping now, openly, my tears raining down on his face, a veil of pain between us as I laid my cheek on his. 'Impossible,' I murmured. 'You cannot love me more than I love you. Just stay with me. I'm going to get you out of here. I'm taking you home.'

89

PRESENT DAY, CAIRO, EGYPT

SOPHIE

Henry took a sip of his tea – English Breakfast with a dash of milk. 'Felix Vulke worked for the SS in Europe and North Africa. He was one of Hitler's favourite assassins. Nadia tried to take him out in Paris and thought she had succeeded. As it turned out, her bullet must have missed his heart by a whisker, although he was scarred for life.'

He opened his wallet and extracted a yellowed newspaper cutting from it, handing it to me. 'Fugitive Nazi War Criminal Arrested', blared the headline above a photograph of a white-haired man in handcuffs being bundled into a car. 'Detectives in Argentina captured Felix Vulke, a 72-year-old German, on Thursday on the outskirts of the capital, Buenos Aires...'

'I got that from the file,' said Henry. 'It seems we have an entire section on Felix Vulke in the embassy archives. He came back to Cairo, you see, for a while in 1955. He was arrested and interrogated by Nico Casanoff, no less, aka Ivan Bosko. Casanoff had the great pleasure of revealing to him that he'd missed the gold strapped to little Céline. Apparently, her grandmother in Djerba did it to hide the most precious items in her dowry, never thinking they would actually take her grand-daughter too.'

'I wish I'd been there to see his face. Did Vulke tell them anything?'

'Nothing of note. In the end, they had to let him go. Orders from on high. After the war, Vulke worked for the Syrians and then General Pinochet in Chile, alongside his old pal Walther Rauff. They also both worked for the BND, the Federal Intelligence Service of West Germany. It was they who insisted on his release.'

'Seriously?'

'I'm afraid so. Mossad tried to catch them both a number of times, as did various other Nazi hunters. The arrests came to nothing. Both men returned to Chile, and Pinochet refused to extradite them. They were too valuable, you see, Rauff less so than Vulke. Rauff's specialty was extermination, but Vulke, he was a cunning bastard, if you'll pardon my French.'

He took another slurp of his tea. Felix Vulke certainly was, by all accounts.

'What about Peter Vulke?' I asked. 'The grandson? Where does he fit in?'

He might have borne a passing resemblance to the man in the photograph, although it was hard to tell. The cutting was old, the man in it just as faded.

Josh took it from me and studied it. 'Same nose and mouth,' he concluded. 'Different eyes.'

The Vulke in the newspaper had eyes that drilled into you even down the years. Hard, bright, rat-like eyes, alight with intelligence and, yes, cunning.

'Ah, yes, his grandson Peter,' murmured Henry. 'According to what I've read, Vulke barely knew him. He took his wife with him to South America. She was a stolid Nazi sort. They had two boys, but Vulke was forever having affairs. Another trait he shared with Rauff. Peter was the son of his eldest who was married to the daughter of another escaped Nazi.'

'What a lovely family,' I muttered.

'Indeed. Peter grew up in Chile but went back to Germany after both his grandfather and father died within a year of each other. He was already connected with a gang of organised criminals. He operated all over Europe, including in London, which is where he started to use his alias, at least according to our people. Vulke means "falcon" in English. He was up to the usual things. Drugs and human trafficking. But he wanted more. Much more. And he'd heard about the lost gold from his grandfather.'

'Why did he want those coordinates so badly?' asked Josh. 'Surely his grandfather knew where he'd dropped it overboard.'

'That was Felix Vulke's big mistake. He relied on one of his men to note down the coordinates and keep them safe. Unfortunately for him, that same SS officer was transferred to Dachau to oversee the camp and took the coordinates with him, scribbling them on the back of a photograph. Vulke was away on another mission carrying out a raid to rescue Mussolini from the castle where he was being held captive on Hitler's orders. By the time he got back, the officer was long gone. Someone found that photograph when Dachau was liberated. As luck would have it, that someone was an OSS officer named Jim Taylor, who realised what the numbers on the back might signify and gave the photograph to Nadia.'

'Colette's Jim?'

'My great-grandad,' said Josh.

'That's right. Apparently Nadia destroyed it and wrote them on the back of a picture of Tom instead. Or rather, she wrote half of them. The other half, as you know, was in her notebook.'

I smiled. 'Clever Nadia.'

'That wasn't the cleverest part. She knew by then where

Rauff had ended up that day, so she doctored another photograph and pretended that was the one found in Dachau, writing coordinates on the back of it for Corsica as the supposed location of the gold. Ever since, treasure hunters have been trying to find it without success.'

'Until now.'

Josh's eyes met mine. 'Until now,' he echoed.

'So what will you do?' asked David, who had been sitting listening to all of this, whisky in hand, a peculiar little smile on his face.

Another look to Josh, taking in the acquiescence in his gaze. 'Do? Nothing. We're going to do absolutely nothing. Too many people suffered for and because of that gold. The original owners are long gone, and it would be hard to trace their descendants. Besides, I really do believe it's cursed. I think it's best to leave it where it is.'

I picked up the photograph with the numbers on the back and turned it over, gazing into Tom's eyes laughing up at me. 'I can understand why she loved him so much.'

David smiled at me. 'She'd be so proud of you.'

I returned his smile. 'You think so?'

'I know so.'

There was something in his voice. A note.

'You knew, didn't you?' I whispered.

Josh looked from me to David. 'Knew what?'

'I found a letter on board the boat along with Vulke's passport. I'm pretty sure Ben had it on him the day he was killed and Vulke took it from him. Probably hoping it would reveal something about the gold, which it did, in a way. Nadia wrote it for me to open on my wedding day, and she dropped some hints in it, talking about Eden as "her greatest treasure". But that wasn't the biggest revelation. Nadia, you see, was actually my great-grandmother. She and Tom had a daughter, Gaby, who was born eight months after he died. Gaby was my grandmother, but Nadia had what sounds like a breakdown, and it was Tom's parents who raised her. That's why Nadia left me Eden along with everything else.'

'Gabriella Molyneux,' murmured David. 'My cousin.'

I stared at him. 'Of course. So you and I are related?'

'We are. You can put all of that in your book, Josh. Now run along, you two. Go out and have some fun. You deserve it after all you've been through.'

Josh held out his hand. 'Shall we?'

No need to answer. We walked hand in hand out the door.

90

7 FEBRUARY 1943, CAIRO, EGYPT

NADIA

Three days. For three long days, he hung on, all the way back to Alexandria and then Cairo, on to the villa, where we set up a bed in the library, unable to risk the stairs. Most of that time he drifted in and out of consciousness, stirring only when the doctor came to extract the bullet. His cries then were awful, subsiding at last when the chloroform kicked in. I watched him afterwards, floating in a sleep that was not a sleep, his face ghostly pale, his breathing too slow.

As the night wore on, I read to him, plucking his favourite from the shelf. Not the plays this time but the sonnets, bitter-sweet, full of everything I wanted to say. How much I loved him. How angry I was that he was leaving me. And I knew he was leaving me with every laboured breath, his hands plucking now at the sheets, his lips moving as if he had so much to tell me too, although not a single word fell from them. At last, I turned to *Romeo and Juliet,* knowing how much he loved it, hoping he could still hear me through the haze that hung over him, heavy now like a shroud.

I read through the entire play, savouring the poetry of the language, doing my best for him. But it was when I read these lines that I finally broke: "'Good night, good night! parting is such sweet sorrow, / That I shall say good night till it be morrow.'"

The tears were rolling down my face unchecked, the sobs coming in gasps, so loud I didn't hear him call my name at first. When I finally did, I looked up to see him gazing at me with such love I almost dissolved again.

'You're awake.'

He managed a crooked smile. 'I am. Come here. Come closer.'

I leaned over him as carefully as I could, laying my cheek beside his where he indicated, listening as he murmured to me.

'I want you to promise me something.'

'Anything.'

'Promise me you'll go on, Nadia. You'll live your life for me too.'

'No, no. Don't say that.'

'Hush. You and I know the truth. I'm dying, my love. I would do anything to stay with you, but I can't. It's the only way I can live now, in your heart.'

His words were coming slower and slower, great pauses between them.

'I promise.'

'Good.'

Another pause, so long I thought I might already have lost him. And then he opened his eyes once more, looking beyond me, smiling at something through the window before turning his gaze back to me. 'I love you so much. I have always loved you.'

'I love you too. Don't go. Please don't leave me. I will always love you.'

But he could no longer hear me. He was already walking

ahead of me into a place where war no longer existed. Where all his pain had disappeared and peace now embraced him in her tender arms. Where I could not follow. At least, not yet.

I carried on kissing him until I felt gentle hands at my shoulder, urging me to let go. I still could not relinquish him.

'He's gone, Nadia. Let him be.'

Nico, his voice gentle but raw with pain too.

I looked up, staring blindly out of the window. It was a new day. A new dawn. One without Tom in it.

As I gazed out at the courtyard, I thought I saw him standing there for a moment, holding a child by the hand. He raised a hand in farewell and then turned, leading the child into the sun beams that were pouring through the window, covering us in liquid gold. I glanced down at his face, bathed in that golden light, and fancied I saw him smile. Only then did I release him from my embrace, knowing that I would hold him in my heart for as long as I lived. This was our place now. Our Eden. The place where our love had been born and blossomed. A love that would carry on beyond death, beyond everything. Forever.

91

PRESENT DAY, CAIRO, EGYPT

SOPHIE

We stood once more on the bridge, watching the boats skitter across the river like dragonflies, their sails translucent as wings. I thought back to that other boat where we had so nearly lost our lives. 'I came here because of Ben. And Nadia. I know it sounds fanciful, but I feel like they both wanted me to come to make sure people knew what really happened.'

'It doesn't sound fanciful at all,' said Josh. '"There are more things in heaven and earth", as we both know.'

I smiled. 'I love it. You're a tough guy who quotes Shakespeare and can hack his way into most things.' Including my heart.

He put his arm around my shoulder and pulled me in closer so he could drop a kiss on the top of my head. 'I just love you.'

I froze, his words reverberating around my head, not sure what to do or say. Or how to feel. Josh was so very special to me, but Ben would always occupy a place in my soul. Was there room for both of them? I had no idea. All I knew was that you didn't heal all at once. It happened in layers, like the dust motes that had settled all over the villa, softening the edges, although they were still there, somewhere, underneath, waiting for a ray of sunlight so they could dance again.

He must have sensed my confusion because he drew back just a little. 'Why don't you go and get some rest at your hotel and meet me later, at the villa? I have a surprise for you.'

I let out the breath I hadn't even realised I was holding in. 'You do?'

'Yes, but I need to go and do a few things first. Let me walk you back. I wanted to say hello to Mohammed as well.'

Mohammed was, as ever, busy tending to his beloved hotel. We found him polishing up the brass bowls which were dotted around the place, carefully tending to each nook and cranny of the intricate patterns etched into them so that they gleamed. They still didn't match the light that shone from his face when he saw us.

'We've come to thank you,' I said. 'Without you, we would never have found that evil man.'

As Josh switched to Arabic, explaining what had happened, I watched the shadows cross Mohammed's face. They were the same shadows that had haunted Nadia for the years that followed Tom's death. The shadows that were now dispelled, never to return. When Josh finished, Mohammed stood with his head bowed for a moment. Then he turned to me, taking my hands as he gazed at me. 'Nadia. She very proud of you.'

I felt the tears prick, managing a watery smile. 'Thank you.'

He nodded just once, reaching out to lay his hand on my cheek one more time. Then he picked up his polishing cloth and went back to his work, ever diligent.

'I'm glad Nadia had people like Mohammed to turn to,' I murmured as we walked away.

'People wanted to help Nadia. She was remarkable. As are you.'

For a moment, with his back to the light, I could have sworn

I was looking at Tom rather than Josh. 'I'll see you later then. What time?'

'Six o'clock. On the dot.'

I gave him a mock salute. 'Yes, sir.'

As it turned out, I was five minutes early. I dawdled outside the gate, looking at the villa, at its crumbling beauty and the jungle that had once been a glorious garden. Could I ever restore it to its former glory? I wasn't sure.

'There you are.' Josh was bounding down the front steps, the evening breeze stirring his hair, the scent of roses and eucalyptus wafting on it. 'Come on in.'

We mounted the steps hand in hand, Josh commanding me to close my eyes once we were through the front door. Then he led me blind through the house, my senses tuning in to each footfall, turn and bend for clues, until at last he announced, 'You can open your eyes. We're here.'

I knew before I did that we were in the ballroom. It had its own smell. Its own atmosphere. Its ghosts.

When I opened my eyes, the light from what seemed to be a thousand candles glowed from every corner, glinting off the chandeliers above, casting their reflections in the windows as dusk fell outside. In the centre of the dance floor, Josh had spread cushions and a rug, on which he had placed a picnic basket. There were more roses scattered around the rug, their scent mingling with those from the garden permeating the room through an open window. He led me over to the rug, keeping hold of my hand as I sank onto the cushions.

Josh sat too, reaching for the bottle chilling in a silver bucket full of ice. 'I know you like champagne.'

I smiled at him. 'I love it.'

He poured me a glass, our fingers brushing as he handed it to me, stirring all my senses. 'Wait. I forgot one thing.'

After flicking the switch on a mini speaker, he hit the button on his phone. Music filled the room. I recognised it at once – 'In the Mood'. I put my champagne flute to one side. 'Shall we dance?'

As we moved together across the ballroom, they began to emerge from the corners, sweeping and whirling around us, their faces alight with love and laughter. There was Tom with Nadia. My Ben. My mother and father. A host of other faces. One a gorgeous woman with green eyes. Colette perhaps? I hoped so. I hoped they were all together again, just as I was here, with Josh, heart to heart, my feet finding their way, knowing I had finally come home.

92

ONE YEAR LATER, CAIRO, EGYPT

SOPHIE

I stood outside the summer house, surveying our handiwork. The lawn stretched away from me, neatly clipped, a swathe of green.

'Are you ready?' called Josh.

'I'm ready.'

He hit the switch and water spurted from the fountain, reaching higher and higher before cascading down into the pool below.

I let out a cheer. 'You did it. We have life.'

He strode over to me with a grin on his face, wrapping his arms around me to cradle my belly. 'We most certainly do.'

I looked down at the gentle swell of it, placing my hands on top of his. This time next year, our child would be crawling across the lawn. Or at least sitting on it. Four months to go. It was a scary prospect. As well as a thrilling one.

I tilted my head back for a kiss. 'I love you.'

'I love you more.'

I would have happily stayed like that forever, but I could hear someone calling from the gate.

'You stay here and play with the fountain,' I sighed. 'I'll go and see who it is.'

A woman in a jade-green dress was standing there, her elegance belying her years.

'Hello,' I said. 'Can I help you?'

She turned her gaze from the house to me, and I noticed how her eyes matched her dress. She smiled. 'I certainly hope so.'

Her voice was husky and accented. American, I would guess, although, from her appearance, I wouldn't have been surprised if she'd emigrated from here. Her cheekbones defied her years, as did the vitality that oozed from her. 'My name's Céline Hudson. I believe my grandson Josh lives here?'

'Céline? Oh my goodness,' I cried, flinging the gate open. 'I thought you weren't going to be here until later. Come on in. It's so lovely to meet you at last.'

The next moment, I was swept up in an enormous hug. 'You must be Sophie. You're every bit as beautiful as he said you were.'

I heard Josh come up behind me. 'Grandma! You're here. Why didn't you call me from the airport? I was going to come fetch you.'

'Don't be silly. I got a cab. Besides, I can see you have a lot to do here.' She smiled, reaching up to give him a kiss as he enfolded her in his arms. 'It's so good to see you both. Although I see now there are actually three of you to visit.' Her eyes dropped to my belly. 'How wonderful. Another baby born here.'

'Isn't it? But let's not stand out here. It's hot, and you must be tired after your journey. Follow me.'

I led the way up the stairs and into the house while Josh offered his grandmother his arm, carrying her suitcase in his other hand.

Céline gasped in admiration as she caught sight of the transformed entrance hall, its walls freshly painted a pale, golden yellow to offset the colourful pictures and kilims we'd hung at various heights across them. 'What a wonderful place,' she exclaimed.

'Thank you. We've been working on it for nearly a year, Josh and I.'

'A home for your little one. Josh, I cannot believe you didn't tell me about this. When is it due?'

I could feel myself blushing, more with pleasure than embarrassment. 'Four months to go. I can't wait.'

'I'm sorry, Grandma,' mumbled Josh. 'I wanted it to be a surprise.'

'Well, it sure is that. A wonderful one.'

We were standing by the entrance to what had been the ballroom now. I flung open the door. 'Why don't we sit in here and have a proper chat?'

Another intake of breath from Céline. I beamed. The ballroom was my pride and joy, a space now brought back to life with love, its walls cream to act as a blank canvas for the paintings and drawings that would be stuck to it, tables with chairs set round them filling up the space. In the far corner, the tuned piano sat ready, while a large sofa and armchairs occupied the one opposite, acting as an area where staff could sit and spend time one on one with a child.

We took our seats there now as I waved my arm, encompassing the room. 'We're turning this place into a kindergarten and primary school for displaced children. There are a couple of charity villages on the edges of the city where they live but a shortage of places like this, so we decided to open one.'

Josh slid his arm around my shoulders. 'It was Sophie's idea. She's the teacher. I'm just the handyman.'

Céline laughed. 'I doubt that very much. Although your grandad, he was very handy. Could make or mend anything.'

Her voice caught.

'He sure was,' murmured Josh, their eyes meeting in memory. Another family trait, it seemed. Loving well.

A distant bell chimed through the house. A couple of minutes later, Mohammed popped his head round the door. 'Mr David here to see you.'

Seconds later, David bounded through with a spring in his step, carrying a book. He stopped dead when he saw Céline. 'I-I'm sorry to interrupt. I had no idea you had guests. I just wanted to bring you a copy hot off the press, Josh.'

Josh's eyes lit up as he took it from him. 'No need for apologies. This is my grandma, Céline. Grandma, may I present David Molyneux? I've been writing a book with him, all about this place. I think you're going to love it. At least, I hope you will.'

Céline was hardly listening. Instead, she was gazing at David with a quizzical smile. 'David? Is that really you?'

David stepped forward and took her hands in his. 'It most certainly is. Céline and I used to play together as children,' he added, glancing round at us. By the way he could scarcely tear his eyes from her, it looked as if they had a lot of catching up to do.

Mohammed dropped a tiny bow. 'Shall I bring tea, madame?'

'Yes please, Mohammed. What would you like? English Breakfast? Mint?' I turned back to Céline. 'Mohammed knew your mother too. He was a great friend to Nadia. He's just retired from his job at the hotel where he worked all his life. He needed something less demanding to keep him going, so we asked if he would like to come and help us. To be honest, I think he's busier than ever, and he can't wait until the children arrive. He adores kids.'

'He does? Well, that's wonderful. It's about time there was another child running around this house.'

I stared at her. 'You said something about that before, about another child being born here.'

'Well, of course that other baby born here was Nadia's. Hers and Tom's.'

'My grandmother, Gabriella. She was actually born in this house?'

Céline smiled. 'She was.'

I ran my hands through my hair, feeling the familial threads that tied me to my mother, and her mother before her, tighten, imagining Nadia here, giving birth without Tom at her side, the white noise I hadn't heard in nearly a year filling my head once more, bringing with it words whispered down the years: 'I love you.' A chorus of voices – Nadia, my parents, Ben. I glanced out the window, half-expecting to see a little boy and girl playing outside, but there was no one there. The storybook. Not made up after all but written about her two children, Gaby and Alexander. 'Poor, poor Nadia. She had her baby all alone.'

She patted my hand. 'She did, but I know she loved that baby very much, just as she loved you very much. I visited her in England along with my father. You were only a baby then yourself.'

'You came over from America?'

'That's right. My dad brought me to the States, you see, along with my grandparents. They were destitute after the war. The Nazis had stolen all their money. Dad put them up and shared my care with them. He and Mom gave me a great childhood, and I'll always be grateful to them. It's OK,' she added, 'I know all about his love affair with my biological mother and how Nadia saved my life, just as my birth mom saved hers. I call dad's wife Mom because that's what she was to me. She couldn't have kids, but she treated me as her own.'

She spoke with such quiet dignity that my heart bled for her. She had missed out on so much. And yet, her story had a happy ending too. She was loved and she had created more love in turn. That was all that truly mattered.

I glanced at Mohammed, silently pouring more tea. He must have known too but never breathed a word. Discretion, a hallmark of that generation.

'We can show you round some more after we've had tea.'

'Thank you, my dear. That's very kind. Tell me, have you picked a name for your little one?'

'If it's a boy, we thought perhaps Thomas. We don't yet have a name for a girl.'

She patted my hand again. 'You still have plenty of time.'

As I looked at her hand on mine, a thought struck me. 'I'll be right back,' I said, leaving Céline and David with Josh while I darted upstairs to our room, its torn drapes now replaced, although we had kept everything else pretty much as it was in Nadia's day. I reached under the four-poster bed, drew out a box and carried it back downstairs with me. 'I believe these belong to you.'

Céline looked inside it at the neatly coiled necklaces and the rings laid against the silk lining, my old engagement ring among them. I had a new one now, a pretty Red Sea pearl set in platinum. Nadia's ring belonged with the rest.

'What on earth is this?'

'It's your mother's gold – or rather, your grandmother's dowry, stolen from her by the Nazis.'

She drew a necklace out of the box, holding it up to the light, its pendants dangling as they had done for thousands of years. 'No, my dear. I cannot accept this. These belong in a museum.'

'Then please take them and donate them. Do whatever you wish or what you think your mother would have wanted.'

Céline shut the lid and handed the box back to me. 'My mother would have wanted you to have them. At least, that's what my father told me. You're going to need money to run this place. Why don't you sell them to someone who will look after them? One of the big museums?'

I cradled the box against my belly. 'I'll think about it.'

'You do that.' She smiled. 'Now, I want to hear everything. All about you, this house, how you came to be here. Everything you can remember about Nadia.'

I saw David dart her another glance, one of deep admiration mixed with something else. Nostalgia perhaps. Or something more.

As we chattered on and the shadows lengthened, I could feel them all gathering. First Colette with her green eyes so like her daughter's. And her grandson's. Then Nadia and Tom. With them, the little girl who had grown into my grandmother and the little boy she had buried by the sea. In Ben's place, another man who walked over to Colette, enfolding her in his arms. That had to be Jim. They were all together again, here in the house where it had all started and where Josh and I were creating our new beginning. Eden. The villa full of secrets. Of love too, for that was all that mattered in the end.

I knew that as I watched them fade away, raising their hands to me in a final farewell. They might linger here in the memories that soaked the very fabric of the place, but now they were free to walk together into eternity, forever young and in love. Just as it should be.

Thank you for reading *The Key to the Island House*. If you enjoyed it and want to keep up to date with all my latest releases, just sign up at the following link. Your email address will never be shared, and you can unsubscribe at any time.

www.bookouture.com/amanda-lees

This book was inspired by a painting of a broken vase in a sun-scorched Cairo backstreet. The artist was my aunt, who was posted there along with my uncle, a group captain in the RAF, long after the Second World War. The picture was simple enough – pottery fragments scattered on a dusty road executed in slashes of ochre and burnt sienna that evoked the heat and sense of the place, but it was enough to spark something in seven-year-old me.

Every time we visited my aunt in Devon from the Far East, where I was born and grew up, I would gaze at it, making up stories in my head. How did that vase break? Did someone smash it in anger? I'm still making up stories in my head, only now I put them down on paper, mining those memories along with the people and places I stumble across every day.

Another long-held fascination of mine is with crumbling, abandoned buildings and their secrets, especially if those secrets hide the truth about spies and their daring missions, along with the love affairs and hard partying that went with the territory. Villa Eden actually existed, along with its colourful inhabitants, although I have, as ever, changed names and amalgamated the real-life characters to create fictional ones who have their own adventures alongside those based on historical fact.

During the Second World War there was a group of spies billeted in a villa on Gezira island in Cairo who partied like there was no tomorrow in between fighting the enemy and carrying out acts of extraordinary bravery, not to mention cunning. Dudley Clarke, one of the few characters to go by his real name in the book, was a master of deception who led A Force in Cairo and ingeniously fooled the enemy time after time, creating entire fake armies, fleets and bomber groups.

Agency Africa, the Franco-Polish intelligence agency in North Africa that is mentioned in the book, also existed and was a highly successful operation led by 'Rygor' Słowikowski, whose work facilitated the Operation Torch landings in North Africa that ultimately paved the way for D-Day. Nadia is based upon a glamorous Polish noblewoman who lived in the real-life villa and worked alongside these people, sharing her room there with her two pet mongooses and falling for the man she later married, an SOE officer.

Above all, this is a book about how the secrets of the past can unlock those of the present, including murder, intrigue and love both lost and found. North Africa and Egypt fascinate me in different ways, their cultures so ancient and diverse, full of the myths and legends which also appear in the book. I wanted to echo the great love stories which are timeless in the way they resonate with us, as well as the secrets so many families conceal and which can either drive them apart or bond them tightly forever. Nadia and Sophie's stories are inextricably intertwined, as all our stories are, beholden to fate as well as to the choices we make.

I want to add a note on family – I refer to Nadia as Sophie's great-aunt throughout the book. That, according to genealogists, is the correct title rather than great-great aunt. Writing a book that spans generations is complicated enough without worrying about details like that, but I do, as I do in all my research. What's more important, though, is the story, and I hope you love it as much as I have loved writing it. These characters have found their way into my heart. It's going to be hard to let them go.

Thanks,

Amanda

www.amandalees.com

 facebook.com/AmandaLeesAuthor

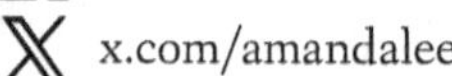 x.com/amandalees

ACKNOWLEDGEMENTS

It takes a team to write a book, and I am lucky enough to have a brilliant one. First, there is my agent and friend, Lisa, who is not only one of the most stylish people I know but one of the kindest, as well as being fierce, fabulous and a force to be reckoned with. The same goes for her own equally amazing team in Patrick, Zoe, Jamie and Elena.

Then there is my wonderful editor, Natalie, and the team at Bookouture, who get my books out into the world with the extraordinary skill and dedication that sets them apart. There is a list of them at the back of this book, and I am grateful to each and every one of them for their genius in bringing it to life.

Thanks, as always, to my fellow author buddies who keep me going through the long, coffee-fuelled days and nights, and especially to the crew at the CWA, who somehow manage to make board meetings fun.

As ever, there is my constant inspiration, my daughter. I love you, and I am so proud of you, as the dedication on this book attests.

To the friends and family who have been there for me through times dark and light – Julia & Phil, Andrew, Josa, Guy, Ed, Murat, Ann, Kevin, Jackie & Sam, Clare and Sean along with so many others – thank you. You are my rocks.

Above all, thanks to the women and men who served, and gave their lives in service for, their countries and our freedom, including my father. We will never forget you.

PUBLISHING TEAM

Turning a manuscript into a book requires the efforts of many people. The publishing team at Bookouture would like to acknowledge everyone who contributed to this publication.

Commercial
Lauren Morrissette
Hannah Richmond
Imogen Allport

Cover design
Ami Smithson

Data and analysis
Mark Alder
Mohamed Bussuri

Editorial
Natalie Edwards
Charlotte Hegley

Copyeditor
Laura Kincaid

Proofreader
Jennifer Davies

Marketing
Alex Crow
Melanie Price
Occy Carr
Cíara Rosney
Martyna Młynarska

Operations and distribution
Marina Valles
Stephanie Straub
Joe Morris

Production
Hannah Snetsinger
Mandy Kullar
Nadia Michael

Publicity
Kim Nash
Noelle Holten
Jess Readett
Sarah Hardy

Rights and contracts
Peta Nightingale
Richard King
Saidah Graham

Dear Reader,

We'd love your attention for one more page to tell you about the crisis in children's reading, and what we can all do.

Studies have shown that reading for fun is the **single biggest predictor of a child's future life chances** – more than family circumstance, parents' educational background or income. It improves academic results, mental health, wealth, communication skills, ambition and happiness.

The number of children reading for fun is in rapid decline. Young people have a lot of competition for their time, and a worryingly high number do not have a single book at home.

Hachette works extensively with schools, libraries and literacy charities, but here are some ways we can all raise more readers:

- Reading to children for just 10 minutes a day makes a difference
- Don't give up if children aren't regular readers – there will be books for them!

- Visit bookshops and libraries to get recommendations
- Encourage them to listen to audiobooks
- Support school libraries
- Give books as gifts

There's a lot more information about how to encourage children to read on our websites: **www.RaisingReaders.co.uk** and **www.JoinRaisingReaders.com**.

Thank you for reading.